W9-APK-238

"I cannot wait to see where Ms. Feehan takes us next."
—Fresh Fiction

"Packed with adventure . . . Not only is this a thriller, the sensual scenes rival the steaming bayou. A perfect 10."
—Romance Reviews Today

"Daring. . . . Fresh . . . Who knows what the next book will bring?" —HeroesandHeartbreakers.com

"Explosive! The sexual chemistry is literally a scorcher."
—Fallen Angel Reviews

"The fastest-paced, most action-packed, gut-wrenching, adrenaline-driven ride I've ever experienced."
—Romance Junkies

"Wow! . . . . Made me hungry for more."
—The Best Reviews

"Sultry and suspenseful . . . swift-moving and sexually charged . . . In short, it is an electrifying read."
—*Publishers Weekly*

"Brilliant. The sexual energy . . . is electrifying. If you enjoy paranormal romances, this is a must-read."
—Romance at Heart Magazine

"Intense, sensual and mesmerizing." —*Library Journal*

"[An] erotically charged romance." —*Booklist*

Titles by Christine Feehan

COVERT GAME
POWER GAME
SPIDER GAME
VIPER GAME
SAMURAI GAME
RUTHLESS GAME
STREET GAME

MURDER GAME
PREDATORY GAME
DEADLY GAME
CONSPIRACY GAME
NIGHT GAME
MIND GAME
SHADOW GAME

HIDDEN CURRENTS
TURBULENT SEA
SAFE HARBOR

DANGEROUS TIDES
OCEANS OF FIRE

LEOPARD'S BLOOD
LEOPARD'S FURY
WILD CAT
CAT'S LAIR
LEOPARD'S PREY

SAVAGE NATURE
WILD FIRE
BURNING WILD
WILD RAIN

BOUND TOGETHER
FIRE BOUND
EARTH BOUND

AIR BOUND
SPIRIT BOUND
WATER BOUND

SHADOW KEEPER
SHADOW REAPER
SHADOW RIDER

JUDGMENT ROAD

DARK SENTINEL
DARK LEGACY
DARK CAROUSEL
DARK PROMISES
DARK GHOST
DARK BLOOD
DARK WOLF
DARK LYCAN
DARK STORM
DARK PREDATOR
DARK PERIL
DARK SLAYER
DARK CURSE
DARK HUNGER
DARK POSSESSION

DARK CELEBRATION
DARK DEMON
DARK SECRET
DARK DESTINY
DARK MELODY
DARK SYMPHONY
DARK GUARDIAN
DARK LEGEND
DARK FIRE
DARK CHALLENGE
DARK MAGIC
DARK GOLD
DARK DESIRE
DARK PRINCE

COVERT GAME

CHRISTINE FEEHAN

JOVE
New York

A JOVE BOOK
Published by Berkley
An imprint of Penguin Random House LLC
375 Hudson Street, New York, New York 10014

ISBN: 9780451490117

Berkley hardcover edition / March 2018
Jove mass-market edition / October 2018

Printed in the United States of America
1   3   5   7   9   10   8   6   4   2

Cover illustration © Craig White
Cover design by Judith Lagerman
Book design by Kelly Lipovich

For Zara. I love you with all my heart.

FOR MY READERS

Be sure to go to christinefeehan.com/members/ to sign up for my private book announcement list and download the free ebook of *Dark Desserts*. Join my community and get firsthand news, enter the book discussions, ask your questions and chat with me. Please feel free to email me at Christine@christinefeehan.com. I would love to hear from you.

ACKNOWLEDGMENTS

I couldn't have written this book without the guidance of Dr. Christopher Tong. Thank you for allowing my heroine to take on your background in education and creativity in artificial intelligence. I appreciate the time you took helping me to understand so much about that field and machine learning. Thank you Neil Benson of Pearl River Echo Tours for patiently taking me into the swamp and showing me all the cool places where you grew up. I appreciate you giving me a love and understanding of the state, the swamp and the invaluable lands as well as the people. As always, thanks to Sheila English and Kathie Firzlaff for getting me through such a terrible loss and Brian Feehan for keeping me on track. I couldn't do this without Domini Walker and Denise Tucker. Thank you to both of you.

THE GHOSTWALKER
SYMBOL DETAILS

SIGNIFIES

shadow

SIGNIFIES

protection against evil forces

SIGNIFIES

the Greek letter psi, which is used by parapsychology researchers to signify ESP or other psychic abilities

SIGNIFIES

qualities of a knight—loyalty, generosity, courage and honor

SIGNIFIES

shadow knights who protect against evil forces using psychic powers, courage and honor

nox noctis est nostri

THE GHOSTWALKER CREED

We are the GhostWalkers, we live in the shadows
The sea, the earth, and the air are our domain
No fallen comrade will be left behind
We are loyalty and honor bound
We are invisible to our enemies
and we destroy them where we find them
We believe in justice and we protect our country
and those unable to protect themselves
What goes unseen, unheard, and unknown
are GhostWalkers
There is honor in the shadows and it is us
We move in complete silence whether
in jungle or desert
We walk among our enemy unseen and unheard
Striking without sound and scatter to the winds
before they have knowledge of our existence
We gather information and wait with endless patience
for that perfect moment to deliver swift justice
We are both merciful and merciless
We are relentless and implacable in our resolve
We are the GhostWalkers and the night is ours

1

Zara Hightower stepped into the town car with tinted windows, sliding along the leather seat, positioning her briefcase at her feet on the floor. She gave the man who slid in beside her a small smile and looked out the window, ignoring the way her heart wanted to accelerate. It was always this moment, when she was so close to her goal, when her body wanted to betray her. She never let it. Never. She was very, very good at staying in control. Breathing. Keeping her heart rate perfect, adrenaline at bay.

The car moved forward, and her head went up alertly. "Wait. I need my interpreter. She always travels with me."

The car kept moving. The man beside her, Heng Zhang, turned his head and gave her a small, polite smile. "Miss Hightower, you do not need an interpreter. I speak English."

"I'm aware that you do, Mr. Zhang, but I require my own interpreter. I made that very clear to Mr. Cheng when he invited me. I was given assurances when I agreed to speak with his people. I've turned down his request four times, and will do so this time as well if you don't stop this car immediately, turn it around and get her."

She kept her voice smooth and even. She had a certain reputation to uphold. She never lost her temper. She never raised her voice. She was always polite. She cut people down sweetly, so sweetly they almost didn't realize at first that she was telling them off. She was an expert at that as well. Seeing as how she was considered one of the world's leading minds in the field of artificial intelligence, those around her should expect that she could hold her own with anyone, but they always took one look at her and judged on appearances. Like now. Zhang made the mistake of looking her up and down and giving her a look that said she was nothing in his eyes before turning away from her and looking out the window.

In her head, she went through the moves that would end his life and then the driver's. She would use one hard-edged chop to the throat, hard enough to drive through the trachea. Or she could just scratch his arm accidentally. Smile and apologize. Then, when he slumped on the seat, for good measure she could follow up by taking his gun and shooting the driver in the back of the head, shooting Zhang to be certain and then taking control of the car. One, maybe two seconds was all she'd need.

Zara sat very still, appearing as she always did. She looked like a beautiful model with her long legs, oval face, flawless skin, large slate blue eyes and long red gold hair that fell down her back, thick and unusual, sheets of it falling below her waist, looks that most reporters ended up commenting on when they should be listening to what she had to say. Still, her looks enabled her to get her work done. She shouldn't complain. It was her looks that often kept her alive.

She turned her head and looked out the window, resisting the impulse to kill Zhang for his smug, superior attitude. They probably had a camera on her. She let her mind drift, uncaring of the direction they were taking her. She knew where Cheng's lair was. He was famous in the district, his building a fortress. The government tolerated him because he paid them well and gave them all sorts of reasons to keep him protected. Cheng bought and sold secrets and shared them often enough with the government to buy their protection.

Once at the facility, the car pulled into the underground parking garage, went through three guard stations and pulled right up to a private elevator. Zhang got out first and went around to her door. For a split second, Zara debated whether or not to have it out with them right there in the parking lot by refusing to move from the car. She knew they would force her, but she also knew they wouldn't kill her.

Cheng needed her. He wanted the information she had. He had kept doubling the price each time she refused to come to his private facility to give her talk on the VALUE system, as she called her project, and its uses in the business world. He thought he had bought her with his more than generous offer, the one that would set her up for life if she accepted it—or get her killed.

She slid out of the car without looking left or right, and followed Zhang into the elevator. Neither spoke as they were whisked up to the middle floor where Cheng waited for her. She was stopped as she stepped off. Two guards with automatic weapons took her briefcase and pointed to a door. She stepped through it into a narrow cubicle. Immediately her entire body was scanned for listening devices, weapons and cameras, anything that might harm Cheng in any way.

Zara knew Cheng was paranoid, and deservedly so. He had his hand in every criminal activity around the globe that had to do with running guns, drugs or political secrets. He had top minds working for him developing all kinds of weapons that he sold on the black market. What he didn't develop, he stole. She knew every paper in her briefcase would be scanned and copied before it was returned to her. She'd come prepared for just such a thing. Those papers were "encrypted." No one could break the code because there wasn't one. In reality, the code was nothing but sheer gibberish, but it would give Cheng's people something to keep them busy.

She was taken from the cubicle and marched through an open floor where there were several desks leading the way to Cheng's office. He stood in the doorway, all smiles, as if she should be pleased to meet him even though he'd broken their rules.

"Miss Hightower, how good of you to come," he greeted.

She stopped moving a few feet from his office, forcing Zhang and the two guards to stop as well. "My interpreter?" She didn't smile. She kept her gaze fixed on Cheng without blinking, something she'd practiced for a long time. She was very good at it.

"I'm sorry." Cheng didn't sound in the least remorseful. "You must understand I have many enemies. I don't, as a rule, allow any outsider into these facilities. There are always industrial spies. We won't need an interpreter."

Stubbornly she didn't move an inch. "Don't you think you should have let me know you changed the conditions? I'm uncomfortable without her. When I come to Shanghai, I always use her and have grown used to her."

Cheng stepped back to clear his doorway, waving toward his office. "Please come in, Miss Hightower. My staff has made you tea, which I believe is your favorite drink."

She stood for several seconds, letting them all worry. Zhang stepped close to her. "Miss Hightower." He waved toward the office.

She looked at him coolly. Haughtily. Every bit as arrogant as his boss. "I'm deciding. I added this additional talk to my agenda, and as you both are aware, I've had a very tight and exhausting schedule. I did this as a courtesy. I don't need the money. To have your boss break his word so quickly is disconcerting to say the least."

Zhang switched instantly to his native language. "Do you want me to take her up to the interrogation room? Bolan Zhu can extract the information you require from her."

Cheng shook his head, a small, humorless smile on his mouth, one that reminded Zara of a cold-blooded reptile. "Don't be so bloodthirsty, Heng. She will cooperate."

"I apologize again, Miss Hightower."

"I dislike others speaking in a language I can't understand," Zara said, still not moving. She had understood every word they said. Her resume never stated that she was gifted in languages. That was kept a secret for instances just like this one. She admitted to knowing a few pertinent words in the languages of countries she traveled to often, but was careful not to let on that she understood without her interpreter. Her heart had jumped at the name Bolan Zhu. He was extremely good at torturing people.

"Zhang was only asking after your comfort. We knew you would have trouble without your interpreter, so we tried to think of other ways that would assure you would enjoy your visit with us," Cheng lied smoothly. "We thought a tour of our labs was in order. Understand, this is a great privilege, one not extended often."

As in never. A tendril of unease slid through her. He wanted her evaluation. She understood that. He wanted to hear what she was doing in her chosen field of expertise. She understood that too. She had the feeling that seeing his labs, especially his computers, the ones that stored all that data, the secrets he blackmailed or paid others to get so he could sell out countries—including his own—to the highest bidder, would earn her a bullet in the brain.

She kept her eyes steady on Cheng's face. Zhang didn't

matter. He would carry out his boss's orders, but he wouldn't act on his own. He didn't take her as a threat.

"Miss Hightower, I realize the circumstances are unusual, but if you would just come into my office and hear me out, I would appreciate it."

She felt Zhang stiffen beside her. He didn't like his boss asking. He was used to the man ordering others and if they didn't obey, punishment was swift and brutal. The fact that she was a woman and an American probably offended him even more. Deliberately she made certain to stand as tall as possible so she could tower over Zhang. He was particularly short, and she knew it irritated him that she was tall. Cheng was the same height as she was in her heels.

Zara flashed Cheng a small smile and walked past him into the spacious office. She took the chair he indicated and sank into it, deliberately crossing her legs. Zhang didn't like her, but he appreciated her looks. Doing the leg thing always kept others from thinking she was brilliant. She'd found out that most people didn't think looks and brains could go hand in hand.

Cheng seated himself across from her, not behind his desk, clearly trying to create a much friendlier atmosphere. He picked up a file and scanned it quickly. "This is very impressive. I see you went to MIT as an undergrad and then got your PhD at Stanford in Computer Science. Your subfield is machine learning?"

He made it a question, but Zara didn't respond. Instead she looked slightly bored. She was really good at that particular look as well. She'd perfected that and the wide-eyed innocent look she was certain she was going to need very soon.

"I see you teach at Rutgers University. Why not private business? You could make a lot more money."

She shrugged. "Money bores me. I realize it makes the world go around, but I don't spend much time in the real world, Mr. Cheng. My mind prefers other pursuits." Which she supposed was the strict truth. She didn't think about money because she didn't have to. She thought about other things like life and death. Like survival. "I spend most of my time working on things others don't understand, and that's all right. My programs, hopefully, will be a contribution to the world."

"There isn't a lot here about your earlier life."

She frowned at him. "What does my earlier life have to do with my work?" She kept her voice mild, as if barely interested. She kept her heartbeat the exact same rhythm, and that took just a little extra work, but she knew it was possible her vitals were being monitored just by her sitting in the chair he'd chosen for her.

"I like to know everything about anyone I do business with."

"I'm not a businesswoman, Mr. Cheng. I lecture. I get paid to lecture. I give talks on exciting new breakthroughs in the world of artificial intelligence. That's what I thought you wanted from me, and knowing anything other than my credentials is not really helpful. I can assure you, my credentials speak for me. I'm regarded as one of the leading experts in AI and machine learning. I thought you were aware of that."

"I'm very aware of that, Miss Hightower," Cheng assured. "It's just that you're far younger than I thought you'd be. I noted your age, of course, but thought it was a typo."

His gaze flicked several times to Zhang, and more than ever she was certain they were somehow determining if she was lying or not. She liked cat-and-mouse games. She was good at them. She was fairly certain his secretary, or whoever prepared the report on her, wouldn't dare give him a report with a typo. His secretary wouldn't survive the hour.

"My age does sometimes give people pause, but I graduated with honors, I assure you," she said with a small shrug as if she didn't care whether he believed her or not. She uncrossed her legs to switch them, drawing their attention immediately. Once comfortable, she moved her foot, clad in a sexy blue high heel to match the blue jacket she wore, around in lazy circles. That always seemed to mesmerize males. It worked with Zhang, but not with Cheng.

"You disappear for long periods of time."

He made it a statement, so she smiled sweetly at him as if waiting for a question, making him ask.

He sighed. "Where do you go?"

She shook her head. "I don't really think what I do in my downtime is any of your business."

"You're more of a consulting professor for Rutgers. I want to know where you go, Miss Hightower. You're asking me to trust you around my researchers."

She stopped the lazy circles, planted both feet solidly on the floor and leaned toward him. "Let's get something straight, Mr. Cheng. I'm doing you the favor, not the other way around. I said no over and over. I made it clear I wasn't interested in your money. You may think I agreed to speak to your people because the money was too good to pass up, but it was because you intrigued me. You were that persistent. I thought the research mattered to you. If you keep insisting on playing this silly game, I would very much like you to ask your driver to return me to my hotel."

"Have I offended you with my questions?"

Zhang interrupted, once again in his language. "Let me take her to the interrogation room, Mr. Cheng."

"That's it." Zara stood up, glaring at Zhang. "I can't believe how rude you're being when you *invited* me here. Please return my briefcase and escort me down to the car."

Cheng stood as well. "Mr. Zhang will be leaving us.

I'm sorry for his rude behavior. Mr. Zhang, send in Mr. Zhu." He indicated the door with a jerk of his chin and it said something for the fear his people felt, even those closest to him, that Zhang hastened toward the door.

"Please sit, Miss Hightower. I'm used to people trying to spy on us, stealing what we've worked hard to develop. Just a few weeks ago, a spy escaped with valuable information. It set us back months."

Zara kept her heart from accelerating, but it was difficult after hearing the name Bolan Zhu twice. She knew all about him. He was Cheng's right hand and probably far more feared even than Cheng. He was the interrogator sent in for difficult subjects. Most people never got near him. He was the man Cheng trusted more than any other. Little was known about Zhu, until he served with the army.

Zara decided it was better to appear to cooperate than have Bolan Zhu threaten her. It was one thing for Zhang to do so, but Zhu was a different matter altogether. She sank into the chair and gave a pretty little moue with her lips. "I'm sorry. I think I'm being temperamental because I'm tired and your Mr. Zhang wasn't the most welcoming."

Cheng looked up as Zhu walked through the door. Bolan Zhu was tall and wore a very expensive suit in a dark charcoal. He gave Zara a small smile as Cheng introduced them.

"So nice to finally have you here, Miss Hightower," Zhu greeted. "Cheng has spoken of you often. He is a great admirer of your work."

Clearly the man was as charming as he was lethal. Her information on him included the fact that he enjoyed traveling abroad and when he did, he visited clubs nightly. He was considered quite a ladies' man, and Zara could see why. He was extremely handsome. She gave him a smile and sat a little straighter.

"That's nice of you to say," she murmured, lowering her lashes. She felt rather than saw the two men exchange a look. They bought that she was a little affected by Zhu's good looks and charming manner.

"Miss Hightower was just going to tell me where she disappears to when she isn't at the university, which is often," Cheng said.

"It's a little embarrassing," Zara said, acting reluctant. She snuck a quick glance at Zhu as if talking in front of him was the reason she would be embarrassed. "I work very hard for long periods of time without sleeping or sometimes eating. I realize it isn't the best thing for my health, but I just can't remember to eat or sleep when I'm on to something. I've been known to wake up in the middle of the night and use my walls for paper to write on. I often take breaks, sometimes just a couple of weeks, but often longer, to regroup. I go on retreats where I don't have access to a computer, phone or television. I have to shut out the world entirely. Sometimes I sleep for twenty-four hours straight."

"That makes sense." Zhu jumped to her defense. "Cheng told me you were a child prodigy, one of the leading AI experts at a very young age."

"It's such a fascinating idea," Zara said, pouring enthusiasm into her voice, hoping neither man would realize she hadn't answered the question of where she'd been. Only what she'd been doing. "Artificial intelligence is a growing field, covering so many things that could be useful. People have the mistaken idea that it is just robotics— although that alone is amazing and forward-thinking—but it's so much more."

"We spend some time and energy on robotics here," Cheng said. "You think that's a waste of time?"

"No, of course not. It's just that artificial intelligence can be used in a much broader scope. I don't want any student to get bogged down thinking in a box, just thinking one thing. Already we have small examples of machines learning. They can help so many people. On a small scale, people stuck in houses can just ask their devices to order food or supplies for them. If an elderly man or woman falls in their home, they can call out to their device and have it call for an ambulance or family member. The possibilities are limitless."

There was genuine enthusiasm in her voice. She sat up straight and her face lit up. Her eyes did. She was very aware of the changes in her and allowed them. She wanted Cheng and Zhu to see she was exactly what she said she was, a very young professor who believed in exploring artificial intelligence.

"Why did you choose a subfield like machine learning versus something else, like robotics?" Cheng asked.

"I like machines. I like programming, not that I do much of that anymore myself, but numbers speak to me. Machines are logical." Her long lashes fluttered and she made a small face. "I get carried away when I talk about my work. Please forgive me. What else do you need to know before I give my talk to your people, Mr. Cheng? I don't want to take up any more of your time than I need to. It's getting late, and I'm certain your employees need to get home."

"They would wait all night to get a chance to ask questions of you, Miss Hightower," Cheng said. "Your briefcase has few papers we can understand. Your code appears to be unbreakable. Did you devise it yourself?"

She burst out laughing. "The few papers you can understand are used for my talk. The others are sequences of numbers I put together when I'm working out a problem in my head. It soothes me."

"Hasn't anyone ever stopped you, believing it's a code of some kind?"

She shrugged. "It's happened, but eventually they real-ize it's nothing but me doing something repetitious that helps me think."

Cheng's brows came together and he regarded her with skepticism. "Didn't you have trouble coming into the country with those papers?"

"I only had a couple of papers with numbers at the time and someone assured those holding me that it's no code but random sets of numbers repeated over and over on several pages. That ensures everyone thinks I'm a little eccentric, which I probably am."

"That doesn't make sense," Cheng said, suspicion in his voice.

"It does if she's OCD," Zhu pointed out, looking straight at Zara. "Those random numbers are repeated in sets of three."

Zara didn't change expression and she kept her heart rate exactly the same—a nice steady rhythm as if she didn't have a care in the world. As if she wasn't sitting in a room with two deadly vipers ready to strike at any mo-ment. Zhu's answer meant he'd looked at those papers.

A timid knock announced the arrival of the tea. It was Zhu who physically got up and opened the door. Zara found that fascinating. He didn't call out to the woman carrying in the tray; he got up and took the tray from her. She never entered Cheng's office, and Zhu lowered him-self to carrying the tea tray. He set it on the small table in front of Zara. She knew she was really in trouble. Zhu didn't care what others thought of him. He didn't stand on protocol or ego. That made him very, very dangerous.

Was Cheng so paranoid that he didn't allow anyone into his office? Probably, she decided. "I don't mind pour-ing the tea for everyone," she said, pitching her voice low, almost submissive. "I don't know if that would be offen-sive to either of you. I'm unsure of the custom when there is no other woman in the room."

She knew Cheng would never pour her tea. He'd already stepped far back as if that would save him from having to do such a menial task in front of her.

Zhu had no such problem. He simply smiled at her and shook his head. "We are very modern here, Miss Hightower. I have no problems pouring you tea." He suited actions to words, picking up the little pot and pouring the liquid into three cups.

She watched very carefully, making certain he didn't put anything in the tea. He poured quickly and efficiently, his long fingers looking incongruous on the small cups. He was mesmerizing. Frightening, but mesmerizing. Bolan Zhu was a very scary man. He appeared modern and sophisticated, very charming with his white teeth and startling green eyes. His shoulders were wide, filling out his suit beautifully, and when he walked, he seemed to glide.

She noted that he served Cheng first and her second. They weren't quite as modern as they wanted her to believe. She took the cup of tea, observing that Zhu's index finger touched the rim, sliding around it in one continuous motion. The drug was on the outside of the cup, not the inside, but it was where her lips would go no matter where she placed them. Zhu also took a cup and deliberately brought it to his mouth and drank. Cheng also drank. Both watched her.

Zara had a couple of choices. She could drop the cup and "accidentally" break it, or she could drink it and hope they weren't trying to kill her. She suspected Zhu would interrogate her and whatever drug he'd just introduced to the rim of the cup would compel her to tell the truth. She lifted the cup to her lips and sipped. She had to take the chance. She knew if she didn't, Zhu would probably incarcerate her, and that wouldn't go well for her at all.

"Have you been taken around the city at all?" Zhu asked.

"No. I haven't had time. I've been here four times, and mostly I see the inside of hotels or facilities where I've been asked to speak," she said, taking another sip. She looked at the liquid in the teacup. "This is exceptionally good. I don't think I've ever had this before and I order tea all the time."

Zhu sat in the chair closest to her, and Cheng seemed to fade into the background. "All our teas are made from one single plant, did you know that? It's actually an evergreen shrub that can grow into a small tree and live over a hundred years. It grows in southeast China and the leaves are harvested year-round."

He watched as she sipped at the tea. She smiled at him. "Well, it's excellent."

"Why did you come here?"

"I was invited, of course. I don't like to travel that much anymore, so I only go where I'm invited." She frowned. Something was definitely working on her brain. She had to puzzle it out fast. "That's not exactly true. I turn down a lot of invitations as well. I travel to the countries I'm interested in. Ones that are beautiful, but then I don't get to see them because I'm working."

Was she babbling? It sounded like it to her, but the words just tumbled out. She had to rein it in. Think. Force her brain to process whatever it was, and work around it. She was good at repeating numbers in her head. That would lessen the effect of the drug on her. She watched the reactions of the two men and realized they expected her to babble and blurt things out. Well, she could do that.

"You find our country beautiful?"

"Don't you?" she countered. "It's so *alive*. I love the people." She didn't have to lie about that. "There are so many things to love." She put her fingers over her mouth as if embarrassed. "I'm sorry. I don't usually carry on this much." She took another sip of tea, careful to keep her mouth in exactly the same place. She didn't need a larger dose of Zhu's truth drug. Was it a new strain? Something that didn't slow her mind. It had to be a new strain. This wasn't making her slow and sleepy. It wasn't slowing her brain at all. What was it doing to her? She continued to count sequences of numbers in her head and solve intricate problems. It helped to clear her mind of the effects of the drug.

Zhu leaned into her, took her teacup from her and placed it on the table. Very gently he turned her hand over and stroked her wrist once. Something slithered through her mind, something unsettling that coiled hotly in her belly. He was looking at her differently. Not with the eyes of a viper, but more like a predator—a wolf or a tiger, something with teeth about to pounce. Her heart jumped. Stuttered. His fingers pressed into her wrist, right over her pulse, and she forced calm when she felt more threatened than ever.

"Do you wish Mr. Cheng harm?"

Her gaze leapt to Zhu's face. "Harm? Of course not. He seems a very nice man. He asked me to talk to his employees. I thought perhaps they would benefit from my work." She needed to blurt something out. Something true. "You have a really beautiful mouth. I should know. I notice mouths all the time." That was a truth that seemed to come flying out. She put her hand over her mouth again and tried to pull her arm away at the same time.

Zhu smiled at her and clamped his fingers around her wrist, but so gently she almost didn't realize he was holding her still. "Thank you. I was thinking the same of yours. What is the true reason you've come to see us tonight?"

His voice was extraordinary. She almost told him so, but that calm she called on, the one that kept her heart from beating out of control, thankfully prevented her from blurting out that he was mesmerizing. Spellbinding. "I came to talk about a new project my team has developed to Mr. Cheng's chosen researchers, the ones he thought would be interested in my work."

Her eyelashes fluttered at him because she knew it was expected of her. She wasn't a flirt. She never flirted because it would be fruitless to flirt. She couldn't have a relationship with anyone. She was forever alone. Now that her best friends were gone, she was truly alone.

"You look sad."

Those long fingers stroked her arm, sending more ripples of awareness snaking through her. It was more unsettling to her than if he'd put a gun to her head. "Do I? I guess I was thinking sad thoughts."

"Tell me."

"I lost my best friends recently." She lifted her chin, making her eyes go wide in seeming surprise that she'd blurted out such a personal detail. "That's personal and not pertinent to what I need to be doing here. Please take me to this group. It's already late, and I'm getting tired." It wasn't the drug making her tired, but she knew it made her susceptible to Zhu and his mesmerizing voice. She could feel his pull on her. She kept up the numbers running in her head, combating the drug in the only way she could.

Zhu immediately pulled back and looked at Cheng, who nodded. "Mr. Cheng thought you might like a tour of the facility. He's very proud of it and the work environment he's created here. It's a haven of sorts for his people. They're very loyal to him. He provides apartments, day care, and even exercise rooms." He stood up and gently tugged on her hand until she was up with him.

The touch of his skin on hers sent an electric current sizzling through her. What was that? She hadn't experienced it before. Not. Ever. The drug wasn't a date rape drug, but it was something that made her respond chemically to him. In her mind, she gave a delicate shudder.

She knew such things existed and they could even be permanent—causing the woman or man to be obsessed with the person giving off the pheromones.

Zhu led her out of Cheng's office, one hand on the small of her back. She'd never been so aware of another human being in her life as she was of Bolan Zhu as he walked her through the facility. She noted that several floors were avoided and most of the people failed to greet Zhu—in fact they kept their eyes downcast.

It was definitely pheromones. Some kind of drug that made her physically susceptible to him. His fingers burned through her clothing right into her skin. She snuck a glance up at him. His breathing was much better than her own but not quite normal. He'd had to touch the drug with his fingers before administering it onto the rim of the teacup. He'd drunk his tea. Had he touched his fingers to his mouth? She couldn't remember. Her body had grown hot. She was almost too uncomfortable to listen to the sound of his voice.

Zara managed to ooh and aah in all the right places, but it was clear to both of them that she was struggling against her attraction to Zhu more than she was paying attention to the things he was showing her. After all, that was the point, wasn't it? She kept that uppermost in her mind so she wasn't too ashamed of herself for the fight she had to put up to not give in to the drug's effects. And she kept solving number problems in her head.

Before her talk, she had him take her to the ladies' room. She threw up like she did every time before she gave her talk. From experience she knew, once she got started, she would be fine, but the idea of standing before colleagues, others interested in AI work, always made her feel incredibly sick. She knew if Zhu was aware she was ill, he would think she had something to hide. He would never consider it nerves. She carefully rinsed her mouth and ate the strong peppermint candy she always carried before rejoining him.

"I'd like to take you on a tour of our city," Zhu said as he brought her to the auditorium where they'd set up a podium for her. Her briefcase was there, sitting right beside the glass of water provided for her.

"I'd love that." She'd be long gone, thankful she'd escaped with her life.

He took her straight to the podium, and Zara immediately slipped into her role. She hated everything about her life but this—talking about what she loved and believed in with those interested. That, more than anything else, always allowed her to escape the horrible shyness that made her the worst traveler ever. She had developed the character everyone saw and believed, and she hid behind her. Once she got past her nerves, she could settle into explaining the program and why it could be so helpful on so many levels.

Zhu stood to one side. Close. Beyond the lights she could see half a dozen men with automatic weapons at the entrances. She pretended not to, but it was a very definite fight to keep her heart rate normal.

At her introduction, conducted by another very charming man in a suit, the applause was enthusiastic. She wondered if Cheng had threatened all of them—applaud her loudly or my goons will shoot you.

"Good evening. My talk is called the VALUE system, the program you'd love to have as a partner. I think you'll see why in just a moment . . ." She trailed off and scanned her audience. She'd given her talk dozens of times already and knew it was cutting-edge. They would be hanging on every word if they were really interested in artificial intelligence and what it could do for them.

She reached out to the machines on the first floor. The computers. Touching them with her energy, that psychic gift Dr. Whitney had so carefully enhanced. She could talk to machines, and they listened with rapt attention just as these people were listening. She had the ability to serve as a wireless conduit between the remote computers and her wireless hard drive. She instructed the remote computers to transfer their data from every one of the computers, floor by floor, and store it in the PEEK-carbon nanotube hiding the SSD in her brain.

"AI game-playing systems since the 1960s have been fixated on winning. Every twenty years there is a quantum leap in AI programs' ability to win. Arthur Samuel built the first self-learning program in 1959, a program that learned how to play checkers increasingly better over time. The program reached a respectable amateur level status of play by the 1970s. Fast-forward twenty years, and in 1997, you could watch the deep learning program, Deep Blue, beat the reigning world chess champion, Garry Kasparov—an amazing accomplishment! Fast-forward another twenty years, and in 2017, you see Google's deep learning program, AlphaGo, beat the reigning world Go champion."

It took time to transfer the amount of data stored in the computers in Cheng's facility. It would take as long to destroy every hard drive to ensure the man had none of the data on the GhostWalker program given to him by the treasonous senator Violet Smythe. Zara kept her voice even and calm, so that later, when Cheng and Zhu compared it with other speeches she'd given, there would be no difference. Inflections would be the same. She wasn't under undue stress. She couldn't possibly be the reason they lost the data on every computer. She was incredibly thankful for her mind's ability to work on solving number problems. In doing so, it had lessened the effects of the drug they'd given her enough for her to control the systems in her body.

"But here's one thing we have yet to see . . . What about a program that could learn to intentionally *lose* when playing a little boy, so that boy could experience winning? What about a program that could learn how to propose 'win-win' solutions for itself and someone else? What about a program that knows that 'you can't always get what you want' and learns how to 'get what you need' by making good trade-offs given limited, competing resources—time, money, people, materials, et cetera?"

The idea had been talked about for years. For trade, such a program would be invaluable. It was expected that there would be a breakthrough sooner or later, but to be able to stand in front of them and announce it had been accomplished was exciting. Every. Single. Time. She had to be careful to never lose sight of why she was really there. She needed the information in those computers. She'd done this so many times, but she'd never had to destroy the hard drives. Most businesses or universities had no idea she'd taken anything out with her when she went because she only gathered information; she never left evidence that their computers had been touched. Destroying the hard drives of every computer in the building would definitely raise alarms.

"In this talk, I'm going to describe a program, the VALUE system, which integrates an entire suite of learning techniques, some old and some new, to do just that. The VALUE system integrates: the inverse reinforcement learning techniques of Russell and Ng for learning the value of others, our earlier deep learning techniques for creating and refining negotiations and compromise in a two-party circumstance, our new supervised learning techniques for reformulating design spaces based on human guidance with acceptable trade-offs."

She launched into her talk, trying not to get lost in the excitement of the artificial intelligence world and the endless possibilities that always consumed her mind when she allowed herself to become fully immersed there. She had a job, a much more important one, in terms of serving her country, saving lives and getting out of there alive.

As each of the computers gave up its data, its hard drive destroyed itself, wiping out all documents, making certain no trace remained. It was a big facility, but she was used to delivering her talks while making the data transfers. She was certain the flow of information to her would never be detected, so she was never nervous. It was a matter of instructing the machines in any chosen building to cooperate. She didn't need to hack in, or figure out passwords. She just needed a wireless environment. Destroying the hard drives after was a much riskier thing to do, and she'd never done it before. That left footprints. No one could prove she had anything to do with the losses, but she was there. On-site.

Zara let her enthusiasm for her work show, in her voice, her mannerisms, the way her face lit up. She wanted to be animated, and she was. Her mind had finally let go of her curious obsession with Bolan Zhu, the need to focus on her academia and the particular program she was spearheading overcoming the last remnants of the drug. This program was her "baby" all the way, and she was totally immersed in that world and had been for a long while when the sirens blared loudly. Instantly, the room went electric. Zara stopped speaking to look around, allowing her heart rate to accelerate just as everyone's had to be. Her audience stood up in silence and began filing out of the room like robots.

Zara gathered her papers and turned to Zhu. "What's happening?" Fear crept into her voice. Just enough of a note that she hoped Zhu would think was normal under the circumstances. She had to keep collecting the remaining data and destroying the hard drives as she went. There was no protection from her unless the wireless was shut down. Only half a floor to go and she'd be finished. She had no way of knowing what data was in what computer on what floor, but even as Zhu reached her, gathering her into him, she kept up the transfer and destruction.

"We have to get you to safety and then I'll check it out," Zhu assured. "I can't imagine a drill being scheduled, so this is more likely a glitch in the system or someone left chemicals out when they shouldn't have. Don't be alarmed." He escorted her to a small room.

No windows, Zara noted. She heard the lock turn when he left her. She didn't bother trying the door. Sinking down onto the chair, she glanced at her watch, noting the time. She wanted to press the stopwatch, but she forced herself to leave it alone. She had time, but it would run out fast if she didn't get out of Cheng's facility. She knew his lockdowns could last a week or longer.

She told herself her mission was important to Whitney. He wouldn't allow her to die, not when what she had in her head was so valuable to him. Calmly, she finished the data transfers and destroyed all remaining hard drives in the building. She could be calm because she had something for her mind to work on, but the moment that was done, fear poured in and she rocked herself in terror.

2

Gino Mazza rested one hip against the wall and regarded his best friend and team leader, Joe Spagnola. Joe shouldn't have been up, running around, let alone called to the Pentagon just to get their orders directly from Major General Tennessee Milton, the man overseeing the Air Force's Division of GhostWalkers.

He knew Joe. They'd been kids together. That seemed so long ago. Gino had grown up in an extremely wealthy family, so much money it had been said they could buy a small country if they wanted. That money hadn't done them much good when their home had been invaded and his parents and grandparents from both sides had stood in front of him and been shot down one by one for their efforts to prevent the men from kidnapping him. It had been his twelfth birthday. He'd been shot three times and left for dead because, once you killed the family, who was going to pay the ransom?

Of course, each family member had one heir. Gino. He inherited a fortune from his grandparents on his father's side. Again, on his mother's side. Then from his parents, and he received everything from his mother's private trust. He got everything and he had nothing. He would much rather have had his family back. He'd turned his back on the money, detesting that someone valued it far more than the lives of his family.

Gino carried scars from those three bullets. He had earned a hell of a lot more since, but those scars ran the deepest. They reminded him every day that families could be fragile. His parents had been decent people—no, *good* people. He thought of them every single day and wondered what he would be like if they'd lived. Most certainly he'd be a better man.

Joe Spagnola's family had taken him in. The two fathers had known each other since they were children. It was Joe who'd found Gino and saved his life. Life was very different after that. Ciro was head of a crime family and was every bit as ruthless as Gino's father was kind. How the two men were best friends remained a mystery, but it was Joe's father, not the police, who'd found the men who had wiped out Gino's family. The men were tortured mercilessly before they were killed. They died hard, and Gino watched it all.

Joe and Gino were sent to the best schools. They also were required—and that was a polite way of saying it—to learn martial arts from dozens of trainers, the best in the world. Boxing and street fighting followed, and they trained for hours every day. They learned how to use a variety of weapons: knives, sticks, guns, everything Ciro and the trainers could conceive of.

Gino followed Joe into the Air Force and from there, pararescue training. Then the GhostWalker program. If there was one thing both men knew how to do, it was to take care of themselves. Until Joe tried to save a woman from herself. Senator Violet Smythe had stuck a knife in Joe and twisted it for good measure, making sure to do as much damage as possible. He was still healing and had no business getting on planes and flying to Washington at the major general's insistence.

"Major General received a personal call from Dr. Whitney," Joe announced, looking around the room at his team—at the nine men serving under the major general with him. None of them liked the idea that Dr. Whitney, the man who had created the GhostWalker program, would dare to call their boss.

Whitney wasn't sane. They'd all agreed on that. Worse, he was a megalomaniac with far too many friends in high places and way too much money.

"It seems one of his GhostWalkers has gone missing. She was sent to Shanghai to Cheng's facility there, the one Bellisia barely escaped from with her life. Whitney's agent apparently managed to wipe the computers of all data, including everything Cheng had on the GhostWalker program, but she's being held prisoner. He wants us to go in and get her out."

There was a shocked silence. Mordichai Fortunes cleared his throat. "Wait. Whitney wants us to work for him? After all the shit he's pulled on us, he wants us to do a job for him?"

"Doesn't he have his own little army?" Rubin Campo asked. His voice was mild. Gino had never heard him speak above that soft, accented tone.

"Yeah, he's got an army," Joe agreed. "But they aren't like us. Cheng is a powerful man with a lot of clout in Shanghai. Whitney's soldiers are more like tanks. Or robots. They self-destruct very fast. You all know that. He's still experimenting, and his experiments have gone in another direction. We don't like Whitney, but the fact is, one of us is a prisoner in enemy territory and in danger. She's a GhostWalker, the same as we are."

Gino noted Joe looked uneasy when he glanced at Ezekiel Fortunes. The two had clashed when Ezekiel had met his wife, Bellisia. Joe had ordered her incarcerated briefly, just until they finished an important mission they were running. Ezekiel hadn't liked it and he'd let Joe know. Gino straightened from his lazy pose against the wall. He made the move subtly, silently, gliding into a better position to defend Joe if there was need.

Ordinarily, when they were having a meeting, it was understood that Joe was in charge and no one contradicted him. He gave orders and they obeyed. That was military life. The thing was, they weren't ordinary. They only had one another. There were four teams of GhostWalkers, but each of those four teams were somewhat isolated from other military units. That meant sometimes the lines blurred for them when they talked to one another. Or like now, when Joe was about to say something he believed Ezekiel clearly wouldn't like.

"Whitney called Major General the moment he was informed that his agent hadn't returned to her hotel. He said it was imperative we get there as soon as possible to get her out due to Cheng's reputation of torturing and killing anyone he doesn't like."

Gino figured it stood to reason Cheng wouldn't like an industrial spy, let alone one that would wipe out the data on GhostWalkers that Cheng had worked so hard to collect.

"I spoke at length with Bellisia and she assures me that she knows the woman; her name is Zara Hightower. Apparently, Zara has always been Bellisia's closest friend."

There it was. Bellisia was Ezekiel's wife and he was very, very protective of her. Gino kept his movements subtle, but he was careful to be in a place he could move fast to intercept any aggression on either part if necessary. Ordinarily, Joe could protect himself, but his wounds had been serious. He doubted Ezekiel would really do anything to try to hurt Joe, but Gino had been protecting him since they were children, and the habit wouldn't die.

"Zara works outside Whitney's seeming control quite a bit of the time. She was allowed to go to school, and he sent her to the best. A childhood prodigy or something. You know how Whitney loves brains. She taught at Rutgers and now works mainly consulting. She is invited all over the world by businesses to give talks on artificial intelligence and her particular subfield, which is learning machines."

"So, she's given a tremendous amount of freedom," Mordichai said.

"You talked to Bellisia without talking to me first?" Ezekiel sounded mild enough.

Gino inched closer. Ezekiel was never good when he sounded that calm.

Joe ignored Ezekiel and focused on Mordichai. "Certainly more freedom than most of his women. She's written up in all the journals and her name is everywhere in conjunction with artificial intelligence."

Wyatt nodded and glanced across the table at Trap. "She and her team have developed some leading-edge programs in her field."

Trap rubbed the bridge of his nose. He was considered leading-edge himself in researching new drugs for various diseases as well as in quite a few other fields. "I remember reading, very early on when she was a professor at Rutgers, one of the youngest, just a kid, she was creating some kind of knowledge compilation program to teach other programs to learn faster or something along those lines."

"Which is?" Malichai prompted.

"You would tell the knowledge compiler what kind of program you wanted, what it would have to do, and the knowledge compiler would automatically write the program for you. She had four of her PhD students working on different pieces of the overall program. It was in such a way that each student had an important and exciting research problem they had to solve as they were constructing their piece of the overall program."

Wyatt nodded. "It was a win-win situation for both her and her students. They got their PhD dissertations and she got her program."

"Now that knowledge compiler program she built with her students back then is a piece of her current VALUE system," Trap added.

"She's the real deal, Joe," Wyatt continued. "Smart as hell. I had no idea she was a GhostWalker. Never met her. Did you, Trap?"

Trap shook his head. "We traveled in different circles, but I started at the university when I was in my teens, obviously before her. When I heard of her, I kept up with her progress, just to see how she was doing. She's younger than me, but after I read about her, I wanted to see how well she did for herself."

"I would think Whitney would make sure none of us ever met her," Ezekiel said. "Just my wife. Bellisia. Her best friend. My *wife*. The woman Joe talked to without talking to me first. I thought we had multiple discussions about that, Joe."

"If we did, I don't remember, Zeke," Joe said, finally turning to face him. "Bellisia had no problem telling me the things I needed to know without you holding her hand. I didn't bite her. We just talked."

"Like anyone's going to bite that woman," Malichai whispered in a too-loud voice. "If she bites you back, it's over, as in you drop dead."

"Don't think he's worried about you biting her, Joe," Mordichai announced. "Zeke's got himself in trouble and he's worried she's going to be looking for love in all the wrong places."

Ezekiel wadded up the sheet of paper in front of him and threw it at his brother. "Shut the hell up."

Gino relaxed, allowing the coiling snake inside him to

unwind. He should have known Ezekiel's brothers would take care of the tension that hadn't quite worked itself out between Joe and Zeke.

"So, getting back to the problem Major General sent us," Joe said. "We know for sure that Zara Hightower is one of us, and right now she's sitting in Cheng's fortress. If we don't go get her, the chances that she will survive are zero."

"Did Whitney admit to planting the same virus in her that he planted in Bellisia?" Ezekiel asked. "Does she need the antidote?"

"No. Funny that he managed to leave that out when he talked to Major General," Joe said. "Bellisia stated Zara was never allowed to leave without the virus capsule in her."

"How do we know that's true?" Diego asked. "Whitney might have told Bellisia and the other girls that. This Zara could be working for him and leading us into a trap. For all we know, Whitney could have sold us to Cheng. He sold out Ezekiel."

"No," Joe denied. "He didn't. That was all Violet." He touched his abdomen, unconsciously smoothing his fingers over the wound the senator had inflicted when she'd betrayed them all. "She sold out Zeke and the rest of us when she gave Cheng the GhostWalker program. Whitney's insane and he's willing to do just about anything to experiment, but he is a patriot and he wouldn't give us up. That much I believe, and so does Major General."

Wyatt groaned. "That means we're going to China to rescue this chick. Do you know how much trouble I'm going to get into from Pepper if I leave right now?"

"Major General didn't give us any choice on this one, although, of course, it's all volunteer."

A little snicker went up around the room.

"Whitney said he'd allow us to keep the woman without his trying to get her back if we rescued her. One more

GhostWalker, a brilliant one at that, a female—of course Major General is going to make the bargain. Neither Whitney nor Major General wants Cheng to recognize that she's a GhostWalker. He'll take her apart if he finds out," Joe said.

"No wonder Whitney didn't tell the general about the virus. He figures we'll rescue the woman and then she'll haul ass back to Whitney as fast as she can go so she doesn't die. If she doesn't make it back and dies before she can get there, at least Cheng doesn't have her. Whitney wins all the way around," Mordichai said.

"Aside from what Bellisia thinks, Joe," Gino said, "do you think we can trust that this woman isn't working with Whitney and that's why he wants us to go in after her? He could just let the virus kill her. There has to be more here than any of us are seeing."

Joe sighed. "Nothing with Whitney is straightforward. Nevertheless, we can't leave her in Cheng's hands. This is a suicide mission as far as I can tell, so in spite of what Major General says about mandatory, this is volunteer basis only. If you do agree to go, you would have to leave in three days at 21:00 that evening."

Gino knew if there weren't enough volunteers, Joe would go. That meant he was going either way. He couldn't let Joe go, still healing from the wound that nearly ended his life.

"Three days doesn't give us very long to train," Ezekiel pointed out.

"Right now, construction is huge in China, particularly in Shanghai. Apartments are going up for the elderly. Several American contractors are working with crews there and have been for a while. New workers move through there all the time. You're going in as workers scattered among several different crews. Our equipment is being transported with the equipment needed for the construction project. You'll have to leave when the next crews are changing out so there is no suspicion. This company is already established and they bring in new workers and equipment all the time," Joe stated.

"How big a team do we need?" Ezekiel asked.

"It has to be small. Five-man team. If it goes to hell, less men to get out."

"I'll go," Ezekiel said immediately. "This is Bellisia's best friend. She talks about her all the time."

"I'm in," Gino said immediately.

"Count me in," Draden Freeman volunteered.

"Not doin' much in this next week," Rubin said with a small shrug.

"Likewise," Diego added, which wasn't a shock to anyone. Rubin and Diego watched Ezekiel's back whether he liked it or not. It probably had something to do with him looking after them when they were all on the streets.

"I had a hankerin' to see China," Mordichai objected.

"Me too," Malichai added.

"Too late," Ezekiel said. "We've got our five-man team."

"Well, shit," Mordichai said. "That woman of Trap's is still tryin' to learn to cook and on her night, I swear the woman's tryin' to poison us all. I might pay one of you to stay home this trip and give me a break."

"My woman's going to hear what you have to say, Mordichai, and she'll tie you up to the ceiling," Trap threatened.

The others hooted because it was a very real possibility.

Joe waited for the laughter to fade. "Major General has given his permission to incorporate the women if you need them as backup or in any other capacity. Cayenne and Bellisia, obviously not Pepper, Wyatt, so don't give me that glare, although she did try to pay me to ship you out."

That brought smiles. Pepper was in her first trimester and already Wyatt was a wreck. Even with being a doctor, he was nervous, standing over her, ordering her around, walking with her three times a day, watching every bite of food that went into her mouth, making certain she was taking her prenatal vitamins and generally hovering. It wouldn't have surprised Gino if Pepper had tried to bribe Joe to send Wyatt out on a mission.

"Was that Whitney's idea—to send the women—or Major General's?" Ezekiel asked.

Joe frowned. "Good question. If Whitney planted that seed, it would be best not to let them anywhere near Shanghai. If it is an ambush, they'd be right back in Whitney's hands—or worse—Cheng's."

There was a small silence. No one was willing to risk their women, but on the other hand, Bellisia and Cayenne were both lethal and would be a huge asset if needed.

Ezekiel shook his head. "I don't like it. Too convenient. Whitney wants them back. He's not getting them. I know Bellisia would want to go to help Zara out, but until I know Zara isn't working with Whitney to make that happen, I want Bellisia right here where she's safe. Cayenne as well. Mordichai will just have to put up with their cooking."

This time it was Ezekiel who waited for the laughter to fade. "We need intel on where she's being held. Do we have any?"

"Whitney turned over all his intel on Cheng to Major General and he's sent it to us. You should consult Bellisia as well to double-check it. She might remember more than she already gave me. She was actually there and might have a better understanding of where they could be holding Zara. She said the top floor, nearest the roof, was where they took prisoners they interrogated, so her best guess was that they would hold her there," Joe said.

Ezekiel was all business. He nodded. He took having four of his colleagues, brothers really, entrusted to him very seriously. "What did she tell you about Zara?"

"She goes in without a weapon. She's an industrial spy, not a government spy. She can't take pain at all. Bellisia said if Zara hadn't been so brainy, Whitney would have gotten rid of her a long time ago. He wants them all to be stoic. No matter how much he tried to condition her to pain, she couldn't take it."

Gino knew exactly what that shit meant. The woman was subjected to pain in order to gain a higher tolerance for it. That was Whitney's fucked-up way of thinking. He'd like to put a cap in the bastard's head. Torturing girls. Children. Experimenting on them because he found them in orphanages and considered them throwaways. Yeah, he wanted to go to Shanghai.

"What do we know about Cheng?" Ezekiel asked.

"Bernard Lee Cheng was born of an American mother, an actress, and a very ruthless businessman there in Shanghai. His mother was beautiful and his father powerful. Between the two, he had contacts in both countries and grew up to be very, very powerful, more so even than his father," Joe said. "He inherited the business from his father and has built it beyond anyone's imagining. There isn't a secret anyone has in any government that he doesn't eventually find out about."

"And Bolan Zhu? What do we know about him?" Ezekiel persisted.

"Cheng's right-hand man," Joe said. "He's a little murkier. Served in the military and acquired a certain reputation. He's the enforcer for Cheng and scares the shit out of just about anyone he comes in contact with. His expertise is taking apart people, and he does it efficiently. There's very little about his personal life. Like Cheng, he doesn't have a permanent woman, but there have been many. None last more than a few weeks for either of them. Nothing is known about his parents. Nothing at all. His life started there in the military as Bolan Zhu, but his earlier childhood was wiped out."

Joe looked around the room. "There's nothing about this that's good. Not one damn thing. I don't like that Whitney called Major General personally. I don't like that Major General suggested the women go along. I don't like that we can't get to you if things go to shit, and the number one thing you can count on is things always go to shit."

Ezekiel shrugged. "You keep everyone safe here and we'll get the job done and bring her home."

"Be prepared for a virus. Gino, you're on the woman. You can find the capsule and hopefully get it out before it breaks open. If not, you'll only have a couple of days to figure out the antidote. Whitney wasn't generous enough to give us one," Joe said. "If she's working with Whitney and is any kind of a threat to us, Bellisia, Cayenne, Pepper or the children, kill her."

Gino nodded, although there was a nasty taste in his mouth. He didn't like killing women. It was a line he'd drawn, but sometimes, out of necessity, it had to be crossed. When that happened, it stayed with him. He could put away the others, but women haunted him. He remembered each of the few, the circumstances and the way they looked crumbling to the ground. He looked away from the others, but he nodded all the same.

No one could be allowed to be a threat to their family. The men in this room, their women and children and Wyatt's grandmother, were family. They had one another and fought together and pooled resources to stay alive, carving a fortress out of the swamp in order to better defend themselves against anyone trying to harm them.

"You'll go in with the contractor's crew, and once in Shanghai, you won't have much time, so orient yourselves immediately. For those going, you'll do a night jump, HALO from a commercial charter plane, the company working in Shanghai uses. You'll land on the roof of this building. You'll have to watch for the series of water tanks, so you'll need to land north to south with the predicted winds."

A high-altitude, low-opening jump—a HALO—at night was done often, but this would be a precision landing with no room for error, and if there was a guard on the roof . . . The room went silent. A jump like that might really be a suicide mission.

"What kind of security they have up there?" Gino asked.

"Cameras, no guard. That's where Rubin is going to come in. You'll have to jump first out of the plane, Rubin, and disrupt those cameras as you're coming down."

Rubin nodded, but Gino looked at Joe sharply. They had two men with the particular psychic ability to disrupt electrical equipment and Rubin was one of them. His brother Diego was the other. How had Joe known they'd volunteer? He'd known exactly who would go. Probably, he was counting on all of them volunteering. No one would leave another GhostWalker behind in enemy territory, especially one who had risked her life to save the rest of them. A woman. Damn Whitney to hell for using women.

"We know she's being held on the top floor, but we don't know the room. That floor will be heavily guarded with cameras everywhere. It will require both of you to take those cameras out while the others take down the guards. Gino, Draden, the two of you do your thing that you never explain to any of us and find where she is fast. Get her out of there." Joe sighed and looked around the table at his men. "This is a non-sanctioned op. You can't kill anyone. We take only less than lethal arms. In and out like ghosts."

Ezekiel nodded. "We understand, Joe."

"That being said, if you have no choice, if it's them or you, kill them," Joe said. "And get the hell out fast. Leave no trace if possible, so it's thought to be an enemy of

Cheng's. He'll know the GhostWalkers came for her, because Violet gave us up, but the government won't."

"We'll get the job done quietly," Ezekiel assured.

"You'll need to carry a lot of gear on the jump because you'll be using the powered paragliders to leave from the rooftop. Anyone who prays, now is the time to start. You'll need favorable winds. With good winds, you should get close to thirty miles with the gliders. That should get you to this park, right here on the map. That will put you a quarter mile from the embassy. You get her there, and they have to help you, we're golden. With any luck, you're at the embassy before any authorities are notified with some bogus story Cheng comes up with."

Powered paragliders were heavy. This was getting worse and worse. A small landing target with a series of water towers on it. A high rise, which meant winds. In the city. Gino shook his head and looked around him. The others were thinking the same thing he was and it wasn't good. Their chances were looking worse every minute.

"How is her disappearance going to be explained as well as her exit from the country?" he asked.

"We've got that covered. She was very ill and went to the embassy for help. They flew her out of the country to get medical aid for her. Someone from the embassy will go to her hotel room and collect her things. Cheng will know who took her, but what's he going to say to the authorities? They aren't going to like him kidnapping an American professor who is famous in her own right. He can't very well admit to that."

Ezekiel nodded. "Everyone get some rest and be back here at 7:00 so we can get to work. We want to run this precisely. We'll need the rest of you to help us have a mock-up ready of the building, rooftop and floor. Gino, she'll be going out with you on the glider. If she's in bad shape, and we'll have to expect that with Zhu on board, you're not going to have much time to prepare her for the escape. She may be unconscious. And it has to be said, it's possible she's already dead. If so, we take her body out of there."

Gino shrugged. He was strong. Extremely strong, enhanced strong, and he'd started with that trait long before Whitney got creative. He could deal with the woman, unconscious, dead weight or not.

"If she's alive, she may fight you," Joe said. "Bellisia didn't trust us at first, and Zara has no reason to either. She'll have been in their hands three days by the time we can get there. In Zhu's hands, three days is likely to be a lifetime, especially for someone who can't take pain."

"She'll tell them what she knows," Diego said, rubbing his hand along the barrel of his rifle. He carried the weapon just about everywhere he went, like a security blanket. "And they'll stop working on her." His tone was hopeful.

Gino knew it wouldn't matter if the woman gave Zhu everything. He'd want to make certain there wasn't more. The torture wouldn't stop until she was dead.

"I don't think she will," Joe disagreed. "According to Bellisia, she might be terrified of pain, but she doesn't break. Her best defense is ignorance. Her cover is solid because it's the truth or as close to it as possible." He looked to Ezekiel. "Stay, let's go over this so you can look to see if there's any holes in my plan."

Ezekiel nodded. Gino studied the two men. All differences had been put aside for the mission. They were good. He walked out of the room, Draden pacing along beside him. Draden was considered the epitome of what a man should look like. He'd made his way through college and grad school on modeling. He'd been in high demand for some of the most high-end companies imaginable. The ladies loved him, calling out to him as he passed them on the street. Draden ran most nights, sometimes with Gino, but mostly alone. Whatever demons drove him, they were deep. Mostly, he kept to himself, even among the Ghost-Walkers, just as Gino did.

"This is a bad one," Draden observed.

"They usually are." Gino was noncommittal.

"She's a beautiful woman. Has brains too," Draden continued.

Gino paused and looked at him. "Spit it out."

"Just saying you want me to take over if the job needs doin', I will. Won't like it, but I'll live with it. You don't sleep so good."

Gino didn't know how to feel about the offer, but Draden wasn't going to have to do his job for him. He decided to be grateful. Brothers did that, noticed when something didn't sit well and tried to help out, but Zara Hightower was his responsibility and he wasn't shirking. Draden didn't sleep much better than he did, if at all.

"Thanks, man, I appreciate the offer, but it's mine to do if necessary."

Draden nodded and peeled off, heading toward the road. He ran before he slept. Always. Sometimes miles. Sometimes all night. The man rarely slept and seemed like a machine. Gino shook his head and headed toward the house. He wanted to find his laptop and research Zara. There was something about her that caught at him.

He wasn't like the others—well—maybe Wyatt, a little bit. He didn't want a warrior woman. Bellisia and Cayenne were lethal. Pepper was as well, in her own right, but killing had a vicious backlash for her and was dangerous. She did it if she had to, but all of them were aware the consequences for her could include death, so it was a last resort.

Gino knew if he had a woman, he wouldn't want her anywhere near killing. He'd killed enough for both of them. He didn't want his woman trying to stand in front of him like his parents and grandparents had done. He'd watched them be mowed down, one by one. It was never happening again. With the help of Ciro, he'd shaped himself into a killing machine. He was quiet and deadly. He never picked a fight. He faded into the background whenever possible, but he could take apart a man if needed and not look back. He didn't need or want his woman to be anything like him. Listening to Joe and the others talk about Zara, it had occurred to him, just crept right into his mind, that she wasn't anything at all like him.

Wyatt's three little girls came running out of the house straight at him. All three. He didn't know the first thing about kids. Hadn't thought to find out about them either. Not in this lifetime, but these three little girls blew right past that notion and wormed their way into everyone's affections—his included.

He crouched low as they got to him so they could fling their arms around him. Triplets. Hard to tell them apart unless you knew what you were looking for. Beautiful little girls with their dark, thick curls, skin like their mother and eyes like their father. They had been deemed mistakes and had been scheduled for termination. Pepper had gotten one out of their prison, and Wyatt and their team had rescued the other two—and Cayenne.

"Where are you going?" he asked.

"We're going to hide in the swamp and see if Daddy can find us," Ginger, the spokesperson for the three, said.

"Did Pepper or Nonny give you permission?" he asked. "It's late. Past your bedtime." They were dressed in nightclothes, which meant Pepper had put them to bed. They were little escape artists.

The triplets looked at one another. Gino shook his head, lifted all three of them up and stood. "You three. Ginger, you're such a little ringleader."

She grinned at him, completely unrepentant. "I know. Nonny says I keep everyone on their toes."

"You're not walking on your toes, Uncle Gino," Cannelle pointed out.

Although extremely intelligent, the children were very literal. He kept a straight face. "No, you're right. It's a saying, remember, Pepper explained that concept to you?" He kept striding toward the house, picking up speed, not wanting them to realize he was taking them back inside before it was too late.

"How are we supposed to know when it's a saying?" Thym protested, patting his face with her little hand.

That did something to him. He liked that her hand was so tiny, brushing over his rough shadow. She seemed intrigued with the dark sandpaper along his jaw, rubbing at it over and over. His heart melted just a little when he'd been so certain it was made of stone. It was the three little girls who had given him back some humanity.

Pepper burst out of the house, glaring at her little ones. "You do *not* get to take advantage of me throwing up in the bathroom, you little hooligans."

They didn't have to ask what a hooligan was. Pepper called the triplets that often, and the word had been explained. Gino set them on the porch just as Wyatt's grandmother stepped outside. She smiled gently at the girls and seated herself in the rocking chair, and gestured, using her pipe, toward the three little rockers Wyatt had made for his girls.

"Girls, your mother wasn't feelin' well this evenin', was she?" The tone was mild.

Gino's stomach turned to knots. How did Nonny do that? She didn't raise her voice, but just by the tone and words, you knew she was disappointed. No one ever wanted to disappoint Nonny—especially the triplets. Their little faces dropped as they all obediently sat in their appointed rockers.

"I wanted Daddy to come and find us," Ginger said,

her lower lip starting to quiver. "He works all the time now."

Gino leaned one hip against the post. Pepper, Wyatt's wife, was gorgeous. Not just gorgeous, that didn't begin to describe her. She was exotic. Sexy. Every movement she made was sensual. She was enhanced that way, and sometimes just looking at her hurt. Right now, she looked beautiful but very tired. Her pregnancy appeared to be a rough one.

He wanted to put his arm around her and offer her a little sympathy like any brother might do for his sister, but one didn't touch Pepper. There was something on her skin that could cause a man to need her. They were all very careful around her. Fortunately, her husband watched over her, and he came up behind Gino and went straight to his wife.

"Hey baby. Did they wear you out today?" He brushed gentle kisses over her mouth and then sank into a chair and pulled her down onto his lap. "You girls were good for Mommy while I was workin'?" he asked.

Ginger, Cannelle and Thym looked at one another and then shook their heads. Ginger looked down at her hands. "We snuck out of bed while Mommy was throwin' up and were goin' to hide in the swamp and make you find us," she said. "We don' like you gone so much."

There was a small silence while Wyatt regarded his children. Gino went on into the house, giving Wyatt and his family privacy. The men were all building homes close, with Trap's home the fortress to defend should they come under attack, but most of them were still using the Fontenot home as a barracks until the buildings were complete.

Gino went down the hall to his room. He didn't have to share with anyone and he pulled off his boots immediately, grabbed his laptop and sank down onto the bed.

There were hundreds, no, thousands of entries about Zara Hightower. She'd been a child prodigy just as Trap had been. Gino wondered if she had the same problems as Trap. Trap had Asperger's and missed a lot of social cues. Draden interpreted for Trap often, and Gino had found himself doing so as well. He studied Zara's face. She was looking straight at the camera, something Trap wouldn't do in a million years.

She was beautiful. He found an image of her in color. That hair of hers was the perfect mixture of red and gold. She wore it long, but usually in a tidy braid down her back. There were only two images of her with her hair outside that braid, and both times the wind was blowing and the sun was shining. The thick mass looked like spun silk gleaming in the sun's rays, more red than gold, but a soft, barely there red.

Her eyes were very large, a slate blue framed with long lashes. Her mouth was generous, her teeth very straight. She had legs that went on forever, and he knew he shouldn't be looking that close—not at someone he might have to kill. He cursed and slammed the lid down on his laptop. What was he thinking? He didn't look at women that way. He hadn't for a long, long while. If he needed relief, he found it for a night and walked away.

The problem was those three little girls. Wyatt's daughters. His wife. Cayenne and Trap. He never thought Trap would get married, but the man was crazy about Cayenne, couldn't keep his eyes or his hands off of her. They shared those soft, intimate looks. She made Trap smile when Gino had never known him to. Then there was Ezekiel with Bellisia. The two were inseparable. And Nonny, Wyatt's grandmother. She was the glue that held them all together. She'd made a home for all of them, and Gino hadn't had a home in a very long time.

Gino knew he wasn't the kind of man to find the happily ever after, because what woman could put up with him? He wasn't like the rest of them. He'd watched the others succumb, even Trap, to their women. When Cayenne wanted to join the men in a firefight, she did it. So did Bellisia. Pepper might be the guardian of the safe room, but she wasn't in it. His woman would be. He had a coldness in him the others didn't. Trap was antisocial, he could be dark and very dangerous, but he didn't have that well inside him that turned to ice and allowed him to do ugly, vile things when needed. Wyatt was way dominant, but again, he didn't turn to a cold, unnatural place when riled. Zeke was always interesting. He was the sweetest man on the planet, but he had a wealth of darkness shadowing him. He had been given that strand of big cat DNA just like the rest of them, so he was a hunter, but to his woman, he was beyond nice.

Gino leapt off the bed and paced across the room to stare out the window into the gathering night. Zara Hightower was physically beautiful the way Draden was beautiful. The kind of looks that were noticeable and turned heads everywhere they went. She would always garner attention, if not with her looks, then with her brains. Gino was a man to fade into the background, and his wife wouldn't be somewhere where a fuckin' goon could grab her and throw her in an interrogation room. With her good looks, she should belong to a man like Draden, one who matched her, but could look after her.

He touched the pane, looking up at the stars just beginning to show themselves. Zara was the type of woman a man might come to crave. To obsess over. If he were the wrong kind of man, he might come to think she could be taken against her will. She shouldn't be all over the Internet. He was tempted to go back and look to see how many stalkers she'd had over the years because he was certain it would be more than one.

He swore again and tore his shirt off, pulling it over his head with one hand. The bullet holes from when he was a child were prominent on his chest, but along with them were dozens of other scars. He had them and he'd earned every single one. He wasn't pretty nor, by any means, handsome. He was scary and he knew it. He had cultivated that stillness, that coldness he'd been born with in order to survive. Enhancement had grown all traits, good or bad, and that coldness had spread, obliterating most of the good he had left. The things he wanted from a woman weren't for the likes of a woman like Zara.

He was restless, edgy, moody. He needed to be sharp for this mission. Joe had called it. It was a suicide mission. Precision jumping onto the roof of a high rise with heavy gear? Avoiding water towers when the target was already so small? He knew he would go no matter what, even if the others changed their minds. He pulled the laptop to him, even though he knew he shouldn't. He was one of those men becoming obsessed with Zara Hightower and he didn't even know why.

3

The Louisiana swamp had a magic all its own. Gino knew not everyone would find it that way, but for men like the GhostWalkers, it was the perfect refuge. There was a beauty to the land, a rhythm that got under a man's skin and soothed him when he was a predator and needed space and a hunting ground. There was that same wild that called to him, a place to fish and hunt and an opportunity to live off the land if necessary.

Gino liked the humidity and heat and the fierce weather changes. He spent time learning the canals and waterways as well as his way around the various islands and large tracts of swamp. He liked to be alone, and the swamp provided him with ample opportunity. He liked the people even though he didn't interact much with them. Most were good people, eking out a living, working hard to provide for their families. They worked hard and played just as hard.

He found himself cursing the heat and humidity that he liked so well as they built the exact replica of the jump site, thanks to Bellisia's intel, up on top of Trap's home. Trap had a huge cement warehouse he'd turned into a home. The roof was flat, a good place to put up the series of water towers and mark where all five would have to land when they jumped. The build went up fast in spite of the light rain that did nothing to relieve the heat.

The rain brought the fresh smell of the swamp, the perfumed flowers mixed with rotting vegetation. Shirts off, they worked fast to get the site ready so they had as much time as possible to practice the jumps. Just looking at the marks they would have to hit—all five of them—made Gino's heart sink. He'd done many dicey missions, but this one was going to be bad. He wasn't the only one feeling that way.

"Zeke," Rubin said, after walking the length of the rooftop they'd mapped out with the water towers now sitting right in the way of their landing. Just that one name. A protest. An exhale. Saying that name said it all. Rubin stood on the edge of the roof they'd cut more than in half and then made it even smaller by adding the banks of large water towers. He stood for a long time, mathematically calculating their odds.

Gino knew the odds weren't good. He'd already made those calculations and he hadn't added the additional complication of it being a night jump.

"Boss, how the hell are we supposed to make this jump with all that gear? Power paragliders aren't small and just with us it's already a tight fit."

Zeke shrugged. "It will be just like doing a tandem with a person strapped to you, only smaller."

They all exchanged long, silent looks. Mordichai shook his head, swore under his breath, walked to the edge and spit. It was his older brother leading the suicide mission. "You're going to need a couple of us there to collect the fuckin' bodies, Zeke." He meant it as a joke, but it was too close to the truth, so no one laughed.

Zeke shot him a look that told him to shut the hell up.

"Is there a possibility of doing this with less men?" Gino asked. "Even dropping one, we might fit better up on the roof. Leave Draden or Diego behind. Draden is the biggest, takes up the most room." He didn't want to examine his reasoning for pushing to leave Draden behind. It shouldn't matter who stayed, but somehow it did.

Zeke took his time thinking it over and then shook his head. "We'll practice the jumps on the ground until we all hit our marks and then we'll start jumping on the roof without the equipment first. We have today to get this right, and we will because it's necessary."

Gino nodded. Zeke was the boss and his word was law under the circumstances. If he said they needed everyone, then they did. Cheng wasn't a normal businessman upset because he'd caught an industrial spy he would hand over to the authorities. He was a notorious criminal willing to torture and kill perceived enemies, let alone someone he caught working against him.

Gino had taken the time to read everything Joe had on the man. He seemed to be unraveling, or he was just that paranoid. He was known to shoot lab techs for messing up. He lined up workers, picked a few he claimed were working against him and they disappeared, presumably to be tortured and then killed. He locked down his office building periodically for weeks at a time, refusing to allow the workers to go home.

He had cameras in private apartments, spying on his workers at all times. His private security forces were drawn from ex-military, men who knew what they were doing and didn't mind bullying or roughing up innocent civilians. He paid well. He seemed to the outside world to run a model business with day care and living quarters for his people. It was known to those around the world who knew his true character, that those children lived under a threat and their parents were his most loyal employees.

"This is sketchy at best, boss," Draden pointed out.

"Joe said it was going to be a suicide mission. If you've got a better plan, I'd fuckin' love to hear it."

They looked at one another again. No one was going to back out. They had to get the woman out one way or another. She'd shut down the sale of their program, preventing terrorists from getting their hands on Whitney's work or from having any intelligence on the GhostWalkers. Even Cheng would have begun experiments to have better soldiers guarding him. Or maybe he'd sell his soldiers. He was capable of selling human beings. If the information they had on him was correct, he did it often with the sons and daughters of the hapless employees he thought had double-crossed him.

Zeke sighed. "We'll figure it out on the ground," he repeated. "We'll practice it all day and then do a couple of night jumps to get it right. We have to start traveling tomorrow to make that deadline of meeting up with the workers going to Shanghai."

The rain ceased, which made wielding hammers easier. The rest of the unit not going continued to set up a site inside the building that was a mock-up of the floor Bellisia had seen. She knew nothing about the inside of the rooms, but the floor was basically the same as the lower floors. The positioning of elevators determined the layout of the floors, so that was easy. It was impossible to tell where all the guards would be, but she'd seen enough of the floors to know where the standard placement was.

The heat and humidity added to frayed tempers as the day wore on. They practiced their spots on the rooftop, making the dry run over and over. The first jump, without equipment, was a disaster. Trap had a landing field not far from his home with a large hangar that housed several aircraft including a smaller plane that would be similar to the one they had to use. Malichai piloted. All of them could fly a plane or helicopter if necessary, but Malichai had particular talents, and Zeke didn't want to worry about anything but the jump.

If the first jump was any indication, this wasn't going to work, at least in Gino's mind. They all managed to stay out of one another's way, but he felt as if he'd never made a jump before—it was that bad—and he didn't even have the heavy equipment with him. Still, they'd all gotten on the roof without an incident. Zeke called for the equipment. He wasn't going to mess around. He wanted them prepared.

They barely had time to see to their gear before Malichai took them up again. Gino didn't think the first jump with the heavy equipment went any better than the first dry jump. He cursed as Diego slammed into him, nearly sending both of them over the edge of the roof. He was going to be hurting like hell on the plane ride to China.

"That didn't go well," Diego announced. "I felt like I was a first-time jumper. Sorry, Gino. I just ran out of room."

"I was all over the place too," Rubin admitted.

"Me too," Draden said. "The weight really pulled me off balance."

"Yeah," Gino added. "Even after I pulled my canopy, steering wasn't great."

"We're fucked," Diego said. "Wonder how Valhalla is this time of year." His voice dripped with sarcasm.

Zeke looked them over. "Repack your gear; we'll break for lunch and go up again in an hour and thirty. Eat, boys, you might not get another chance until we're in the air, and Nonny did the cooking."

That improved things as far as Gino was concerned. Nonny's meals were always something to look forward to. He knew when they were leaving for a mission, she came up with special dishes, everyone's favorites and loaves of freshly baked bread. Nonny was part of the reason he had begun thinking about having his own family. She was the epitome of what many men would want, a partner to walk beside him, one who could defend her children, to help carve a life out of the wilderness. She had hunted and fished right along with her husband, and later, after the accident that took her son and his wife, she had raised four wild boys herself with no money, her man in the ground.

Her meals alone were worth gold. He sat at the table, quiet as usual, letting the talk swirl around him, hearing it, but not really listening to the camaraderie of ribbing one another and telling old war stories to take their minds off the fact that it was more than likely some of them weren't going to be coming back.

He thought about Zara and what was happening to her. He had no idea why just the images of her had gotten to him, but more and more, he couldn't stop thinking about her. He was obsessed with finding everything he could on her, and he'd spent most of the night reading the articles he'd found online. It wasn't a good thing, especially since he'd been tasked with putting a bullet in her head if she was working against them. Still, he couldn't stop worrying about what was happening to her. That was another unusual thing for him. He didn't waste time on things he couldn't change.

Joe's dad was a criminal. Straight up. A member of organized crime. Not just a member, but a boss. Neither Joe nor he could change that. Joe's father, Ciro, and Gino's father, Jacopo, had served in the Marines with Sergeant Major Theodore Griffen, and the three had been friends ever since. Gino had benefited from Sergeant Major's abilities and connections. Ciro had run down those who had killed Gino's father and made them pay. He had been the man to condition Gino to seeing torture and being able to shut down his mind and not view the recipient as anything but the slime they were. He considered, with his father's two friends looking out for him, that his father was still there in spirit. He wished his father could see Zara Hightower.

Ciro had been the one to insist he be taught to take care of himself, with hands or weapons, to keep himself in good physical condition. He had taught Gino that the world wasn't always black and white or a man all good or all bad. He'd always recognized the cold well in Gino and had talked to him often, telling him to accept himself, but to find something to balance that side of him.

Ciro loved his wife and son. He loved Jacopo and Gino. He was capable of love, and Gino knew he was as well. He'd pushed that side of him down for so long, refusing to think about it because in their line of work, men didn't always come back and sooner or later, putting his life on the line so often, his luck was bound to run out. Then they'd found the swamp. Nonny. Wyatt's family. Trap's woman. Bellisia. It was hard to get around the fact that they were building homes, permanency.

He had a lot to offer a woman. He hadn't touched his family's money—and there was a wealth of it and growing every day. He'd never needed it. He didn't want a woman with him because of money. His choice was the military and now the GhostWalkers. There was no getting out of the program because no one could undo what Whitney had done to them. The government wasn't certain what to do with them. They were dangerous, but they also were loyal, and they cut down on the deaths of soldiers when they were sent into the field. His woman would have to put up with military life. The only difference was, each team was able to choose their permanent location.

"You've gone a million miles away, Gino," Joe said. "You okay with this?"

Gino knew Joe was talking about the order to end Zara's life if she was a threat to them. "Don't know," he muttered truthfully. He could lie to anyone but Joe. "Don't like it."

"It's just a contingency," Joe reminded softly. "In case she isn't like Bellisia. She planned an escape with Bellisia and one other woman, but they never could be in the same place at the same time. Whitney always sent one of them out along with the threat of a deadly virus implanted in them, held the other two up to be sent to the breeding program if things went wrong."

"Whitney's still got one of them." Gino sighed. Loyalty was a huge reason the women stayed, unable to leave when they knew leaving would cause suffering to friends or others who had been raised as siblings. He understood loyalty. He felt it, first toward Joe, and then the other GhostWalkers in his unit, and lastly the ones not in his own unit.

Joe nodded. "I'm sorry, Gino, I should have asked someone else."

Gino shook his head. He already thought of the woman as "his." That meant if she had to be terminated, he would do it himself, quick and clean so there was no chance she ever saw it coming and suffered. "She's my responsibility all the way. I'll see to her."

Something about the way he said it had Ezekiel's head turning toward him, those eyes moving over his face assessing him. He stared back, keeping his expression blank.

"Gino, when the others go out, drop back and talk to me," Ezekiel ordered.

Gino nodded, but he cursed under his breath. He was blowing it. He wasn't a man to give anything away and in the space of a few seconds, both Joe and Ezekiel were worried about him. Joe's father had taught him the importance of keeping his thoughts to himself, yet in a very short time, he was giving away too much.

The talk continued, no one wanting to draw attention to the fact that both of the commanding officers had questioned him. He listened to Malichai and Mordichai tease

Trap and Ezekiel about their women's ability to cook and how they were lucky to have Nonny as an instructor. Wyatt's wife, Pepper, had a little more time with Nonny, and although in the beginning she had been pretty bad at cooking, she was getting the hang of it.

He waited for Ezekiel, a little wary, but managing to lounge by the door looking lazy and relaxed. Another thing he had to thank Ciro for. Ezekiel was a hunter, through and through. He stalked up to Gino without hesitation, his eyes giving off a faint glow, much like a cat's might. The two walked out of the house together, the others moving ahead in a group to give them privacy.

"You think I'm a threat to Joe?"

The question startled Gino because he was expecting something altogether different. He shrugged. "You're a threat to anyone making your wife uncomfortable. That's the way it should be, so no judgment, but Joe's in a bad place right now and I think he's looking for a fight."

Gino could see that his answer shocked Ezekiel. The man stopped dead in his tracks, ran a hand through his hair and glanced back toward the house. "Shit, Gino. You're right. Why the hell didn't I see that?"

"I've known Joe since we were kids. His dad was best friends with my father since grammar school. When the murders happened, it was Joe who found me. They saved my life when Ciro took me in and raised me as his son. Joe's a little older than I am, so I guess I looked up to him and I learned his every mood. His expressions. I can read him like a book." The trouble was, Joe could read him just as well.

Ezekiel shook his head. "Thanks for letting me know, but just so you know, I may have gotten upset with him if Bellisia told me she didn't like his questions, but I wouldn't ever attack a man, a friend, when I know he's wounded. If you'd thought about it, you know me too well to think I'd do that."

"Before the enhancements, yeah, I get that. None of us can predict what we might do now. You need to hunt. It's in you now. It was always in me, even before the murders, but you got that in you, Zeke. We have to watch out for one another. Your brothers covered you, and I covered Joe. Next time, you might have my six while I'm taking Mordichai's."

Ezekiel flashed him a smile. "You're a good man, Gino."

Gino regarded him soberly. "No, I'm not. I try to be. I want to be. But I'm not. Joe's a good man. I think we were born into the wrong families. He never wanted to be a part of his family's business, and I would have followed in Ciro's footsteps. In the end, I looked after Joe for so many years I just followed him into the service."

"And you're still at it."

Gino nodded. "This mission, Zeke. You're married. Maybe you should turn it over to one of the others. Let them take it. I'm an officer. A surgeon. I can run it and you stay back this time."

Ezekiel clapped him on the shoulder. "You know I can't do that, but thanks for the offer. We'll bring her home."

Gino wondered if Zeke still thought the same thing when the next two jumps proved to be a nightmare. No one hit their mark on the first jump with the heavy power paragliders attached to them. The second jump wasn't much better, and Ezekiel lost patience and growled orders at them, reminding them they still had to simulate the actual rescue and this was the last jump before their practice night jump. The man definitely wasn't happy with them.

"Get it together. Focus. There won't be room for mistakes up on that roof. One of you fucks up and goes over, we're all dead. Every single one of us and the woman, so hit your damn marks," Ezekiel snapped.

Gino pushed down amusement. Growling sometimes worked, but Zeke could look like a Bengal tiger when he wanted. Joe always spoke softly. Zeke did the same, but the two were so different in their delivery. Joe had the way of his father. He could be scary with that soft voice. Zeke growled, looking every inch the predatory male he was.

Somehow Ezekiel's order was followed and every one of them managed to hit the mark with their bulky and very heavy equipment on the third try. They repacked everything and went into rescue mode, ready to simulate the actual retrieval of the prisoner.

Rubin jumped first and disrupted the cameras as he came down, hitting the roof and hurrying into position as soon as he removed the powered paraglider. His brother was on his six, hand on shoulder at the door. Gino moved into position. He would go in first, checking for guards, making certain the way was clear. Draden stepped up, his fingers working magic on the lock, and then dropped quickly into the last position, watching their backs. Ezekiel was positioned right after Diego.

They moved quickly and silently down the stairs leading to the floor. It was Gino who signaled all clear so they could open the door onto the floor, while Rubin disrupted the cameras. Small glitches only. The lights flickered, so that it seemed perfectly logical that the cameras would be having trouble as well.

Once on the floor, they split into two teams, Draden and Ezekiel going to the left and Rubin, Diego and Gino going to the right. Each room would have to be checked. Draden had gifts similar to Gino's and would be the one to hopefully know the positioning of any guards.

Gino had to strain, using his gifts, the ones that burned his eyes but allowed him to see beyond walls. He could feel for the energy that told him someone was behind a door waiting and just how focused they were on their job. He moved with authority, with confidence, along the hall. Sensing someone behind a door, he signaled to the others. Diego nodded and he and Rubin stood to either side of the door.

To the left of the door, Gino told them. *One man.*

The count was silent, but the moment Diego got the door open, Rubin exploded inside, was on the "guard" and took him down with a tranq. They hadn't wanted to take down any guards, just in case there were radio check-ins, but they had to check each room that was occupied.

They repeated the same entry and operation several times until it felt smooth. They broke for dinner and prepared for their night jump. They'd only do one and then they'd have to repack gear to be ready to leave.

They ate dinner at the Fontenot house—all of them. The entire family together, and as promised, Nonny and the women fixed a feast for them. It was plain Cajun cooking, which meant it was amazing. Gino looked around the table. These were good people, all of them. He liked them. They were loyal, true to their word, warriors ready and willing to fight for one another and yet quick to give a hand to a neighbor.

Did he fit in? He was never certain. Wyatt was the closest thing to him, and Wyatt was a good man. Gino had a cold edge that set him apart, and yet the triplets kissed and hugged him, accepting him as their uncle just as they did the other men. Pepper looked at them all with affection, although she stuck very close to Wyatt and never touched any of them physically.

Cayenne was beginning to overcome her anxiety around them. She'd lived alone in a cell for too many years, and it had taken her longer to warm up to the idea of one big family. She and Trap never seemed to be able to keep their hands off each other, and she looked to him for cues around the others, which was laughable, as Trap was the most antisocial man Gino had ever met.

Ezekiel and Bellisia were good together. She was a tiny little thing, but very strong and, like Cayenne, lethal as hell. Gino liked watching their interaction. He liked all three women and the way they were devoted to their men.

He sat back in his chair, smiling at Pepper when she poured him a cup of coffee.

"You don't have to wait on me, honey," he said.

"I know. That's why I do it. I can't wait on Wyatt or he'd expect it every time." Pepper tossed her wild mane of dark hair—it was almost as thick as a man's arm when she braided it. It had a faint darker pattern strewn through the silky mass.

The men erupted with laughter at Wyatt's expense. He just wrapped his arm around his wife's waist as she tried walking past him and pulled her down onto his lap. "You wait on me," he announced, nuzzling her neck. "Anything I want. Anytime I want it. Everyone knows you worship at my feet."

"I do not." Pepper pretended to struggle.

Gino noticed that her butt wiggled around all over Wyatt's lap. He liked that for his friend—that a woman loved him enough to show him.

"Maybe not my feet, but you do worship other parts of me."

"Wyatt." She punched his shoulder lightly and buried her face in his neck. "I do worship you, but I think it's gone to your head."

The men, including Gino, burst out laughing. He could tell Pepper had no idea why they were laughing, or that Wyatt could have come back with something even more embarrassing.

He wanted that, he realized. What Wyatt had. What Trap had. What Ezekiel had. He even needed it. Sooner rather than later. He knew he grew colder every day in spite of having the little triplets following him around, asking him to do bird calls for them and teach them to track animals in the swamp.

He loved the triplets' company and sometimes sought the little girls out when he was feeling particularly shadowed. Nonny always seemed to notice. Once she'd ges-

tured at him with her pipe while she was rocking away on
the porch and told him he needed a good woman. He
hadn't replied, but at the time, he'd thought a good woman
wouldn't have him. A woman like him, one dark enough
to accept him, would only drag him down further and he
couldn't afford that. He was looking for just the opposite
of him. He was searching for a woman who made his
world light up when she smiled.

He excused himself and went out to the porch to look
at the night. He loved nights in the swamp. The sounds of
the insects, the slide of alligators through mud to get to
the water. The bellows of the bull alligators. The plopping
of snakes as they fell from low-hung cypress branches
into the water. The swamp seemed laid-back when it was
really teeming with life. It was a long way from the city
where he'd been born and raised.

He was surprised that Joe had taken to the place. Joe
was much more civilized than Gino. Gino was primitive
and a little savage, and Joe was charming, sophisticated
and easygoing. Joe seemed to love the swamp so much he
didn't want to leave. Like Gino, he spent hours a day exploring when they had the time. The team had bought up
as much land around the Fontenot home and between
Wyatt's home and Trap's as possible. There was one tract
of land they couldn't get, a prime piece they'd offered far
more for than it was worth, but so far the owner hadn't
bitten. Joe was obsessed with that piece of land.

He liked birds. Who knew? Big bad Joe Spagnola liked
birds. The tract of land was home to quite a few. He went
there often with his binoculars and watched them. Gino
knew, because when Joe went into the swamp, he followed. He was used to protecting his foster brother, and
having the man traipse around in a dangerous area didn't
have Gino quitting his bodyguard ways any time soon.

"You got somethin' on your mind, Gino?" Nonny

asked as she pushed open the screen and slid out onto the porch, pipe in hand.

"A few things," he admitted. He'd come to know Wyatt's grandmother, and he was fairly certain the Fontenot boys had gotten psychic gifts from her. It was useless to try to hide things from her.

She was small now, looking frail, with her silver-spun hair and her thin body, but she worked all day, never shirking, even when they all tried to anticipate what she might need or want. She slipped into her favorite rocking chair and regarded him over her unlit pipe.

"You're a much better man than you think. And you're deserving of happiness just like all the rest of them." She announced it as if by her decreeing it, that made him a good man.

She made him smile. He turned toward her, leaning his back to the porch post. "How do you know I'm a good man, Nonny, when I don't know it?"

"I see more than most people. I see you struggle, but you don't quite understand that sometimes, in this world, someone like you is needed. You go with a clear conscience and you find your woman. She needs you and your strength. We're not all made the same. Cayenne is all warrior. Bellisia can be a warrior but isn't thrilled with it, where Cayenne feeds off it. Killin' makes Pepper sick. She still will stand up and do what's needed, but it does sicken her. Does that make her weaker? Or does it make her the strongest of all of us? I don't rightly know. But I do know there is a woman needing you."

"My brand of loving wouldn't be easy for anyone, Nonny, let alone the kind of woman I want."

"It's need that matters, Gino. Find the kind of woman you need. Wanting can fool you."

He nodded because he knew she was right. He'd thought a lot about women and what would be right for him. He wasn't ever going to be easy, and the last thing he needed was a woman who would spend her life opposing him at every turn. He wasn't a man who liked a fighter as so many of his brethren did. He needed someone who would soothe him, quiet the dark demon when it began to emerge. A fighter wouldn't do that for him, and any union with the wrong woman wouldn't end well.

"My family has money, Nonny. So much. You have no idea how much money. I haven't touched a penny of it, although I offered it to the others to help with purchasing land for us. Or to buy weapons to keep the little ones safe. I mostly forget about the money, until I meet a woman. In the last few years, I haven't met one who hasn't already known about the money and deliberately set out to meet me with one idea in mind."

She laughed softly and lit her pipe. The scent was soothing and somehow fit with the swamp. "There are good women in this world, Gino. Hardworking, caring women who prefer to be partners with a man."

"Don't want a fuckin' partner, Nonny," he said before he thought. He ducked his head. "Sorry for the language, ma'am."

"I raised my own boy and then four grandsons. Language never bothered me none but it was fun to make them think so. A partner can be many things. I worked alongside my husband because there was need and I'm that kind of woman. Cayenne will fight beside her man. Your woman will find her place with you and whatever that is, it is a partnership with each of you having your role. You just need to make her feel loved and cared for. Communication is important, not just in the bedroom, but mostly out of it. You have that, you'll have no problems."

He wished she was right. He hoped she was right. He was damned tired of being alone. "I think it's your swamp, Nonny. It's cast some kind of spell on all of us."

She looked around her, out over the water and into the

thick trees and foliage. Her rocker creaked softly, adding to the symphony of the insects and frogs. "It is beautiful here. I spent my days here, Gino, and never longed for another place. I love the beauty of it. The mystery. The wildlife. Most of all, the people. There are good people here."

He let himself grin at her, teasing her a little. "I suspect you loved the lazy bayou at night with your sweetheart."

She flashed him an answering grin, looking a little mischievous. "You wouldn't be wrong. My man made my life good right up until the day he passed."

"I'm happy for you. I'd like to think my father did the same for my mother. Believe me, having gone without a woman of my own so long, I'd know to look after her if I found her." He broke off abruptly when Draden joined them. It was one thing to talk like this to a woman in her eighties in the cover of darkness, but not in front of one of his fellow GhostWalkers. Likely, he'd never hear the end of it.

"Draden," Nonny greeted. "Did you get enough to eat?"

"Yes, ma'am," he said. "If I didn't run so much, I'd be putting on all kinds of weight. Where did you learn to cook like that?"

"Growin' up here, in the old days, we didn't have much. Hunted, fished, crabbed, even shot alligators for food. Had to cook for my brothers and sisters. I was the youngest by a good few years and they were all workin' tryin' to help so I was home tendin' to the food and house."

She'd worked hard all her life. As far as Gino could see, she was still working. But she was happy. She was a woman who wouldn't have looked at a man's bank account to judge his worth. She looked at whether or not he would take care of his family. Working hard, bringing passion to his woman. Those were the attributes she looked for in a man.

He wanted a Nonny, but not the fighter. He half lis-

tened to Nonny engaging Draden in conversation while he
stepped back out into the night, thinking of Zara Hightower and wondering what was happening to her. His gut
knotted with dread. Reading the file on Cheng was like
reading a man's descent into paranoid madness. Cheng
was rarely seen in public anymore, but if he was, he surrounded himself with bodyguards.

Gino didn't quite understand men like Cheng. What
was he doing it all for? Stockpiling a fortune he couldn't
take with him. Keeping to himself so he had no friends or
family. Trading his government's secrets as easily as he
traded those from foreign countries. Loyal to no one, not
even the country he was born and raised in. In the end,
what was the point?

Zara was being tortured. He knew she was. Cheng
would never lose that data and let a foreigner leave his
country. After, he would have to kill her. Even if she never
admitted she was spying for Whitney, or running a mission, Cheng would still have to kill her. How could he
not? He couldn't rely on her not talking about being de-
tained and tortured. She might have the United States
lodge a protest on her behalf. Cheng's government would
have no recourse but to investigate. No, he had to kill her.

How long did she have? He was suddenly anxious to
get started. They were making one last night jump, and he
wanted to get it over and get on the road. He was a doctor,
a damn good surgeon, and he had a healing touch. That
was always a shock to him because his hands killed. Not
just killed outright either. Ciro had taught him that sometimes killing cleanly didn't send the right message. If you
wanted others to pay attention and fear you, killing
cleanly didn't get you what you wanted and you did it
another, very ugly way.

He didn't like inflicting pain on anyone, but he didn't
mind either. He could shut down. He had shut down when
intruders had murdered his family one by one in front of

him. When they shot him three times and left him for dead. Over money. It had all been over money. He detested that money more than anything else. They had broken in with the idea of taking Gino and ransoming him back to his parents. His parents and grandparents had refused to let him go. They wouldn't step aside.

Gino remembered trying to push them aside and get around them, so no one would get hurt, but his father had quietly stopped him. He'd shaken his head and told the intruders very softly that he wasn't giving up his son. That was a man taking care of his family. He hadn't resisted, or tried to hurt the intruders, he'd simply said no.

Being nice didn't work with some men. Being nice was equated with weakness. Gino had made certain he would never be equated with weak. Like Ciro, he learned to be strong and feared. He wanted to be feared so no one would touch the people he loved. So no one would ever try to do to his child what had been done to him. Money cost him his parents and he'd turned his back on it. That was ironic, because now he was far wealthier than his parents had ever been. What was more ironic was the fact that he'd shaped himself into a man to be feared so no one would touch those he loved—but he was so cold and dark no woman would ever love him for himself.

The sky was clear tonight, and the moon shone over the water. A light fog moved through the forest, giving the interior an eerie glow when the sky and water were both so clear. He stared into the trees, looking at those fingers of fog pointing toward him. He didn't believe in signs or fate the way Nonny did. She saw signs in everything from rings around the moon to horny toads jumping across the road.

"We're coming for you, princess," he whispered to the night and hoped she heard him. Hoped she could hold on. "*I'm* coming for you and nothing will stop me. Not heaven. Not hell. I'm not leaving you in that place." He'd already made up his mind she wasn't working with Whitney, and that was plain stupidity. He wasn't a stupid man. It didn't matter. "I'm coming, baby, just hold on a little longer."

That was another thing he had to consider as he made his way back to the small airfield where they'd go through the jump one more time before they packed their gear for the night. Zara Hightower was smart. Way the hell smart. Like Trap smart. She was used to being in the spotlight, and he didn't want that life. He didn't want any one of his family members to ever set themselves up as targets. That wouldn't happen. She traveled the world, giving her talks. She might need that. Still . . .

"Won't make a difference, princess," he whispered again. "I'm coming for you. Just hang on."

The jump went far smoother than he expected. They knew the feel of the power paragliders as they steered their chutes down to the rooftop. Each knew where he had to come down to avoid hitting the others. They were out of their gear and into formation in minutes, cameras disrupted, and then they went through the entire routine of finding the prisoner. Every movement was planned in advance including what to do if she wasn't able to walk.

"Good job, everyone," Ezekiel said. "Okay, everything is set with getting out of here and joining the work crew. We leave at twenty-four hundred hours. You have two and a half hours to get everything ready and reset. Adjust your gear, get your chute repacked, do whatever you're going to do, but be back here on time ready to kick ass and get our girl back. You can sleep on the plane, it's a long journey. And remember, the minute you leave here, you are no longer soldiers, you're construction workers."

Gino inclined his head and went to work. He knew exactly what he was—and he was neither.

4

Already three days had gone by and no one had come looking for her, or if they had, Cheng had given a plausible explanation for her disappearance. Zara knew she was going to die in this hellhole. If Cheng didn't have her killed, she wasn't going to escape in time and the virus Whitney had planted in her would begin to make her sick. It wouldn't be an easy death. Whitney had made that clear. She would die screaming, writhing in pain. She knew she wasn't a good spy. She wasn't stoic like some of the girls. She hated pain.

Whitney *detested* her. He had the moment he realized she was useless for his purposes. She'd been two years old the first time she was really hurt and screaming in pain. She saw the disgust on his face, and after that, he introduced her to pain, trying to build her tolerance. The other girls tried to shield her, but he was insistent. None of his attempts worked—and over the years there had been many. This was going to be bad.

Zhu had questioned her multiple times that first day.

She had been pushed around a little, and that horrible little toad Heng Zhang had stared at her several times with an ugly grin that promised he was going to personally administer pain to her. There was no confessing. That would earn her a death sentence. She'd have to brace herself for more torture. The very idea made her sick.

They'd used chemicals on her the second day and her insides still were raw and shaky. The chemicals had raged through her body, blistering and burning with horrific consequences. She writhed in pain, screaming, trying to outrun her insides as they twisted and burned as if a blowtorch were cutting a wide path through her. Zhu had restrained her to keep her from hurting herself, and twice he'd wiped the sweat from her face with a cool cloth that only added to her misery because the moment he took it away, the flames felt hotter on her skin.

He'd stripped her clothing away, leaving her bare and vulnerable, afraid of being raped. Of being humiliated on top of being tortured. It was the longest day of her life, the questions coming at her until she was so confused she could barely hear him above the noise in her head. The drugs messed with her mind, so sometimes she didn't know her own name.

Zara had endured pain before, Whitney had seen to that, but it was nothing like the chemicals Zhu kept injecting her with throughout the long day and most of the night. She knew she'd resorted to begging. Anything to make it stop, but he was relentless. He never raised his voice, it was always the same low tone, demanding she tell him the truth. The questions he asked her bounced in her head like Ping-Pong balls. Each time they hit the side of her head, it felt like a blow.

Strangely, toward morning, Zhu sat her up, his arm supporting her, holding a bottle of water to her lips, forcing her to drink the cool liquid. Those times he'd given her water, he was always unfailingly gentle. He was impersonal, as if he hadn't noticed she was naked. He didn't threaten to rape her. Once, when Cheng came in to see the progress, Zhu covered her body with a blanket to prevent the other man seeing her. She wanted to cry in gratitude, which was insane since Zhu was the one who had taken her clothes.

She woke alone and thirsty, her body hurting beyond belief. Every muscle. Every joint. There was a terrible taste in her mouth and even brushing with her finger didn't get rid of it. She didn't know what she'd said or done the day before. She only knew she didn't want a repeat of that torture or anything like it that Zhu had devised. She also knew she was going to die here. She actually felt she might welcome death from the virus, although if Cheng did an autopsy, he would find the SSD in her brain and might find a way around Whitney's protections, and everything she suffered would be for nothing.

The one chance she might have was Zhu. Shockingly, while her strange reaction to him when he'd slipped her a drug on her teacup had faded completely, his reaction to her seemed to increase the more he was around her. She was well aware his attraction to her wouldn't stop him from doing his job; he'd certainly proven that. He had subjected her to hours of chemical interrogation and hadn't batted an eye that she was in terrible pain while he'd done it.

Cheng was angry. No, angry wasn't the right word for what he was. Over the last couple of days, he'd discovered the exact extent of the damage done to his computers. Every secret he'd collected over the years, the locations of guns, of traffickers, of drug routes, all were wiped out. His precious data on the GhostWalker program he'd sacrificed his men for was gone. Someone had to pay, and she was fairly certain that someone was her.

Several times she heard gunfire reverberating on the floor and knew others—innocents—were being interrogated and probably killed. The screaming individuals in agony really got to her. Her heart stuttered as she considered maybe someone was coming to try to rescue her. She couldn't sit still and jumped to her feet, hope blossoming. She paced unsteadily across the room, wishing she had a window to look out of. They hadn't even given her a view. Just four walls. It felt as though she were suffocating.

Footsteps. Many people. She closed her eyes and tried to will a rescue team to open the door. She hurried back to the bed and pulled the thin blanket over her. Heart pounding, she waited. The lock thudded. Clinked. The door handle rattled. The door opened, and Zhu's broad shoulders filled the doorway. Her heart sank. Of course no one would come for her. Who would? Whitney? He made it clear, when one of them went out on a mission, they were alone. Get in. Get out. Come back or die.

Bolan Zhu stepped inside and she shrank back, one hand to her throat defensively. He didn't look as though he'd come to free her. He threw her the clothes he'd taken from her. "Get dressed."

She didn't wait to see if he would leave. She knew he wouldn't by the way he folded his arms across his chest. He kept his eyes on her the entire time. Her heart shivered inside her body and the tremors started. She'd never been so afraid of a man in her life. She pulled on her clothes, praying that he was going to let her leave. The moment she was finished, he reached out, took her arm and began to pull her toward the door. Suddenly, the four walls felt like protection, not a prison.

"Please tell me what's going on. I don't understand what you think I could have done. I was with you the entire time," she protested, trying to hold back, trying to reach one spark of humanity in him when he was completely unreachable.

"Come with me willingly or you will regret it," he said.

It was his tone, a soft whisper that was issued in a firm,

unyielding manner, that told her he wasn't playing around. She went immediately, terrified he was going to torture her again. He took her down the hall to the elevator without saying another word. She couldn't control the tremors running through her body, and she didn't try to stop her wild heart. They would expect her to be scared. A professor of a university accused of wiping out an entire building full of data would be scared.

As soon as she entered the room on the second floor, she knew what they were going to do. There was an MRI machine. They were going to look for signs of treachery on and in her body.

"Strip." Zhu stepped away from her. "Everything."

Zara looked to him and then around the room, feeling helpless. She'd been helpless her entire life. She considered forcing him to kill her right there, just as a final show of defiance against Whitney, Cheng and Zhu. All three. She hated feeling weak, at the mercy of men who used her for their purposes. She wasn't real to any of them. She was a tool, nothing more. She didn't because she was a GhostWalker and if they had her body and took it apart, which they would, she would be endangering every other GhostWalker and her country.

She stepped away from Zhu, looking at the floor. Strangely, there were spots on it. Small, round, rust-colored spots. Tears? Blood? Bloody tears? She unbuttoned the small flat abalone-shell buttons and let her blouse slip from her shoulders. She didn't try to seduce Zhu by making it a striptease. He'd already seen her body. He'd taken the clothes from her once before. Had he forced her to dress just so the guards wouldn't see her? A small concession. She wanted to think that. She needed to think Zhu was trying to look out for her, but she knew he wasn't. He was the one torturing her, causing her untold pain. She simply undressed, folding her clothing neatly and placing each item on the little table just to the right of

the door. Her bra and panties were last. She hesitated before she unhooked her bra and then shimmied out of her
lacy panties.

Zara refused to cover up with her hands. She'd done
that the day before and it hadn't done her a bit of good.
She stood, shivering, completely naked in front of Zhu,
her gaze on those strange spots dotting the floor. Waiting.

Zhu handed her a thin hospital gown. She put it on
without looking at him.

"Miss Hightower." He spoke her name low. Compelling. When she didn't look at him, he switched tactics.
"Zara, look at me."

She took a breath and raised her eyes to his.

"If you're hiding anything, you need to let me know
now."

"What would I be hiding? And where?" She sounded
bitter. She felt bitter. There was no getting out of this. She
was terrified because no one was coming for her and after
subjecting her to all of this, wouldn't they have to prevent
her from talking even if they determined she was innocent? She was going to die. She had to decide how she
wanted to die. She couldn't rile Zhu, he was too disciplined, and he clearly dissociated himself from his victim. The guards were more susceptible. She could taunt
one until he shot her. But what about her body? How
could she die and not leave evidence behind of the Ghost-
Walker program? She was intelligent, she had to find a
way, but right now, she was so scared it was all she could
do to stay standing.

Zhu shook his head and stepped to the door to call in
the tech. Her heart pounded even more as they strapped
her down. This was the moment of truth. They had done
a full body scan twice now, using the CT scan machine
before they'd administered the chemicals. She'd been
wanded repeatedly. Now they were going to scan her
brain. This would be the telling moment.

She was put inside the machine and she closed her eyes, trying not to feel claustrophobic. The solid-state drive implanted in her brain had no movable mechanical parts. The SSD was far more resistant to physical movement and shock than a metal hard drive would be. Without the spinning disk, there was no whirring in her head to drive her insane.

The SSD was made of a newer material called PEEK-carbon that was radiolucent to X-ray, CT and MRI scans—at least Whitney told her it was. So far, she'd passed the X-ray and CT scans. She had, of course, done research on it and knew it was 30 percent carbon fiber reinforced polyetheretherketone.

Whitney had built a nanotube from PEEK-carbon. Using the nanotube, he created an SSD that he claimed was invisible to X-ray, CT and MRI scans. To power it, he used the same idea as was used in pacemakers—the body's movements. The generator was made of the same PEEK-carbon material and sat on a flat sheet of the same right beside the SSD. Although it was tiny, she knew it was a lot to miss with a scan. She had to rely on Whitney's assurances that the SSD wouldn't show up, no matter how they tried to search for it.

She allowed her breathing and heart to swing out of control because it would be unnatural not to. She'd shown she was terrified. She'd made it appear as if she were close to going into shock, and maybe she was. She could be cool and calm in most situations, but not when torture was looming. Not after the chemicals Zhu had given her. She still felt the burn through her body and tasted the agony in her mouth.

To get through the brain scan, she concentrated on trying to figure out what drug Zhu had used on the teacup and why she was no longer feeling the effects but he was. Whitney had developed some secret pheromone formula that was unique to two people in the program. His desire had been to pair them so when they were sent into the field together, their distinctive psychic gifts and the physical enhancements he chose for them complemented each other and made them a much more lethal combination.

Zhu wasn't a GhostWalker, so how had he managed to get ahold of Whitney's secret project when no amount of hacking had found the program used by him? And why was it working against Zhu? He was clearly attracted to her. Could it be natural and not part of whatever truth serum Cheng had devised? She didn't want to think Zhu capable of something so mundane as to be generally attracted to a woman.

Could she use his attraction to her against him? She didn't think so. He was too disciplined and she didn't doubt for a minute that he would put a bullet in her head if Cheng demanded it. Better a bullet than more torture. He hadn't hesitated to inject her with nasty drugs and sit by all day while she screamed, cried, begged and pleaded.

She knew it wasn't good when they took her out of the machine. She heard more gunshots just outside the door, the bullets fired in rapid succession, and this time the body that fell hit against the wall to the room with the MRI machine. Zhu, impassive as always, handed her clothes to her and told her to get dressed. She did so in silence, watching blood seep under the door.

Zara felt a little faint, but better a quick death than being tortured again. She didn't think she could go through it again. She didn't believe for one moment she would get lucky enough to be let go. She was fairly certain the tech was murdered because he'd given Cheng results the man didn't want to hear. She stole a glance at Zhu. He looked unconcerned, and that was even more terrifying than knowing Cheng just indiscriminately killed a tech because he didn't like the results the man had given him.

Zhu placed his lips against her ear. "You keep quiet, do

you understand me? Unless I tell you otherwise, keep your mouth shut."

She nodded her understanding, although she didn't understand at all. She kept dressing as quickly as she could. The moment she was finished, Zhu took her arm and opened the door. The body of the young tech lay slumped over beside the wall and directly in front of the door. He lay in a pool of blood. She let out a single sound of despair and closed her eyes, turning her face away.

Cheng paced the hallway, a gun in his fist. He talked fast, an angry staccato, lashing out at his hired soldiers, berating them over and over. He halted abruptly when Zhu pulled her out of the room and around the dead body. She kept her eyes on the floor, visibly shaking. What had made Cheng so angry? The fact that they found something, or they didn't?

Cheng stalked over to her, his face contorted like a madman's. He regarded her silently for a long moment. She didn't dare look up. She tried to look as cowed as she felt. He raised his gun hand and everything in her stilled, braced for the impact of the bullet. Instead of a bullet, he slammed the gun into her face, hitting her temple on one side and then across her cheek on the other, pistol-whipping her. She tried to get away from him, but Zhu caught both arms and held her immobile in front of him. Blood ran down her face. She felt light-headed when he stopped.

"Take her to the interrogation room. I want you to beat the truth out of her. Make it hurt, Zhu. Beat her within an inch of her life, but keep her alive. If that isn't successful, use the cane and then the whip. You wield it with such proficiency. I want to know how this was done." Cheng spoke in English, wanting her to know what was coming.

Zhu didn't respond, but pushed her toward the elevators. They had to skirt around a pool of blood. Halfway to the elevator, another of the soldiers lay on the floor, dead.

She stumbled. Zhu wrapped his arm around her waist, holding her up as they entered the elevator. She tensed, wondering if she could kill him and get out. She knew the place was on lockdown, and soldiers guarded every point of entry.

"Don't."

She must have tensed up, ready to fight. Her head exploded with pain with every movement, but she had to try. She couldn't just let him torture her. This was going to be bad, worse than the chemicals, and she'd never done bad well. She wasn't stoic. She was loud and cried like a baby. She was the last person that should ever guard secrets when torture was involved. She had to try. She had to protect the GhostWalkers.

Before Zara could make a move, Zhu punched her hard in the stomach. Very hard. She doubled over and heaved. He didn't let her fall to the ground, not even when her legs turned to rubber. Nothing like taking the fight out of her fast. She knew that move and why he'd done it.

She tried to bring her head up fast, hoping to hit him under his chin, but she was disoriented from the pistol whipping and Zhu easily avoided her attempt and hit her a second time. Pain exploded everywhere, refusing to stay confined to her head. She'd had training, years of it, but then Whitney told her to forget her training in situations like this one and react like a terrified woman. He'd made her practice that for the last few years. Training warred with survival instincts. She forced herself to bite, to hit feebly, to carry out the stupid, stupid cover that wasn't really a cover, but was really her.

She lost track of how many times he hit her. It was methodical and done coolly, completely impersonal. So much for attraction and how much goodwill it would buy her. When they reached the upper floor where her room was, he dragged her out of the elevator by her hair, taking her right past her room, to another, three doors down, where he shoved her inside.

She landed hard on the floor. There were bloodstains there. A fingernail. Clearly no one believed in cleaning up after themselves. She knew she was a little hysterical, but she tried to get to her feet and face him because really, damn him. He could go to hell. She didn't realize she was shouting it at him until he hit her again, right across the face, right where Cheng's gun had cut her cheek open.

Zara heard her breath hiss out of her lungs. Then he hit her breast and all air was gone. The pain was excruciating. She tried not to let him see, knowing she would be giving him more ammunition, but it was impossible not to scream. Tears mingled with blood on her face. She lost count of how many times he hit her breasts, then moved lower, attacking her ribs, back up to her breasts and then her face.

There was no way to stand, but she realized they weren't alone. Someone held her in place for Zhu. He didn't look as if he'd even broken out in a sweat when he finally stopped. She was dragged to the wall, her hands jerked above her head so high she was on her toes, wrists bound tightly.

She heard Zhu's voice asking questions, but she couldn't make out the words. It wouldn't matter anyway. She didn't have anything to tell him. Her eyes were swelling shut in spite of the fact that her body had taken far more punishment than her face. He'd slapped her more than punched her in the face, but her body hurt so badly she didn't think she could breathe through the pain. How did spies do this?

His voice stayed a soft, almost gentle tone. He pushed back her hair, his fingers stroking her swollen cheekbone. A bottle of water was held to her lips and she was forced to drink. It was cold and wet and tasted faintly like blood.

He kept stroking back her hair, murmuring soothingly to her. Then he held the bottle to her lips again. She drank because he gave her no choice.

The questions started again. Her name. Where she was from. Her education. She wanted to scream at him. She was written up in all the journals for her work. What was wrong with him? He already had that information. Her head wouldn't stop its vicious pounding. The pain made her so nauseated she couldn't keep from dry heaving. She'd already been sick all over the floor.

Zhu wiped her face gently with a wet cloth. "Pay attention, Zara," he said. "Answer the questions."

She shook her head. "I don't know what you want me to say."

"The truth."

That horrible pounding in her head increased, and this time, there was that strange ripping sensation in her mind, as if Zhu was there, trying to tear the truth from her. "I'm a professor at Rutgers," she blurted. "I don't understand any of this. Cheng invited me to give a talk on the program my team and I developed, the VALUE system. I was doing that when the alarms went off and something happened that I still don't really know or understand."

He hit her. Hard—so hard everything became even more blurred. There was no place on her body that wasn't sacred. She lost track of time. She must have lost consciousness because he threw a bucket of water over her and yanked her head back by her hair. "Stay with me, Zara, this is important."

Once again, he held water to her lips. It hurt to drink. Her lips stung and her throat felt raw and damaged from screaming. She didn't even know what she screamed, only that she did. He soothed and petted her. He whispered to her. He let her lean into him. Then the questions started again and that ripping sensation in her head increased. Whatever new drug Cheng developed to force truth from his victims added to the jackhammers piercing her skull. It had to be in the water he gave her. She began reciting mathematical problems in her head over and over to combat the effects of the drugs. For all she knew she recited them out loud. She was beyond caring if she did.

He viciously stripped the clothes from her body, ripping them into long rags, and that made her cry harder because she knew she didn't have any other clothes. They couldn't send her back to her hotel naked. They were never sending her back.

He spun her around. She heard a whistle like something moving fast in the air. It hit her across the backs of her thighs and pain exploded. The cane. He was caning her. She'd heard of it, of course. It was common practice on prisoners. Never in a million years had she ever considered she would have to endure it. He hit her so many times she lost count. There wasn't a place on her back, buttocks or thighs that he spared. Sometimes he hit in the same place several times until she couldn't even scream because the pain was so excruciating.

Then he repeated the gentle handling, pushing back the damp hair from her forehead, whispering to her, holding the water to her mouth. Again, the questions began. She was so disoriented, she couldn't think to answer him. She just wanted to lie down and go to sleep and never wake up.

He dragged her legs back, so that her feet were propped up on something she couldn't see, the tops of each foot resting in a notch so the soles of her feet were exposed. When the first strike hit the arch of her foot, pain exploded, so excruciating she knew she might black out. She wanted to let go and faint. Nothing could ever hurt that bad again. She was wrong. He spent a great deal of time caning her feet, arches, heels, the balls of her feet, sides, toes, finally the tops. She was sweating profusely, sobbing, her breath wheezing out of her by the time he put down the cane and offered her more water. She choked on it, tried to turn her head away, refusing to drink, but he caught her hair, tipping her head back and forcing the water down her throat.

He let go of her and she tensed, waiting, hanging by her wrists, facing the door. She couldn't stand any weight on her feet, so she had to take her full weight on her wrists. She couldn't see and that made him scarier than ever. It was terrifying to wait for what he would do next, and she knew it was something terrible when he spun her around to face him. He stood for a long moment, letting her see what looked like a long bullwhip. Then he swung. The lash hit her across both breasts, cutting into her soft flesh. She jerked hard against her wrists, nearly tearing her arms out of the sockets, screaming again, her voice so hoarse she didn't recognize it. She'd thought the cane was agony, but the whip slicing into her skin, cutting her open, was far worse.

She had no idea how long he kept at it. She lost consciousness twice and both times there were buckets of ice-cold water thrown over her to revive her. He started up again immediately until there wasn't a place on her body that wasn't bleeding, bruised, swollen or throbbing with agonizing pain. She quit screaming. She couldn't think beyond the pain. When he stopped to ask her questions, Zara tried to answer. She pleaded with Zhu to believe her.

Then he was hitting her for the fourth session with the whip, and her mind shut down completely. She hung there limply, unresponsive, almost in a catatonic state, but she was aware of Zhu cursing as he cut her down. From a great distance in her mind, she was surprised that Zhu didn't get one of his subordinates to take her body down and drag her to her room. Instead he let her fall into his arms. He opened the door to find Cheng pacing back and forth in the hallway.

Cheng regarded her bloody body as if she were a bag

of trash Zhu was about to throw out. "Well?" he demanded.

"She doesn't know a thing," Zhu said. "I've been doing this a long time, and she wouldn't have been able to hold out. She's not built for pain. She isn't stoic and she didn't have the opportunity to destroy the computers." He kept walking straight to Zara's room.

Cheng swore loudly as he trailed after them down the hallway. "It had to be that intruder, the one we never found. A delayed virus of some sort introduced into the network? Or we have a traitor right here in the building, one that works for us."

Zhu laid Zara on the bed. It hurt so bad when the sheets touched her back she wanted to roll over, but he prevented her with a hand to her stomach. Pouring water onto a cloth, he held it over her face, wiping blood and tears from her swollen cheeks and mangled lips.

"Kill her or send her to Moffat. He'll sell her to the highest bidder. She's beautiful, so he'll owe us a favor," Cheng ordered. "She would be perfect for his club."

"I will be keeping her for myself," Zhu said. "I have plans for this one."

Cheng stopped his pacing and swung around. "You've never wanted to keep a woman."

"I do now. She'll do what I want, and you'll have the benefit of her mind. She can develop programs for you instead of giving them away to anyone who wants them. I researched her carefully, Cheng, before I gave you the report. She's brilliant and would be an asset to you. Even had the computers not been harmed, she would never have left this place."

"Can you control her?"

At the question, Zara forced her swollen eyelids to part a minuscule amount, just enough to see the two men. Why it was important to see them, she didn't know, but they were deciding her fate. It sounded as if Moffat was a human trafficker, but staying with Zhu after what he'd done? Her entire body shuddered with pain and rejection of the idea.

"Why would you ask me such a thing?"

If she hadn't been watching from such a distance, Zara would have shivered in fear at the look on Bolan Zhu's face. He was extremely handsome, but in that moment, he looked a demon, invincible and very dangerous even to Cheng.

Cheng sighed. "This was a blow, Bolan, a huge one for us."

For us. Zara heard that clearly. Cheng and Zhu were more than boss and number-one interrogator. Cheng sounded as if Zhu was more of a partner than an employee. Cheng stayed safe while Zhu traveled the world doing his bidding. That didn't make sense, but her mind wasn't working properly so she didn't know if she was even hearing right.

"Who is looking at the cameras?" Zhu asked.

"I had a full team on because she was here. We don't let outsiders in and usually I have three per floor, but I had six in each control room. The tapes have been reviewed. No one tampered with them. They don't show anything amiss."

"I'll talk to the heads of each of the departments," Zhu said. "If one of them is hiding something, I'll know it."

Cheng turned on his heel and started out of the room, but paused in the doorway to look back. "Are you certain your need of this woman hasn't blinded you? Perhaps one more round again with chemicals."

Zhu stood up slowly and stalked Cheng. To Zara's shock, Cheng gave way, backing up with a placating hand. Cheng was the man everyone feared, yet now she was certain everyone was looking in the wrong direction.

"Do you believe I can be blinded by anyone, let alone this American woman? She's beautiful and has a brilliant mind. She is young enough for my every need. I have searched for a long while to find the perfect partner and the moment I read her file, I knew she was the one—and that was without seeing her. She was never going to leave this place. Had she been guilty, I would still have kept her, but she would have paid for that indiscretion for a very long while."

"Bolan . . ." Cheng broke off when Zhu shook his head.

"Do not insult me again. We have built the perfect empire. Your role suits you as mine suits me. We had a setback. It's a bad one, but we can overcome it the way we have overcome everything else in our path."

"How are we going to explain her disappearance?" Cheng asked.

"I will keep her here, locked away where no one can find her if they start looking for her. We have to make certain it appears she returned to her hotel. I'll set it up so it will look as if she'd been robbed in her hotel room. There's enough blood to make it real enough for the cops. Later, when I take her as my wife, we will explain her defection."

Cheng inclined his head and scurried away. Zara was left with the man who had beaten the shit out of her. She knew she was lucky to be alive. Every breath she took hurt, but her ribs weren't broken. He was that good. He'd gone for maximum pain, but he hadn't done any permanent damage.

Zhu closed the door and came back to her, sinking his weight onto the mattress beside her. "Zara." He brushed back wet strands of hair from her swollen face. "Can you hear me?"

She didn't want to admit she could. She was afraid to stay still without answering him. She swallowed hard and barely inclined her head. Just that small movement made her head explode. She made a hopeless sound she couldn't take back, and fresh tears flooded her eyes.

"I want you to feel everything I did to you and know this was me being easy on you. It could have been so much worse. You might not feel gratitude now because you can't conceive of the ways I could make you suffer. Just know I was careful with you. I'm going to leave you now to take care of your disappearance. When I return, you'll know you belong solely to me. I can do whatever I want with you. You don't want to ever make me angry or disappointed in you. Not ever, Zara."

His fingers had been stroking her inner wrist, but settled over her pulse as he gave her orders. She couldn't respond, she was too terrified and her entire body hurt so bad she was afraid to move a muscle. His fingers continued again, as if the wild beating of her heart satisfied him.

"When I return, I'll give you pain pills and clean you up. In the meantime, I want you to think about every part of your body because it belongs to me. I can make you feel good or I can make you feel very, very bad." He leaned down and brushed a kiss over her swollen eye. "I like that you don't like pain. It pleases me. I enjoy inflicting pain. You need to remember that at all times. When I ask you to do something, you will obey me immediately. Do you understand?"

She didn't answer because she couldn't find her voice. She was too terror-stricken. He caught at her bloody, stripe-covered breast and squeezed until she gasped in anguish.

"Do you understand?" he repeated, his voice as mild as ever.

She swallowed again and attempted to nod. The movement sent hammers crashing down on her. A moan escaped, and she hated herself for giving him the satisfaction she saw in his eyes. He did like that he hurt her. He was allowing her to see the cruelty in him—the craving to see her just like this, mewling in pain, barely human, dependent on his goodwill and her obedience in order to keep from getting worse. She thought Whitney the epitome of a monster, but she was wrong. So very wrong.

"Don't roll over while I'm gone. I know caning hurts, but your back has no cuts. I was careful to leave you with one side to lie on. If you roll over, the sheet will stick to the lacerations and it will be very painful when I have to pull it off you, especially if my errand takes too long and the blood dries."

When she made no sound, he leaned over her. "Did you understand what I said to you?"

She nodded hastily. She wasn't making the same mistake twice.

"Good girl. You forgot to thank me for taking it easy on you. Cheng expected a much worse beating for you."

She took a breath. Let it out. "I'm grateful." God. She wanted him dead. She wanted this monster of a man out of her life. Away from her. She didn't know a human being could hurt so bad and still live. She fought down the need to kill him. If she did, Cheng would take her apart and all of this would have been for nothing.

He rubbed his hand down her body from her breasts to her mound, skimming deliberately over the open lacerations the whip had caused. "Each of these cuts is shallow. You won't have a single scar from this."

She knew immediately what he expected. She wanted to spit in his face, but she knew better. "Thank you."

He smiled at her and held the bottle of water to her again. "I am angry at Cheng for hitting you with his gun. You shouldn't have any permanent damage, but if you do, he will pay."

Did he expect her to thank him for that as well? She couldn't say another word. He would have to torture her and hear her screams, but she wasn't talking because she didn't have anything left.

Zhu seemed to know her breaking point. He slipped his arm behind her back, making her cry out as he put her in a half-sitting position. "You have to hydrate, Zara. You shouldn't fear what will happen to you, your new life. Once you understand that you will do as I say, you will be given the equipment needed and you can research all you want. You will be able to discuss your findings with others who will be excited about your projects and aid you in finding the answers that are important. There will be plenty of money so you will have the best of whatever you need."

She drank from the bottle and allowed the little slits in her eyes to close all the way. Her eyes hurt like hell anyway. He kept her drinking until she couldn't swallow and the water ran down her chin. He didn't wipe it away any more than he cleaned up her bloody body.

"Remember what I said to you about turning over. I will be very angry if I have to soak the sheets to get them off you."

She made a sound in her throat to indicate she heard him. Pain swamped her. Enclosed her in a horrific cocoon. Her body refused to stop shivering, the tremors going through her, rocking her. She knew she was close to shock if she hadn't already tipped over the scales. All the water she drank, even after the several times of humiliatingly losing her bladder in the interrogation room, meant she would have to find a way to crawl to the bathroom, and he knew it. Did spies get treated this way? If so, why would anyone voluntarily sign up?

She'd been in an orphanage and Whitney had all but bought her. She knew a great deal of money had exchanged hands because he told her all the time what a disappointment she was for the price he'd had to pay—how much he'd lost in his pitiful gesture of kindness. She had discussed with Shylah and Bellisia, her two best friends, what a horrible megalomaniac Whitney was, and she'd cried because she'd been considered so useless to him. It hadn't mattered that she'd gone to the university so young and excelled. She couldn't take pain. She was a baby when it came to the slightest wound on her. The lightest of blows.

Zhu pushed back her hair again and stood. She felt the movement rather than saw it, and it took everything she had not to cringe. She was blind and writhing in pain, unable to stay still, but every movement made her hurt worse. She couldn't imagine the damage Zhu could inflict on a prisoner he truly wanted to harm.

She couldn't imagine anyone defeating him. *Anyone.* She didn't know anyone as strong as Zhu. What kind of man could stand up to someone so evil? She certainly couldn't.

"No one will enter this room while I'm gone, not even Cheng. He knows you're under my protection."

She wanted to scream and throw things at him. She could only mewl a little in abject terror and total agony. His voice never changed. He had to be a complete sociopath. Her mind was in such chaos, for the first time in her life, she couldn't think of a way out. She didn't acknowledge she heard him. If he hurt her more, so be it. She couldn't speak, only keening wails escaped her throat. An animal in pain. He'd reduced her to that and he'd said he was going to keep her.

Whitney had forced her to do his bidding, and now she was in Zhu's hands. Something had to be terribly, terribly wrong with her. How could Zhu have the face of an angel? Not a fallen angel, an actual angel. He was beautiful. No one would ever take him for a monster.

She heard the door close, and she let herself cry. Sob. Tears poured down her face and mixed with the blood from where Cheng had struck her with his gun. The tears stung but she barely noticed. She thought to move, but her body protested, refusing to obey her. She tried to think about soldiers, captured during war. They were tortured far worse than what she'd had done to her. If they could endure it, surely she could. But she knew she couldn't. She couldn't ever do this again. The only good thing was, the virus would kick in soon, a week, maybe two at the most. The bad thing was, when she died, they might find the SSD. Hopefully they wouldn't figure out how to get the information out of it. Could she endure two entire weeks with Zhu? She wasn't certain, but she made up her mind to kill him before she died, and then somehow, she had to figure a way to keep them from taking apart her body.

Zara wanted to curl up in a little ball and never move. She wanted a safe haven she never had to leave. Someplace where no one hurt her. Someplace where she could have a semblance of a home. She wanted to be someone else, anyone but Zara Hightower.

5

Gino looked at his watch. 01:55. He put out his hand. Rock solid. It was a silly leftover habit from his childhood when Ciro checked to see if he was able to continue no matter the difficulty of what he was seeing or doing. In the beginning his hand had shaken a lot, but slowly, over time, he'd become completely able to control his nerves and even his heart rate.

The charter plane was small, and they were cramped inside with the power paragliders, but he took it as a good omen that they'd managed to get this far without discovery. Their gear had gone through customs with the heavy operating equipment the construction company had brought over. No one had noticed anything amiss. No one had suspected they were anything but workers for the company, not even the other personnel.

"Ready," Ezekiel called. "Rubin, you're up."

Rubin had nerves of steel, or maybe he didn't have any. His brother and he were from a poverty-stricken section of the Appalachian Mountains. They'd survived by hunting, killing with one bullet because they couldn't afford to waste ammunition. After the last of their family was gone, they'd made their way to the streets of Detroit, where they ran into Ezekiel and his two brothers. Ezekiel had taken them in.

They'd been teenagers and had no clue how to survive in a city, but they'd learned fast. Both were soft-spoken and had lazy drawls that somehow gave people false impressions about who they were and what they were capable of.

"Okay. Good luck," Ezekiel said. "See you on the roof. Stand by . . . Go."

Rubin went out without looking back, falling into the dark sky. Farther below, the city was lit up with so many lights, Shanghai blazed like a sun.

Diego followed his brother without hesitation.

Draden shook his head. "I hate this shit," but he launched himself out of the plane.

Gino went next, making his jump smooth. There was the wind, a vicious hit on his body, but unlike Draden, who didn't like the drop, Gino had always relished the freefall. Moving through the sky, hearing the whoosh and then silence. A perfect silence. For a few seconds, he was part of the universe along with the stars and moon. The night. Part of the reason he loved being a GhostWalker was their creed was so true. The night belonged to them, and falling through the night sky was just a small part of that.

He hit his mark on the roof, but just barely. A gust of wind caught at him at the last minute, trying to blast him off target. It caught Ezekiel full on. He was coming in right after Gino hit, and Gino moved fast to clear a path. Gino and Draden caught at Ezekiel to steady him so the wind pulling at his chute and the weight of the power paraglider didn't take him over the edge of the roof.

Man, that was ugly, Ezekiel said. *Everyone good to go?*

Each responded telepathically.

Two up, Diego said.

Three up, Draden added.

Four up, Gino reported.

Five up, Rubin reported.

Okay, drop the gliders here. Gino, keep your medical pack, you may need it.

Like he was going to forget that. The others had traveled light out of necessity.

There's a camera on that door, Rubin, Ezekiel reminded. *Be careful approaching it.*

Camera's already disrupted, Rubin reported. *Starting electricity glitches.*

Draden moved to the keypad and lock. He had the door unlocked, and Gino moved to the front of the line. He "felt" for the energy behind the door and looked briefly beyond it, his eyes burning as he did so. *Guard on the lower stairs to the top-floor corridor.*

They moved in silence, careful of the slightest sound on the narrow metal stairway. One sound would blow everything before they were even close. If they took out a guard and he had to report in, that would alert security that something was wrong. If they didn't take him out then he would be between them and their escape route.

Take him out. Ezekiel made the decision.

Diego slid past Gino, his feet whispering on the stairs. Rubin covered the sound. He moved around the corner and in one motion, shot the guard with a tranquilizer dart. Rubin caught him and dragged him into the stairwell out of sight of anyone walking by.

Gino scanned the hallway. *All clear.*

Ezekiel nodded. *Draden and I are taking left. You, Rubin and Diego have the right side. Move fast. We've got*

*to find her and get her out in record time. When she's
found, we'll converge on her location, and head back to
the top as a unit. Questions?*

They shook their heads and Ezekiel signaled them to
move out. Draden took the lead, Ezekiel on his six. Like
Gino, Draden could sense the energy of an enemy. He
would know when someone was behind a door. That was
no guarantee. Gino had more than once missed someone
while training. It could happen, and his brothers' lives
depended on him not making a mistake.

Knowing Zara was held somewhere on this floor made
their task easier, but not knowing how many guards or
their locations was extremely difficult. They were playing
a very expensive game of roulette, one that could cost
everyone their lives. Every step, every doorway was a new
spin of the wheel and they would have to play it all the
way down the long corridor and back up again. Gino just
hoped they were on a hot streak tonight.

When they had to take a guard down, they knew they
risked being heard or seen. Each time they had to do it
increased the chances of them being discovered. If a radio
call was not answered, they knew someone would come
looking. The best thing to do was not to touch anyone. In
and out like ghosts. The problem was that was easier said
than done. In the end, in spite of all enhancements, they
were still human beings with limitations. This floor, and
the surrounding area where they were keeping Zara prisoner, was bound to be more heavily guarded.

Anything, Zeke? Gino asked.

They were going door by door down that unexpectedly
long hall. So far it was very quiet. Too quiet. They still
had to worry about an ambush. Whitney very well could
have set them up. What his reasoning could be, none of
them knew, but it was such an unusual situation, him asking for help from the GhostWalkers after all the shit he'd

pulled on them, none of them were feeling particularly confident in his motives.

We're stuck about twenty feet from where we split. There's a guard standing here talking to someone over his radio. Sounds like he's giving a goddamned dissertation to someone on the other end. We can't proceed because if we tranq him, whoever is on the other end of that call will know something's wrong.

Gino found himself cursing under his breath. The knots in his stomach were pulling tighter. The woman needed them to find her *now*. Something was off. Not enough guards. Had they moved her? Where the hell were the guards? One in the stairwell and one a few feet down the hallway didn't make sense.

The floor was essentially planned in a circle with the elevator being at the twelve o'clock position. The middle consisted of a long solid wall dividing the two corridors. It was an odd floor plan, but one Cheng seemed to favor. A gun could be shot down that long straight corridor easily, so maybe it was all about defense. Or offense.

Zeke, can you screw with the battery to drain it so they have to go and replace it?

Shit. I should have thought of that. Thanks, Gino.

There was a small silence while Gino waited, counting his own heartbeats.

Yes, it worked, he's leaving.

Gino, Rubin and Diego inched their way another few feet until they came to another door. This one housed a few men. Three? Four? Gino wasn't certain, the energy was blending together, but he felt them. He held up his fist and then indicated the room was occupied. He was feeling something else. Smelling something else.

He was a hunter, just like the others, enhanced with cat DNA, and his sense of smell was very acute. This was metallic. A coppery scent. Blood. His heart sank. He hoped to hell it wasn't Zara's blood he was smelling. It was possible this was Zhu's private torture chamber. He wanted to believe that some other poor son of a bitch was on the receiving end of Zhu's brand of torture that he'd read about. The man rivaled every war criminal known to the world.

Gino couldn't make himself believe the blood belonged to anyone but Zara. *His* Zara. So, yeah, he wasn't as fucking detached as he should have been. Putting a bullet in her head wasn't going to work for him. If she was operating for Whitney, helping him set up an ambush for the GhostWalkers, no doubt she'd been emotionally blackmailed into it or brainwashed. Whatever the reason she was there, they had to get her out. *He* had to get her out.

He didn't stop to think why he was so drawn to her when he hadn't even laid eyes on her. If he looked at that too closely, he knew he'd be in trouble. He didn't want to know the reason. He didn't even care. He was taking this thing one step at a time, and the first step was locking himself down with discipline. He couldn't yank open the door to the room where he was certain *five* guards were inside playing cards, instead of working as they should be, and spray them with hundreds of bullets until their bodies were riddled with holes like he wanted to do.

I found the guards playin' cards in a room here, Zeke. What the fuck? I thought they were all terrified of Cheng. Why are they so sure they won't get caught? Gino posed the question to Ezekiel.

Could be they know they're safe for the moment. There was speculation in Ezekiel's voice. *Find her fast, Gino.*

He didn't need to be told twice. The laid-back guards could be a setup. He moved around the room with Diego and Rubin. Heading quickly down the hall, he kept his hand lifted, palm hovering toward each door they passed in order to feel the energy. Movement caught his eye and he dropped low, signaling Diego and Rubin.

Guard ahead. Two doors, standing just inside the alcove. The scent of a cigarette drifted to him. What the hell? These men weren't on high alert. They didn't appear to be expecting trouble at all. It occurred to him, Cheng didn't believe anyone would try to come for her. Or maybe she hadn't broken. Maybe he didn't know yet that she was the one to wipe his computers clean.

Diego inched into position, slithering along the hallway, moving fast, using toes and elbows to propel himself forward, his tranq gun already aimed and in position to fire. He was so accurate, Gino would have bet he could shoot the wings off a fucking fly. Rubin set himself for a burst of speed as Diego released the dart. It hit the side of the guard's neck, the needle delivering straight into the carotid artery, so the drug would take him fast. Rubin leapt to catch the guard and his weapon, dragged him into the deeper shadow of the alcove and positioned him in a chair that was against the wall.

She's here. Be careful on the approach, Zeke. There are several guards on this side massed together and they're bound to decide they need to do their jobs. Gino sent the warning and stood just outside the door the guard had obviously been watching.

He inhaled, taking the scent of blood and fear into his lungs. No, not fear. Terror. He'd been in enough hotspots and had caused men to feel petrified to know what terror smelled like. There was a taste to it. It was tangible. And it was coming from that room in violent waves. He pushed down the need to rush in and forced himself to get a feel for the energy in the room.

Hostility. So much fear beating at him. Zara was panicked, but she also was feeling extremely determined. Gino opened the door cautiously, sending in soothing energy to try to offset her fear. There was blood all over the bed. A trail on the floor leading presumably to the bathroom. His heart caught in his throat.

His body warned him and he stepped back automatically even before his brain fully registered the threat. An object whooshed toward his groin, just missing him by a scant inch. He caught at it and tugged hard. She came out from behind the door on her knees, falling toward the ground. Stark naked. Covered with dark, purple bruises just rising all over her swollen body. Her back, buttocks and thighs were a mass of purple and black stripes. Long. Ugly. Deep. He swore as he caught her, preventing her from hitting the ground.

Get the guard's shirt. Screw that. He didn't want anything touching her skin from this place. Not one thing. *Forget I said that.*

"Zara, my name is Gino Mazzo. I'm a GhostWalker, and we've come to get you out of here."

The tension didn't diminish at all. She pushed at him. He understood. If she could see him through the slits in her eyes, he wasn't pretty. He tried again, keeping his voice low, afraid she would hurt herself more if she fought him, or alert the other guards.

"Bellisia sent us to get you out. She gave us the information on this place. We don't have time for you to fight me. There are guards all over," he whispered to her as he gently turned her over, cradling her to him.

Fuck. Fuck me, Zeke. I'm going to fuckin' burn his house down. And rip whoever did this to her from limb to limb. He knew a lot of ways to kill a man. He knew even more to hurt one. If this was Zhu's work, he deserved a taste of his own medicine.

The whip had torn her flesh, long stripes of open wounds from just above her breasts to the tops of her feet. He hadn't looked at the soles of her feet. How she'd even managed to crawl in an effort to attack someone was beyond him. She'd had to drag those lacerations on her knees and shins over the tile. No wonder the floor was smeared with blood.

Her eyes were all but swollen shut. He thought she could see out of the slits, but both eyes were black, her nose was swollen and on one side of her face her cheek was ripped open; on the other, her temple. Her fingers bunched in his shirt.

"He's coming back soon."

The terror in her voice shook him. This whole fucked-up mess shook him. Who did this kind of damage to a woman? What kind of courage had it taken for her to crawl through the room, find a weapon—the cane the fucker used on her—and wait on her lacerated, bleeding knees for a try at her attacker? She had to know it would fail. What was she trying to do? Get herself killed? His heart stuttered. Of course that was what she was doing.

Rubin, get me warm water fast. There in the bathroom.

"Baby, I'm going to lay you down right here on the floor. I need to address these cuts and then I'll get a shirt on you and get you out of here. You with me?" He kept his voice soft, pressing his mouth to her ear, trying to convey the sense of urgency and the need for silence.

She shook her head. "Go."

"Two minutes, baby," he whispered, already pulling out the antibacterial field dressings. Ignoring the way she shook her head, he began to wipe her down with one of the wet cloths Rubin handed him, hating that Rubin used a second one to start at the bottom of her feet and work his way up. Gino knew he was feeling far too proprietorial over her. Under the circumstances his reaction to her was inappropriate. They had to do whatever it took to get her out of there fast.

Gino kept the strokes as impersonal as possible, especially as he moved over her generous breasts, down her rib cage and belly to her sex. He was gritting his teeth by the time Rubin met him at her thighs. They tossed the cloths, and both started again with the antibacterial pads, cleaning the wounds. Next, he bandaged them lightly with gauze, having first put a salve on the field dressings.

Her body shuddered continuously while they worked. Gino found himself sweating. He ripped off his jacket, pulled his tee off one-handed, and shrugged back into his jacket almost all in one move. "Okay, Zara, you're doing great. I'm going to put this shirt on you. I know it's going to hurt, but as soon as it's on, we can get you out of here."

He was aware that Ezekiel and Draden had joined them. Along with Diego, they were guarding the hallway. Gino could feel the precious minutes ticking by. She tried. He could tell she wanted out of there, but she couldn't lift her arms very well. The whip marks covered her entire front and arms, the cane marks her entire back, legs and feet.

"Sorry."

The whisper broke his heart. "You're doing great, princess. Let me dress you." He even tried for impersonal when he spoke, but he knew he failed when he got a sharp look from Ezekiel. Like Gino, Ezekiel was a doctor, and he knew Zara was a mess. There would be no walking on her feet. Very gently he put her arms in the sleeves and pulled the shirt over her head. She whimpered, but immediately pressed her lips together to stop the sound. Her body never stopped trembling. The shaking had turned so violent he was afraid she might have a seizure.

"This might hurt a little, but we have to get you out of here. You can't make a sound, understand?"

She nodded.

Gino shifted his medical pack and Ezekiel took it from him to shoulder it. Taking a deep breath, Gino reached for her, getting an arm behind her back and one under her knees. He lifted her, cradling her close, trying to shelter her with his body, trying to convey they would get her to freedom. He was up on his feet and nodding to Ezekiel.

Draden took the lead, Diego followed. Gino with their

package was in the middle with Ezekiel and then Rubin in the rear. Draden could feel ahead for the guards. Rubin was still disrupting electricity and cameras, not enough to alarm the security personnel, just enough to alert them that glitches were happening throughout the building and the problem would have to be checked out in the morning.

Ordinarily, Gino would have packed out the wounded on his back to keep his hands free. He elected to give control over to Ezekiel and the others in order to keep Zara's front from rubbing along his shoulder and making the lacerations worse while he took her out of there.

Halfway down the hall, a door slammed, and they froze. At the same time, the elevator began to climb from the parking garage toward their floor. Immediately, Zara stiffened in his arms. The shivers, running through her body indicating pain, turned to tremors so strong she nearly jumped out of his arms.

She began to struggle, making small mewling noises, her head turned toward the elevator. Gino didn't understand how she even knew it was moving, or how she saw it through her swollen eyes, but she was beginning to lose it.

Shut her the hell up, Ezekiel snapped. They had to keep moving, and up ahead were guards. If she gave them away, they were all dead. *I don't care what you have to do.*

"Stop it now," Gino hissed, his mouth against her ear. When she didn't stop, he took her earlobe between his teeth and bit down hard. It was that or knock her out, and that was coming next. He wasn't going to let them all die, nor were Cheng and Zhu getting her back.

Startled, her attention went from the elevator to him. "Keep your eyes on me. Stay quiet or everyone is fucked." He kept his voice low, a mere thread of sound, but it was commanding. He meant it.

She stayed tense, her eyes bouncing beneath those

swollen lids. The sight of her so terrified turned his stomach. He had to gain control, get her to choose his brand of authority over her terror of her captors.

"Zara, you fuckin' do what I tell you. You look only at me. No matter what happens, you keep centered on me. I'll get you out."

Her breath came in ragged, labored puffs, her fear of whoever was in the elevator so strong, he didn't think he could overcome it long enough to get them to safety.

"You don't stop, you give me no choice but to knock you out." He'd put pressure on her carotid artery and give them a few seconds to clear guards and make a run for it. "Look. The fuck. At me." He enunciated each word when her terrified gaze started to slide toward the elevator.

It took a moment before she settled and it was infinitely slower than he would have liked, the seconds ticking by, seconds they didn't have. The group kept moving though. They had to be on the roof before the elevator reached the top floor and anyone realized anything was wrong.

Take out the guards. Ezekiel issued the command, knowing full well they were racing the elevator.

Diego, Draden, Rubin and Ezekiel went on the hunt, moving fast now, counting on the element of surprise as they came right up on the five guards exiting their card game. Four darts went in accurately and Rubin hit the fifth guard as he was lifting his gun. They double-timed it, moving fast, heading for the stairs.

One guard approaching the stairs.

Hell. A shift change? They'd taken out the guard on the stairs entering the building. If this was his replacement, the elevator could be holding an entire new set of guards. The sound of boots hitting the floor was loud as the guard ran toward the stairs, calling out in his own dialect.

Why haven't you answered? He's on his way up.

Whoever that guard was, he had tried to warn the guard in the stairwell of presumably Cheng's or Zhu's arrival. When the guard didn't answer, he'd rushed to warn him in person. Diego shot him with a dart as they rounded the corner. He didn't bother to pull the body out of sight. They just stepped over it and kept going up the stairs to the roof.

Gino glanced at the elevator. They only had two more floors before Zara's torturer would join them. He was tempted to hand over Zara to one of the others, fall back and put a bullet in the fucker's head, but he kept going, holding her close, trying not to jar her as he took her up the stairs fast.

Draden jammed the door to the roof after them as they all raced to their power paragliders. Ezekiel took Zara as Gino strapped himself in. Then she was put into the harness as carefully and quickly as possible. Ezekiel clipped her to Gino's torso.

"Hold on as best you can. Keep your face buried in my jacket. The wind is going to feel fierce. We've got a distance to go," Gino told her.

Diego and Rubin were away, heading toward their destination, a park about thirty miles from the building. They had to have favorable winds to make it, and Gino sent up a quick plea to whatever gods might be listening as he took his glider right off the building, following Diego and Rubin. Behind him, Ezekiel and Draden trailed them.

They weren't out of the woods. Ordinarily, Gino would have kicked back and enjoyed every second of soaring through the night sky. He loved it. He'd always loved the peace up there, especially at night. It was quiet. Serene. He wasn't a laid-back kind of man. He spent a great deal of time watching, always on guard, and up here, in the sky, he could fully relax, even with a woman strapped to his chest. Unfortunately, he knew it was possible they wouldn't quite make the park, not unless the winds rushing behind them, pushing them, were favorable. Even if they made it, they still had to make the run, a quarter of a mile at least, to the embassy.

Whoever was in that elevator would find the tranqed guards and know they had to have used the roof to escape. Cheng had a lot of clout with the government. He wouldn't be able to say he had taken Zara prisoner, although he might claim she was an industrial spy. Gino kept his eyes on the woman as they rode the night together.

She hung limply in the harness, and that worried him. He didn't have a way to reassure her. He could only watch over her, and hopefully she felt him there, felt his resolution to keep her safe. She probably equated him with Zhu, talking so roughly to her. He was rough. He didn't have it in him to be gentle and refined like his father had been. He had no charm. That hadn't gotten his father anywhere.

It had been Joe's father and the three bullets that had nearly ended Gino's life along with the dead bodies of his family that had shaped who he was. He was more Ciro's son than Joe was. Joe was more Gino's father's son. Maybe they'd been born into the wrong families. Hell. Gino found his gaze drifting back to the woman.

There was a pull that had never been between him and a woman before. It was strong. Too strong for his liking. He fucked hard. He fought harder. He did whatever job had to be done without flinching. Women didn't influence him. He had been taught respect, first from his own father and then from Joe's, but no one led him around by his dick. This one . . . He shook his head trying to figure out what the pull was and why it was her. It had been there since the moment he saw her picture and read the file on her.

Landing was going to be an issue. He needed to stay out of the trees inside that park and away from any objects on the ground. They hadn't been able to check out the park itself, so there were no specific landing marks to hit.

He had to trust their leaders, Rubin and Diego, to find them a clearing for all five of them to put down, drop gear and make a run for it.

Their contacts at the construction company had a large van already waiting and the men would pack away the power paragliders and rush them back to the construction site where they would be broken into pieces and put into the bins with broken equipment to be shipped back to the United States. If it wasn't clear, the driver would keep moving. There was no way to trace the gliders back to the construction company.

The glider came in low over the park, skimming brush. He winced, hoping his woman didn't have her bare, dangling feet ripped up by leaves and twigs. The soles of her feet had been damaged by the cane and there had been three whip lacerations where Zhu had torn the top of her foot open. Gino found that strange when the man had taken such care not to leave lasting evidence on her body. Her feet were never going to be the same.

Rubin and Diego dropped their paragliders and ran back to help him as he guided his to ground. They caught at Zara, unhooking the clip and harness before Gino had a chance to stop the thing moving altogether. Between the two men, they managed to pull her free and out of the way. Already men were hauling Rubin's and Diego's gliders to the van.

Gino heard Zara cry out, a small, keening wail that tore at him. He wanted to rip Rubin and Diego in half. He dropped the equipment, went straight to her and gathered her up, swinging her into his arms and set off at a jog toward the embassy, Rubin and Diego running in front and back of him, matching his pace exactly. Ezekiel and Draden caught up, Ezekiel moving into position directly behind Gino so that Diego brought up the rear. Draden added into the formation, not missing a beat, jogging right past Gino and the others to take the lead position.

They were used to running in formation. They constantly scanned their surroundings, were aware of all traffic on the street. Gino knew by now, Zhu and Cheng would know Zara was gone and she only had one place she could go—the American embassy. All they had to do was drop an army of their guards into a car and haul ass to the embassy to stop them from getting her inside those gates. Not only was that a very real possibility, it was a probability.

The embassy loomed up before them, the high fence surrounding it. Soldiers went on alert, watching them running toward them. A car's tires screeched around the corner.

"Americans! Open the gate! Open the gate!" Draden called out. "We're Americans." They didn't slow, but doubled their pace, Gino holding Zara tightly to him. Rubin moved over to the street side, running with him, hiding their package from the car rushing toward them. Draden had his military ID out, waving it at the guard.

"Captain Ezekiel Fortunes," Ezekiel identified himself as they came up on the embassy.

The car screeched to a stop and Cheng's men poured out, armed to the teeth, running at them. The embassy gate swung open and Draden stepped inside, spun around and watched as Gino, with Ezekiel and Rubin, sprinted inside the gates. Diego kept up the rear, and like Draden, spun around to face Cheng's security guards and their weapons. The guards closed the gates right in their furious faces.

"Sir," one American sentry said to Ezekiel. "I'm required to see your ID."

"Captain Ezekiel Fortunes," Zeke snapped. "We need to get this woman inside. She's been tortured. We all are carrying our IDs, so give us an escort inside and we'll each show them immediately." He handed his over. "She needs medical attention."

"Yes, sir."

Gino felt Zara stir in his arms while Zeke sorted their identities with the guard at the gate. He wasn't listening. The tension in her ratcheted up another notch. Her body shuddered. Shivered. "Need your coat, Rubin."

Rubin immediately shrugged out of his jacket and helped Gino wrap the shivering woman in it. She had her head turned away from Gino's chest and was looking out the gate toward the security guards. Her breath left her lungs in a long rush of fear. Gino not only heard the small whimper of terror, but felt it. His eyes followed the turn of her head to the sleek car that had pulled up in front of the gates. A man slid out of the leather interior.

Bolan Zhu. Gino recognized him from his photographs. He looked like a movie star, his dark hair slicked back, his suit immaculate. He simply stood on the walkway, eyes on Zara's face. Gino turned her so she couldn't see the bastard. They all knew the big son of a bitch was the one doing the torture for Cheng. If her reaction to him was anything to go by, she was petrified of the man.

Deliberately, Gino locked eyes with the bastard. Let him know where the true threat was. Zhu could beat a defenseless woman, but it was something altogether different to come at a man looking forward to the altercation. He didn't smile. Not even a taunting smile. He didn't feel like giving him that much of a warning. He just stared at the fucker and then, contempt on his face, leaned down to nuzzle the top of Zara's head.

"I'm right here. I've got you," he whispered. "You're safe."

She shook her head and pressed her swollen face against his shirt. "I'll never be safe."

"Princess," he said softly. "Look at me."

She raised her head and peered up at him. He felt the impact all the way through his guts—through that monster punching at him to get out and rid the world of a man like Zhu who would commit such a crime against an innocent. Zara Hightower needed protection, not the cold monster lurking inside him, but he knew it was the same thing. His monster was her protection.

"I take care of what's mine. He won't get his filthy hands on you again. That's my promise to you."

He held steady while those little pinpoints of what was left of her eyes searched his. She must have caught a glimpse of that demon inside of him, the one ready to be let loose, the one punching and stabbing to get free.

"You understand me?" Because he was telling her so much more than the words conveyed.

She swallowed again and nodded.

"Keep your eyes on me. Don't look at him. Don't think about him. A man like that is beneath contempt."

She nodded again, and once more, Gino lifted his gaze to Zhu's. The bastard was staring at him, stupid enough to think he might be intimidating. Zhu thought Gino was like the others, a white knight. Maybe he would have been, but that was long gone, ripped from him when he was a child and he'd been shaped into something completely different. He was a demon now, still rescuing the innocent, but with so much more in his arsenal.

Zhu refused to look away, or go away. He wanted Zara to be afraid of him. The man didn't realize she'd already recognized the monster in Gino and was willing to give herself to him for his protection. She saw. She believed. That was enough for Gino.

Gino turned with Zara in his arms, cradled close to his chest by his heart, and he walked away without once looking back.

The moment he was inside, he was a different man. He was an officer. A doctor. A surgeon, and he expected complete cooperation. He showed his ID but had no patience for the rest. "I'm a doctor," he snapped. "This is my patient. No one touches her until I know she's safe and has been treated. Take me to a private room where I can treat her."

"Her name?"

"Zara Hightower."

There was a small gasp. The military guards, Houghton and Hurley, exchanged shocked looks. "*The* Zara Hightower?"

Houghton was already moving, not waiting for an answer. Gino followed him. "Zeke's arranging a flight out of here as soon as possible on the first scheduled plane back to the United States. We have to get her out of the country before the authorities realize she's gone."

"She can't just leave the country without . . . There are protocols. She's a guest here."

Gino sent him one look over Zara's head. It was enough. Gino let him see the demon, the one from hell ready to do damage to anyone opposing him. Houghton pulled open the door to a suite with a bathroom. Gino indicated the bed with his chin. Rubin and Diego had followed while Ezekiel went to make hasty arrangements to leave the country. Draden stayed with him to ensure his safety.

It was Rubin who ripped back the covers to expose the sheets while Diego ducked into the bathroom to run hot water onto cloths. He brought back towels.

"We'll need clothes for her for later. Something soft. Don't worry about underwear. Her body's too torn up."

Houghton's gaze found Zara's lower legs and thighs with their terrible striping. "Who the hell did this?" Anger was in his voice now. On his face. Yeah, he didn't much like seeing a woman, an American at that, treated to torture.

"Houghton," Gino said softly. "We have to get out of here before he goes to the government. You'll need to find us a plane out."

Houghton nodded and left them. Gino jerked his head toward the door and Diego and Rubin obeyed his silent order. Zara wasn't too aware of her surroundings, the trauma throwing her into shock, but later, he didn't want her to be embarrassed every time she looked at his friends.

"All right, princess, it's just the two of us. I'm cutting off this shirt and treating your wounds. First, I'm injecting you with morphine. I need to know if you have any allergies." He hadn't read that she did. Her body hadn't once stopped the terrible shivering, some of the tremors so severe she looked as if she was having a convulsion.

"Zara, when I ask you these questions, baby, you have to answer them so that I can help you. Understand?" He smoothed back her hair. In spite of her ordeal, that hair was every bit as soft as it looked. More even. "We have to clean you up fast and get you back to the United States where I know you're going to be safe. I'm taking you to Bellisia." He figured it wouldn't hurt to remind her that her best friend was waiting. "I need to take the pain away for you."

Another shudder went through her body. He saw her eyes shift to his face. "Trying." She managed. "So scared."

"I know you are. You're doing great. We're almost out of here. Any allergies?"

She shook her head. Gino didn't wait, but injected her with morphine. He was almost desperate to take away her pain. Her fingers traveled up his chest and found his jacket, curled there and held on. That little gesture disturbed him as nothing else could have.

She didn't look away from his face. Not once. Not when he injected her. Not when he could see the drug take her, not when he cut his own tee from her body.

"What's your name?" Her voice was whispery soft. Trembling still, but the terrible tremors were easing with the drug floating her.

"Gino. Gino Mazza."

"Thanks for getting me out," she said softly, her voice beginning to slur, letting him know she was already drifting. Her fingers clutched at his arm. "Don't leave me."

That was distinct. Very distinct. Her lashes, caked now with sticky infection, fluttered, but refused to go down. She was waiting for his answer. Refusing to give in to the painkillers.

"I'm not going anywhere. I'll be right here, standing guard."

Her eyes searched his face. Something in the hard angles and planes gave her reassurance. He was certain that close scrutiny would have frightened anyone else.

"Go. To. Sleep." He made it an order.

A ghost of a smile touched her lips. She relaxed completely, still holding his hand, but her fingers went slack and those lashes finally drifted all the way down.

6

Zara didn't want to open her eyes. *He'd* laid cooling cloths over her swollen eyes and face, soaking them in something each time they warmed and placing them back over her eyes. Gino. Gino Mazza. She woke often, too terrified to sleep. He murmured soft words of encouragement and tried to get her to sleep. She knew she was at the embassy, but she wanted out of the country. She knew what kind of influence Cheng and Zhu had. She couldn't go back there, and she wasn't going to sleep until she was safe far, far away from them.

There had been a delay and she knew Gino wasn't happy about it. At the same time, she was running a fever and he gave her massive doses of antibiotics and told her it was just as well they weren't flying in the air for hours while her body was so torn up. He was rough, bossy, scary, and sometimes, the things he said to her echoed the orders Zhu had given her. Zhu's voice was always gentle, Gino's not so much. That comforted her, that even when Gino was trying to be gentle, there was a note in his voice that said he could handle anything. Anyone. He could handle hell coming at him.

She didn't need or want nice. She needed scary. Dangerous. Someone capable of stopping Zhu. She needed strong. Confident. A man willing to do things that Zhu was willing to do if necessary. She knew there weren't too many good guys that were like Gino and she wasn't about to get too far from him.

She'd been given painkillers, really heavy ones that gave her relief and allowed her to drift off, but all she saw when she closed her eyes was Bolan Zhu. He terrified her. She woke, every time she fell asleep, crying her eyes out. That added to the raging headache. Through it all, there was his voice. It had a rough note to it. Deep and raspy. Not the voice of an angel. The owner of that voice didn't have the face of an angel either. More like a beautiful devil. She didn't want him to leave her side and every time he tried to, to her utmost horror and humiliation, she'd grabbed his hand and clung.

Clung. Like a baby. She was one of Whitney's Ghost-Walkers. A reject maybe. One that was useless as a soldier. She'd proven that. She certainly hadn't been stoic under torture and as tortures went, hers had probably been mild in comparison to what happened to most others. Cheng had acted as if Zhu had taken it easy on her. Zhu had acted the same.

A shudder ran through her body and she tightened her fingers around *his*. Her guardian devil. Gino. She wanted him to be real, a terrible demon, and she didn't care if he was sent from heaven or hell to save her. He'd done it. He'd come for her and gotten her out. He'd carried her to the roof, strapped her to his chest to fly through the air, run with her to the embassy and gotten her inside.

Zhu had come for her, staring at her, determined she come back to him. She knew he wouldn't stop coming. Not ever. It wouldn't matter if she was in China, or the

United States, he would come for her. If he ever got his hands on her . . . She shuddered. It would be bad. So bad.

Strangely, Gino even used some of the same phrases when he talked to her that Zhu did. He wanted her to answer him when he asked a question. He insisted she look at him when he spoke to her. He had a way of dictating to her, using his voice to command her. With Zhu, she'd been terrified. With Gino, she was comforted. She felt as if Gino would take care of everything for her, make certain she was safe and secure.

She knew she was becoming too dependent on him, and it wasn't fair to him. He did everything for her. He had to take her to the bathroom. See to her every need. She was horrified and humiliated, but he didn't let her be that way. He was gruff about it, telling her to knock it off and that it wasn't a big deal. He didn't let others see her without her clothes and he even managed to tame her hair. He seemed to know when she was uncomfortable and anticipated her every need.

She found herself thinking about Gino as a man. His eyes. She'd looked up at him, and his eyes had caught her attention. Cool, nearly black eyes. Like obsidian. Gleaming like a cat's. Fierce like a cat's. Just as cool. His lashes were unexpectedly long and for some reason, she'd fixated on that. Held it to her. Did demons have long lashes?

They were going on day four and she still refused to let him leave her side. She couldn't help it. She expected Zhu to climb through the window and take her back. She was desperate to get out of China, although to be honest, she didn't think that would stop Zhu from coming after her. Gino had moved, trying to let go of her hand, and she refused to let him.

"You have to stop shivering or I'm going to have to climb in bed with you and share body heat," he warned.

"I was just going to step out of the room for a moment."

He sounded serious. She didn't care. She wasn't losing

him. She shook her head and tried to squeeze his fingers. His hand was significantly larger and stronger than hers, but he didn't try to break away from her. He sank down onto the bed again.

"You're killing me, Zara. We've got you safe. We'll get you home and Bellisia will take good care of you. Everyone will. You'll be doted on like every beautiful princess should be."

She wasn't beautiful anymore and she wouldn't be ever again. She couldn't bear to look at herself in the mirror over the sink in the bathroom. It wasn't about whether or not those marks would leave scars or fade altogether; they were there, below the surface of her skin. Bolan Zhu had put them there and no matter how her skin healed, or how often she scrubbed, she would never remove what he put on her. Another shudder went through her.

She hated that she was such a coward—and she was. She couldn't stand being in Shanghai. She couldn't stop being terrified long enough to fall asleep. Seeing Bellisia would be wonderful. Brilliant. She couldn't wait, but if her demon was thinking he might leave her, he had another think coming. She wasn't certain, even if they were free and clear of Zhu, she would be able to let Gino go. That wouldn't be happening until Zhu was dead, so it wasn't happening at all.

"Not Bellisia." She wanted to make that clear.

His hand swept back her hair, slid into the thick strands and massaged her scalp. "What does that mean?"

"You take care of me. Not Bellisia." She didn't care if she sounded needy or demanding or if he was sick of her. It was Gino who would keep her safe. He was her only chance and she wasn't about to be separated from him, even if it was his idea. She wanted to be tied to him. She wouldn't have minded if he handcuffed them together or tied her to him with a rope or anything else as long as he couldn't break that tie.

She heard his soft laughter. He bent his head toward her, his breath warm against her skin as he brushed his lips over the swelling of cheek. "You're going to be a little monster, bossing me around."

She hadn't thought about it that way, but she was okay with bossing him as long as he stayed close and kept Zhu from her.

The sound of the door opening had her stiffening. She struggled to open her eyes. Panic set in when she realized there were cool bandages over them and she couldn't see. She reached up to rip them away and Gino caught her hand. He had insisted on putting cool gauze soaked in something over her eyes every half hour.

"Leave it, princess," he commanded, his voice an absolute authority. All trace of amusement was gone. "What is it?"

"Trouble, Gino. Boss wants to talk to you," Rubin interrupted.

Zara knew. He was there. Zhu was there at the embassy and he was going to force them to turn her over to him. A small, terrified whimper escaped. She didn't even care that Gino might think her a coward. Let them all. Let everyone think that. She knew she was a coward and she wasn't going to make apologies for it. She tried to throw herself sideways. All that mattered was escaping. Getting out of bed and running. Hiding. Shanghai was a big city. She could lose herself there.

Gino's arm clamped down around her waist. "Stop, Zara. How many times do I have to repeat myself? He's not getting you. I'm taking you out of here one way or the other."

"You have to follow orders," she whispered. "Everyone has to follow orders."

"Ma'am, excuse me," Rubin said softly. "We're not exactly known for followin' orders. We're takin' you home with us no matter what these people say."

"The embassy has to fly us out of here," Zara protested, but she subsided beneath Gino's restraining arm, although she was still tense.

"We're already looking into alternatives, just to give us options and diversions," Rubin explained. "Gino's handling it."

"Shouldn't have to keep saying the same thing, Zara," Gino said. "I got you out, you're staying out."

She almost bit her lip, but it already hurt, so she licked it instead. "Would you take the wraps off my eyes?" She wanted to be able to see. "Please?"

"Not yet. I want that swelling to go down. Give me a second to see what's so important and I'll be right back." His fingers touched her face very, very gently, so gently she barely felt the whisper of his skin against hers, but it was enough to send her stomach tumbling off the edge of a cliff. She'd never had a reaction like that before to anything, and it shocked her enough that she froze and just nodded, hoping he wouldn't notice her accelerated heartbeat.

She should have known better because it seemed Gino noticed everything. His fingers brushed over her inner wrist, right over her pulse, came back and stayed. She resisted the urge to pull her hand away and instead, held her breath.

"Princess, I swear to you, I'll get you out of here."

Grateful he thought her heart had gone into overdrive because she was so fearful, she managed to nod her head to show him she'd be fine until he returned. She wasn't, but Zara could justify being a clingy baby for only so long—then she'd lose what little respect she had left for herself.

The mattress shifted as Gino got up. Zara curled her fingers into the cool sheets. They felt so good beneath her back. The painkillers Gino gave her were surprisingly effective when she hadn't thought anything could take away that all-encompassing pain. They held off the worst of the agony inflicted by Zhu.

The moment she allowed herself to think of the man and what he'd so casually done to her, her entire body shuddered. Shivers started again. Gino had managed to stop them by his presence. He seemed . . . dangerous. Predatory. Invincible. There was that same energy Zhu had given off, only Gino felt different when he was close to her, his energy merging with hers. He felt protective and even possessive toward her. She didn't know what the possessive part was all about, but she needed protection desperately and he felt as if he could shield her. He was a rock. Solid. Steady. An anchor she'd never had before and wanted to keep.

Zara detested that she counted each second Gino was away from her, but she couldn't stop. She'd never thought of herself as a needy person. Her best friends were Bellisia and Shylah, two women she'd grown up with from the time she was an infant. They weren't born of the same blood, but they were sisters. She often, over the years, had wished she was more like the two of them.

She hadn't excelled at being a warrior like the others. She'd come in last at everything—well, with the exception of running. That was her one call to fame. Whitney despised her for her lack of talent, although she learned quite a lot and was proud of her capabilities—she just wasn't quite as fast as her "sisters" in a battle. They coached her of course. Both girls were generous with their help, but she wasn't wired for combat.

She knew Whitney would have gotten rid of her had it not been for her brain. Once he realized she had something to offer, he stopped her training and began to devise a different path altogether for her—but no matter how well she did on the outside, he made it known to everyone she was a failure and inferior to the rest of them.

Her fingers stroked the sheets, clutched at them. She

couldn't stop the nervous habit she'd never been able to get rid of, no matter how many times Whitney had told her he was done with her over her inability to stay still. She silently counted, drawing air into her lungs and breathing it out. Maybe she should go looking for him—Gino. She desperately needed him with her. Time stretched out and her heart began to accelerate. Not too fast at first, but beating harder, finding fear so that the acceleration started slow but ended up galloping.

Maybe he was sick of her clinging to him. Maybe Zhu and Cheng had made an appeal to their government, and to avoid an international incident, the American consulate was going to order her turned over to Zhu. What could Gino really do if that order was given? He'd have to turn her over to Cheng.

Panic welled up. She felt dizzy, unable to catch her breath. Her hands and fingers tingled, numbness setting in, and that panicked her even more. She knew she was shutting down, terrified that Gino had left her alone and the real monster was coming. She braced herself for the attack, held her breath until she nearly fainted for lack of oxygen. She drew her feet up, struggling into a sitting position, not wanting to feel so vulnerable when he came. If she could make herself small, keep her legs and feet away from him, he might not be able to do as much damage.

"Zara. What the hell is wrong?"

Gino's voice made her jump. She hadn't heard him come in. But then she hadn't heard him go out. Maybe he was part of some larger conspiracy, one of the many mind-tricks Whitney played on the women to see how they would handle a situation. She wrapped her arms tightly around her drawn-up knees and shook her head.

The mattress shifted as he sank down onto it beside her. She wished she could stop shivering, that air would find her lungs so she wasn't gasping like a fish. It was humiliating to know he was seeing her panicked and out of control.

"Baby, listen to me." Gino's voice was soft, a whisper of sound, but it was all command.

There wasn't anything else she could do—or wanted to do—but listen to him. She needed to hear his voice. That take-charge, reassuring tone that made something shaky and scattered all over the place, deep inside her, begin to settle.

"You have to find one person to trust through this, and I'm asking you to let that person be me. I'll get you home safe. As long as you're with me, no one is going to get to you, harm you, or take you back."

She reached up and caught at the wrap around her eyes. She had to see him. She had to know he meant what he said, and how could she do that simply relying on her ears? She heard truth in his voice, but she needed to see it. His hand closed over hers very gently, but she couldn't move her fingers let alone get rid of the bandage.

"I need it off," she said, willing him to understand.

Apparently, he did, because he pushed her hands down and then his returned to the dressing. He slowly unwrapped the gauze and took it down from her face. She blinked a few times, surprised she could pry her eyelids open. She lifted her lashes completely for the first time since Cheng had hit her with his gun and Zhu had added to the mess by beating the shit out of her. Whatever Gino had used over the last few days had taken the swelling down dramatically.

Gino Mazza was intimidating. He had the widest shoulders and a chest that went on forever. It wasn't that he was massively big, just muscular. She didn't know a man could have so many muscles. The tight tee he wore stretched over so much definition she was afraid to breathe. His face was carved, as if from some immovable matter such as marble, or better yet, steel or iron. Granite.

She didn't know, only that it worked. He was both beautiful and terrifying to look at. She'd never seen eyes so intense. So compelling. If he walked into a room full of people, she was certain everyone would stop what they were doing to look at him. He was that scary—and that enthralling. If she wasn't counting him hers, believing him to be her protector, she would have been screaming for help.

He had gorgeous eyes. She'd noticed them before when she could barely see through the tiny slits she'd been able to make; now, she was staring full-on into those black, obsidian eyes. They gleamed. Shone. Almost as if there was a red or blue flame beneath them.

"I don't like you leaving me." She knew there was a reprimand in her sulky voice. She hated what that revealed to him.

"I told you I would be right back, princess. I was gone less than ten minutes."

Could that be true? It had to be longer. It seemed a lifetime. She nodded to let him know she was listening. She willed him to keep talking. His voice steadied her as nothing else could.

"What did they want?" It was bad news. There was nothing on his face to give it away, but she felt his energy and he wasn't happy. His expressionless mask hid his feelings from the world, but she would always know the truth, because he couldn't hide his moods from her. Every emotion was part of his energy whether he liked it or not, and when his energy merged with hers, she felt everything he did.

"Nothing I didn't expect," he assured. "Cheng went to his friends in the government and complained about you, said you ran and hid inside the embassy and that you took valuable information on something he was researching for them. That it pertained to agriculture, but that in doing their research, they had discovered a new, biochemical weapon that could cause untold harm. They want you and the information back immediately."

Her heart sank. She pressed her palm tightly over her heart. "I knew they'd do something like that. Does the embassy want me handed over?"

"The Chinese government doesn't want you handed over. It would be risking an international incident. They also don't want Cheng angry with them. He provides them with all kinds of information they wouldn't get otherwise." Gino swept his hand down her head, his fingers finding their way to the nape of her neck where they massaged to ease the tension out of her. "We're leaving now for the airport."

"Zhu will stop us."

Gino shrugged, not in the least concerned. "He can try, but we're slipping out a back way and we'll have a military escort. Even if the Chinese were lying, and they weren't, they aren't going to want a shootout with us on their streets. They want you out of here so they can tell Cheng you were already long gone. I don't think they believe Cheng about the biochemical weapon either."

"I just want to get to American soil." She knew Whitney would be waiting, but she didn't want to think about that until she had to. She just had to get out of China and Zhu's reach and then she'd deal with the rest. She didn't doubt for a minute that Zhu wouldn't stop coming for her. She tried to tell herself that once she was on another continent, he would leave her alone, but she knew better.

Her fingers found the dark tee stretched so tightly across Gino's chest. Her fingers were shaking, but she dared to touch him, to gather the material into her palm and close her fist around it. "He'll follow," she warned, hoping he wouldn't think she was a hysterical female. She knew she was acting like one, but she couldn't make herself stop. "Zhu will follow."

He nodded his head, his hand coming up to hers,

catching her wrist between his thumb and index finger as he held her fist to him. "I'm well aware of that. He let me know with that little macho bullshit stare-down at the gates that he wasn't going to let it go. Don't worry, princess. One thing at a time. First, get you on the plane out of here. While we're in the air, I'll continue to work on you. You're already healing fast. Your feet are the worst. The rest is deep bruising and lacerations. I know it hurts like hell, but there won't be any permanent damage, unless it's to your feet. He wanted your body flawless, but he didn't want you to be able to run."

Her heart clenched wildly in her chest. He believed her. He knew Zhu was coming after her. That was both terrifying and wonderful.

"After we're home, I'll get you to safety and we'll sort things out."

Safety was wherever Bellisia was. Bellisia had managed to escape Whitney. Zara wanted to see her as soon as possible. Once the capsule with the virus broke open, she wouldn't have much time. If Bellisia could tell her how she survived, maybe she could stay. Otherwise . . .

Her gaze jumped to Gino's face. She didn't want to be away from him. Never in her life had she felt safe, not until she was in Gino's presence. "I'm putting you in danger." She had to at least acknowledge that she knew what she was doing to him, what she was asking of him.

His smile was slow in coming, but when it did, it was gorgeous. It took her breath and sent her stomach into a slow roll. "Baby. Really? What the hell do you think I do for a living?"

She hadn't thought about that. He was a GhostWalker. She knew Whitney was extremely proud of the Ghost-Walker program and the soldiers who had volunteered. Unlike the girls he'd gotten from an orphanage to experiment on, these men had patriotically decided to serve their country. The experiments were done over and over on the disposable girls until Whitney felt he'd gotten it right, then he performed the operations on the male soldiers. GhostWalkers took on extremely dangerous jobs.

Still, it wasn't about Gino being a GhostWalker. The others with him were GhostWalkers, and they didn't feel the same to her. Gino was different. Colder. Darker even than the others. Scarier. Not in terms of what he could do, but what he was willing to do. She needed that coldness to keep her safe.

"I suppose that was a rather silly thing to say."

"Nothing you say is silly," Gino assured. "You're scared right now, which is very understandable." He glanced at his watch.

She was determined to be honest with him and she hoped he'd always be honest with her. She cleared her throat. It wasn't going to be an easy admission. "Gino?" She had his attention. He always looked straight at her and seemed to give her his entire consideration. "I'm afraid of everything. All the time. I hate being in public. I'm always afraid. I don't want you to think I get any better than this because you'll just be disappointed."

He leaned forward and brushed her forehead with his mouth. His lips. They felt soft yet firm. Cool yet quickly heating. His breath was warm. "Zara, I have no expectations, so you can't disappoint me. That said, I don't like you being afraid because it isn't necessary, not when you're with me."

She looked down at her hands. One still clung to his shirt, like a little child's. The other was a fist in her lap and she could still see and feel those fine tremors, which meant, because Gino was so observant, he would see them as well. "I'm no fighter. I know you think we were all trained, and I was, but I'm not like Bellisia. Ask her. She'll tell you."

"She told me she loved you. That you were her sister and you had a gentle soul. She asked me to protect you and I will, with my life. It isn't necessary for you to be a fighter. We have them. I'm one. You be the calm in the eye of that storm for me. I could use that. When I lose my mind, and I will, you can center me."

Her gaze searched his. He meant it. He wasn't patronizing her, he actually meant it. The relief was tremendous. She took a deep breath and let it out. "I can do that." They were connected, and that connection was strong enough that she was certain she would be able to find a way to soothe him if he needed it. Still, he seemed awfully cool under fire, unlike her.

There was a knock on the door. "Look alive, Gino, we're leaving in five."

"Wrapping her up now, Draden. Rubin, did you pack the supplies I asked for?"

"Got them here, Gino."

The voice was so close it made her jump. She hadn't known there was another man in the room with them. He just seemed to come right out of the shadowed area near the windows. Had he been there the entire time? She was afraid he had. She hadn't taken her eyes from Gino to even look around the room. She would never have made a good soldier and no matter the training, she still wouldn't. She could defeat an opponent—but only with the element of surprise. She had knowledge, but she wasn't fast enough nor did she generate the power the others had. She could kill, but just thinking about doing so turned her stomach.

"Babe, you're going to have to let go of me so we can move," Gino said.

She felt the heat rising under her skin. She tried to snatch her hand back fast, but Gino's fingers tightened around her wrist, holding her to him. He waited until her gaze jumped to his. "Stop worrying about the little things. I like you holding on to me. Understand?"

She didn't but she nodded anyway. His eyes burned through her to brand her somewhere deep.

"I'm going to wrap you up in the sheet and carry you out of here. My boys are going to surround us. No one will get to you. Understand?"

He seemed to say that to her a lot. Zara nodded again even though she was used to worrying about everything— especially the small stuff. He removed the IV that dripped a painkiller into her along with fluids and then he stood, planted a knee on the bed, tucked the sheet under her, lifted her easily and rolled the sheet closer around her body, then cradled her close. He did it so quickly and efficiently she wondered how many women he'd rescued. She didn't want to sound jealous or possessive, so she didn't ask him. She caught him around the neck and held on as he carried her out of the room.

Rubin followed them, and just outside the door, the others were waiting. The one he called Draden as well as two others.

"Zara, this is Rubin and Diego, they're brothers. Our boss, Ezekiel, and you've met Draden. They all serve with me in my unit. This is Zara."

There were a lot of murmurings of "ma'am." She felt a little underdressed to be meeting people. She flashed a small, strained smile to the group of them and then subsided against Gino's chest.

"Can you wait to use the bathroom until we're on the plane? I should have gotten you there right away when I knew we would have to leave fast."

She nodded. She would definitely wait. She wanted on that plane more than she wanted anything. At her agreement, they moved quickly, in perfect step, Gino in the middle of the formation, through the hall toward the back of the embassy. A corridor led down another hall, and they went out a back door to a waiting vehicle with the back passenger door open. Gino, with Zara in his arms, slid onto the seat and someone closed the door.

She found her heart accelerating all over again. This

was either going to go smoothly or all hell was going to break loose. Chinese soldiers could ambush the car. If Cheng got wind of their leaving, if anyone was in his pay in the embassy and they found out, his security force, all ex-military, could ambush the car on the way to the airport. Cheng could have his guards waiting at the airport.

Gino's arms tightened around her as the vehicle began moving. "You're not breathing."

"This is nerve-wracking." It didn't seem to be for him. She swore his pulse hadn't gone up at all. It was the same steady, reassuring beat it had been all along. His breathing hadn't changed either. Her breathing, however, was coming in ragged puffs she couldn't control. Panic was beginning to set in all over again.

"Zara."

"I'm trying." She was. She'd warned him.

"You're cool as a cucumber talking in front of hundreds of people. I could never do that," Gino said.

"I throw up every single time before I go out there to talk," she confessed.

"That makes you even braver. You still get your sweet little ass out there and you give your talk, which, by the way, I can barely comprehend."

She liked that he called her ass sweet, although she wasn't certain if she should be as happy about the ass part as she was. "Once I start talking about the developments in AI, I can't help but forget where I am or how many people are watching. I like sharing because it's the future and there are so many wonderful uses."

"I listened to a few of your talks they had online and I have to admit, I could hear the enthusiasm in your voice. I hadn't thought too much about artificial intelligence, but you made it so interesting, I started studying it to learn everything I could."

She liked everything he said to her. He made her feel as if everything she did was all right. Not just right, but extraordinary. Or perfectly okay if she wasn't good at something. He gave her that as well.

"Breathe, baby. Look to me when you get stressed. Every time. I'll be close." His fingers caught her chin in a firm grip, but one so gentle her heart turned over.

He lifted her chin so her eyes met his. Outside the shadowed windows, the brilliant lights of Shanghai burst past like long, colored streamers. Inside, it was the two of them, separate, even, from the driver. Gino's eyes were very black, so bottomless, a fathomless abyss that she found herself falling into. His eyes were every bit as mesmerizing as his voice.

"I want you to understand what I'm telling you. When we get home, I'll be close. You get scared for any reason, you look to me. I'll be there and you'll know you don't have to worry."

He was offering her the very thing she had dreamt of her entire life. She had just wanted to feel safe—even if it was for just a few minutes. She hadn't felt safe as a child. She'd known at any moment Whitney would come to subject her to pain and call her worthless and selfish. It wouldn't matter how hard she tried, she would fail and he would be disgusted with her. During her teenage years, the pattern had worsened, especially when she was attending schools. It seemed the more she succeeded on the outside, the uglier Whitney was to her when she returned. The more he demanded. There had never been a place of safety.

"Zara." He said her name softly. "I realize you don't know me very well, but I'm a man of my word. I've offered you my protection. All you have to do is say yes, and believe. It really is that simple. Actions will bear out what I'm saying to you."

She didn't wait, didn't dare take any chances he would rescind his offer. She was so terrified of Zhu, and she knew he would come for her. She had to make that clear to Gino before she accepted his protection—and she wanted to accept immediately.

"Zhu isn't like anyone I've ever met, Gino," she whispered, glancing toward the front seat and the driver. She didn't want anyone to overhear her. "I think he's a true sociopath, and he's capable of extreme violence without feeling any emotion. He'll come after me, and if you're standing in his way, he'll hurt you."

Gino was silent so long she was afraid he wasn't going to answer her, that he'd finally decided she wasn't worth all the effort he'd gone to. He didn't look away and she couldn't. She had to sit there on his lap, his arms tight around her, just staring into his eyes, her heart beating so hard it felt as if someone was taking a hammer to her chest.

"Do you think I'm a sociopath?"

It was the last thing she expected and she actually gasped, already shaking her head in denial. "No, of course not. Clearly, you have the ability to feel. Maybe too much."

"How do you know?"

"Your energy merges with mine and I can feel your emotions, or at least catch glimpses of them. Can't you feel mine?"

He didn't answer her. He stared into her eyes for another long minute. "I can do the things he can without feeling a thing, Zara, although not to a woman. I don't know why there is a distinction for me, but it doesn't mean I'm not capable of beating the shit out of someone. Or torturing them. I have. I will again. I've put bullets in men's heads. I'm not the good man you think I am."

She recognized a warning when she heard it. She'd already known he was a demon, rising from the depths of hell to save her. Maybe she'd end up going down with him into those fiery flames, but at least she'd be safe on Earth and not shivering in a little ball all night alone in her bed if she stayed with him.

Her hand slid out of the sheet to reach for his hair. The dark, wavy mass was wild and unruly and the only thing on him, other than perhaps his long lashes, that brought any relief to his rough, hardened features. "You're a better man than you think you are, Gino. I would choose you every time."

"Mean it, Zara. Don't say it to me because you're afraid I won't see this through for you. I will. I'll stash you somewhere safe and . . ."

"No!" The protest burst out of her, an explosion of breath, of heart, of her wildly churning stomach. "No, Gino. I'm going to stay with you."

She didn't trust anyone else, not even Bellisia, to keep her safe. No, it was more than that. Maybe Gino wouldn't succeed against Zhu, although she believed he had the best chance, but that feeling of safety he generated empowered her. She knew, once she wasn't hurting with every breath she drew, she could live what little life she had left enjoying herself, rather than being terrified.

She wanted to see how Bellisia lived. She'd like to take a walk and taste freedom without worrying she might be late and one of her friends would be punished.

"Okay, baby, just remember I gave you every chance to bail on me."

She nodded and snuggled deeper into him, burying her face in his neck. He didn't shove her off him, but let her. She needed the reassurance. She liked him holding her. She knew Shylah didn't like to be touched, and Bellisia hadn't either. Zara had felt that way after the years with Whitney. No one had ever touched her in a kind way. There was always pain associated with touching. Not with Gino.

"Level of pain?" Gino asked.

"About a four right now, very tolerable," she said, because she didn't want him to think she was a big baby. She could handle a little pain if she needed to. "I don't want to move. The drugs are working, Gino. Any more and I wouldn't be able to think straight."

"You don't need to think straight. I don't want you in any pain at all. There's no need for it."

The vehicle was slowing and she craned her neck to see out the window, suddenly scared all over again. "Why are we stopping?"

"No worries, we're at the airport. The driver will take us to the plane. A customs official will be waiting to get us on the plane and out of here as fast as possible. The government doesn't want you here. They really don't want an incident any more than we do. We have fully loaded weapons and an escort. If we're attacked anywhere, it would have to be explained."

"Cheng has a lot of clout."

"Yes, he does, but you're an international treasure. You give talks all over the world. This wasn't your first, and most of the officials think it's ludicrous to think you're a spy. You are very open, giving away important research to businesses in foreign countries that are interested. We took photographs as proof of what Zhu did to you. Can you imagine the outcry if that was made public?"

She would be utterly humiliated. She didn't make a sound, but stared at him with what she knew could only be a horrified look.

He bent his head and pressed a kiss to her temple, right over the spot Cheng had slashed her with his gun. "There will never be a need for anyone to see those pictures, Zara. Cheng is known to be a paranoid man. If you were already gone, they don't lose face with anyone. The matter is out of their hands and therefore resolved."

She hoped he was right, although she knew they had to have shown those photographs to government officials, otherwise the Chinese wouldn't have acted quickly to get her out of their country. Still, she knew what clout Cheng had. She couldn't imagine customs looking the other way as she was raced up to the plane, covered in a sheet that even now was spotted with blood. She forced herself to breathe, matching the rhythm of his lungs. Slow and even. Steady. She couldn't hyperventilate. "My passport was with my briefcase. Cheng took it from me." Panic hit hard.

"You're fine. I'm telling you, baby, we're getting you out. Your passport will hold up."

Zara felt as if she was holding her breath the entire time they waited for the plane to take off. First, they had to go through customs. It was unlike any customs she'd ever gone through. The man all but waved them through with the briefest of glances at documents. He carefully averted his eyes from Zara's sheet-covered body. Gino still hadn't put regular clothes on her, afraid they would rub, but she knew he had some. She was so used to the sheets that she hadn't asked to put them on and now she wished she had.

Gino carried her onto the plane and took her straight back to where they'd set up an area designated for medical aid. He set her in the wide chair very gently. The pressure on her back and buttocks and the backs of her thighs made her gasp. She hadn't tried to sit on anything but the soft mattress at the embassy.

"Once we're in flight, I'll get you settled in the bed and give you a good dose of morphine," he said, seating himself beside her. "You'll be able to sleep, hopefully for most of the ride. It's long, Zara, a good seventeen hours."

"Tell me about yourself," Zara said. She needed the sound of his voice. She was looking out the window, noting the line of cars moving very fast toward the airport.

He shrugged. "I'm not the most interesting man in the world. Don't have your brains."

"That's a relief. I don't like people trying to prove they're smarter than I am. I'll concede every time, even if I know they're full of crap. It gets so old. Do I really care?"

"Usually men, right?" Gino asked, giving her a small grin.

She noted he had a small dimple. It was intriguing in the middle of all that rough. She was a little shocked that she hadn't noticed it before. "Yep. However did you know?"

"Competition. Ego. You name it, men have it." He reached for her closest hand, the one she'd been twisting into the sheets wrapped around her. He wrapped his hand around hers and brought it to his chest. "I'm an only child. My grandparents on my dad's side lived with us, but my mother's parents were very close, neighbors, so I went between houses all the time. My father served in the Marine Corps and was best friends with Joe Spagnola's dad, Ciro. They served together in the Marines. Joe serves with us in the Air Force pararescue GhostWalker unit."

She couldn't look away from his face, certain he was about to tell her something important. At that moment, the plane began to taxi down the runway. She looked out the window to see the line of cars turning onto the road leading to where the airplane had been waiting for them.

Her breath caught in her throat and she curled her fingers tighter into a fist within the sanctuary of his hand. He pressed her fist harder against his chest. "Look at me, not out there, princess," he reminded. "I know you've had to count on yourself, but you aren't alone anymore."

"He planted a virus in me," Zara blurted. She shouldn't have. She should have kept her mouth shut. She had at least a week or longer to get back to Whitney before the capsule broke open. She just wanted to see Bellisia. Now she didn't want to go back at all. Now she considered it might be worth it to let the virus take her if she could just have a few days of freedom—with Gino.

"I'm well aware," Gino said. "When you were unconscious at the embassy, I did a full body scan. I knew what I was looking for because he'd done the same to Bellisia. He planted two capsules, Zara. The first and a fail-safe.

He wanted to make certain you were dead. He knew we'd look for the first capsule and hoped we didn't find the second. He also planted two trackers in you."

"Cheng did a full scan as well as a brain scan, and he didn't find anything." She held her breath. She had more to hide than capsules of viruses and tracking chips.

"Because they're attached to your ribs and Zhu beat the holy hell out of you. They're encased in a new kind of PEEK-carbon nanotube that is invisible to X-rays, CT scans, and MRIs, but Zhu beat you so hard, he dislodged both of the nanotubes and the capsules were just peeking out. Once I go in, I'll be able to remove the capsules as well as the tracking chips."

"Go in?" she echoed faintly.

He gave her another small, reassuring smile. "I'm hell on wheels as a surgeon, baby, and that's me bragging, pounding my chest and acting like an egomaniac just to impress you."

She couldn't help but laugh. They were in the air. The cars were sitting on the ground, watching them go. For the first time since she'd been taken prisoner by Cheng, she felt absolute relief.

7

Gino and his fellow GhostWalkers had brought clothes for Zara with them from the embassy. Just a long skirt Gino had approved, one that wouldn't rub over the bruises or lacerations. He hadn't bothered to have them find shoes for her—her feet were far too damaged. She dressed on the plane with his help and he did his best to be a gentleman, an impersonal doctor, but he knew he failed miserably. Her top was cotton, a thin material that buttoned down the front. There was no underwear, but she didn't seem to care, acting grateful for something to wear other than a sheet.

He'd been careful to keep her covered with that sheet whenever anyone else entered her room. He told himself it was because no woman wanted strangers, even doctors, to see her naked when she was unaware, but he knew it was because he felt possessive of her. That was new for him and unexpected. He'd spent five days and nights with her now, taking care of her every need and instead of being bored out of his mind, or done with the entire business, he craved more time with her.

Her breasts moved under the thin material of her blouse, drawing his attention. That wasn't supposed to happen, not when they had a long ride home from the airport. Gino didn't believe for one minute that Whitney would give Zara up. That meant they'd most likely get hit on the way home. Ezekiel and Draden pored over a map of the area, so they could take alternate routes. They also called for some of the other members of the team to meet them halfway and escort them home. He couldn't be thinking about Zara's body when they might get hit at any moment.

Gino didn't tell Zara any of that. She was floating a little, looking out the window at the landscape as they rushed past. She leaned into him, her head on his shoulder, her eyes searching his face.

"You're beautiful," she said, touching the dimple at the side of his mouth.

"You're a little out of it," Gino told her, but he didn't remove her fingers, now stroking gently over the dimple and tracing scars that dissected the heavy shadow on his jaw. Her fingers felt like a caress. He should move them. He should move her altogether away from him since his body was beginning to give him a really hard time—literally. At first, he just ached. Now his cock hurt like a son of a bitch, but that didn't matter as much as having her head on his shoulder did.

Every time she took a breath, those breasts moved. That wasn't something he was eager to share with his fellow GhostWalkers. He had the urge to cover her up, but he knew he would take the worst razzing of his life. It was going to be bad if the looks he was getting from Draden and Zeke meant anything. Rubin and Diego rarely talked, but he caught them looking once and gave them the death stare. Rubin returned a faint grin; Diego rolled his eyes.

"Isn't he beautiful?" Zara persisted dreamily, looking at the two men seated opposite her.

"Yes, ma'am," Rubin said. "We say that very thing to each other every day."

"And so sweet."

Gino wondered if he leaned forward and took her breast into his mouth right there, right through the thin material of her blouse, if she'd still think he was sweet. Probably. She'd most likely cradle his head to her chest and he'd be lost. He had to get a grip.

"We were just talkin' about how sweet Gino is the other day, weren't we, Draden?" Ezekiel chimed in, looking up from the map.

"Keep it up," Gino warned. "None of you will wake up tomorrow. At least, if you do, body parts will be missing."

Zara's lashes fluttered and a ghost of a smile curved her lips, bringing attention to her mouth. He wanted to groan when his cock pushed hard against the material of his jeans. It was much more difficult to control his body when he'd never had a problem with that before. She had that lower lip that just begged to be sucked—or bitten.

"Woman, don't encourage them." He growled the order at Zara and was rewarded when her smile went from small to a little bigger. That smile could stop men in their tracks. Maybe even stop wars. He'd walk through fire for one of those real smiles.

Zara leaned into him, her body melting into his. Her head found his neck and nestled there. Yeah, she was floating and he didn't care. He'd take whatever he could get. He'd made sure he was the one to see to her every need. He carried her to the bathroom, her slender arms around his neck, her face buried in his neck out of embarrassment, but he'd shut that down with a few harsh commands. Still, he'd done it enough times that she was beginning to joke a little when he took her.

She couldn't stand on her feet yet, at least not without

a lot of pain, and Zeke agreed with him that the tendons were damaged. He didn't give her underwear because of the whip lacerations. The long skirt hid everything. The blouse should have but didn't, mostly because he was very aware she wasn't wearing a bra. He tried to be a gentleman and not notice the shadow of the curves beneath the thin material, but it was difficult when his mind seemed consumed with her. Now, his body was all too aware of her as well.

He kept her close to him not just there on the seat, but in every other situation, on the long plane ride from Shanghai, to the Louisiana airport and now in the car heading for their final destination—the fortresses they were building in and around the swamp.

Drone flying overhead. About two miles out. Looks to be heading your way. I can take it out in about two minutes.

That was Mordichai. He was good with a sniper rifle. Ezekiel had alerted the home team that they were coming in, most likely hot, with the enemy on their heels. They knew they'd be ambushed. It was only a matter of where, not if. Whitney was full of shit, telling the major general that he would leave Zara to them if the GhostWalker team rescued her. He'd make his try before they got home, hoping his supersoldiers could take on a smaller force.

Take it out, Ezekiel ordered. *Trap? Cayenne? You spot anyone in the surrounding swamp?*

As always, Ezekiel sounded calm, almost serene. He could explode into action in a heartbeat, but never seemed that way until it was too late. He didn't sound tense, not even confined in a car with a small team and Zara. They liked to be out in the night, where they did their work under the cover of darkness—not to say they couldn't do the same work in daylight hours.

Took out three of Whitney's supersoldiers, Trap reported. *They're armored. You'll have to go for the throat to kill them. These men are souped-up. I'm talking really revved, Zeke.*

Of course Trap would give the report. Cayenne rarely talked to anyone but her man. Sometimes to the women. Mostly she observed.

Look alive, gentlemen, Ezekiel warned them all. *We're about to enter the party zone.*

Drop me, Draden said.

The car slowed. Adam Cox had picked them up at the airport. He had been one of Whitney's soldiers, but he hadn't liked what the man was doing to the women. He had come after Bellisia but hadn't returned to the fold. He stayed to work with the GhostWalkers.

Could have eyes on us, Ezekiel warned.

Not for long, Mordichai said.

They didn't hear the shot, but they saw the drone fall from the sky just ahead of them. The car came to a rolling stop and Draden was out and running into the swamp. The man could run for miles and not get winded.

Gino was better outside the car. They all knew it. Ezekiel looked at him but didn't order him out, which was a good thing. Gino didn't know if he would obey the order or not.

"Best chance is me outside, princess. We're about to be attacked. Whitney's looking to reacquire you. We knew that would happen and we're prepared, but I can serve us better outside the car. You okay with that?"

Zara's long lashes lifted and she looked right into his eyes. He could read fear there. She sat up very slowly. "Just let me out. They'll come for me."

Gino shook his head. "He doesn't get you."

"I have a virus in me anyway."

"One I can remove," Gino pointed out. "You stay. This is our best chance, but I want you on board with the decision. I'm not deserting you, I'm trying to help save you."

Her gaze searched his for several long moments and

then she slowly inclined her head. The movement was barely perceptible. He was very reluctant to leave her, but he glanced at Ezekiel and nodded. At once he could feel the car beginning to lose speed again.

He caught Zara around the nape of the neck and pulled her close to him. "You stay close to Zeke. I'll come for you in a few minutes." Before she could say a word, he settled his lips over hers. The moment he did, his heart went crazy. A roaring started in his ears. Loud. Taking away his hearing. Robbing him of all his senses with the exception of feeling.

He felt far too much. He'd kissed a lot of women. It had never been his favorite thing, but he gave them that. Kissing seemed intimate—too intimate to give to one-night stands, but if they expected it, he gave that to them. Kissing Zara was something altogether different. His heart pounded. His stomach somersaulted. Heat exploded through his body, rushed through his veins until he thought he might burn in hell for all time. Maybe one burned in paradise, because kissing Zara was something he could do for a lifetime.

Ezekiel cleared his throat, and Gino instantly lifted his head. He set her on the leather seat, and let her go abruptly because otherwise he was certain he wouldn't be able to do it. The car slowed to that snail's pace and the door swung open. Gino dove out, rolled to his feet and slipped into the swamp. The car—with his woman inside—moved ahead without him.

There was a rhythm to the swamp, and over the last few months, Gino had become accustomed to it. He knew the sounds, the way the insects droned, the slight rustle of leaves as mice, shrew and other little rodents scurried along the floor, scavenging for food. He had learned to become part of it, to pass through the swamp without disturbing any of the creatures. He did so now, moving fast, listening as he went, allowing the animal DNA in his body to tell him where the enemy might be hiding in wait.

He came across a dead body. Draden's work. He kept going, keeping his passing as silent as possible. He felt at home in the swamp. Anywhere outdoors. When he was inside, he felt confined, trapped. Most nights he slept outside, on the roof, on the porch, wherever he couldn't be easily spotted. How was that going to translate to having a woman? A woman like the one he needed? One that needed taking care of.

He knew most people would say that wasn't a partnership, but for him, it was. Already, Zara gave him a sense of a purpose. Of home. Of affection. To him, giving attention and care was showing love. It didn't matter if others thought his particular needs were fucked-up. He was fine in his own skin. He hadn't thought he'd find the perfect woman, but Zara fit with him. He didn't know what she'd be like when the threat to her was over, but for now, she fit him.

He wanted—even needed—his woman dependent on him. He wanted her looking forward to his coming home because the things he did for her, no one else would ever do. He wanted to wrap her up in a silken cocoon and give her everything she ever could need or want. He needed her world to be him. He hadn't thought such a thing was possible until he'd met Cayenne and had seen her with Trap. She didn't see anyone else. He wanted that for himself. Cayenne was a warrior woman, but still, that aside, Gino wanted his woman looking at him the way Cayenne looked at Trap.

The attack came from his left, but he'd known the soldier was there, waiting, hunched down in the brush. He'd felt his energy, a large mass that didn't belong in the swamp. The man exploded into action, leaping toward Gino, hoping to overwhelm him with a blitz attack. He had both hands on his semiautomatic, swinging the weapon in front of him as he came at Gino, his face a mask of determination.

Gino hurled the knife on the move, not slowing his run, his stride exact. The snap of his wrist as he threw the blade added power. The knife was one of his favorites, perfectly balanced, and he hated to lose it, but he didn't have time to retrieve it, not with Zara's freedom hanging in the balance. He had a gut feeling that if Whitney couldn't reacquire Zara, he would have her killed. He didn't know why he felt that way, but his instincts were usually right.

Zeke, left my favorite knife in an asshole's throat. Want it back if possible.

I'll tell the cleaners.

Thanks.

He was coming up on another one. He timed his steps, veered to his right, throwing the knife underhanded, but using the same hard wrist action that always assured the blade would go in accurately, deep, and do the most damage. The big soldier took several steps and then went to his knees, shock spreading across his face.

Whitney's men were armored under their skin. They didn't last long. He used rejects from his GhostWalker program for the most part. The men couldn't stand up psychologically to the enhancements. They went downhill fast. Whitney had changed up his experiments, moving into trying new things, like body armor. That had sped up the deterioration of his supersoldiers.

Found their nest, Mordichai reported. *Four waiting about one klick from your position, Zeke. You're heading toward them fast. Two spread out just ahead of the nest, two behind it. Gino, you're clear. Draden took out the others.*

Where one of the others might have joked about not leaving any behind for the rest to be in on the fun, Draden rarely said anything. He just got rid of the enemy and left their bodies where they fell.

Gino, you're coming up on the two just in front of the nest. Draden's taking out the two from behind. Malichai is with me and we're going to take the four in the nest.

It's too damn easy, Zeke said. *Look for a vehicle. These are his sacrifices. Find the real threat.*

The shots rang out over the swamp. Four in rapid succession. Mordichai didn't have to report that they'd hit their targets, all of them knew they had. Gino nearly ran right into the first soldier waiting in ambush for him. He was hidden in a patch of elderberry bushes. He came up fast, reaching for Gino, determined to get his hands on him. Gino took several steps to the right, unable to get a good angle on the soldier.

It was useless to waste ammunition on him. Unless he managed to get a throat shot, there would be no putting him down. The soldiers were slow, but immensely strong. He felt the energy of the second soldier just before the bastard plowed into him. He hit with the force of a freight train, knocking Gino straight at the other soldier.

The first soldier caught him in a bear hug, squeezing hard, turning him so his partner could stab him with a knife. Gino used his feet, planting both boots' soles hard into the oncoming soldier's chest. He used his enhanced strength, driving the man away from him, hoping to crush through the armor plate, but knowing it wasn't going to happen.

Using his speed and strength and the force, he continued his momentum, pushing off the soldier's chest and flipping over him, wrenching his arms free as he did so. He landed on the soldier's back, took his head in a firm grip and jerked. There was an audible crack. He landed behind the dead man and held him in place as a shield to take the barrage of bullets.

Simultaneously, over the head of the remaining soldier, he saw the silk of a spiderweb descending from the tree surrounding them. One of the thick gnarled branches glistened with silken strands, the anchor for the silky rope snaking down toward the soldier. It wasn't alone. More lines were cast. Gino couldn't help but admire the way Cayenne threw the silk. She was an expert at it.

The first looped around the soldier's neck, never once touching his skin, so he had no idea he was in any kind of peril. The second dropped over the barrel of his semiautomatic at precisely the same time she pulled the first one tight. The silk, stronger than any steel, tightened around the enemy's vulnerable throat and he was dragged upward, off his feet, as the second line stripped the gun from him.

Gino dropped the soldier he'd killed and turned toward the road. *Are we clear? Thanks, Cayenne. Always admire the way you use that silk.*

Whitney had never conceived that his creations, once out of the lab, might turn on him. Cayenne had been scheduled for termination. They'd always been afraid of her, but Trap had sprung her loose and now she was with the other GhostWalkers. In a fight, she was invaluable. Silent. Deadly. Just what they needed.

Don't like this, Ezekiel said. *Stay away from the car, Gino. I think . . .*

The sound of an explosion rocked the night. Gino swore and turned back toward the sound. *What the hell, Mordichai?*

His heart accelerated with every step he took. Calm and cool deserted him completely. That hadn't happened since he was a kid with his family falling all around him. He realized, in that moment, as he ran back toward the car, he'd already let Zara in. Somehow. Someway. That damned fast. She was in. She was his.

Has to be a drone. They fired from a mile or more out.

Find the fucking thing and get rid of it, he ordered. He leapt over a fallen, rotting tree trunk and stopped himself from bursting out onto the road.

The car was surrounded. The road was gone in front of the car, leaving a gaping hole where it had been. No one moved. The soldiers couldn't get into the car, and Ezekiel wouldn't hand Zara over to them.

"Zara, no one else has to get hurt," one of the soldiers said. He glanced at his watch. "You don't have much time before you make up your mind. The next round takes out the car and everyone inside it."

Gino could tell by his voice the soldier meant exactly what he said. If he put a bullet in the man's throat, killing him, it wouldn't save them. That would be the signal to fire. *Don't let her get out. The second you do, they'll blow the car.*

They're going to blow it anyway, Ezekiel said calmly. *Her only chance is to go with them. You can recover her once she's out of here.*

You're not disposable. The moment she's out of the vehicle, they'll blow the car. Gino shook his head. He had to resist sending another plea to Mordichai or Malichai to find the drone. The two were Ezekiel's blood brothers. Rubin and Diego, both inside the vehicle, had been raised with them. If Mordichai or Malichai could find the drone and take it out, they would.

The window rolled partially down. "How do I know you won't kill everyone in the car when I get out?" Zara asked.

Zeke, she can't walk.

He'll have to reach for her. Hold her. The other two we can take. The timing has to be just right.

"Whitney doesn't want them dead. He wants you home. Alive. You can't survive here. You know that. Come home, Zara."

Gino willed her not to open the door. Once she was in the open, if they had a sniper, and most likely they did, she could be taken out at the first sign something was going wrong.

"She can't walk," Ezekiel said. "She was tortured and her feet messed up."

The soldier's body jerked, clearly reacting to that news. "Zara, did you give them any information?"

Gino frowned. Information? What information? She'd gone in to destroy their computers, wipe the drives clean so there was no chance of Cheng having data on the GhostWalkers. They didn't need him selling the intelligence to the highest bidder. So, what information could Zara have that would make the soldier tense up like that?

"Of course not. I'm going to come with you, Damon, but if you hurt these men in any way, I won't go with you. I've got a weapon and I'll use it on myself. You know me, you know I will."

Gino heard the resolve in her voice. *This is fucking crazy, Zeke. Stop her.*

It's our only chance, Gino. They don't know you and the others are out there.

Tell her I don't want her to go. Tell her now. Tell her to stay with me.

Ezekiel clearly relayed the information. Like Gino, he was stalling for time, hoping Mordichai or Malichai found the drone before time ran out on them.

She says she has the virus implanted and would die anyway.

I can remove the capsules. I can find an antidote. It's what we do. I told her that. She knows I won't let her die. Gino felt almost desperate enough to rush Damon. Once he did, the other GhostWalkers, already silently surrounding the vehicle, staying in the cover of trees and brush, would move in with him. They could easily kill the soldiers surrounding the car, but the drone would fire and take out all of them.

It had been years since he'd felt so vulnerable and he didn't like it. He didn't like that Zara wasn't in his control.

He'd put her under his protection and he wasn't about to fail her.

Tell her I'm going to keep them from taking her. Even if they get her now, they won't get out of the swamp with her.

They'll put a gun to her head, Gino.

I'm aware of that. He was accurate with a knife. More than accurate. He knew there were few alive better than he was, but was he willing to bet her life on that? Especially now, when he realized she was already a part of him? Hell yeah. He'd bet his training, his dead calm when he needed it. *Tell her.*

She said she's counting on it.

That settled him. Her belief. Just that. She was counting on him. Believing he'd come for her. *Be ready,* he warned the others.

The door began to open slowly. Damon spoke into his radio. "Delay strike. She's coming out. Shoot only if they make a move against us."

Got something. Got something, Mordichai reported. *Eastern sky. Nearly two klicks out. Bastards staying low, but it rose just for a second, enough that I caught the movement. Can't take it out because it sank again, but it would need to rise to make the shot. I've got a lock on it now. The moment it comes up, I'll take it out.*

Everything depends on that shot, Mordichai, Ezekiel warned.

Sheesh, Zeke, his brother said, *just add more pressure. Malichai is backing me up. It's going down.*

Need Malichai to help out here.

No, you don't. Joe's lying up here, and he's got your six. You awake, Joe?

Mordichai. That was all Joe said, but it was enough.

The team was in place. They had a plan. They worked together all the time, so much so, they always knew what the others were going to do before they did it. Cayenne was new to them, but they were beginning to get a feel for her strengths and how to use them. Bellisia was still too new and would be defending the house, Nonny, Pepper and the children.

"Zara, don't blow this by doing anything stupid," Damon said.

Gino had the idea that the soldier was pleading with her and he didn't like it. At. All. Something was off.

"I can't do much, Damon," she said. "I can't put my feet on the ground." She pushed the door open and tried to straighten her legs to show him her mangled feet.

"What the fuck did they do to you?" the soldier burst out.

"I'm on painkillers," she answered. "I just can't walk, but I won't slow you down."

Damon signaled to one of the other soldiers who was guarding the rear of the car. He moved warily, not liking being so exposed, but he came around to Damon's side, wincing a little when he saw Zara. Her face was still very swollen, but at least she could open her eyes now. They were black and blue, as was most of her face, and the swelling was still horrendous.

Damon shoved his weapon around to the back, letting it hang from his shoulder strap while he reached for Zara. Her breath hissed out in a long rush of pain, and Damon hesitated before bringing her in close to his chest.

"We don't want to kill her," Damon told Ezekiel. "We're going to take her home. She'll be well cared for there."

"She'll be a prisoner," Ezekiel pointed out. "She seems to matter to you. Don't you mind that she's a prisoner?"

"We're all prisoners in some way, and she has more freedom than most. Sir, stay in the car. It's safer for you. If you get out, you'll be shot. I give you my word as an officer that your crew and car will not be fired on if you stay there for the next five minutes."

"You know we can't let you take her," Ezekiel said softly.

"She'll die if she stays here. Her only chance is with me," Damon said.

Gino definitely didn't like that. The soldier hadn't said with Whitney or that her only chance was to come back; it was with him. As if he had some proprietorial rights to her, including the right to keep her safe. So safe, the other soldier was pointing a gun at her head. When Damon stepped back, the soldier stepped with him, mirroring him as if they were dancing.

Find their sniper, Gino ordered. *No one can safely leave that car until you do.*

He's down, Trap reported. *Cayenne swept the trees, all clear.*

"Bring the car now," Damon ordered. "Tell the helicopter to meet us at the rendezvous location."

Of course there was a car. There had to be a car. Damon and the others needed an escape route. They'd need a car and a helicopter. Where would the helicopter meet them? What possible places, close, were there?

Find that helicopter and take it out, Ezekiel ordered.

The gun never wavered from the exact location on Zara's skull. *Exact* location. Gino noticed small details like that. Every step they took, that gun was relentless, aimed in the same spot, as if that one spot was more important than any other spot on her head. Like her temple. No, this was specific. He filed that information away. They'd done an MRI, looking for the virus capsules, and Whitney had used a new PEEK-carbon nanotube to hide it in, knowing it wouldn't show up in a scan. So, what if something else was hiding there as well?

Zeke, you let them get too far from the car, you're risk-

ing them blowing it the moment you exit. That was Mordichai.

You miss that drone shot and we're all going to die, Ezekiel said.

Miss? I don't fucking miss. Mordichai sounded outraged.

Gino knew that was their way, talking it up, joking, giving each other shit when the tension mounted. His eyes were on Damon and the soldier walking with him away from the vehicle. The door was still open, Ezekiel sitting on the edge of the seat, both feet out of the car.

"I'd like to move my men to the side of the road, no weapons," Ezekiel said.

Damon shook his head. "Sorry, man. We have to follow the plan. Whitney doesn't want to hurt anyone, just get Zara back."

Why would he need Zara back? What about her was so important that he sent pawns to be massacred and a crew to retrieve her? Why? The question nagged at Gino. The GhostWalkers had Bellisia. She had escaped. For the most part, once the women were gone, they were left alone. Whitney would make a try every now and then, but the general consensus was Whitney was keeping them on their toes, mostly testing his supersoldiers against them, not all that actively trying to get the women back.

Gino matched every step Damon made with Zara. He walked backward, away from where there was a hole in the road under cover of the swamp. Any minute a car would be driven up to collect them. Damon kept throwing expectant glances over his shoulder. Gino relaxed, suddenly realizing why the car wasn't coming. Draden was loose in the swamp. You never wanted Draden after you, not for any reason. He didn't know how to stop coming at you.

Three. Two. One. Ezekiel did the countdown.

The men remaining in the car popped open all doors

and came out shooting, rolling on the ground, each targeting a soldier. Gino was on the man holding the gun to Zara's head. He'd outpaced him, getting a perfect line to his throat, not willing to take any chances. One tiny knife went straight through the space where the trigger met the weapon, severing the trigger finger. The second knife, thrown a heartbeat after the first, hit the soldier in the throat and buried itself there.

Gino was already running, knowing Damon would turn back toward the car, expecting the drone to fire, to blow it up. He ran *between* Zara and the possible bomb. He didn't stop. He trusted Mordichai, but it would be stupid not to take precautions. He moved fast, slamming his body hard into Damon's, driving him backward. At the same time, he reached for Zara.

She wrapped her arms around his neck without hesitation and he kept going, running for the relative safety of the swamp, aware Damon had a semiautomatic and knew how to use it. Right now, it was pointed between his shoulder blades. He knew, because he had that itch that warned him.

He heard the bullet hit Damon's head, and Zara cry out almost simultaneously with the sound of Joe's rifle. Gino kept running. Once in the thick brush, he took to the ground, trying to protect her as they went to earth. Even so, he knew he'd jarred the hell out of her body. Her breath was coming in ragged pants and she bit off a moan of pain.

"Sorry, princess," he whispered as he set her on the ground. "Lie flat." He lay over her, his body covering hers, his gun out and ready, although the others had disposed of the soldiers.

More shots rang out. Two. A third. *Drone down. Helicopter in air, heading your way,* Mordichai reported.

It wasn't as easy to bring down a helicopter as the movies made it look. They'd done it, more than once, but it wasn't easy. Mordichai, Malichai and Joe would concentrate on three targets. The pilot. Probably Mordichai, the best of the three. Malichai would go for the tail rotor, and Joe would go for the engine. He was counting on Mordichai. The moment Mordichai killed the pilot, they would load Zara back in the car and get the hell home.

Gino felt her body heave under his. He frowned. "You crying?"

There was a small silence and he imagined she was making up her mind whether to admit it to him or not. His hand found her face, fingers tracing the tears there.

"Trying not to," she admitted.

A surge of adrenaline hit hard. "Damon? You like the guy?"

"Most of the soldiers aren't very good to us," she answered slowly—slowly enough that he knew she was reading his mood. "They know eventually Whitney will insist we go into their breeding program and we'll have no choice. They're . . . vulgar. Not dirty and kind of sexy, if you know what I mean, but just rude and vulgar. They treat us like we're so much less than they are. Damon was one of the few who wasn't like that. He treated us with respect."

Gino took a breath. Let it out. He swept his hand down the back of her head. "I'm sorry, then, that they had to cap him, baby."

She struggled with tears, managed to press back another sob and nodded. "Damon would have followed orders, Gino. He would have killed me, both of us. Me and himself. He wouldn't have allowed you to keep us alive."

"Why?"

"Why?" she echoed.

"Yeah. Why? Bellisia is with us and he hasn't cared all that much. Cayenne and Pepper are with us too. And the little viper chicklits."

"Little viper chicklits?" she repeated.

He rubbed his chin on top of her hair. "That's what some of us call Wyatt's triplets, just to annoy Pepper. They pack venom in their bites and when they're teething, the little munchkins like to bite."

"How extraordinary."

"Why would Whitney be okay with us keeping the other women and the children, but not you? He promised the major general that if we went to get you, he would leave you alone."

She turned her head in order to look up at him. Her face, so swollen, was an abomination after seeing the photographs of her flawless, soft skin. He stroked his finger gently over the terrible bruise where Cheng's gun had struck her. He wanted to go back and kill the bastard.

"Whitney did that? He called a major general about me?"

Gino nodded. "Our boss, Major General Tennessee Milton. Whitney called him and Major General gave the order to Joe, but it was voluntary status only."

"Why?"

He didn't hesitate. "It was unsanctioned and considered a suicide mission."

Her breath caught, and then she asked, "But you volunteered. Why?"

"Everyone did."

"Why did you?"

Shit. He didn't want to tell her that. The truth would make him sound like a stalker. "Not sure I want to give you that, princess. You're still making up your mind about me."

"I already made up my mind about you," she whispered. Her gaze slid away from his.

His gut clenched hard. "Baby, you know I'm not leaving it there. Look at me."

Her fingers dug into the dirt, pulling up a few rotting leaves. "Tell me why you volunteered."

He sighed. "You look at me and I will, but I'm warning you, I look like some kind of stalker."

"That's good."

The amusement in her voice surprised him. It was shy, but it was there. "Read everything about you I could get my hands on. Got every image the Internet had available. It's all on my personal laptop. Fell hard. Long fall, Zara, and surprising, but the real thing is far, far better than anything I could have thought I saw on the Internet."

"I'm not like that." There was hurt in her voice now, and she closed her eyes and turned her face away from him.

"Like what?" He kept his hand in her hair, fingers working her scalp. He half expected her to be upset that he'd gotten every piece of information available about her onto his computer, but hurt wasn't the emotion he anticipated at all.

"Like what you see on the Internet. I detest traveling. I know I'm not supposed to waste my brain and all that, I've been told enough times how selfish and worthless I am for not being grateful for my opportunities, but I can't help how I feel. I'm not like that superconfident woman you see on the Internet, Gino. I'm not her."

"You don't have to talk in front of everyone in order to not waste your brain, Zara. Trap is the most intelligent man I know. Wyatt runs a close second. They do all kinds of good. They don't talk about it, or give speeches. Trap would light himself on fire before going public like that."

She turned her head back toward him. "Really?"

He brushed a kiss along that long, wide bruise. "Absolutely. So, baby, I've got to ask you again, why is it that Whitney would rather have you dead than with us?"

"He always plants a virus in us before we leave the compound. That way he ensures we have to return."

She was telling him the truth, but definitely hedging. "Yeah, we know that. So why send Damon as a safety net?

He promised Major General. Going back on his promise to Major General isn't a smart move or a good political one. Whitney still has friends in the White House. If Major General, a very popular man by the way, goes against him, he might lose those friends. So, again, Zara, why does Whitney want you dead or back with him when he leaves the others alone?" Gino poured icy cold into his voice, wanting her to know he meant business.

She didn't answer him.

"You know you're going to have to trust me sometime."

She still didn't answer him.

Two boots planted themselves right beside their heads. Gino looked up to see Ezekiel staring down at them. "You two going to play in the dirt all night or come on home?"

Gino was going to choose home for them, but he wasn't going to drop the subject Zara wanted so desperately to avoid. And he wasn't going to forget that the soldier had trained a gun to one specific spot on her head.

8

Zara looked eagerly out of the car window, desperate to see Bellisia. When Bellisia had failed to come back to the compound, she was terrified that her best friend was dead. Shylah and she had spent hours alternately crying and then trying to convince each other that Bellisia was alive and had managed to escape. Eventually, Whitney's anger and his retaliation—separating Zara and Shylah— had Zara believing Bellisia was still alive. She couldn't wait to see her. She had so much to tell her, and she needed her advice on what to do about the information she had stored and locked in her brain.

Zara recognized their driver, Adam Cox. He'd been a soldier for Whitney and, after Bellisia disappeared, Adam and his partner Gerald Perkins had been sent out, presumably looking for her. They had never returned. Seeing him driving the car made Zara uneasy. If she hadn't been able to read Gino's energy so easily, to merge her own energy with his, she might have become suspicious, but there was no way for Gino to hide the fact that just the mention of

Whitney brought that cold demon inside him close to the surface.

Bellisia stood outside the two-story house the vehicle drove up to. She looked beautiful. Radiant. Tears welling up, Zara clutched Gino's hand. "I can't believe she's really alive. Whitney wouldn't tell us for sure. I hoped she was. I hoped she really was the one to kill Violet. When we heard the senator had died from being bitten by a blue-ringed octopus when she was diving, I thought it had to be Bellisia, but there was no way of knowing for certain."

The car came to a halt, and Zara threw the door open. She swung her legs out of the car before Gino could stop her.

"Zara, what the hell do you think you're doing? You can't walk, remember?" He caught her around the waist to keep her from trying to leap out.

She'd forgotten. For just that one moment she was so happy to see her "sister" that she forgot Zhu, the torture, everything but hugging Bellisia. Bellisia looked toward the car and her face lit up. Zara had forgotten how beautiful she was, and how her smile could light up the sky. She was very small with blue eyes and pale blond hair. Already, she was in motion, leaping off the porch and running toward the car. Zara braced herself, her answering smile hurting her sore face.

Bellisia ran around the hood of the car and launched herself into the air. Ezekiel Fortunes caught her, wrapping his arms around her, his mouth on hers. Zara's smile faded. Shocked, she couldn't take her eyes off the couple. Bellisia hadn't even seen her. Her gaze had found Ezekiel and she never looked anywhere else.

"They're married," Gino said. "This mission, you have to understand, princess, it wasn't certain we were coming back. Boss called it a suicide mission, and if you'd seen the jump onto the roof at night with those power paragliders, you'd realize just how close it was with those winds."

She knew he recognized that she was hurt and he was making excuses for Bellisia. He was right too. If she had a husband and that man had gone on a suicide mission, she would be looking for him first. Still, that didn't take away the hurt. All those weeks of thinking Bellisia was dead. Instead she was falling in love and getting married—without her. It embarrassed her that Gino saw her at her absolute worst all the time.

"I'm really tired," she said. "Can you take me inside?"

"Sure, baby."

Of course he would. She didn't look at him. She couldn't. There was no tearing her gaze away from Bellisia and the tears streaming down her face as she looked her husband over so carefully. Bellisia had to have known that if Zara was left with Cheng for three days before the rescue, she would be tortured, but instead of even checking on her . . .

"Zara." Gino's voice was low. She was in his arms, her face in his neck. "Don't. You're understandably upset, but Bellisia couldn't possibly have known what Zhu did to you. When we're on an unsanctioned mission, we can't report home. As much as Zeke would have wanted to tell her, he couldn't."

She'd said it out loud where Gino could hear her. What was wrong with her? Now he really knew what a mean, petty person she was. She should be happy for Bellisia, not feeling alone, miserable and betrayed.

"I always show you my worst side." It came out a whisper. She kept her eyes closed as he entered the house and moved through rooms. She knew there were other people around, but she didn't want them to see her puffy face and black eyes. For some reason, she felt embarrassed and guilty as if she could have somehow prevented Zhu from beating her. "It's not like what happened to me was that bad."

"Zara, stop talking right now. Keep your mind blank,"

Gino ordered. "Stop thinking until I can get you into the bedroom." It was a clear command, issued in his gruff, obey me or else voice.

Zara tried to do what he said, pretending her mind was a slate, and every time she thought about Bellisia ignoring her, or self-pity, or the fact that she was making such a fool of herself in front of Gino, she would wipe that slate clean. Unfortunately, she couldn't stop the tears. Those flooded his neck and soaked his T-shirt.

He kicked a door closed. The thump of his boot on the wood was loud as well as the slamming of the door. He took her to a bed and gently laid her onto her back. She attempted to roll onto her side, away from him, but he had anticipated her movement and stopped her with a hand to her belly. Gentle. Always so gentle. He looked scary and tough, but when he touched her, it was almost with reverence. That brought another fresh flood of tears.

"Zhu tortured you, Zara. He beat you unmercifully with his fists. He caned you. He used a whip on you. The man knows anatomy very well because he inflicted the most pain on you he could without permanently damaging you. He's well versed in torture and, although he was careful not to do permanent damage, he certainly went for maximum pain."

"You can't know that."

"Of course I know that. Aside from the fact that I'm a doctor and I can see what he's done, and of course I know anatomy, I certainly can beat someone with my fists, cane them and whip them. I'm just as well versed in the art of torture as he is—maybe more. I've been dealing with that sort of thing since my family was slaughtered."

Her heart jerked hard. She opened her eyes and looked at his face. God, that face. If a woman could fall for a face, she had. Those unusual, intense eyes. The scruff on his jaw. The hard angles and planes. The scars. His mouth. Slaughter? His family had been slaughtered? She'd been wallowing in her own misery, counting on him. Forcing him to stay with her because of her cowardice, but she hadn't asked him about his past.

"Does that scare you?"

She frowned, uncomprehending.

"That I learned to torture people. That I'm capable of torturing someone. That I have." He refused to look away from her, his gaze holding hers.

She could see he was waiting again for condemnation. He had before, when he'd tried to put her off with scare tactics. To be able to have even a slight chance of combating Zhu, Gino had to know what Zhu was capable of, what he would do to her, to anyone in his path. Gino had to be a fierce ice-cold demon, everything that Zhu was and more. The more was his protective nature.

She shook her head. "It's a little at odds with being a doctor, but I imagine you went to school sometime after you learned your other . . . um . . . skills. No, Gino, you don't scare me. I just am sorry that you lost your family. We're a pair, aren't we? I have no family and you lost yours."

He swept his hand over the tears on her face. "Princess, those tears had better not be for me. Looking at you, I believe I have what I want right in front of me."

Her heart clenched hard and her stomach did a slow somersault. She didn't know if she was willing him to want to be with her, to overlook her cowardice and every shortcoming that was right there in his face, or if she was being selfish because she was so afraid without him.

"I think I'm just tired, Gino. And the pain is getting worse. I don't think the pills last nearly as long as when you give me IV painkillers. Am I being wimpy?" Why couldn't she just ask him straight out? But she couldn't, not until she had something to offer him. Right now, she didn't have much, not even her own clothes. All she had was terror, neediness and tears.

"All right, baby, just close your eyes. I'll darken the room and give you some more meds. Just the beating he gave you, bruising your internal organs, would cause pain. Add the whip and cane and of course you hurt like hell. There's no need." He was already setting up an IV.

Zara closed her eyes with some relief. Her eyes burned from tears, and from the light, from keeping them open, all of it. She hated that she looked so awful and that Gino had to see her that way. "It's been nearly a week."

"Five days isn't a lot to heal your body inside, Zara," he said. "Just go to sleep. The more sleep you get, the quicker you'll heal."

"You have the white knight syndrome in spades," she murmured.

"Don't kid yourself, baby, there's nothing white knight about me."

There was a knock on the door, and she panicked. She could feel her heart accelerate and her lungs burn for air. She couldn't face anyone right now, especially Bellisia, and she knew it was her. "I can't . . ."

"I'll handle it," Gino said. "Just rest."

He already had the lights out and the curtains pulled while she lay in bed drifting on the pain medication with her eyes closed like the coward she was.

Gino swept his hand down Zara's hair, feeling anything but the white knight she named him. He felt proprietorial. No way was Bellisia coming in and taking Zara from him. No one was going to do that. He'd staked his claim on her and he wasn't backing off. He crossed the room to the door when the knock came again.

Ezekiel stood right behind Bellisia, one hand on her shoulder, his face a mask. Gino could tell by his eyes that he knew exactly what Gino was up to, but it didn't matter.

"She's resting right now. I've just gotten her comfortable and she's almost out," Gino said, blocking the door. "I'll let you know when she's up for visitors."

"I need to see her now, Gino," Bellisia insisted. "I won't disturb her, but Zeke told me Zhu tortured her. I have to know she's all right."

"Physically she will heal, although I'm concerned about her feet." Gino stayed in the doorway, blocking access to the room. "Of course, the feet are bruised, but she has hematomas, bleeding in the spaces inside. There appears to be tendon damage, but I can't tell how severe or how permanent it is. I'll know more when I can take more X-rays, do an MRI and a few other tests just to get a good look. Right now, I'm not letting her put any weight on her feet."

"Zeke said he used a cane on her."

Gino nodded. "On her back, buttocks, the backs of her legs and also on her feet. He did a very thorough job of it, so very painful." He managed to sound impersonal when he no longer felt that way. "On her front, he used a whip and he was thorough about that as well, so she's having trouble moving around too much. The beating was very severe, and he did that before the other. He also used chemicals on her and that was before the physical torture." He raised his gaze to Ezekiel's. "She told me that on the plane. I didn't have a chance to give you that information. She didn't tell him a thing about the GhostWalker program. He didn't suspect her of being a GhostWalker."

"Why would they keep her alive, then?" Bellisia asked.

For the first time Gino had to struggle to keep his features impassive. Bellisia had all but implied that Zara had given in to Zhu and told him what he wanted to know. He knew Zara was awake, or at least drifting in and out. She was already hurt and he didn't want her to think Bellisia didn't trust her.

When he continued to stare at her, Bellisia opened her mouth and shook her head, reaching back for Ezekiel's hand. "That came out wrong, Gino. I know Zara. She would *never* give up information, not under any circumstance. She would find a way to suicide before she'd do that. I meant, Cheng had to have had a reason. He never does anything without a reason. Did he plan to sell her?"

That first night in the embassy, when Gino had slept in a chair beside her bed, she'd woken in terror several times. She'd told him Cheng wanted to sell her to a man named Moffat who ran a human trafficking ring and owned some club he used his victims in. She'd admitted she didn't know which was worse, having Zhu keep her or being sold into trafficking.

"Cheng apparently wanted to sell her," Gino said, "but it was Zhu insisting on keeping her. He believed her almost from the beginning, but he wanted to keep her. For himself." Gino disliked saying it aloud. He was too much like the man, mirroring his words, his dark, ugly character. Gino wanted to keep Zara for himself and he planned to do so. He was good at carrying out a battle plan. The more he was in her company, the more he was certain Zara Hightower was the woman for him. .

"My poor Zara," Bellisia whispered. "What a terrible thing for her to have to go through. You said you were worried about her feet. Is she going to be able to walk on her own?"

Gino stepped toward her, forcing the couple to move back so he could step outside the room and close the door, just in case Zara hadn't yet succumbed to the drug.

"She'll walk. I'm just afraid she'll always experience some pain when she does. Zhu was careful not to leave any permanent marks on her skin, but he didn't mind messing up her feet. Probably so she couldn't run from him."

Bellisia frowned and looked back at Ezekiel. "Do you remember I told you how fast she is? No one could keep up with her when she ran. I hope her feet aren't permanently damaged. Have you talked to her about it?"

Gino shrugged. "She's been pretty out of it. She's just

getting to the point where she can go longer periods with lower doses of painkillers. The travel did her in. When she wakes up, I'll bring her out of the room so you can talk to her. She was very anxious to see you."

"She didn't know Zeke and I are married, did she?" Bellisia asked.

Gino shook his head. "There wasn't much chance to talk about anything, Bellisia. She was in bad shape when we got to her. All I cared about was getting her out of there and letting her body heal without pain. The first couple of days, she could barely stand a sheet on her body and even lying down hurt her. I kept her out of it for long periods of time to give her a break. There isn't really a comfortable position for her. She's doing better though."

"Ezekiel and I can look after her now, Gino," Bellisia said. "It must be difficult to take her to the bathroom, and she'll be needing showers and baths soon. I can do that and Zeke can see to her medical needs."

Gino stared down at her for a long time, letting her see the devil in him. Very slowly, he shook his head. "Not happening, Bellisia. I'm taking care of her. She's my responsibility now."

Bellisia scowled. Ezekiel tightened his fingers around her hand, but Gino could see she wasn't going to take the warning. "She's my sister. My responsibility."

"Yeah, I could see that when we pulled up and she sat in the car waiting while you were all over your husband. Zara's mine. She wants to be with me, in my care, and I'm not going to relinquish that just because someone says so—or I have something better to do."

Color crept into Bellisia's face. "I can't believe you just said that. I had to make certain Zeke was all right."

"I got that. So did she. She wasn't all right though. She'd been tortured, unlike Zeke."

"Gino." Ezekiel's warning was just that one word. His name.

Gino didn't give a damn. "She's mine, Zeke. No one's taking her from me."

Bellisia tossed her hair, eyes flashing. "She isn't a doll, Gino. She's a living, breathing woman with feelings. And she's fragile. Vulnerable, especially now. You're not taking advantage of her."

He gave her his most chilling smile. White teeth. No humor. Eyes dead. She had recognized the demon in him when they'd first met. He saw the knowledge in her eyes, but she never said anything to him and was unfailingly polite, but she avoided him if she could. Now he gave a reminder.

He let Zeke see him, although seeing the cold, dark side of Gino wouldn't be news to him. They'd known each other too long. It was just that Gino had never chosen to set that demon in him loose on his fellow GhostWalkers— but then he'd never had anything of his own worth fighting for.

Ezekiel got it immediately and put a warning hand on Bellisia. "Baby, let Zara sleep. When she wakes up, you can ask her where she'd like to be and who she wants looking after her. Gino is an excellent surgeon and he's been taking care of her from the moment we broke into Cheng's lair."

Bellisia stood looking up at Gino for a long time. "She's not like me, Gino. She's sweet and kind and good."

"I'm very aware of what she's like," Gino said, his voice gentling, when he didn't feel gentle. Bellisia was going to fight him, and she was Zara's best friend.

Bellisia nodded and turned away, allowing Ezekiel to sweep his arm around her. In Gino's assessment, Bellisia was all the things she had said Zara was, just in a different way. She made Ezekiel happy, and that alone made Gino like her, but she saw into him and she didn't like what she saw. He didn't blame her. Because he could have been Bolan Zhu.

Gino slipped back into the bedroom and firmly closed the door. They didn't need any more visitors. "You awake?" Her breathing told him she was.

"Thank you, Gino. I put you in a bad position and I'm sorry."

"No problem, princess. I'm never going to mind handling things for you. That's what I do. What I want to do."

She half turned over, the movement awkward, and he remembered she was in that long skirt and blouse that were most likely uncomfortable. "I'll get you into something you can sleep in, Zara." Because he was sleeping in the bed with her, and full nudity might just be a problem for them both.

"Why don't you mind having to take care of me, Gino? It usually makes everyone angry, or at the very least, annoyed."

She sounded a little lost, and his heart turned over. "I like taking care of you. I'll always like taking care of you." Her blue eyes kept looking at him, wide and sad. He shrugged and told her the truth. "It feels like a privilege to me."

"You're a little crazy, you know that?"

He nodded solemnly. "Sadly, I'm well aware."

"I didn't mean it in a bad way, only that you're so sweet to me, Gino. No one has ever been so good to me."

"Baby, that isn't true. Bellisia and your friend were always good to you, and they didn't mind taking care of you either. Bellisia just told me that she would be happy to take over your care. I know you're hurt because she didn't go to you first, but when your man goes off on a suicide mission, or any mission because there's a chance every time that he might not come back, you'll be running to him."

"You're defending her, but it didn't sound like she was being very nice to you."

He shrugged. "I don't mind, not when she's looking out

for you. I'm telling you up front, so there's no misunderstanding, Zara. I'm not a nice man. Bellisia sees that in me. She also sees I'm interested in more than taking care of you as a patient. She doesn't like it. I don't blame her, but it isn't going to stop me from pursuing a relationship with you."

He took the IV from her arm and rubbed his thumb over the spot, watching her for a reaction to his declaration.

"I'm the one on painkillers, and you're the one not making any sense. I don't even look halfway decent right now."

"It isn't about your looks, Zara, although I've seen enough pictures to know you're beautiful. I just don't want there to be any misunderstanding between us. I want you with me. I'm determined to make that happen in spite of knowing there will be a few obstacles, and Bellisia is probably going to be one of them. Having said that, I'm not going to pretend to be someone I'm not. You're going to get the real man so you'll know whether or not you can live with me."

"Are you trying to scare me off?"

He looked into her upturned face and his heart did some crazy somersault in his chest. Her face was black and blue. There was even a little yellow, making her eyes and cheek very colorful.

"No, I just don't want you to think you want to be with me because I rescued you."

"That's a legitimate worry," she acknowledged.

"Or that you believe I can handle Zhu's threat to you and once it's over, you won't need me anymore."

"Like the gunslingers in the Old West. Come clean up the town, you did, thank you, so now leave," she agreed.

He liked that she got it immediately. Even with the drugs in her system, her mind worked just fine. More than fine.

"What about the other way around, Gino?"

He raised an eyebrow and pushed back some of the thick reddish hair spilling around her face. He could spend a lifetime with his hands in her hair.

"I'm not always going to be beat-up."

"No, you're not. And I'm always going to want to take care of you. I'm always going to be that man standing in front of you. Sometimes you might not like it, Zara. That's something you're going to have to decide if you can live with."

"Why me? I don't see how it's possible for a man as courageous as you to want to be with someone like me."

"I've never met a woman braver. You need a home and a family of your own, and if I'm not mistaken, you want to stay in that home and take care of your family. I need that in my woman. I want her to put me first. To put our children first. And, princess, when I come home from a mission, I want you coming to me just the way Bellisia did to Zeke. She didn't do a damn thing wrong. I know you were hurt, but you have to understand, she was right in going to her man and making him know he's everything to her."

Zara pressed her lips together, a little frown on her face. "I know you're right, Gino. Intellectually, I know you're right, but I had no idea she was with him. For me, she disappeared, and I worried she was dead. I was terrified when I was with Zhu, and frankly, I still am. I couldn't wait to see her, and it felt like I didn't matter in the least to her."

"That isn't true. If you could have seen Bellisia's face when I told her what happened to you, you'd know you matter to her. Tomorrow, when you're feeling better, you can meet all the women here. You're going to love Nonny. She's Wyatt's grandmother and has lived here in the swamp all of her life. She's an amazing woman."

"The house smells the way I think a home should," Zara said. "Welcoming."

"I agree. Nonny knows her way around a shotgun, but she's the most welcoming woman I've ever met." At least she hadn't shot him down and told him there was no way she would have any kind of an actual relationship with him. He'd been as honest with her and as up front about his intentions as he possibly could be and she wasn't yelling her head off for Bellisia to come and save her. He supposed he should consider that a win, even if she hadn't thrown herself into his arms and declared undying love.

"Just so you're aware, Bellisia and Zeke would gladly take over your care if you prefer them to me. I told you, but you didn't really address it. I need to know if you want them to handle the rest of your recovery."

She slid back down in the bed. Even with her eyes black and blue, that slate blue staring up at him had his heart accelerating when facing men with guns didn't.

"I don't want them, Gino. I want you." She made it a very firm statement.

"I'm taking your clothes off and inspecting every laceration before I put the tee on you. I'll have to reapply the antibiotic ointment. All this traveling easily could have reopened the worst of them." He wanted it clear he was shifting into caretaker mode.

"You've seen me without clothes often enough that I'm pretty certain you know every tiny laceration and bruise on my body by now."

He caught the slight edge of embarrassment in her voice. "Sit up and let me get your clothes off. They can't be comfortable. And trust me, baby, I'm always happy to remove your clothes. Right now, I'm taking care of you, but later, I'm not going to be so impersonal. It's getting more difficult."

She lifted her arms for him to remove the blouse. He

looked because he'd be a fool not to. He wasn't a saint, and she had beautiful breasts. The stripes across them were definitely healing. He indicated for her to lie back so he could strip the skirt away as well. Her body was gorgeous. Those long legs, the curve of her hips, that tucked-in waist, the little curls almost as red as her hair in the sunshine. His body reacted, which was bullshit when he was a doctor and trying to be professional. He shouldn't be noticing all those details, but he couldn't help it. He already thought of her as his.

"You're definitely healing. I don't like that a couple of these lacerations are being stubborn. By now, they should be completely closed, but you've got a few that aren't, the ones that were infected. I should have stitched them. They were deeper than I first thought." He ran his finger along the line just below the red slashes under her breasts. "You'd been through so much already, but I should have just done it."

"I think you're being hard on yourself. They'll heal."

"Might scar, Zara."

She shrugged. "Maybe. It isn't like I expected to get out of there alive. A couple of scars won't hurt."

He carefully applied antibiotic ointment to each long slash over the front of her body. He cursed Zhu under his breath with each application, not understanding how a man could do this to a woman. She tensed under his hands a few times.

"Am I hurting you?"

"It's all right. Just stings in a couple of places. I told you I couldn't take pain."

She kept her eyes on his face and he felt that impact. He found himself smiling. "What?" Because she was thinking something important. Color crept up her body. He actually felt the wave of heat. That made him more curious than ever. "Talk to me, baby. I want to know what's going on in your mind."

Her fingers crept toward the sheet as if she might draw it up. Clearly she was feeling vulnerable. "Turn over. I want to take a look at the bruising on your back." If she was lying face away from him, it might be easier for her to tell him.

She obeyed him, easing her body over onto her stomach, lying gingerly, making certain to take care as she put her weight on the sheets. That was another reason he was certain she was right for him. She wanted to please him. She did what he asked, even if she was afraid, or in this case, if it hurt. She trusted his judgment. He knew part of that was because she'd had to trust him fast in extreme circumstances, but it was additionally because he came through for her every time. It was also instinctual.

"Now tell me." His fingers skimmed the fierce bruising caused by the caning. Those bruises were in various shades of blue, black and yellow. Most of the damage was done internally, the inside muscles bruised.

"I wanted you to kiss me."

She whispered her confession, and he went still. Her head was turned toward him, one cheek against the sheet, one eye hidden. The other looked up at him through the long fan of lashes. She looked shy. Embarrassed. But she'd had the courage to tell him the truth.

He smiled at her. That smile began somewhere deep inside him because that was where she was getting to him. He started out thinking she was right for him, not that he'd fall for her, but that bravery of hers, when she thought herself a coward, was too much for a man like him to resist. Her brand of courage wasn't the kind everyone could see, but it was there, quiet and just as unswerving as his was. The fact that she would trust him with the truth when it was embarrassing to her, shattered him.

"Trust is a gift, Zara, and I won't forget that you give it to me every day we're together. I won't ever abuse it." That was one thing he could say with absolute certainty.

He wanted a woman to accept him and the things he did, but that might mean she couldn't know what he was doing or where he was going when he went on a mission. He would be up front about that. Zara would be the kind of woman who would understand. "Thank you for giving me your trust and for telling me what you were thinking. Kissing you is hard to stop once I start, but you want kisses from me anytime, princess, you get them. I'll expect the same from you."

Her lips turned up in a faint smile that had the strange effect on him of robbing every bit of air from his lungs. He turned his attention to examining the bruising on her body, but that wasn't any easier. She had a body that just spoke to his.

"You have a gorgeous ass, did you know that?" He rubbed gently over her buttocks, where those long dark lines were.

"No, not really. No one's ever really looked at my . . . um . . . bum."

"Ass, baby. Perfect, beautiful ass."

"I'm glad you like it."

He trailed his palm over the stripes on her upper thighs. Zhu had hit her precisely, laying the cane on almost every square inch of her back, buttocks and legs, doubling up every other stroke. The same was true of the whip. Zhu definitely knew anatomy. Under any other circumstance, Gino might admire his handiwork. Zhu's skills were the kind a man like Ciro Spagnola needed, which was why Gino had them.

"Tell me what you like, Zara. Your favorite things to do." He tugged on her arm to indicate she could roll over again. He had to put a T-shirt on her before he examined her feet.

"I like being outdoors," she admitted, slowly sitting up as he went to his drawer to retrieve a clean shirt. "We had a big barracks, but there were always guards. Every minute of our time was directed by Whitney's schedule until late evening. When I was allowed to go to school, even though he had men watching me, I would go outside at night and just look at the stars. I wanted to see mountains and rivers, forests, waterfalls. Everything. I haven't experienced those things yet. As an adult, he still had guards on me and the rules were even stricter than when I was in school."

He pulled the shirt over her head, noting she had more arm movement than before. The enhancements Whitney had given her aided her body in healing fast. "How long did he give you before those capsules break open? Was there always a set limit he told you about ahead of time?"

She nodded. He went to the end of the bed, sat and picked up her ankles to examine her feet. Zhu had definitely done the most damage there, either deliberately hurting the tendons or uncaring that he did so. Gino was certain the damage he'd inflicted was deliberate.

"Depending on the job he'd given me and where it was, he would change the time. In this case he gave me four weeks. We discussed the possibility of a lockdown because Bellisia had gotten caught in one. I had given talks to three businesses before Shanghai, in three different cities in China. We should have about a week and a half before those capsules break open."

"Have you ever had one break open early?"

She shook her head. "It did, supposedly, happen to one of the other girls. She was doing something for him and didn't make it back. They brought her body home, and she'd died of the virus. He said the capsule broke open early, but Bellisia didn't think so."

"What did Bellisia think happened?"

"They wouldn't let us see her. We tried to sneak into the morgue, but Whitney had posted guards. Bellisia said if it was the virus, we would have been able to see her. Whitney had her cremated so we never knew for certain."

Gino could see her feet were beginning to heal, but they had a long way to go. He didn't want her to put any weight on them. He tested the reflexes and movement, all of which made her wince. Rest, anti-inflammatories and then physical therapy were her best chance of recovery. "You have to stay off your feet, princess. That's important."

"I don't exactly feel like putting them on the ground, Gino. When I move them, they hurt very, very bad."

"That's a sign you shouldn't move them too much," he pointed out. "I'm not taking chances with the capsules breaking open. I'll be taking them out as soon as I finish my reports. I'll get Wyatt to assist me."

She nodded, but he noticed she avoided his eyes. There was something she wasn't telling him, something she *wanted* to tell him, but she had to do it in her own time. He had a suspicion it had to do with why Whitney had lied to Major General and said they could keep Zara if they rescued her. Then there was the matter of the soldier pointing a gun at a specific spot in her brain.

Gino pulled off his boots and climbed onto the bed with her. "I'm going to put you on my lap, Zara." He waited, but she didn't protest, so he picked her up and settled her on him. He wanted her to get used to his arms, the feeling of his body against hers and how it reacted when she was near him.

She put her arms around his neck and looked up at him. Her eyes were that strange slate color, and looking into them, he felt as if he had fallen under a spell. He wasn't a man given to flights of fancy so it was a little strange for him. He wrapped his hand around her throat so her heart was beating into his palm and he tipped up her face to him.

There was that trust again. Shy hunger. Desire. He liked that a fuck of a lot. He leaned his head to hers and took her mouth. She might not have a lot of experience kissing, but the combination of the two of them was so potent, it was as if she lit a match to dynamite. Flames spread through him like a wildfire out of control. He shifted her closer and took complete command of her mouth. She followed his every move. The slide of her tongue sent heat rushing through his veins to pool low and mean in his cock.

He used his thumb to tip her head back farther, giving him greater access. Fire poured through him, erupted in his belly and flowed through his veins. It didn't take long to know he had to pull back when that was the last thing he wanted to do. It took discipline to lift his mouth from hers. He rested his forehead against hers and stared into those eyes of hers.

"I want to keep kissing you, baby, but it's best if we stop now before there's no stopping. Your body isn't ready for anything but rest right now. I'm putting you in bed, and I'm going to take a long shower."

"Does that really work?" There was genuine curiosity in her voice.

"No. I had to take a couple of showers at the embassy, and when it comes to you, no, they don't work, but it might help before I go face everyone."

"You aren't coming back here?"

There was the smallest note of alarm in her voice. Some panic in her eyes. He smiled at her. "I'll be here with you, tonight. Just have to finish those reports, grab food and I'll be in for the night. I promise."

She studied his face for a long time before she nodded and relaxed in his arms.

9

"Your poor feet," Nonny whispered, crouching down to examine them.

Grace Fontenot was in her eighties. Very slender now, so that she looked small and appeared fragile with her thick, silver white hair, braided and looped in a bun at the back of her head. Her skin was thin and pale, the blue of her eyes faded. The color might have faded a bit, but her eyes were sharp and took in everything, including the multitude of gauze strips beneath the thin blouse Zara wore.

Zara didn't want to be rude and pull her feet under her skirt, but everyone was staring and she was embarrassed. She looked around for Gino. The room held women, no men. Bellisia had hugged her too tightly before she got control of herself, and the wounds were throbbing all over again in spite of the painkillers Gino had given her earlier. Now, Bellisia curled up in the chair beside Zara with tears in her eyes. She kept petting Zara because, like everyone else, she didn't know what to do.

Zara couldn't stop looking at her best friend. Drinking her in. She hadn't thought she'd ever see her again, but there were too many people around and she couldn't talk to her alone. The things she needed to say—to know— were locked up tight and she could only sign to Bellisia, using the code they'd perfected after they became aware there were cameras on them at all times, to tell her that she needed to talk.

Thankfully, Bellisia signed back she'd find a way to be alone with her. Ezekiel had given her two more pain pills after Bellisia had hugged her, and she was beginning to feel the effects. Right now, she was beginning to feel very off-balance. As always, when that happened, she looked for Gino.

Wyatt's grandmother took charge. "Back up and give her room," Nonny ordered.

The three women, Pepper, Bellisia and Cayenne, automatically obeyed. It was clear they respected the older woman and her word was law in her home.

Zara took her first real breath since Gino had left her with the women, dragging the scents of the Fontenot home into her lungs. It was . . . comforting in a weird way. Spices, delicious smells drifting from the kitchen. Freshly baked bread. Chicken. The chicken smelled like heaven. This was the way a house was supposed to smell. Inviting. Homey. Not like a barracks and rations. Someday, she was going to have a home like this one and fill it with similar scents so anyone coming in would feel instantly welcome.

"It smells wonderful in here," she blurted.

Nonny looked pleased. "I always like to have somethin' on the stove to welcome the boys after they've been out workin' so much. My boys were always hungry when they were growin' up. The ones I have now don't seem to be filled night or day."

Pepper and Bellisia laughed. Cayenne nodded her

head, her lips curving, but she didn't make a sound. Zara understood. It was difficult to laugh when for so many years, she hadn't had anything to laugh about. Zara had tried to be "normal" with her friends, with Bellisia and Shylah, but she hadn't been happy at the compound or out in the real world. There didn't seem a place for her. She could tell Cayenne felt a little of that.

Zara wondered what, when Cayenne had total freedom now, kept the woman in a place where she was uncomfortable. Maybe for women like them, there was no place to call home. She studied Cayenne while Nonny examined her feet. A part of her saw Bellisia and Pepper looking at her feet with a kind of horror. Both got tears in their eyes. Cayenne's face gave nothing away.

Zara's heart began a slow acceleration. The room tilted a little, and her stomach lurched. Somewhere there was the sound of dripping water and she remembered the water in the bathroom where Zhu had tortured her. The steady drip she hadn't acknowledged until right at that moment. She hadn't noticed it then, probably because she had other things to worry about, but now she knew she would always connect dripping water with the lash of the whip and the whistle of the cane.

Her body jerked. She *felt* the strike on her body. A low whimper emerged, and she hastily pressed her fingers to her mouth. Uneasily she glanced at the windows. It was midafternoon. Gino had let her sleep in and then brought her breakfast in bed. He'd had her nap again before getting her dressed to meet the other members of the household.

Zara knew with all the windows, anyone could see into the house. Anyone. Whitney would get the information she stored in her brain from her, dead or alive. He didn't need her alive, just her body. He would keep coming at her until he got what he wanted, and anyone near her would be in terrible danger.

What of Zhu? He would be coming as well. Gino and the others might think they were finished with him, but they weren't. She saw his face and heard his promise. He would come after her and would take pleasure in killing those around her. Whitney might kill them, but there would be no pleasure in it. He would consider them sacrifices for the greater good. Zhu would enjoy the killing, making her—and everyone—suffer in the process. That would be his enjoyment.

Her body gave a shudder she couldn't hide and she looked around. Needing him. Gino. Her shield. It was wrong to force the man into that role. He had rescued her. Taken care of her. Watched over her. And he'd delivered her to Bellisia and was gone. She knew he was probably sick of her clinging to him. Sick of having to hear her whine. How much whining had she done? She didn't even remember. She was getting a little confused because of the additional pain pills Ezekiel had given her. She had to let Gino go. He was probably hiding out, so relieved to be away from her when she looked everywhere for him and listened with everything in her for the sound of his voice.

What was she thinking? Gino had kissed her. He'd declared his intentions, made it very clear that he intended to pursue her, that he wanted them to be in a relationship. He wasn't the type of man to lie to her. Doubling up on pain medication when Gino wanted her to back off from it a bit clearly was affecting her thinking processes. He'd kissed her. He wanted her. She wasn't going to let go of that.

"Zara, would you like a cup of tea before you eat anything? Tea can settle the stomach."

Nonny asked her the question gently, but Zara had the feeling it was to give the other women something to do besides cry over her. God knew, if they saw the lacerations and bruises on her body, they would really fall apart. She couldn't handle that. She felt like she was well on her

way to healing, with the exception of her feet, but she
knew her body looked as if she'd been through a battle.

She nodded gratefully. She wanted a cup of tea and
then a room that was quiet, and mostly, she wanted Gino.
She felt scared without him. She couldn't help looking
through the windows again, wondering if a sniper was
taking aim at her head right that minute. She should have
told him the truth about what she'd been doing there in
Shanghai. She had to tell him soon. But if she did, he
would have to share the information with whoever ran his
team, that person would share with the major general and
then they'd come for her. There was no way they would
leave the intelligence in her head.

"We'll fix you right up, child," Nonny continued. Her
thumb very gently brushed over Zara's swollen face.

"It's so much better already," she assured the horrified
women. She barely glanced at them. She didn't care how
she looked, although always, when she was in public, her
looks her armor. Now, she needed Gino. Her shield.
"Gino really helped me. I couldn't open my eyes before."

Pepper, Wyatt's wife, returned with several supplies,
sent her a small smile and left again. She was the sexiest
woman Zara had ever seen. Her skin was perfect. Her
eyes, exotic. The color was difficult to describe, one moment almost a lavender, or deep purple, but there was a
strange diamond color that looked like a starburst that
spread through that dark purple. She had a natural pout to
her full lips and thick, dark hair that had strange patterns
in it that seemed to come and go with every movement of
her head, making the silky mass mesmerizing. Zara could
hardly look away.

Gino was around Pepper every single day. He saw that
sexy woman. Small, exotic, so sensual she could steal the
breath from a man or woman. What he'd seen from Zara
was blood and vomit and eyes swollen shut. And don't

forget the bathroom. Repeatedly. Lovely. How could he possibly want her after seeing Pepper?

Cayenne was very small, like Pepper, with dark hair so black that it gleamed blue under the light. When she moved, a rich, red hourglass came and went in the long fall. She had an oval face and high cheekbones. Her eyes were a deep green framed with long black lashes. Her mouth was generous. She didn't say anything, but her eyes were watchful, and Zara had the feeling that if she made one wrong move, Cayenne would pounce and end her life instantly.

Ordinarily, Cayenne would have intimidated Zara. Nearly everyone did unless she was lecturing. Right now, she was so miserable she didn't care how watchful and alert Cayenne was. It didn't matter in the least to her. She wanted Gino. She didn't even care that Cayenne, Bellisia and Pepper were beautiful, petite women. Warrior women, and she was . . . not. She needed him and she willed him to come to her, but once he'd turned her over to the women, he'd walked out without looking back. She knew he hadn't looked back because she'd watched him walk away from her. She'd watched his back until he was out of sight.

It wasn't like she could blame him. No matter what he felt for her, he had to take a break sometime. She hadn't trusted him enough to tell him the truth about the information stored in her head. She took a deep breath and let it out, afraid she might cry in front of the very sympathetic strangers and Bellisia. Was she still upset with Bellisia? Gino had insisted she shouldn't be. As it was, her skin felt clammy. Cold. She could barely catch her breath. She really needed air because she was getting dizzy, and there was a strange ringing in her ears. How long had she been out of the safety of the bedroom? How long away from Gino? Minutes? A half hour? An hour? It felt like an eternity.

"Zara." Bellisia's voice was gentle but very firm, catching her attention. "What is it? You're having a panic attack."

"Where's Gino? Where did he go?"

"I'll get him for you."

Shockingly, that was Cayenne. One moment she'd been leaning her hip against the wall, draped there so casually and still. The next second she was all movement, slipping from the room before Zara could protest. It was one thing to ask where he was, another altogether to have them go get him. She realized these women were going to get her whatever she indicated she wanted.

"How much time did Whitney give you before the capsule breaks?" Bellisia asked.

Zara bit down on her finger to keep from screaming. She needed air. She needed a way out. Why did she always feel like she was less than everyone around her? She didn't belong anywhere. How many times had Whitney drilled it into her that she was worthless? The other girls had something to contribute to their country, but she was a waste of his time. All the effort he'd put into her, and she was always a disappointment.

"Princess, take a breath."

Gino was there, crouching in front of her, eye to eye. She couldn't look at him, but that terrible burning in her chest, the raw soreness in her lungs eased enough to allow air to slip inside her. He moved right past Nonny's protest and lifted her, settled into the wide, comfortable chair she'd been in and put her on his lap. His arms were familiar to her now. Safe. Comforting. She snuggled into his heat, those firm muscles that went on forever.

Instead of forcing her to talk to him, Gino rocked her gently and addressed Nonny. "What do you think about her feet?"

"It's going to take some time to heal," Nonny answered. "I've got some poultices for her face. I can bring down the swelling faster, but her feet are a problem. I'm thinkin' on the best herbs to help them. Has Wyatt looked at them yet?"

Zara didn't want everyone looking at her mangled feet. They were long and flat like two skis. Everyone really had to stop looking at them, especially Gino.

There was a small silence, and she realized she'd said it out loud. Bellisia broke the spell by laughing. "You always say that about your feet, Zara, and it isn't true."

"They are twice the size of your feet."

The other women laughed along with Bellisia. "My feet are twice the size of her feet," Cayenne shocked her by saying. "She's teeny." Zara knew Cayenne was a couple of inches taller than Bellisia, but not much more, not six or seven inches taller.

"But lethal," Bellisia pointed out. "Zara, your feet are just fine. Whitney is an ass. He likes to be the smartest man in the room, and a woman having your kind of brains didn't fit with his concept of women being disposable. He had to make you feel inferior to him—probably to convince himself as well. He did it from the time we were toddlers. I remember him talking about your feet and your hair and what a mess you were even then."

That didn't make her feel any better, now that everyone in the room knew Whitney despised her from the time she was a baby. She couldn't remember a single word of praise from him. Also, Bellisia *was* teeny, even smaller than the other two women. If Zara was standing, she would have appeared a giant next to the others. The Amazon woman. The giant woman in the movies that stepped on cities.

Nonny applied a soothing cloth to Zara's feet and then straightened. She was taller than Zara realized because she was so thin and fragile. She held herself straight, unbending, and she clearly didn't care that she was taller than Pepper, Cayenne and Bellisia. She exuded a quiet confidence that Zara wished she could have.

"I was just asking Zara how long Whitney gave her before the virus is activated," Bellisia said to Gino. "I imagine you or Zeke are going to go in after the capsule."

"He's hiding them now," Gino said. His arms tightened fractionally around Zara, as if he didn't like the idea that she could be in any kind of danger. "He put two capsules in Zara, not just one. I'm going to look again, now that I know what I'm looking for. She told me she had about another week and a half."

The room went silent. She tried hard not to tense up when Gino talked about looking again. She had to confess. Tell him everything before he found the SSD in her brain, but not in front of everyone. She desperately needed to talk to Bellisia alone. "Whitney always gave me extra time to get back just in case something went wrong. If it did, Damon came to me to give me the antidote and he'd inject another capsule to give me the time needed."

"Your time was pretty exact, wasn't it, Bellisia?" Gino asked.

Zara did stiffen. There was no way to help it. He knew she was holding something important back, and he wasn't going to let up until he knew what it was. She had to have a little time to think things through. People killed over the kind of information she carried in her head. Certainly, covert agencies would do anything to get their hands on it. She needed alone time with Bellisia to ask her advice. She knew these people and whether or not they could be trusted.

Bellisia nodded. "Whitney liked us to keep to a timetable, but Zara was different in that she was very exposed publicly. He sent her all over the world, not to spy on governments, but mostly research centers and businesses. He likes to know what others are doing and project further out. He is brilliant, I have to give him that."

Bellisia had inadvertently given Zara some breathing room. She still held herself away from Gino. She didn't know if he could be counted on her side now that he knew she was hiding something from him. He didn't like it, that was for certain. She really wished she was a badass agent like Bellisia. The woman could hold her own with anyone. She wouldn't be trembling and sick because Zhu beat the holy hell out of her. She wouldn't be so frightened that she could barely breathe unless a man held her. She wouldn't be upset that she had disappointed the man she had come to care about. More than any other thing, that was what she hated the most—that she knew she'd disappointed him.

"Lean back," Gino instructed.

She sent him one look over her shoulder, intending to tell him silently to back off. Gino's dark eyes glinted with warning. She refused to be intimidated. What could he do to her when they were surrounded by women, including Nonny, Wyatt's grandmother? A wicked gleam shone in the depths of all that obsidian, and he brushed her hair from the nape of her neck with gentle fingers. He leaned into her, his face disappearing. Zara held her breath. His teeth bit into the nape of her neck. She yelped and muffled the sound by putting her hand over her mouth.

"Something wrong?" Bellisia asked.

Zara glared at her. "You snicker and I'm going to build a robot that gobbles water faster than you can run a bath."

It was a long-standing joke between them. Zara had actually done it and placed the robot in their shared bathroom. It hadn't been easy either. She had to figure out how to dispose of the water and yet not give the robotics' secrets away. She also had to steal the tools to make the robot, one at a time over a period of weeks and months. That was the most difficult part, since Whitney was very precise in his accounting. Fortunately, Zara had learned how to doctor the inventory books without his knowledge—she'd been doing it from the time she was a teenager.

"Not that." Bellisia gave a pretend shudder, her smile wide. It faded fast. "Nonny, can't you make the swelling go down on her face faster? That looks like it hurts."

Weirdly, her face hurt the least of any place on her body. Still, she didn't want Bellisia to call attention to the swelling in front of Gino, not that he couldn't see it. He'd seen her so much worse, but it felt worse in front of the other women.

Gino tugged until she found herself relaxing back into his hold. Now that he was there, she was determined to enjoy herself a little with the other women. "Seriously, Bellisia," she assured. "Gino got rid of most of the swelling in my eyes. I know they're both black and blue, but my face doesn't hurt nearly as much as the rest of me." She wanted them to give him more credit than they were. It almost sounded as if Bellisia had been complaining that he hadn't taken proper care of her.

"Cheng did this to you?" Bellisia asked, her small hands closing into tight fists.

"It was his partner, Bolan Zhu," Zara corrected. "He's a very scary man."

"Cheng doesn't have a partner," Bellisia said. "I read all the data on him. Zhu works for him as a kind of enforcer."

Zara shook her head. "Zhu is definitely more than an employee. If anything, he's the senior partner. Not in terms of age, but certainly in every other way. Cheng pays him deference." She frowned, unsure whether she should share the speculations she'd been turning over and over in her mind with them. On the surface, they seemed far-fetched, given the amount of information on Cheng and the little they had on Zhu. In the end, she decided it would be good to at least give that much to Gino. "I think there's a possibility that they're related."

Gino and Bellisia shared a look, but Zara told herself she didn't care whether or not they believed her, but she really did. Bellisia knew her. She would know she picked up details no one else did. She noticed things. More, she had a feeling about the two men. Her feelings were almost always right.

A small tremor ran through her body at the thought of Zhu. She wished she could forget the look on his face when he promised her that if she didn't do exactly what he said, when he returned, her punishment would be so much worse and she'd suffer for a long time. She was certain running away with the GhostWalker team qualified as not obeying him. He was so handsome and so deadly. For some reason, his good looks made it so much worse that his actions were so horrifying. He terrified her, and she knew it would be years before she dared fall asleep without taking safety precautions.

"Related how?" Pepper asked. "I read the file on Cheng. He seems very alpha, and he definitely is older than Zhu by several years."

"I think they're brothers. Maybe half brothers," Zara qualified. She might as well say what she thought. What did it matter if they all thought she was crazy? Maybe she was. "I know they don't look that much alike. At first, I thought cousins, but they share some of the same movements, but more specifically, identical markers. Their hands, for instance. Their fingers on their hands are too exact. The way they're formed, the length and even width. Both have a flattening on the upper joint of the thumb that's very distinctive and unusual. Cheng isn't particularly beautiful, but he is attractive and the things that make him attractive, his bone structure, he obviously inherited from his mother. Zhu has that same bone structure. He's quite beautiful in a deadly sort of way."

"The only reason I'm not taking offense is you tacked on the 'deadly sort of way,'" Gino said, a trace of amusement in his voice. "You've never described me as beautiful."

Pepper and Cayenne laughed softly. Nonny's lips twitched. Zara pulled forward so she could look at Gino over her shoulder. "I think you're beautiful even if I don't say it out loud." She didn't care if everyone heard. She didn't want his feelings hurt. Her gaze moved over him.

He didn't have an ounce of fat on his body and he had more muscles than anyone she'd ever met, although they were subtler than some of the other GhostWalkers'. His shoulders were wide, his hair shaggy and his black eyes were cool and calm. He had scars and a permanent five-o'clock shadow. He might not be traditionally handsome, but she thought he was far more beautiful than Zhu—or any other man she'd ever laid eyes on.

"Princess."

He didn't believe her. "No, I do. I think I did tell you in the car earlier, when the drugs were kicking in."

"I think they've really kicked in now, but thank you. I appreciate your assessment, skewed though it might be. And if any of you gossipy women tell your man what my woman just said, I'm going to have to plan revenge." Gino pulled Zara closer to him, wrapping her up tightly in his arms. His chin nuzzled the top of her head.

"This is too good to worry about your revenge," Cayenne said. "Trap is *so* going to love me when I tell him this."

"What's wrong with saying you're beautiful, Gino?" Zara asked. The drugs really were slowing things a little bit for her. She felt dreamy. "Is there something wrong with it, Cayenne?"

"Not at all, Zara," Bellisia assured.

"Then why are they laughing?" Zara demanded. She noticed Bellisia wasn't laughing. She had gone silent and looked at her strangely, as if she was suddenly worried. Her gaze moved speculatively between Zara and Gino, and clearly, she didn't like what she was thinking.

"Tea's ready," Pepper announced, trying to change the subject. "Is it for a poultice or for drinking, Nonny?"

"Both. She should drink a cup, and we'll cool the rest. Once it's cold enough, we'll soak her feet and put some on rags for her face."

"What's in it?" Zara asked, suspicion in her voice. She couldn't help it. The tea didn't look like any tea she'd ever had before. More, there were flowers at the bottom of the cup.

"Good things. Pharmaceuticals that will help heal you faster," Nonny assured. "It's sweet and actually tastes good. One of the few I've found that is drinkable without doctoring it too much."

Gino took the cup of tea and sipped at it. "Doesn't taste bad at all, princess. Go ahead and try it." He gave her the cup but kept his hand around hers for support. "Perhaps we might try a little food. She's been on nonstop painkillers for obvious reasons. I think a little food might help."

Zara took a cautious sip. The liquid tasted strange to her, but not bad. She could drink it. She waved her free hand in the air. "I like feeling this way. I don't need help, Gino. In fact, I might be able to walk if I just get the courage to try." She wrinkled her nose. "I'm not very courageous. I could never be a spy. Or do the kinds of things Bellisia does."

"I'm learning to cook," Bellisia said. "That takes serious courage, and you're already good at it."

"I am." Zara was proud of her cooking abilities. "And don't listen to Bellisia. She's *very* brave all the time."

"That's it," Gino said decisively. "I'm taking you to the bedroom before you start telling people about how you attacked me."

"She attacked you?" Bellisia echoed.

"She did," Gino asserted, pushing the teacup closer to Zara's mouth. "First she took a swipe at me with the cane. Nearly took my head off."

Zara started laughing. "Not his head-head. A *different* kind of head."

Gino rolled his eyes and took the cup out of her hand and put it on the table. "You're done. Let's go." He stood up easily, cradling her close to his chest. "Nonny, when it's ready, will you bring the tea to put on her feet and face? I'd greatly appreciate it."

"I have smothered chicken and sausage hot on the stove right now," Nonny offered. "Give me time to make the rice and I'll bring both of you a meal."

"I would appreciate it."

Zara stroked Gino's bristles. "I love the way your face always has this perfect shadow," she whispered conspiratorially.

"Baby, did Zeke give you more meds after I brought you out here?"

She tried to remember. She petted his face again. "He might have. He gave me a glass of water. I really have to go to the bathroom."

Gino laughed softly. "Yeah, baby, he gave you more. I'm going to have to talk to him about this."

She clutched his shoulders. "You said you wouldn't leave, and you did." The hallway was really spinning, making her feel a little sick. If he left her, she wouldn't be able to crawl her way out of there. Her feet were beginning to throb again, pain pounding through her toes and the heel of her foot. It was a terrible sensation because, as if in counterpoint, the ball of her foot felt as if a thousand bees were stinging it. The floating feeling only served to make her dizzy. "I might need to get sick."

The amusement was gone in an instant and he took a detour, turning away from the direction they'd been going to open a door. She could have cried with relief when she realized they were in the bathroom. He carried her straight to the toilet, but shockingly, didn't put her down.

"Um, Gino. Put me on the floor and go." She wasn't in

the habit of sitting on a bathroom floor, but her lurching stomach told her that her body was done with painkillers. He'd spent enough time with her at the embassy and on the plane in the bathroom. Now that she was a little better, he didn't need to be with her. It was too embarrassing.

"That's not happening."

She pressed a hand to her stomach, desperate not to vomit in front of him. "Really, my body isn't used to so many painkillers. I've had more over the last six days than my entire life. Whitney didn't believe we should ever have to use them—me especially. He wanted me to build up my pain tolerance."

Her stomach lurched again and she leaned over and threw up what little contents were in her stomach. It could have been the most humiliating moment she'd had with Gino so far—and she'd had one terrible incident after another. Her hair hung in tangles around her face and fell like a rat's nest down her back. Her face was still swollen, which was bad enough, but when he'd first seen her, her eyes had been nearly closed. Her skin was still green and purple and black. Her feet were mangled, and her body a mess. Of course she had to look—and act—her absolute worst in front of the hottest man she'd ever met, especially when three of the most beautiful women she'd ever seen were just in the next room.

Her eyes burned and she squeezed her lids closed, terrified she'd cry again. All he'd seen her do from the first moment they'd met was cry. "I hate this so much," she whispered. She knew part of her emotions could really be the drugs, but it didn't matter what it was. She didn't want him seeing her like this.

"Are you finished?" Gino asked.

His voice was so gentle that she couldn't prevent a couple of tears from escaping, so she kept her head down and nodded. He carried her to the sink to allow her to rinse out her mouth. She did several times. The moment she was alone she was going to try to put her weight on her feet. She had to find a way to be more independent.

"While we're in here, you may as well use the toilet."

Her heart nearly stopped in her chest and then thudded like a drum. That was the last straw. "Not with you in here." She was firm about it. He'd already been with her in the morning, but that was before she'd met the women of the house. Now, she couldn't bear it if he had to help her.

"I'm not certain how you're going to cope without me. You can't stand on your feet yet. It isn't a big deal. Everyone uses a toilet."

"Not with you in the room."

"It isn't the first time," he reminded.

It was *so* humiliating. Before, she'd been out of it, terrified beyond belief, unable to do anything but writhe in pain. Now, there were three women right in the next room that he saw every day and could compare her to. She shook her head. "Absolutely not. I'll walk back into the bathroom if I have to, but you're not staying here with me." Crawl would be more like it.

He was silent for so long she had to work to keep from squirming. She really had to go now that they talked about it.

With a small sigh, Gino set her on the sink. "I'm stepping outside, Zara, but I swear, you've got three minutes and then I'm back. Get it done."

He was clipped. Abrupt. She realized he was upset. She didn't care. She'd just seen three petite women, all gorgeous and sexy, and realized just how bad she really looked—and probably smelled. She'd thrown up in front of him. She was *not* going to add taking care of her business in the bathroom in front of him to her list of indignities any longer. If a man wanted a mystery, Gino clearly wasn't going to get it with her.

She had to crawl to the toilet because she couldn't take

the excruciating pain when she experimentally put her foot on the tile. She managed to get everything done, flush and crawl her way back to the sink. She hadn't considered the problem of pulling herself back up, so she was sitting on the floor, suffering one more indignity when Gino returned. His face was a mask, all hard lines and planes, as he bent and took her off the floor.

"Gino." She knew she shouldn't comment. She should keep her mouth shut. She detested his silence. The look that said he was upset with her. She didn't want him ever angry with her. He'd done so much for her and she seemed to be repaying him with vomit and whatever else she did to make him look like this.

He kicked open the door so hard it swung viciously, hit a doorstop and came back at them. He kicked it again and strode into the bedroom. "Let it go."

"Did I do something to upset you?"

He stopped right in the middle of the room. She could feel anger pouring off him in waves. His eyes were so black they were scary. "I'm pissed, Zara, not upset. I'm fucking done with you sacrificing your comfort because you think you need to preserve your dignity."

She swallowed back a protest, put her arms around his neck and buried her face against his shoulder. Hiding. She'd wanted to hide nearly all her life, but she'd been thrust into the spotlight—Whitney's retaliation for her disappointing him.

All the girls were so envious. She could leave the compound and see the world. She could go to various cities, go to landmarks, see sites they would never witness in their lifetimes. They told her how lucky she was over and over. Bellisia and Shylah beamed when she came back, so proud of her. All the girls sat in a circle at night and she told them stories of the outside.

The universities had been particular favorites to talk about. She hadn't attended parties, obviously, and Whitney had his men watching her every move, but she'd had the freedom to attend classes, do her projects and mix with like-minded men and women. The other girls had all lived vicariously through her. Sometimes they would tuck a request in her pocket and she'd try to fulfill it, a lipstick from the outside, girly contraband none of them were supposed to have. She had been caught more than once and punished by Whitney. His punishments had been harsh, but they hadn't been anything like Zhu's.

"Nonny thinks your body would benefit from a soak in a tub," Gino said, putting his knee in the middle of the bed and gently depositing her on the sheet-covered mattress.

The anger had receded from his voice and she dared to look at him again. His face was close. His eyes dark. His jaw was tight. A muscle ticked there, telling her his voice might not give away what he was feeling, but the tension was there.

"She says the special herbs would help heal you faster. I know it sounds a little wacky, but I've seen amazing things from her. The old ways worked for centuries before modern medicine, and just like Eastern medicine, Nonny's pharmacy out here in the swamp serves a purpose."

She studied his face, trying to read his mind. What did he want her to do? "I'm really worried about my feet. I need them."

"They'll heal. While you eat, I'm going to ask the women to fill up the bathtub with Nonny's concoction. She swears you won't need pain pills."

"I'm not going to take them anymore. I made a total fool of myself. I can't believe I was blurting out all those crazy things." And vomiting in front of him.

"Do you really believe Bolan Zhu and Bernard Cheng are related?"

She nodded. "Brothers. I don't miss the kinds of things that would genetically link them. They both have the same unusual eyes, bone structure from their mother and those fingers are distinct. I think Bolan is the younger brother and he's very dangerous. Cheng knows it too." She took a deep breath. "I can't stay here long, Gino. You know that. Bellisia isn't going to understand, but there's Nonny and Pepper and Pepper and Wyatt's three children. Pepper's pregnant. Zhu's going to come after me, and so will Whitney."

"Why? Why won't Whitney let up? Every woman here is a GhostWalker and he let them go. Why won't he let you go?"

She shook her head. "I'll tell you, Gino, but later. After my bath." After her talk with Bellisia. She trusted Bellisia implicitly. She had to know if there was corruption here. What she carried in her head was extremely valuable and couldn't be put in the hands of just anyone. Governments could be toppled with the kinds of information Cheng bought and sold. She was certain he had intelligence on terrorist cells. On traitors and agents for various countries. He knew about weapons they had and those countries developing chemicals in spite of the bans.

"We're alone right now, Zara, and I'm giving you this opportunity."

She sighed and looked away from those dark, compelling eyes. He could mesmerize her with them. "I can't right yet. I have to think about this. I can't just . . ."

"What?" he snapped. "Trust me? I parachuted onto the roof of a building for you, carried your ass out of there and risked my life for you. We all did. What more do you need to trust me?"

She blinked her lashes and breathed deeply, turning her face away from him. She was not going to cry. Bellisia wouldn't cry. Neither would Shylah. They were stoic when they had to be. Not her. Not Zara. Whitney could get to her every time. Apparently, so could Gino.

He swore softly and went to the window to stare out

into the night. There was only a shadowed light from a lamp in the far corner illuminating the room, but it would be enough for a sniper to take him out. She wanted him to move. She waited, her heart beating overtime, but he just stood there, his back to her, his anger and disappointment in her coming off him in waves.

"Gino? Could you just please not stand there," she finally burst out, unable to keep quiet even though she knew it was the absolute worst thing to say.

He half turned, his face in the shadows so she couldn't read his expression. "Why?"

"It's dark out there and light in here. A sniper might be able to shoot you." She really did sound like an idiot, but she was too afraid for him.

Gino stepped forward, and she caught his gaze dropping to her hands. She hadn't realized she was twisting her fingers together, a habit Whitney detested. Spies didn't do things like that.

He came to the edge of the bed and reached down to push the tangled strands of hair from her face. "The windows are shaded on the outside and fitted with bulletproof glass. It obviously isn't one hundred percent safe, so you're right. It isn't smart to stand in front of them with a light to my back. Thanks for the worry."

Relief almost made her giddy, but luckily, Nonny and Bellisia came in with dinner.

10

The bathwater was soothingly hot on Zara's tortured skin, and she just let Gino immerse her body in the heat with only a towel wrapped around her. Bellisia and Nonny washed her hair and rinsed it. When the water turned red from the dried blood, they pulled out the stopper, rinsed the tub and refilled it.

"I know why you're so obsessed with water, Bellisia." Zara offered her friend a tentative smile. She still wore the soaking wet towel, but it didn't matter, it was coming off the moment Gino left the room. He wanted to make certain her bruised and aching buttocks could take sitting on the hard surface.

"Gino," Nonny said, pouring authority into her voice. "Give us some privacy so we can get to work on this girl."

Zara wanted to throw her arms around Nonny and hug her. For once, she didn't want Gino close. She was desperate to talk to Bellisia. She would have to let Nonny do her swamp healing, and then she could talk freely.

"You okay with me leaving, princess?" Gino crouched

down beside the tub. "Because if you're not, I'll risk the wrath of the women to stay with you."

"It's indecent," Nonny said.

Something in her voice made Zara look up at her. Wyatt's grandmother didn't look shocked or at all uncomfortable with Gino in the bathroom while Zara was taking a bath. Her statement wasn't her opinion, merely a ploy to allow her to get Gino out of the room. She seemed to know Bellisia wanted some time alone with Zara.

"Sorry, ma'am. You know I have the highest respect for you, but if Zara needs me, I'm not leaving."

That made her feel good. Zara couldn't help it. Something about Gino had her heart stuttering and butterflies winging their way through her stomach. There might have been more of a reaction other places, but she was ignoring that. She was naked in a bathtub, a towel wrapped around her for modesty, but it didn't matter because he made her feel as if his entire focus was on her. He would stay, risking everyone's wrath if she wanted him.

"I'll have Bellisia or Nonny call you when I need to get out," she assured. "Thank you, Gino. I appreciate everything you've done for me. And just so you know, I do trust you. One hundred percent." That wasn't about her heart, but her safety. She did trust him. How could she not? But Bellisia was her sister. It had always been Bellisia, Shylah and Zara. She had to talk her dilemma out with her first.

Gino leaned down and brushed a kiss across the top of her head. "Thank you, Zara, that means a lot to me." He nodded toward Bellisia and Nonny. "Ladies." He sauntered out.

Zara watched him go, appreciating the way his muscles rippled beneath the tight tee. When she turned her head, Bellisia was frowning at her. Nonny was all business, not giving her time to figure out why Bellisia had that particular look on her face. The older woman pinned

Zara's clean, wet hair up on top of her head and then poured a dark-colored liquid into the bathwater.

"You'll need to soak in that for a half an hour. Then you can rinse off and get out. I'll make a paste for your feet and we'll wrap them before you go to bed."

Zara tried to wiggle her toes but stopped when pain shot through her. She was uncertain she wanted paste and wraps on her feet while she slept, but she was willing to try anything in order to heal them. She wanted desperately to walk on her own so Gino wouldn't think he had to carry her everywhere.

She'd never thought much about trying to attract a man. Whitney had made it clear before he sent her off to school that if she wasted her time looking at men, he'd pull her back to the compound fast. Leaving the compound made Bellisia and Shylah so proud of her, and she could contribute to the other women's comfort with contraband and stories. It made her feel like a giving member of their group.

Nonny left the room after lighting an odd-smelling candle, leaving her with Bellisia. The two stared at each other and then both burst into tears, then laughter.

"Did you see Shylah before you left?" Bellisia asked.

Zara shook her head. "Whitney was very closemouthed about Shylah and what he had her doing, but I had a terrible feeling it had something to do with Cheng. He's obsessed with the idea that Cheng was going to sell the GhostWalker program to other governments."

Bellisia studied her face. "But you don't think that."

Zara drew her knees up and rested her chin on top of them. "No. I think Cheng wants his own army. We read about him in the files they compiled for us, but he's far more than what's in those reports. He's far more ambitious. He reminds me a little of Whitney in that he believes he's the smartest man in the room and that he can control lives. He wants that kind of power, just like Whitney does. Turning the GhostWalker program over to other governments doesn't leave Cheng with the firepower he craves. He would want to keep it for himself, develop his own soldiers and send them out if others didn't comply with whatever he wanted. He wants the world to fear him."

"Cheng? Or Zhu?" Bellisia asked.

"Both. They share the same vision." She chewed at her lip for a moment. "Cheng wants that recognition, but Zhu doesn't care about being recognized. He prefers to remain in the shadows. I think he would have wanted the enhancements for himself." A delicate shudder passed through Zara's body. She was afraid to close her eyes and sleep. She knew Zhu would be there looking at her. Reminding her he was coming for her—and he would, she had no doubt of that. "He's incredibly evil."

"You're safe here," Bellisia said, as if reading her thoughts.

She shook her head. "I'm not, and as long as I'm here, no one else is safe either."

"Whitney will give up. He let me stay. At first, he made a try for me, but then he just let the team keep me. I think if I left the safety of them, he might come after me, but . . ."

"He isn't going to stop, Bellisia, neither of them will," Zara said. "Whitney will keep coming for me. If I'm dead, he'll come after my body."

Bellisia sank back on her heels. "You have something he wants."

Zara nodded. "He told me to steal all of Cheng's data. His files. He has secrets on terrorist cells, locations, movements, all that sort of thing. More, he's got dirt on governments, on agents, on presidents and their families. It's his business to know things. All of that was in his files, on his computers."

"And you have it."

"Yes. Whitney knows I have it. I destroyed Cheng's network, deleted everything so it would be impossible to recover it. I wouldn't have done that without first acquiring what was in the computers, and Whitney knows that. He had the GhostWalker file Violet gave him."

"Turn the data over to the team and Whitney won't care about reacquiring you," Bellisia said.

"You aren't thinking it through," Zara said gently. "I've had plenty of time to think about what information I have and what damage it could do if it is in the wrong hands. We have allies, Bellisia. They have agents in the field just like we do. If Whitney gets his hands on this material, he could blackmail our own allies. You and I both know, when it comes to politics, everyone is willing to sell everyone else down the river, and Whitney always wants something."

"Leave out the things you think are potentially a threat," Bellisia said.

Zara took a breath and let it out. "You have no idea the scope of this. I can't leave out things. I downloaded everything. Thousands of files, a lifetime of compiling dirt on governments and individuals. There's no way I could go through the files to determine what is safe to pass on and what isn't. Bellisia, I don't even know if I can actually get them out of my head, which makes me a huge target for everyone the moment it gets out I have this information."

Bellisia scooted back to the wall and drew up her own knees. When they were girls, they'd learned to sit like that and tap out code to one another. "What you're telling me without saying it is that what you've got could potentially start World War Three."

"That's about it."

"Can you destroy it?"

Zara shook her head. "I can't even get it out by myself. Whitney planted what is essentially a storage unit in my brain. It's really an integrated circuit for the sole purpose of storage. It's made from PEEK-carbon so it's virtually undetectable. I'm an industrial spy. Mostly, Whitney wanted to know about the experiments in medical research he was interested in. He sent me in, I downloaded files and got out. No one ever suspected. I didn't touch their equipment so it was impossible to trace me. The companies I stole from didn't even know their research was taken."

"You came home and Whitney removed the information from your head."

She shrugged. "Just that easy, but I don't know how. Then suddenly Violet decides to sell Whitney's prized GhostWalker program to Cheng, and Whitney can't stand it. He sends me in, but he wants Cheng's entire network wiped clean. When the alarms started to go off, I was the only stranger on the premises. Of course Cheng suspects me. How could he not?"

There was bitterness in her voice and she didn't try to hide it from Bellisia. Whitney was the only father figure the girls had. He was cold and unfeeling. He made it clear to all of them that they were expendable and to Zara in particular.

"Does Cheng know you have his information?"

Zara shook her head. "Nope. He has no way of knowing that. I wasn't anywhere near his computers." She rubbed her chin on her knees. "I have to figure out what the GhostWalkers would do with the information before I say anything."

"They're soldiers, Zara. They would turn it over to their commanding officer."

"And he would move it up along the chain of command, right? Whitney has a lot of friends higher up that chain. He'd get it."

"Maybe," Bellisia conceded.

"I don't know who to trust."

"Ezekiel," Bellisia said immediately. "You can trust him."

"Are you saying he wouldn't go up the chain of command? He was running the rescue."

Bellisia's gaze slid away. "I don't know what he would do, but we have to tell him. I tell him everything. That's the way it works between us. If I know it, then so does he."

"Are you saying he tells you the covert missions he goes on?" Zara asked. She suspected that if she and Gino were together, in an actual relationship, he still wouldn't be able to tell her when he went off on some missions.

"Well, no, but that's different," Bellisia hedged.

"So is this." Zara didn't know if she was still very hurt by Bellisia going to Ezekiel first or whether she was jealous because it was no longer Bellisia, Shylah and Zara. She only knew she was reluctant to tell Ezekiel, especially before she told Gino.

If she really was going into a relationship with Gino, if she trusted him with her heart, then she needed to trust him with this information. Still, she'd known Bellisia and trusted her all of her life. That didn't mean that confidence extended to Ezekiel. Gino didn't seem as if he was a by the book kind of soldier. Ezekiel did, even for a GhostWalker.

"No, it really isn't," Bellisia denied. "I wouldn't be able to look my husband in the eye if I didn't tell him about this."

Zara's heart jumped. It felt like a betrayal to her. She knew Bellisia, knew her well enough to know she'd never betray her, but it still felt that way. It wasn't the three women any longer. It was Bellisia and Ezekiel first. Maybe that was the way relationships were between men and women. Zara didn't know enough about them, but it felt as if she'd been abandoned and was alone. She didn't know what she'd been looking for, but having Ezekiel be part of the equation wasn't it.

"You just said Ezekiel wouldn't tell you about a covert

mission he was running. That's what this is, Bellisia, *my* covert mission."

"It's not the same and you know it," Bellisia denied. "You need help, and Zeke could help you. I have to tell him."

She took a deep breath. "I think I have to tell Gino first, before I decide on anything else, including you telling your husband."

There was a small silence. Zara lifted her gaze to her friend's. She was frowning. "What's up with you and Gino?"

Zara's heart missed a beat. She shrugged.

"No, honey, you have to tell me. Gino is a cool guy. I can see the appeal for you. I really can. He's hot as hell. Dangerous. Very protective. He certainly can look after you and make you feel safe, but he isn't at all the kind of man you need."

"Why do you say that? You have Ezekiel. He's a soldier."

"He's a soldier who has evolved. Gino hasn't, and he never will. No matter how much you want him to have moved into this century, he hasn't. He will always feel his woman's place is at home having his babies and sitting at his feet worshipping him. He's intelligent, but he's archaic. You're off the charts intelligent and have so much to give to the world. You need to travel and give lectures, lead the way in artificial intelligence the way you've been doing. He wouldn't want you to do that for one minute. He's the type who would be possessive and probably jealous. He'd keep you under his thumb, and you've had that all your life."

"You make him sound like he'd make a woman his prisoner."

"He would, Zara. I know him. I know what he expects from his wife. He would never be happy with someone like you."

Zara ducked her head to keep Bellisia from seeing that her assessment was shattering her. "You can't know that."

"I do know it. Absolutely I know it. This is your chance at freedom, and Gino would take that away from you as surely as if you were back in the compound. You might be happy for a year or two, but Zara, you're made to set the world on fire and he won't like it. You'd eventually fight him to get free. Men like Gino don't give up their women."

"He's intelligent. I hate that you think I'm so much smarter, Bellisia. You're selling him short." There was a hint of belligerence in her voice, but she couldn't get it out.

"That isn't what I'm saying at all," Bellisia corrected. "I'm saying he doesn't want his woman out in the world. I can go out and fight with Ezekiel, and he believes in my abilities to help defend the triplets or Nonny. Gino would tuck you somewhere safe and expect you to hide with the triplets and Nonny."

"Maybe that's where I want to be."

Bellisia shook her head. "I don't think so, beautiful. You're too smart to want only to be someone's wife and the mother of his children. You want to make an impact on the world. That's your true destiny, and everyone knows it but Whitney. He always wanted you to feel like you can't make it on your own. You don't want to trade him for Gino."

"You're not being very nice. Gino's a good man."

"That has nothing to do with it. You've got a great gift and you were born to change the world. You owe it to the world, but he won't understand that. He would selfishly want to keep you to himself and make all your decisions for you as if you didn't have a brain in your head. He'd insist you be his little submissive in the house and in the bedroom."

"Bellisia, you can't talk about him like that. There's no way you know him that well." Zara's heart was dipping, skipping beats. Hurting. She didn't want to owe the world her gift. She wanted her own little work space with no one around. She knew she was responsible for Bellisia thinking she wanted to set the world on fire. She'd lied since she'd first gone off to school. How could Bellisia and Shylah ever forgive her? She had wanted them to be proud of her, so she'd pretended to love what she did. Worse, she didn't think having Gino make decisions when she didn't want to sounded all that bad.

"Do you know that he comes from one of the wealthiest families in the world?" Bellisia leaned close to the tub. "I'm not talking millionaire here. Trap and Wyatt are wealthy, but they make strides in the medical world. They have patents. They contribute. What do you think he does with all that money? Absolutely nothing, Zara. It just grows and grows for him."

Zara rubbed her temples. Her head was beginning to pound all over again. "You're saying he has no interest in money. Is that so bad?"

"He has no interest in anything," Bellisia countered.

Zara wanted to throw something. "When I was upset with you for not even seeing me when we came back, he defended you, Bellisia. You're tearing him apart, and he defended you."

Bellisia sighed. "I'm sorry. I wish I could tell you something different, but if I had to assess Gino's character, I'd say he was more like Bolan Zhu than any of the Ghost-Walkers. I'm sorry if that hurts, but I need to be honest so you don't make a very big mistake. I can see you're already falling for him, but it's just the fact that he rescued you. It could have been any of them."

Zara knew that wasn't the truth. She felt nothing when she was near any of the others. She hadn't looked at them when they were trying to help Gino with her. She'd felt a connection with him right from the start, and that connection had only grown the more time she spent with him, which was twenty-four seven.

"I need to get out of here. My butt is hurting right along with my head. I expect you to keep my confidence until I decide what to do. That means you can't tell Ezekiel, Bellisia."

"He'll know I'm holding something back and this is big, Zara," Bellisia said, reluctance in her voice and eyes. "I told you, I don't hold things back from my husband."

Panic welled up. "I would never have trusted you if I thought you'd betray me." Zara caught at the edges of the tub as if she could haul herself out of the water. "We made a vow to one another. You. Me. Shylah."

"I know, but if you trust me, you have to trust him. I can't go to him and say I don't trust him enough with this information. It's too valuable and he knows me too well. He has a responsibility to his entire team and everyone who lives here, and so do I now."

"What are you saying? You want me to leave because I bring a threat with me?" Her chest hurt and her lungs felt raw. She hadn't thought anything could come between them. A man had. Would Gino come between Shylah and her if Shylah were to find her way to the Fontenot home? If that was the case, she didn't want anything to do with men.

"No, of course not. I don't know what I'm saying, only that I don't like to keep things from my husband and this is huge."

Zara caught at the plug in the tub, avoiding Bellisia's eyes. All of a sudden, she felt very alone and lost. She thought when she got here, she would have Bellisia, but she didn't. Bellisia's loyalties had shifted to her husband and her husband's team of GhostWalkers. She had to bide her time, get the virus capsules out of her and get gone fast.

"Zara," Bellisia tried again.

Zara flashed her the fake smile she'd perfected over the years. The one she used when the girls gathered around her at night when she came back from one of her "freedom" trips. They always bought the smile because they wanted to believe. It made them happy to think that one of their own was out in the world, free and happy, when they were held prisoner back at the compound. At least one of them was free.

Bellisia took the wet towel and stood up to wring it out. Her gaze jumped to the lacerations all over her body. "Zara." She breathed her name and went to her knees beside the tub. "Zeke told me, but I didn't realize what they'd done to you."

Zara took the clean towel and wrapped it around her body as best she could because she felt very exposed and vulnerable. She didn't want Bellisia staring at her. Lifting her voice, she called out, hoping Gino was a man of his word and that he was in hearing distance. "Gino. I'm ready." She had to end this with her friend before she started crying.

"I didn't mean to upset you," Bellisia said. "I swear, Zara, I'm only looking out for you."

"I know. It's my great mind everyone is always so concerned with, preserving it for the good of all mankind and all." She went for humor, but it fell flat. She was very thankful the door to the bathroom opened and Gino stuck his head in.

"You called, princess?"

"I need to get out of here. My bum hurts." She wished she could be more elegant and not mention her throbbing buttocks, but she really did hurt and it was all she could think of to get him to take her out of the situation.

Gino's gaze jumped from her face to Bellisia's, and then he shut down. His features were once again an expressionless mask. He was across the floor to her in two strides, crouching down to slide one arm under her knees and the other locking behind her back.

"Hold on, baby," he whispered gently.

His voice turned her heart over. So caring. Not about her brain. Not about the storage unit in her brain either. Just her. She wrapped her hands around his neck, buried her face in his shoulder and let him lift her.

"Zara," Bellisia said, her voice tight.

"She's done," Gino said before Zara could summon the will to answer, so she didn't, grateful that he could see her, see that she couldn't take one more moment of her best friend telling her what was good and right for her. Or telling her that her first priority was really her husband now. There was nothing wrong with those things, but they just weren't helping when Zara felt so alone and in need of guidance. Not guidance about whether or not Gino Mazza was the man for her, but about the storage unit filled with data.

Gino carried her out of the bathroom and down the hall, Bellisia trailing after them. "Where are you taking her?" she asked.

"My room," Gino said.

"That isn't necessary, Gino. We're no longer using Zeke's room. Take her there." There was a challenge to Bellisia's voice and an authority Zara hadn't given her permission to have.

That left Zara in a dilemma. Should she back her friend? If she didn't, would Bellisia turn on her and tell Ezekiel even though she'd asked her not to? Her fingers dug into Gino's shoulder and her teeth bit down on his neck. He didn't slow down or break stride. He took her right into his bedroom and kicked the door closed behind him. There was a finality to the sound as the door slammed hard.

Zara lifted her head as he put her down in the center of his bed. Her eyes searched his. "She's going to be very,

very angry with you. She'll tell Zeke you all but kidnapped me."

"If that's what it takes to stop the bullshit, I'm all for kidnapping. What in the hell was she saying that was upsetting you?"

She needed to get weight off her buttocks. She turned onto her side gingerly, still not taking her eyes from his face. "We were always so close. It was Shylah, Bellisia and me. We trusted one another implicitly, which believe me, where we were raised, that was huge to have. I guess I thought it would be the same here. I didn't consider that it would be natural for her to include her husband."

He didn't blink. Those dark, intense eyes never left hers. "You mean you told her something in confidence and she indicated she would tell Zeke?"

Her heart did a strange stuttering that told her she was either afraid of him or very attracted—maybe both. His voice was strictly neutral, but she had the feeling he wasn't happy.

"I'm just not as sure of her as I was."

"Did you talk to her about Zhu?"

"A little." She propped her head up on her hand. "Not about the things he did to me. She didn't ask, and I didn't want to talk about him. She wanted to know if I really thought Cheng and Zhu were brothers, and I do."

"You need to talk about what he did, Zara."

Now his voice was gentle and that got to her. She shook her head. "I want him to go away. Out of my mind. Just for a little while."

"You going to tell me what you're hiding from me?"

"I'm thinking about it. I'm afraid to. I don't know the right thing to do."

He sank down onto the mattress beside her. "You're going to have to sit up for a few more minutes. I need to tame your hair. It's going wild on us."

She rolled over and sat up without thinking why it was

so easy to do whatever he asked. Bellisia was so wrong about him. She couldn't understand why Bellisia saw one thing and she saw something completely different in him.

He unpinned her hair, shifted around behind her and took the brush from the nightstand where he'd obviously put it waiting for her to get out of the bathtub. Bellisia didn't see him—how thoughtful he was anticipating her needs. Zara scooted between his thighs, uncaring that she was only wearing a towel and her back was bare. His fingers skimmed over the stripes of bruises down her back.

"You're healing fast," he told her. "Nonny assures me that her concoction is going to facilitate healing even faster."

"I hope so. I hate that you have to take care of me all the time, Gino. I'll bet you weren't aware of what you'd signed up for."

"I knew exactly what I signed up for, Zara," he contradicted. "Maybe I didn't know the exact extent of what Zhu did, but I knew you were mine."

The brush never stopped moving through her hair, and over her scalp. If he encountered a tangle, he patiently used a comb to smooth the knot before once again using the brush. She'd never had that kind of care before and it was almost too much. Almost. She kept quiet so he wouldn't stop.

"Whatever it is you're worried about, princess, I'm on your side. If you need me to take that off you, give it to me and let me figure it out."

It was an offer, not an order. Gino might have been hurt earlier thinking she didn't trust him, but once she'd said she did, he'd gotten over it fast. She wanted to let him decide what to do with the information she had. She couldn't protect the world from Whitney. If he ended up with the information after what she was doing to try to keep it from him, that wouldn't be on her.

"It would be so easy to hand the responsibility off to

you, but I'm not certain it's right. I haven't lived outside the compound ever. I was allowed out to go to school, but I always knew I was watched. There was no real freedom. I didn't make decisions for myself and certainly not moral ones. I followed Whitney's dictates. If he said I had to steal information, I did it."

She tried to tell him without stating it. She was a thief. She stole data and took it back to Whitney so he could leap out in front of everyone and be the best at everything.

"Zara, I asked for the responsibility. There's a difference. You're not handing me something I didn't want. I'm just saying, if you don't know who you can trust, take a look at the man standing with you. I promised you I wasn't going anywhere and I haven't. I'm with you for as long as you want me."

He braided her hair and secured it with a small tie and then pulled her back until she was resting against his chest. His arms slid around her and held her to him. She rested her head on him, feeling secure. That was something no one else had ever given her.

"If I tell you something important, do you have to share it with the other GhostWalkers? Or take it up the chain of command?"

He nuzzled the top of her head. "I'm supposed to, but I don't always do everything I'm supposed to do."

"Could you give me your word of honor you just wouldn't tell everyone without my permission?"

"I'd like to tell you yes, but honestly, princess? I tend to make up my own mind. I would tell you first what I'm going to do. I'd talk it over with you. I wouldn't do anything until you understood I had your best interests in mind, but I can't promise to get your permission."

She sighed and rubbed her chin on her drawn-up knees. "That doesn't help."

"Would it help if I swore to you that I'd only do something if it was in your best interests? Any decision I make

is done to make your life easier. I can definitely promise
you that. It won't be to further my career or blindly follow
the chain of command. I'm not that man, and just so you
know, neither is Zeke."

Zara looked over her shoulder at him. "I don't know
what to do."

"What does your gut say? You have good instincts."

She was terrified that Bellisia would tell Ezekiel before
she told Gino. Gino was her choice. In her heart, she knew
she'd already made up her mind about him. She might lie
to herself and say she didn't want a man, but she wanted
him. For herself. She never felt alone when she was with
him and she hated letting him down.

"It's in my head." She blurted it out. Her secret. "Whitney planted a carbon nanotube SSD in my brain. The storage unit is made of PEEK-carbon so it can't be seen with
X-ray, MRI or CT scans."

"You downloaded all of Cheng's files into that storage
unit?"

She glanced at him over her shoulder. Her eyes met
his. He gave nothing away, his face a mask of indiffer-
ence. She nodded.

"You'd need a battery. Power."

She turned back so she could rest her head again,
thankful he wasn't jumping around the room at the disclo-
sure, excited to know what she had in her head. "Movements of the body power it. Like some pacemakers."

"What about a generator? You'd need something to
send the power to the storage unit."

She nodded. "From what I understand, it's made of the
PEEK-carbon as well and sits on a flat piece of PEEK-
carbon right next to the storage unit so it's undetectable."

"Of course. Whitney is a master at coming up with
technology that he needs."

"He is," she agreed. "Because he piggybacks on others' technology. That's why he always sent me out to those

businesses involving research. He wanted what they had. Cheng collects information on people, really nasty information that allows him to blackmail them. If Whitney gets that material, he would use it for his own gain. If I could get it out of my head, I'd like to just destroy it all, but there's also information on various terrorist cells, things that could save lives. If I give it to the government, all of the data would most likely fall back into Whitney's hands anyway and I haven't saved anyone."

"You can upload it, can you download it yourself?"

"I should be able to, I can always talk to machines, but he's done something to block me once the information is in the unit. That prevents me from turning it over to someone else."

"How does he get the information out?"

"I don't know. I'm always asleep when he takes it out."

"Under anesthesia?"

She shook her head. "He gives me an injection, I go to sleep fast and wake up to him telling me we're done."

"That's why the soldier kept his gun pointed to a specific part of your brain. He was going to destroy the unit if they had to kill you, rather than letting the intelligence you'd gathered fall into someone else's hands."

"He might still kill me."

"I'm not okay with that, so between the two of us, we'll figure it out. I'm not turning you over to anyone. I'll see what I can come up with. I have to remove the capsules, maybe I can remove the storage unit at the same time."

She shook her head. "He said that was permanent and even he couldn't remove it without damaging my brain. I believed him. I can usually tell his lies from the truth. Most of us can because we've heard them so often."

"So, if that's true, then we know he has a way to download the material without removing the SSD. If he can do it, so can we."

"What are we going to do with the information if we extract it?"

"Not if. We *have* to extract it. As long as you have that information in your head, Whitney will keep coming after you. If anyone else finds out, and if Whitney can't reacquire you, he'll tell someone higher up to get the information from you, then we'll have another huge problem on our hands. We can run, but eventually, they'll catch up with us. We have to remove it, sooner rather than later."

That made sense. The idea that Zhu might find out sent a tremor running through her body. "He's going to come after me no matter what," she whispered.

Gino was silent but his arms tightened around her. His chin nuzzled her head. "You're thinking about Zhu, not Whitney."

She nodded. "He won't let me go."

"Maybe not, maybe he's stupid or arrogant enough to think he can come to our home turf and steal you away from me, but he can't. It isn't going to happen, princess. I'm not leaving your side."

"You'll have to eventually. They'll send you out on another rescue and then he'll come. I know he will." Her voice had begun to swing out of control, just like the rapid beating of her heart. She shoved her fist in her mouth and bit down hard.

"Zara, you're getting worked up for nothing," he objected, his voice a soothing sound that seemed to penetrate her worst nightmare and make her believe he could stop Zhu when no one else could. "We'll take this one step at a time. Zhu is far down the list. I've got eyes on him. He leaves Shanghai, we'll know it. In the meantime, let's worry about removing the virus capsules. We'll do that tomorrow."

He sounded so utterly calm, so completely in control, that Zara was able to breathe deep and feel safe again. He would take care of things. More, he could be counted on. Step one sounded good to her.

"Are you certain there are two virus capsules? No more?"

"I don't believe he put more than two in you, but we plan to study the virus and come up with an antidote. Bellisia said each virus is specific to the person Whitney implants it in, but we'll compare the one he put in you to the one he put in her and see if they're the same or close. That way, if another woman comes this way, we can inject her immediately with an antidote."

She liked that. She liked to think that they were already thinking ahead to saving more of the women Whitney held prisoner. She nodded her head. "Thank you, Gino."

"For what, beautiful? I haven't done much."

"You make me feel safe." It was so much more than that. She took a breath and tried to tell him. He deserved that much from her. "You seem to see when no one else can get past my brain. Sometimes I hate the fact that I'm supposed to be so intelligent. Whitney made certain to point out how worthless to him I was, that my brain wasn't all that . . ."

"Everyone knows Whitney is a self-centered ass, Zara," Gino said.

She couldn't help smiling. He was a self-centered ass. "An egotistical maniac, maybe, as well, but that's not the point. While he was telling me how stupid and worthless I was, everyone else was telling me that I owed it to the world to get my brain out there and do something enormous." She turned her head so she could look at him over her shoulder. "I'm not just a brain to you. I'm a person. So, thank you for seeing me."

His smile was slow in coming, but when it did, her heart gave a funny flip, her stomach somersaulted and deep inside, her womb quivered. God, he was gorgeous when he smiled. When he wasn't smiling he was compelling, hot, and intense, but when he smiled, there was never going to be a way she could say no to him.

"You're welcome, Zara." His hand cupped her chin, his thumb sliding over her bare skin. All the while his eyes looked into hers. "There's never going to be a time when I won't be able to see you. Remember that for me, will you?"

She nodded. "Kiss me." She blurted her request out before she could stop herself, before she knew what she was going to ask, but it seemed to be something she was asking of him on a nightly basis now.

He didn't hesitate, but then he never did. Gino was always decisive. He leaned down and took her mouth. He didn't seem to care that her face was swollen and bruised, he looked right past that in just the same way he looked past her intellect that was supposed to be so superior but only added to her isolation.

He didn't seem to mind that she was inexperienced in the kissing department. He took command instantly. She was fairly certain her entire body ignited at his touch. His lips were firm and cool and warmed hers until she was nearly liquid. His mouth was paradise and she let herself get lost there. He kissed like he did everything else—with absolute confidence.

Excitement coursed through her. She tried to follow his lead and then just didn't care, letting him take her over because whenever she gave herself to him, however she did it, she always got more from him. His kisses were no different. He led her from gentle to rough. From tender to devouring her. She wanted to be devoured. It felt like worship and desire. And then it felt like passion and sin. She wanted that as well. She wanted everything he would give her.

He was the one who stopped first. He lifted his head a scant inch from hers, his dark eyes searching hers. "We're getting out of hand, princess. A little more and I'm going to have you straddling me. You're not ready for that."

"I am." She was certain she was.

His smile was slow in coming again, but when it did, everything in her responded. "No, baby, I wish you were, but when you come to me, it isn't going to be because you're grateful or afraid. You're going to want me for me. That means you have to get to know me. I've told you, I'm not a good man, and you'll have to be able to live with that because once I take you, I'm not letting you go."

His warning should have made her leery. He was echoing the things Bellisia had said to her, but instead, Zara liked him all the more for giving her a warning. She especially liked that if she was with him, he wanted her for all time. She couldn't imagine having Gino for her own. She wasn't gifted in the way Bellisia or Cayenne was. She would never be a soldier, and he was a first-class warrior.

"I can't fight." Again, she just blurted it out without thinking. "I mean I can, but I'm not really any good, not like Bellisia or any of the other women. If I had to defend someone, I could do it, but . . ." Now she was just babbling.

His hand swept over her head and down her back, following her thick braid. His touch was exquisitely gentle. "Zara, I don't want a woman to fight by my side. I'm better out there in the dark, alone. I fight alone. It's what I do best. If I had to worry that my woman was somewhere fighting off an army of men, I'd lose my fucking mind. That's the truth. I'm not made the way some of the other men are."

She knew that was what Bellisia had tried to warn her about. Bellisia wouldn't be able to stand it if Ezekiel wanted her stashed somewhere safe while he went out to fight. Zara wasn't Bellisia and she never would be. Whitney had detested her, calling her a coward, but she'd gone out each time he'd asked and stolen the data he needed.

Bellisia and Shylah had pointed out to her over and over that she did everything Whitney required her to do, and he still called her a coward. She needed to know if her sisters had told her that out of love, or if it was the truth.

"Am I a coward because I hate pain and violence so much I don't want to fight? I want a real answer, Gino, not a platitude."

"No, of course not, Zara. I realize the world has changed into a place where everyone judges everyone else and holds them up to impossible standards. No one takes into account different personalities or things that happened in one's past. If you need someone to take the brunt of the world for you, there's nothing wrong with that. Some men prefer that trait in a woman."

He wrapped her braid around his fist and stared down at the thick mass. "Sometimes, princess, people are cruel when they don't mean to be. You're not a coward. If you were a coward, you wouldn't have gone out time after time and stolen the information Whitney required. You certainly would have told Zhu about the SSD in your head. You would have given up Whitney and even the GhostWalkers. You didn't, in spite of being terrified of pain. He inflicted the worst kind of pain on someone like you. Not just physical, but psychological as well. You didn't break."

She wanted to kiss him again, but before she could act on the impulse, a knock on the door prevented her from saying anything. She reached down and tugged at the blanket she should have been covering up with all along.

Wyatt's grandmother stuck her head into the room. "I brought the poultices for her feet, Gino."

"I'll take them, Nonny." Gino stirred behind her, gently moving her forward so he could get out from behind her.

"And you might put one of your shirts on her. Tomorrow, I'll have the girls go into town and buy her a few things. I'm the only one tall enough to give her clothes, and I'm pretty certain she doesn't want my old lady clothes." Nonny chuckled at her own joke.

"I thought her skin would heal faster without anything between it and the air."

Nonny frowned and then nodded slowly. "If she doesn't mind, it would be best."

"I'll keep everyone out."

"You behave yourself, Gino," Nonny cautioned. "That girl is an innocent."

"I'll protect her. Even from myself."

"I believe you." Nonny handed over the poultices, patted Zara on the head and went out, leaving them alone, the way Zara preferred.

Zara couldn't help but think Nonny thought Gino was a good man.

11

"Where are we going?" Zara asked. She desperately wanted to go *somewhere*, anywhere, just to get out of the house. The walls were closing in on her. Gino and Wyatt had removed the two capsules, preserving them so they could study the virus Whitney planned to infect her with.

The swelling was gone completely from her face and most of the colors had faded. The bruising from the caning had subsided, and the lacerations from the whip had mostly healed. There were one or two places on her body that Gino wasn't happy with, but even those wounds were closed and healing, although tender.

Over the last week, Gino had taken the utmost care of her. She found herself thinking of him constantly. She hadn't been alone with Bellisia, not once during the last week. She didn't know if Bellisia needed time to think things over and was avoiding her, or if she was training with Ezekiel and the team, but Zara was worried that too much time was slipping by. Whitney wasn't going to give them much longer before he came after her again. He had to be obsessing the way he did when his plans were thwarted.

"I'm going to take you on a picnic," Gino said. "It's hot and humid today. We may even get rain, but that won't really cool things down. I asked Nonny to fix us a picnic lunch. I knew you needed to get out of here and I thought I'd show you the swamp. It's beautiful. You'll appreciate the cranes and other types of birds and wildlife."

The idea of leaving the house and getting out into the swamp was so appealing she nearly leapt out of bed, until he gave her a stern look and she subsided, but she flashed him a huge smile.

"Put your hair up off your neck. I'm going to cover you in mosquito repellent."

She immediately pulled her hair up, put it in a ponytail and then added another tie in order to twist the thick mass into a knot on top of her head. Gino sat on the edge of the bed and began to rub the mosquito repellent into her shoulders and the back of her neck.

"We're going to have to address the problem of extracting the information from the SSD, Zara. We need a little help. Trap is unconventional. He doesn't think like a soldier. He would never tell anyone, and he's extremely smart. We could use his brain. Wyatt's a lot like him. Intelligent and a bit of a rogue. I know you haven't spent any time with them, but they would be my choices for help. What do you think?"

Zara chewed on her lower lip, thinking it over. Everyone talked about Trap as if he might be the smartest man on the planet. Wyatt too. It was possible the three men might just find a way to extract the information. "I don't know, Gino. I'd like to talk things over with Bellisia again. I know we didn't do very well the first time, but her opinion matters to me and I'm not so jealous and hurt anymore. I think I have a better understanding of relationships and what she was trying to tell me."

Gino rubbed the repellent over both arms, making certain to get the backs of her hands. "That's a good idea, princess. Let's get on that as soon as possible."

Zara nodded her head, trying not to react to the feel of his hands on her. The more she was with him, the more she found it was impossible to control the way her blood seemed to heat, moving through her veins like thick molasses. She'd never experienced deep, needy hunger that made her edgy the way she felt around him.

A sharp rap on the door had her jerking the sheet up to cover her body. She'd grown used to wearing just a T-shirt in bed and nothing else around Gino, but company was altogether different.

"Come in," Gino called out, but his hand settled around the nape of her neck as Ezekiel and Bellisia came into the room. Ezekiel closed the door, giving them privacy in the busy household.

Zara smiled at her "sister," relieved to see her. "I was just telling Gino I wanted to see you," she said. "I'm so glad you came."

Bellisia leaned in to kiss her on the cheek. "Me too. I've been training and haven't gotten the chance to do anything but peek in on you while you were sleeping."

"Gino told me. He has this thing about me taking naps." She smiled up at Gino, her stomach doing a slow somersault when she found him looking down at her.

"It helps you heal faster," he said. He slipped off the bed to give Bellisia more room. Taking a position against the wall alongside Ezekiel, he continued. "Your internal organs were bruised from the beating and caning. They have to heal as well. Sleep helps."

Ezekiel smiled at Zara. "You're looking so much better. How are you feeling?"

"Whatever is in Nonny's poultices is definitely helping. I have to admit taking baths in tea water and flowers feels strange, but it seems to be working," Zara admitted.

Bellisia paced close to the bed, looking her face over and moving the sheet to look at her legs. Zara wanted to pull the sheet over herself, suddenly uncomfortable. "I'm much better."

"You still have lacerations," Bellisia pointed out. "You do know, Zara, that Gino isn't the only doctor here. Ezekiel is a doctor. There are a few others. If you want more than one opinion, you could get it without stepping out of this room." She looked around the room with a small frown. "Why aren't the window shades open? It's always so dark in here." She marched over and immediately raised two of the three shades, glaring at Gino. "You're not a prisoner, honey. You need light and fresh air."

Zara blinked at the sudden change in lighting. She'd been the one to insist that Gino keep the shades pulled. The longer she was there at the Fontenot home, the more she worried that Zhu would come, or a sniper would find a way to kill Gino because he was with her.

"We were going on a picnic," she said. "Gino asked Nonny to fix us a lunch. I'm really excited about seeing the swamp."

"I came to ask if you want to go with Zeke and me to see the house we're building," Bellisia said.

Zara caught Ezekiel's frown out of the corner of her eye, and she knew Bellisia well enough to know she wasn't telling the truth. There was concern on her face, in her eyes, and her gaze kept shifting to Gino. Clearly, she was still worried about Zara's relationship with him.

"I'm sorry, hon, but we've made these plans," she said, very carefully, not wanting Bellisia's feelings to be hurt. "Nonny made the lunch . . ."

"At Gino's orders," Bellisia burst out, openly glaring at him.

"Babe," Ezekiel said, his voice gentle.

"No. She has to know what's going on. Seriously, Zara, he tells Nonny what you can eat that day. He goes in every single morning and comes up with a menu. It doesn't matter what the rest of us are eating, he decides what you can and can't eat. He decides when you sleep and who can come in and visit you. That's not right."

The accusation tumbled out of her, and Zara could feel her very real concern. She knew Bellisia, and right then she was close to tears. Crying was something her "sister" rarely did. She looked to Gino to clear things up, confident that he would.

"I consult with Nonny on the menus," Gino told Bellisia. "She knows local herbs and dishes that would be more conducive to healing the body. Nutrition is more her forte than mine, so I follow her advice. I certainly am not the one making up the menu."

"The point is, Gino, you don't consult Zara."

"I think more to the point, I don't consult you," Gino said quietly.

Small blue rings appeared faintly under Bellisia's skin, and Zara sat up straighter, suddenly afraid for Gino. "I don't mind the menu. The food is good and if it makes Nonny and Gino feel better to have me eat a certain way right now, I'm okay with it. Nonny's an exceptional cook and everything tastes wonderful."

Bellisia threw her arms into the air. "You're missing the point. Think about it. Gino is keeping everyone from getting near you and he has to stop. I've talked to Zeke about removing him from helping with your care." She glared at Gino.

He shrugged. "You can try it, Bellisia, but it isn't going to stop me. No one is going to stop me but Zara. She has only to say she would prefer someone else and I'm gone."

Zara's heart jumped. Instantly her breathing turned ragged, so that it felt as if with every breath she took, her lungs burned. She shook her head, her gaze going to Gino's.

"Relax, princess," he drawled. "Didn't I just say I wasn't going anywhere?"

Bellisia's frown deepened. "Don't you see that you're becoming too dependent on him, Zara? This isn't you. You're the kick-ass, independent woman who's going to rock the world. You're not the one having panic attacks because your boyfriend doesn't want you making your own decisions."

"Zeke." Gino's voice was quiet, so quiet it made Zara's heart pound in alarm. "Take your woman out of here before I put her out."

"You try it," Bellisia snapped. "One bite from me and you're a dead man."

"Bellisia." Ezekiel just said her name, a warning note in his voice, and color swept up her neck into her face.

That wasn't good enough for Zara. She forced her body out from under the sheet and turned so her long legs were over the side of the bed. "Don't you dare threaten him. I mean it, Bellisia. You're my best friend. I love you, but you don't get to talk to him like that, and you better never threaten him again. *Never.* Do you understand me? I'm not without my own ability to kill and if it came to that, I believe in revenge. You know I do. You touch him, you dare inject him with venom, your man is just as dead."

"Someone has to protect you, Zara. You're not thinking straight."

"No one has to protect me. The virus is out of me, and I'm doing quite well. I can think for myself."

Ezekiel put his hand gently on Bellisia's arm. "Come on, baby. We all need a breather. You've been worrying yourself sick over Zara. Obviously, she doesn't feel like a prisoner, and I told you all along, Gino is a good man and will take excellent care of her. Let's go for a swim and then you can sleep for a while."

That made Zara feel like crap. Bellisia would be worried. She loved Zara and Zara wasn't acting the way Bellisia thought she should—or would. That was on her. She'd misled Bellisia and Shylah deliberately. Bellisia didn't have all the facts and Zara didn't want Gino to judge her harshly. Still, it didn't make sense that Bellisia was so against Gino. She watched the two leave the room and then she raised her gaze until she met Gino's. "Why doesn't she like you?"

He shrugged. "She doesn't like Trap much either. We're not the type of man women like, Zara. Trap has Asperger's and can't read social cues. He doesn't give a damn most of the time, but it does upset him when he screws up with one of us or especially Cayenne. Draden has always interpreted for him because he's very good at reading people whether they want to be read or not, and I have that same trait." He shrugged. "Bellisia has an idea for your future. She's fierce about it. She also has very real concerns. She thinks you're my prisoner and I'm going to make you into some kind of sexual submissive."

Zara shivered, wondering what that would be like with Gino. "She regards herself as a feminist and wants me to be one as well."

"Just because you don't want to conquer the world doesn't mean you aren't a feminist. A true feminist wouldn't tell other women what they should or shouldn't do. They would support their decisions. This isn't about Bellisia being a feminist, princess, it's about her worrying herself sick about you. You'll have to find the time to talk to her without me in the room. You can be open and honest, and she'll settle down."

He stood up and stretched. She watched because she always enjoyed seeing the way his muscles moved every time he did. There was something to what he said. She hadn't thought about that.

He moved close, reached down, pulled her legs apart

and stepped even closer, wedging his hips between her thighs. It was an intimate thing to do and her body responded with damp heat and blood pounding through her clit.

"I think you may have left a couple of very important things out when you were talking to me about your ability to fight."

She swallowed and avoided his eyes. "I told you I could fight. I trained just like everyone else." She couldn't control the blush and she knew he saw it. He never missed anything.

"I'm not talking about combat or weapons training, baby. I'm talking about that little bomb you just dropped when you were threatening Zeke, and I'm fairly certain you know that's what I'm referring to."

She glanced up at him from under her lashes, trying to judge how angry he was—or if he was at all. It was impossible. He didn't give much away. His gaze was steady on hers. Compelling. She sighed. There was no getting around Gino when he wanted something. He'd just stare at her until she caved.

"Okay, fine. Bellisia has a venom. I do as well. It's kind of a fail-safe. Whitney's first idea with us was combat. He wanted to see what we could do in the field together, an all-female team, water, desert, climbing, air, whatever was needed. There were two other women with Shylah, Bellisia and me. They were killed first time out. He was furious. They'd tried to escape rather than fight his army of supersoldiers." It had left the three of them to fight alone against the team he'd sent against them. "After that, when we were sent out, he held one of us back."

"You're stalling."

She was. She hated telling him the truth because she knew he'd look at her differently. Right now, he looked at her as if she needed him—and she did. He looked at her as if she could be the center of his world—and she knew she could be if given the chance. Her ability to drop someone in seconds would change everything.

"I can call up venom under my nails if necessary. One
rake and my enemy is dead."

He studied her face. "You had the ability to kill Zhu
and you resisted. You allowed him to torture you."

She nodded. "I had to. If I didn't, Cheng would know
for certain I was an agent. He didn't believe I was. Zhu
convinced Cheng I was what they thought I was—the
woman who developed the VALUE system and came to
various businesses to talk about it and answer questions.
As long as my cover was intact, the GhostWalker program
was safe. If they knew I was an agent, Cheng would have
a GhostWalker to take apart and study. I couldn't allow
that to happen no matter what."

He shook his head. "And you say you're not brave." He
caught her chin with two fingers and lifted her head. His
mouth brushed hers gently. "So, when I've got you coming apart in my arms and screaming my name while you
rake my back with your fingernails, are you going to
make certain you keep that venom under control?"

Her heart accelerated. It was a wonder she hadn't had
a heart attack around him yet. She nodded. "I think I can
do that, but I've never actually been that out of control.
Maybe we should try to find an antidote before we try it."

"What poison did he use?"

"Deathstalker scorpion, but he multiplied the strength
of the venom. It's lethal under most circumstances. I try
to control it, but it doesn't always work, depending on my
level of panic."

"You had to be panicked when Zhu was torturing you."

"There were others to think of, Gino. All of you. Bellisia and Shylah. Every person Whitney experimented on.
We don't need another Whitney, and trust me, Cheng would
have been far worse with his experiments. Whitney is a
patriot; Cheng has no one he is loyal to, unless it's Zhu."

"I can't get over you, woman, thinking you aren't brave. Does Bellisia know you have enough venom to protect yourself if needed?"

She nodded. "She encouraged me to try to learn to control it. She thought if I was out on a mission and someone did catch me, I could possibly scratch them lightly and get away. I'm not that good. I would never harm an innocent person or take the chance of harming one in order to protect myself like that. They'd never find the SSD, so they could never prove I stole their work. If I'm caught, I just have to ride it out, and in this case, it was a rough ride."

She looked down at her hands. "When we were on missions, it wasn't easy on either Bellisia or Shylah. I hated killing others. I could take them down, but I rarely could make myself finish them off. Bellisia or Shylah had to do it, whichever one was with me. The two of them covered for me all the time because Whitney detested that I couldn't do what he wanted. He would keep me up for days, having one of his soldiers screaming at me while I stood at attention that all I had to do was scratch the enemy's arm or neck or any part of his body and he was dead. Bellisia and Shylah sometimes lied and got caught and then they'd be punished in front of me."

Now he knew what a thief, a coward and a fraud she was. Yes, she had venom, but no, she didn't use it. Deep down she knew she could under extreme circumstances, like saving someone else's life. She would do it to save Gino. Or Bellisia. Or not do it to save them.

"Let's go for our picnic." Abruptly he changed the subject.

She was desperate to get out of the room. "Yes, please. I'm really excited about our trip. I like it here and want to get to know everyone better, but being inside is making me crazy."

"Give me a minute to finish putting the mosquito repellent on you."

He was touching her legs now, smoothing on the repellent. His hands were large and calloused. She liked the way his fingers glided over her skin, almost possessively. She wanted him to be possessive. "You stay here at this house," she said, trying to sound casual. "Do you have a home somewhere else? A place that's yours?"

He had turned away, rummaging in a drawer. "I've got a few of them. I bought property up by Trap, in the swamp. I've got a crew building now. All of us are establishing homes here. We're building a fortress, trying to put the Fontenot home in the middle. Wyatt has three kids and another on the way. He's got Nonny. We all claim them as family as well, so we're working to ensure their safety. Trap's place is nearly impenetrable now. That's our go-to in an emergency. I want to be close to that so my woman and any children we have together can get there fast. This is the swamp so underground tunnels require a lot of work. The water table is very high and it's dangerous, so we're coming up with other solutions."

He turned back to her with a fresh shirt. This wasn't the usual T-shirt. The blouse was a pale mint color with a small laced edge up either side of the front, closed by knotting the lacy edges under her breasts, really more of a cover-up than a blouse. It was hot outside. Sultry. The humidity in the swamp was off the charts. "Put your arms up."

Zara did so and he pulled the shirt she'd been wearing over her head and tossed it aside. He always was impersonal when he dressed her, and that was a little annoying. Still, it made it easier on her, so maybe it was easier that way on him.

The blouse was sexy, no question about it, and she wasn't certain who had bought it. He hadn't left her side for very long, a couple of hours here and there, maybe while she slept. It was very difficult to slide her arms into the sleeves and have him settle the material over the swell of her breasts and tie the knot just below them without reacting. Her nipples peaked, two hard temptations, pushing at the thin material as his knuckles rubbed her sensitive skin.

"There's a matching thong and sarong." He crouched down on the floor and put first one foot and then the other into the thong, pulling the scrap of mint green up to her thighs. "Can you lift up, princess?"

He wasn't as unaffected as his features said. His eyes had darkened with desire, with a lust that took her breath away as his gaze moved up her body. She lifted off the bed and he slid the thong over her hips, settling the thin mint lace just under her belly button.

"Turn over."

Heart beating hard, she complied with his order, rolling over and stretching out on the bed. His hand smoothed over her buttocks and then settled the little scrap of lace between her cheeks. His fingers dug into her flesh for a moment. "Does that hurt? At all? Tell me the truth, Zara."

She had to fight for air. "No." She didn't want him to take his hand away.

"I love the way you look laid out like this on my bed, sexy as fuck, woman. I'm warning you right now, as of today, things are changing between us." He smoothed his hand over her buttocks again and then caught at her arm to help her roll over and sit up.

Zara looked up at him, her body feeling hot and flushed. Deep inside that persistent throbbing beat at her.

"I've given you every opportunity to say you want out, and you haven't taken it. You could have asked Zeke and Bellisia to take over, but you didn't. Why?"

She touched her tongue to her lip, and his eyes went predatory. "I want to be with you."

"Do you understand what being with me means, Zara? You're almost completely healed. There's only your feet and resting them a couple of more weeks should have you walking. Maybe not running, but at least walking, and with physical therapy you'll be good. You don't need me as your doctor."

"I know." She did. She was terrified he'd decide she only wanted to stay with him because he'd rescued her. She knew that was what Bellisia thought, but the more time she'd spent with him, the more she wanted to be with him.

"Once you're mine, baby, there isn't any going back, so you be damn sure I'm what you want."

Just his voice, that soft bite, could command her complete attention no matter how quietly he spoke. A shiver went down her spine and little fingers of desire danced over her thighs.

"You are." She felt very daring telling him, but she meant it. She wanted what she'd had these last couple of weeks, this man, solid and confident, standing by her side, or in front of her. She didn't feel less around him, he made her feel more. "I'm certain, Gino."

His hand cupped the side of her face, his thumb sliding along her jaw. "I'm certain as well, princess. You're going to feel overwhelmed at times, and afraid. When you do, you come to me. You tell me what you're thinking and feeling at all times. That's important to me. I want to know the things that matter to you. The things you want. I'm talking about everything from household items to what you want or need in the bedroom."

She found herself blushing, but she nodded to let him know she understood. He always seemed to want her to talk to him and when she did, he listened to her. She hoped Bellisia had that from Ezekiel. They'd had each other and Shylah at the compound, but not a single person ever listened to a word they said, or cared when they were hurting or hungry or needed anything.

She needed to make the effort to reassure Bellisia she was happy with Gino. She also needed to make the effort to get to know Ezekiel. Misunderstandings were piling up and she was certain it was her fault. She loved Bellisia. She should never have lied to her about liking to travel.

She loved her work, and truthfully, she loved talking about it with anyone interested, but she didn't love the airports and people, the hotels and people, the strangers in the businesses. All those decisions when any moment she could say or do the wrong thing. She hated those. Bellisia would have understood. And she'd probably be more understanding of Gino as Zara's choice. It wasn't fair that she was expecting Bellisia to like Gino when she hadn't even taken the time to try to get to know and like Ezekiel. She vowed to talk to Bellisia when they got back home.

"Let's get your sarong on and get moving. I want to show you so many places in the swamp. I've put cushions in the boat, so hopefully you'll be comfortable."

"This is kind of see-through, don't you think?" She couldn't keep the amusement out of her voice. More than once, he'd hastily covered her up when someone came into the room and the T-shirt she was wearing had hiked up her thighs.

"It's meant to be a bathing suit cover-up. I didn't want you wearing the suit yet and having it press too tightly against your skin. This will hopefully make you feel covered, but still be cool enough. No one's going to see you where we're going."

She hoped not, because it was really see-through. Still, it made her feel beautiful, sexy and very desirable, something she wasn't used to, but wanted more of.

He reached for her, and helped her to stand gingerly on her feet. Pain flashed through her immediately but she stayed very still while he tied the mint, lacy sarong around her hips. It was just as thin as the blouse. She felt feminine and very sexy, but that was probably just the way Gino looked at her, not the clothes.

"Is this outfit the type of clothing you like me to wear?" Her voice sounded shaky and shy even to her.

"I love how you look right now, baby, but it's only for me. When we're alone together. Otherwise, you're covering up when we go out in public. I like the clothes you wear on your trips, they're classy."

"I chose them," she said, happy he liked the things she liked. The smile faded. "I like skirts. I'm kind of girly in how I like to dress."

"I like your 'girly' look, Zara. You want to wear skirts, wear them, as long as they aren't so short I want to yank you into the nearest closet and have my way with you."

She laughed. "You're so crazy. I like long skirts, but I wouldn't mind going into the closet with you, so I might go short if I think it would get me you."

"You have me, Zara. Anytime you want. When we're alone, I'd like you wearing the kinds of things I choose for you. You're so beautiful, and I like seeing your body. You going to give that to me?"

"It will take me some time to get to know what you like, Gino, but of course." Because who didn't want to feel sexy? It was exciting to think he wanted her to wear sexy lingerie for him. She wanted to be able to surprise him occasionally once she learned what he liked.

"I enjoy buying them for you, baby, but you'll get a feel for my preferences after a while. Until then we can shop together." He gave her another smile. "I won't mind if some of the time you go without your panties in your long, elegant skirt when you're talking to a roomful of brainiacs. I can sit there and wonder, is she? Or isn't she? The idea makes me hard as a fuckin' rock."

"You're so crazy." But she loved it. Loved the way he could make her feel so sexy and wanted.

"We've got to get moving, princess. I don't want to wait too long. Where I'm taking you is a distance away."

He put a tote bag with two towels sticking out of it into her arms and lifted her into his. He always cradled her close, tight against his chest. She inhaled him, taking his scent into her lungs. "I love the way you always smell." She was used to him carrying her and she buried her face in his neck, feeling very daring when she gave in to the impulse to touch her tongue to his skin, tasting him. She'd wanted to do it almost since she'd arrived at the Fontenot home, but she'd resisted.

He paused in the hallway, just outside the door to their room. "You're going to get yourself in trouble."

She lifted her head and looked into his eyes. "What happens when I get in trouble? Is it good or bad?"

"That depends." He started walking again. "We'll see what you think when it happens."

Just for that nonanswer, she scraped her teeth along the pulse beating so steadily in his neck. It wasn't fair. Her pulse was beating out of control, and his was as stable as a rock. She heard his breath hiss out in a long rush, but he didn't say anything. Satisfied that she got to him and that the terrible need building in her was also wreaking havoc with him, she lifted her head to catch that first glimpse of the river stretching out in the sun.

She could understand why Nonny and her husband had chosen this spot all those years ago. Sitting on the porch, one had the view and it was breathtaking. She could be happy sitting on a porch with Gino, holding hands, watching the sunset as she imagined Nonny had done with her husband.

"The land you bought, Gino, does it have river frontage?"

"Yes. It was important to have direct access to water, land and air."

"I was thinking more of porches in the evening," she admitted. "I guess I should think more about defending our home from Whitney and Zhu and anyone else who might come for us."

"You think about the sun setting and the two of us sitting on our porch. That's the point of you being with a man like me, Zara. You don't need to worry about whether or not you and the children are protected. If you know me, and you will get there, you'll never have to ask yourself that question."

He stepped carefully into the boat with her cradled against his chest. She didn't know how he could remain so balanced, especially with her in his arms. The boat rocked, but his body seemed to just go with it, uncaring as he stepped to the center to place her carefully on the thick cushions.

"Tell me if that feels all right. It's important to always tell me the truth. Few things get me pissed, Zara, but lies can get me there fast. There isn't any need for lies between us."

She nodded, knowing he meant every word of that. He was doing his best to show her who he was, so she understood what he expected in the relationship. He wanted her to do the same. She didn't know what to expect because not only hadn't she ever been in a relationship, she'd never seen one. She knew that was another reason Bellisia worried about her choosing Gino so fast. Bellisia knew Zara was going to have to follow Gino's lead, but what she didn't understand was that took all the worry and fear from her. She didn't have to be afraid she was doing the wrong thing.

"My bum feels quite all right, thank you, Gino," she informed him, swiveling around, trying to see everything all at once. She loved being outdoors, and the scenery was beautiful.

"We've got everything I think we need, including food. Drinks are in the cooler on ice. I brought a jacket for you just in case we come back late, and there're weapons in the locker right at your feet."

Her head went up, her eyes meeting his. "Are you expecting company?"

He shrugged. "Not really. Just being cautious. I like to plan for every contingency. Hang on, let's get moving."

The first fifteen minutes of the boat moving up the river toward the bay had her laughing and turning in her seat, trying to take in all the birds. Large white cranes walked on long legs in shallower water and others were in the trees on either side of the water. Everywhere she looked, there was something happening. Trees gave way to brush and then saw grass. Tall cypress trees rose up out of the water, knobby knees reaching toward the center of the river.

The current had picked up now that they were out in the open away from homes. The shallower waters gave way to deeper channels. She turned her face up to the sky and laughed. "Gino, thank you for this!" she shouted to him.

He put his thumb up, grinned at her and kept steering the boat straight down the river, clearly heading somewhere prearranged. Excitement skittered through her. She loved that she felt safe with Gino. She'd never felt safe, not even with Bellisia and Shylah. They hadn't either. Whitney had made certain of that. She wanted Bellisia to feel this safe with Ezekiel, and she wished, with all her heart, that Shylah could find her way to freedom and land somewhere safe, if not with them.

The boat slowed and she looked around her. They had gone through so many twists and turns, going into canals and even one shallow waterway that was a little scary—she'd been afraid the boat would get hung up—she wasn't certain where they were, but it didn't matter. The sandbar was right out in the sun and the water was pooled in a crater right in the center of the bar.

"The crater is formed of mostly smooth rock, looking like one solid piece about seven feet across and as many feet wide. You can look right down to the rock floor. It can't be more than five feet deep, maybe five and a half in the deepest center," he informed her. "Nice, clear water, no alligators."

"Wow. So cool," she said as he cut the engine to the boat. She loved the swamp. It was very humid, and a small bead of sweat trickled between her breasts.

"Wait right there," Gino cautioned as he made his way to her. He handed her a water bottle and then pulled the boat onto the sandbar before spreading a blanket and carrying the tote, picnic basket and drinks cooler onto the little bar.

Zara watched his every move, her breath caught in her throat. She could barely take her eyes off him. He'd given her so much. There was freedom in allowing him to make decisions when she had no idea how to live outside Whitney's compound. Still, she had to talk to Bellisia about Ezekiel, Trap and Wyatt. It wouldn't be right to put that burden on Gino without first consulting her "sister" about the other men.

He took the weapons from the locker next, and she found herself looking carefully around their little spot of paradise. Even here, deep in the swamp, surrounded by the intricate canals, a place she was lost in without Gino's guidance, he still worried about someone coming after them.

"Do you think Whitney has another team close by? Or Zhu? Did the person watching him tell you he's left Shanghai?" Apprehension crawled up her throat.

Gino didn't answer at once. He came back to her, moving like the predator he was, that fluid stalk that took her breath and made her heart pound. He stepped onto the boat, his weight making it rock slightly so that she clutched at the edge of the long bench seat she was perched on. He came right to her, crouching down so he was eye level with her.

"Princess, do you think, for one moment, I would take a chance on losing you? I went out this morning with three others scouting. No one has come near our piece of the swamp. Not close to Trap's, not where I'm building, not near Zeke and Bellisia's build, and not near the Fontenot home. If I thought you were in any kind of danger right now, I would have you locked up in the panic room. They'll come, but not today and not here. No one could have followed us the way I came, not without me noticing."

He picked her up and she wrapped her arms around his neck, relaxing into his hold. She could enjoy their afternoon together without worry. "Where was everyone?"

He must have known she was talking about Bellisia. She desperately wanted to talk to her and straighten things out between them.

"Zeke took Bellisia to the bay. He said sometimes she needs to swim in salt water. He's been keeping her hydrated. Apparently, she has a difficult time if she's not soaking in water daily." Gino put her down on the blanket. He was gentle about it.

She didn't hurt nearly as much as she had before. It was easy to be aware of the difference when she was sitting on a sandbar, with only a thin piece of material and a blanket between her and the ground. Granted, he'd brought a thicker blanket, but her bottom didn't hurt at all when she put her weight on it.

"Nonny took Cayenne, Pepper and the girls into town to shop, so they have a large escort," he continued.

Zara was elated that all of them had gone into town together. That meant life could be somewhat normal, even if they had an escort to do it.

"Is it always this humid?" Little beads of sweat formed on her skin and trickled down the valley between her breasts. She was grateful she wasn't wearing tons of clothing. The rock pool looked very inviting.

Gino nodded. "Pretty much. I'm used to it now."

"I'll get used to it too." She took the bottle of water he handed to her and drank, letting the ice-cold liquid slide down her throat. Her gaze flicked from the pool back to him and found he was looking at her throat as she swallowed. The blood in her veins turned to a slow, molten heat, moving through her entire body. Tension coiled deep. She had to do something or she was going to start begging for more kisses. It seemed like she was always asking him to kiss her and really, it had to come from him. "It's hot."

"You can cool off in the pool."

She nodded. It seemed like a good idea. Already he could see her nipples were hard right through the nearly transparent material of the bathing suit cover-up. "I'd like that."

Gino immediately rose and carried a small flat cushion to the edge of the natural rock basin. He added two folded towels, tucking several weapons into one of the towels. She watched him, her heart in her throat, shocked at how much pleasure she got just being with him, just anticipating spending the rest of the day with him.

12

~

Gino glanced down at Zara's face as he lifted her into his arms and carried her to the edge of the pool where he'd put the cushion for her to sit on. "You want to go in, you let me take you in. Don't just drop down. The floor of the pool is hard rock."

She was so beautiful, she took his breath away. He didn't understand how she could be looking at a man like him, not when she was intelligent, gorgeous, sweet beyond imagining and so perfect, but he wasn't about to throw away his one chance at happiness.

"Will do. It's stunning out here." A slight breeze had kicked up, just enough to fan her face when the humidity threatened to keep her from breathing.

"Listen to it," Gino said and dragged off his boots and then his jeans. "The swamp has its own sound. Its own rhythm." He was going to let her see what she did to him, get used to the idea of his naked body. He'd seen hers a hundred times, tempting him. Looking at her now, he had no idea how he managed to resist her.

He wasn't wearing a stitch by the time she stopped looking around at the scenery. She nearly squeaked but managed to suppress the sound before it got loose. Her eyes dropped to his cock and went wide with shock. Then her mouth opened. He very casually tossed a towel beside her on the rock and after throwing his shirt to one side, sank down beside her.

He threaded his fingers in her hair. "Haven't you ever seen a man's body before?"

She swallowed and nodded. Kept staring. "You're absolutely beautiful. Your body." Her tone was almost reverent.

It was the last thing he expected her to say. He had scars. More than a few. Muscles. Clothes hid his strength, but he knew his body could be intimidating.

"I grew up in Whitney's compound. He didn't believe in a woman being modest. We were put on earth to serve a man. We were used for experiments. Emotions didn't matter to him, in fact, they only got in the way."

"Women serving men. Don't know about that. I got myself a beautiful princess. If anyone is serving anyone, it would be the other way around." He massaged her scalp, loving the feel of all that hair, like silk. It gleamed red in the sun. The gold was there, like the sun's rays. His heart threatened to beat out of his chest, which shocked the holy hell out of him. He was a man always in control and yet, with Zara, that control seemed to go right out the window.

"Gino." She took a deep breath. "I really want this. I do, but you're never going to fit."

He couldn't help but smile. "I'll fit, baby. You'll be ready for me by the time we get there, I promise. Keep breathing. Listen to the music around us. I want you to relax, not be afraid of anything. We don't have to do a single thing until you're ready. If that means a month from now, or two months from now, I'm okay with that."

"You are?"

"I'm not going to lie, Zara. I want you with every cell in my body, and I think you can see that." His cock was harder than he ever remembered it and he hadn't touched her yet. Just looking at her in that sheer top, her breasts teasing the hell out of him was enough to make his blood thunder in his ears.

He circled his shaft with his fist, wishing it was her hand, but knowing he had to take it slow with her. Sweat dotted his forehead. More trickled down his chest. His gaze jumped to her breasts, where a small bead ran down that intriguing valley. Her nipples were taut, not flat. She was aroused, he could tell by the change in her breathing. The last thing he wanted was for her to be scared of his body.

Gino cupped the side of her face, turned her toward him and took her mouth. He forced himself to be gentle, coaxing her response, not taking it. One hand slipped over her breast, over her heart to feel it flutter. Her lips were cool, her mouth hot. She leaned into him, wrapping her arms around his neck to bring him closer. He didn't move into her, controlling her body the way he controlled the kiss.

Heat rushed through his veins, a silken fire that moved through every cell, infusing him with her, so much hotter and stronger than he expected with his gentle, very tender kiss. He fought himself, as need pulsed through him and hunger coiled deep. Her mouth was addicting, her taste elusive, like some fine wine he couldn't quite catch all the various subtle flavors of. He needed more. So much more.

She dug her fingers into his shoulders, kissing him back, her mouth soft, chasing his, wanting more. Frantic for more. He liked that. He even needed it from her. Forcing himself to stop, he lifted his head and smiled at her. "You're not going to get your way yet, princess." Because

God help them, if she pressed her body against his right now, his control would go up in flames.

Little beads of sweat dotted her skin and he wanted to lick every one of them off. Trace the ones running between her breasts and find the tight buds that pushed against the sheer material. He was torturing himself by getting her that cover-up.

She looked up at him, those long lashes fluttering, sending little flames burning through his belly. "Why?"

He slipped off the rock into the pool and reached for her. Hands around her waist, he pulled her into the cooler water. He needed it more than she did. It didn't help. Nothing was going to help. He'd been obsessed with her from the moment he'd read the file they had on her. The moment someone had said her name.

Living with her these weeks, lying on the floor beside the bed, or in it with her, inhaling her scent, feeling her soft skin, looking at all those curves, had made that obsession grow until he could barely stand being away from her. He wanted to know where she was and what she was doing, if she was happy, if she was upset. He told himself it was insanity, but it didn't matter, intellect didn't take away the intense emotion he was feeling for her.

The water felt good on his hot skin. Even better, it soaked through the thin material of her sarong and blouse until it was so transparent, she might as well not have been wearing a stitch. He didn't let her feet take all her weight, but allowed her to stand, the water and his hands holding her.

"Why?" she repeated, a little more demanding.

He laughed softly. "You're going to be a handful."

"You're not answering me," she pointed out.

He took her hand and guided it to his cock. She closed her fingers around the hard shaft and looked up at him shyly. Expectantly. Lust swept through him. His cock felt like a steel spike, and in her hand, it grew even more, hardened even more until she looked intimidated, but excited all the same. He could see desire growing in her eyes. Her breasts moved temptingly with every ragged breath she took.

"That's why, Zara. I'm not having your first time with me be out here, and I'm not nearly as in control as I thought I could be. Playing is one thing, but we're going to have to be careful."

Zara scowled up at him and turned her face against his bare chest and tasted his skin. He tasted the way she expected—amazing. Perfect. All Gino. She had read countless books on sex. She'd read the Kama Sutra, and just about everything else she could get her hands on. She was, after all, very good at research. Nothing prepared her for the real thing. The way she would feel with her body so close to his. With his cock, thick and hard, in her fist.

She pumped that hot, rigid part of his anatomy, feeling that silken glide. The water wasn't nearly as cold as it needed to be to keep her from feeling like she might go up in flames. He might think he was going to control every situation, but Zara wasn't about to let him. Not when it came to having sex with him. She knew all about temptation, and she was determined to drive him to the very brink of his control—and beyond.

Her mouth traveled over his chest, her tongue finding every defined muscle, tasting, sucking, using her teeth very gently to nip him and then her tongue to ease the sting. Every time she did it, his breath hitched in his lungs and his cock jerked in her hand. She kept the pumping up, her fist lazily gliding, while her mouth moved over his chest. If it wasn't driving him crazy, it certainly was taking her close to the edge and she loved the feeling of wanting him. He was becoming a need, not a want, his body hot, hard and all hers. Tension coiled hot inside her, drawing tighter and tighter. All the while her clit pulsed and throbbed in need.

Her tongue flicked his nipple and then she suckled there, her tongue dancing over him. She lifted her head and looked up at him from under her long lashes. "Does playing include me doing this to your cock?"

His shaft, enclosed in her hand, thickened, widening in spite of her tight fist, heating until she thought he would scorch her palm. He felt like a combination of silk and steel.

"If you want it to." His voice was husky.

"I want," she said, and pushed her body closer to his while her hand left his shaft and dropped lower to caress the velvet texture of his sac. His balls were tight and hard, just like his cock. She rolled them gently, exploring with her fingers and palm while she kissed her way up his throat. She moved one leg so she was straddling his thigh, pushing against him with her nearly naked body. That thin strip between her lips didn't do a thing to stop her from feeling his bare thigh against her clit. She rubbed back and forth.

"Zara." There was warning in his voice.

She ignored it and kissed his throat, then his jaw, before pulling back to look up at him. She knew he'd look down and see that transparent material over her breasts, her nipples erect, every breath rising and falling for him. His dark gaze left her face and she heard his breath rush from his lungs. Her hand found his cock again just as his hands both came up to cup her breasts, pushing them together and right out of the open edges of the cover-up. Then his mouth was on her breast and her world went up in flames.

She cried out, shocking herself with the intensity of feeling. She had no idea her body could feel so good, so needy and so desperate all at one time. His hand was on one breast, kneading and massaging, his mouth on the other, sucking, his tongue and teeth alternating, doing something delicious that sent spikes of electricity straight to her sex.

"Wrap your legs around my waist." He hissed the command against her nipple as he caught both of her arms, tugged them up and put them around his neck.

She felt the heat of his breath against her skin. Obediently she lifted her legs around his waist, ankles hooking behind him.

"Are you all right, Zara? I need to hear you say it."

She was nodding, but she managed to get out a verbal answer. "Yes. Absolutely." And she was, there wasn't even a twinge of pain on her breasts. Only pleasure. And she wanted more.

She leaned back, throwing her head back as he latched on to her breasts once again. She pressed her mound tight against his abdomen, wishing it was his cock. Her hips bucked when his teeth pulled at her nipple. There had to be a straight line to her sex, because every time he did it, a lash of sizzling heat struck her clit and then continued deep into her core. That stroke set flames roaring through her until she was nearly writhing in his arms.

He cursed, and set her up on the edge of the pool again, prying her hands from around his neck. Pulling himself out of the water, he caught her up and took her to the blanket before she had time to get out a word. "You'd better tell me if anything hurts, Zara."

The warning in his voice should have scared her, but instead, that firestorm in her got loose and swept through her body until she couldn't breathe or think. She just needed. His voice was sexy, nearly hoarse with a desire so dark it seemed like pure lust. She wanted that. Wanted him to feel the way she did—desperate.

"I will, just do something. I need you right now, Gino."

"Baby, we haven't even gotten started." His hands were

at the knot below her breasts. He dragged the cover-up from around her, wrung it out and laid it on a rock in the sun. He pulled off the sarong and did the same thing. The tiny thong was gone with a quick jerk of his hand, leaving her body bare to him. "You are so fuckin' beautiful, woman. Just looking at you gets me hard."

"I want you in my mouth," she said. "Please, Gino. I've thought about it a lot and want to learn exactly what you like. Let me try. You can tell me what to do. I like when you do that because then I feel as if I'm not going to do anything wrong."

All those books had given her tricks to try, and she and her sisters had laughingly practiced on bananas, but it wasn't the same as the real thing. He was much bigger and harder than anything she'd tried practicing on. She also hadn't counted on the fact that she was really desperate for him. She craved the taste of him, the hot feel of him in her mouth. She hadn't expected that.

"You sure, princess? I'm not small."

She wasn't blind. She shifted to her knees and circled his hips with one arm.

Gino thought his head was going to explode the moment her hand slid around the base of his cock. Her body was beautiful, the lacerations faded other than two places that were still raw and red looking. He would have to be careful when he touched her, to make certain he didn't get carried away when he caught her hips in his hands.

His fingers bunched in the silky hair she'd fastened on top of her head. "All right, Zara, just do a little exploring. Don't use your teeth, but everything else is going to feel good."

Her eyes came to his and all air blasted out of his lungs at the look she gave him. Not shy, not even innocent. She looked sexy as hell, a teasing temptress bent on his destruction. And damn him to hell, he was okay with that. He was willing to be destroyed by her.

She opened her mouth and let him guide his cock right in. He watched the head disappear and then another inch. His girth stretched her lips around him, and reality was far better than any fantasy he'd had over that bow of a mouth. That hot, moist cavern was tight, and he pumped, thrust his hips deeper while her tongue did some crazy twisted dance over his shaft. He'd thought he was going to have to go with extreme care, but she was already taking over, sucking at him until he thought the world was going to come apart before they even got started.

"I thought you didn't know what you were doing." He had to grit his teeth and struggle for control. She was that good. She looked sexy as hell with his cock sliding in and out of her mouth, her lips stretched so wide and her eyes on his. Her breasts were perfect, nipples tight buds, and between her legs, moisture gleamed in her red curls, showing him she was definitely into what she was doing. He wanted that picture etched in his mind forever.

She slid her tongue up his shaft and smiled at him with the crown right against her lips. "I read a lot and then I practiced."

"Who the fuck did you practice on?" He knew better than to ask. He'd want to hunt them down and cut out their hearts.

She licked him like he was a fucking ice-cream cone while he waited heartbeat after heartbeat. His hand fisted tighter in her hair, a little warning. He always knew he'd be a jealous man, but he wasn't prepared for the monster in him rising, right then, adding to that roaring of his blood in his cock and the thunder of chaos in his mind.

"Silly man. Not who. What. Bananas and cucumbers are the only things I had, so I made do. Hopefully I learned. I was all about learning to please my man."

She was going to kill him. He wasn't surviving this woman. He caught the back of her head and guided her once more onto his cock. "Need more, baby." His princess looked more than royal, with her hot little body and a mouth full of his cock. She was the kind of woman a man wanted to keep in his life and if he didn't, he was just plain fucked-up. Gino knew her worth and he wasn't about to ever be that fuckup. He was going to make certain she came first for him.

Then he couldn't think anymore. Every altruistic thought left his head as she began to move on him, her mouth so hot and tight that he swore streaks of fire were running from his groin to his spine, racing up to his brain and down to his toes. His fingers gripped her hair harder, fisting there, guiding her now, his hand working with hers.

He could feel her fingers digging into the muscles of his butt, pulling him into her, while her mouth tightened and her tongue stroked and danced. Then he was there, hitting the back of her throat, and she fought to control her gag reflex. She managed and he didn't pull her off as he held himself in paradise for a few heartbeats longer before he let her have air.

"What kind of book taught you this? And don't fuckin' try to answer." He was already making it impossible, pushing deep into that hot, wet world of pure pleasure. He loved watching himself disappear into her mouth, watching her wet lips stretch and her eyes widen as he fed his cock to her.

She was doing things he'd never experienced, things no doubt she'd read in books, but they were driving him right out of his mind. He'd had blow jobs, many of them, but nothing like this. He had no idea if it was because he was already so far gone on her or because she really was that good. And it was that fucking good. Any more and he was going to blow.

"Have to stop, baby, or you're going to be swallowing, and most women aren't down for that." He couldn't quite pull her off him. He should. He knew he should, but he couldn't.

She didn't stop, and all that pent-up seed, despite the many times he'd relieved himself in the shower, came boiling up like a fucking volcano and he blew big. Blasted like rockets. She did her best as he pumped long ropes in her mouth. She took it too, his woman, swallowing him down as if he was feeding her candy. It was sexy as hell to him, seeing his seed sliding out of her mouth and down her chin.

"Gentle," he cautioned when her mouth still suckled. He was more sensitive than he'd ever been.

She followed his warning carefully, her mouth gliding over him as his cock relaxed, although he wasn't as sated as he thought he'd be. She was too damned sexy, and what she'd just done for him was the most amazing gift she could have given him. He was going to find that book, frame it and put it on the wall.

He eased his hands out of her hair. "You okay?" His fingers found his seed on her mouth and chin, scooped it up and fed it to her. She obeyed his silent command and licked his fingers clean. "Need to know, princess, are you okay?"

She nodded, her gaze still on his. "Was it good for you?" There was anxiety in her eyes, in her voice. She didn't have a clue.

"Holy fucking mother, woman, what do you think? I've never had anything so good, and it was your first time."

She smirked. "I practiced a lot."

"What else did you practice?"

"I tried to smuggle all of us toys, you know, vibrators so we could feel what it was like, but I got caught. I spent two weeks in solitary for that one."

"That man was a bastard." He handed her a bottle of water and watched her throat work. "You ever try to deep throat one of your substitutes? Relax your throat and swallow it? Hold it there for a minute or so?"

She nodded. "It's harder than you think it might be. I

practiced that a lot too. Bellisia or Shylah would convince
my guard I needed bananas when I was in solitary to keep
my blood sugar up. I was there quite often until I got better at smuggling contraband, so I didn't have a lot of other
things to do."

He let out a groan. "Woman, you're killing me. We're
going to get some contraband and I'll show you all kinds
of things we can do with it. I like the idea of watching you
get yourself off with a vibrator. Or me getting you off
with one while you practice that deep-throating tech-
nique. The images you're putting in my head are never
going to go away."

"Good images, I hope." There was that smirk again,
but she deserved to smirk.

"Better than good. I'm going to do something with you
that I bet you haven't tried." He waited until she drank the
full bottle of water. "Lie on your back. If anything hurts,
you tell me immediately, understand, baby? We'll find
another position, we won't stop, so don't think that and be
stoic. This isn't about pain, it's all about pleasure."

Zara swallowed hard, her heart accelerating out of
control. He looked so powerful. All those muscles. Without clothes, she could see every muscle in his body—and
he had a lot of them. Part of her was excited to see what
was going to happen, and another part of her was filled
with trepidation. She lay back slowly and found she had
to shade her eyes against the sun when she tried to look at
him. That gave her the impression of the mask, his face
dark, the shadow on his jaw pronounced, his eyes so black
they gleamed at her like a marauder's.

He pulled her thighs apart, fingers tight on her skin,
not letting her move once he created space for his body.
When he slipped between her legs, he lay on his belly and
used his shoulders as a wedge to keep her thighs apart.
Her breath caught in her throat. She wasn't certain she
could actually pull air into her lungs.

"Gino?" She needed reassurance. Fear skittered down her spine. She loved doing things to him, but wasn't so certain how she was supposed to react when he did things to her. She'd read about that too, but even when she touched herself, nothing huge had happened. Now she felt totally vulnerable.

"Trust me, Zara. Just give yourself to me and relax. Let me show you how good this can be."

His tone was that strange dark one that both mesmerized and compelled her to do whatever he asked. She took a deep breath and allowed herself to sink into a place where she felt free to turn everything over to him. It was such a dichotomy, the fact that she could be afraid and yet feel safe with him. Maybe "fear" wasn't the right word; maybe it was "trepidation," because she didn't know what was coming.

Her sex clenched the moment his gaze went from her eyes to her body. Just the expression on his face sent liquid heat moving inside her. He looked feral, more savage than human. She loved that particular expression, especially since his features were stamped with pure possession. The lines in his face were sensual, purely carnal, lust mingling with hunger and need. She liked that she was his and that he thought of her that way.

She felt his breath first and her entire body jumped. Air rushed from her lungs. She felt the hard bristles along his jaw move up her thigh, first one side and then the other until desire danced up her legs and filled her core. Soft kisses on the insides of her thighs drove her wild. Stinging nips, soothed by his tongue, sent jagged shock waves whipping through her body. Then his mouth was on her and he was devouring her, as if she was the finest, most exotic candy in his world.

Zara was unprepared for the sheer feelings overwhelming her. She had no idea her body was even capable of reacting with such fire and sensitivity. Every stroke of his tongue, the raking of his teeth, the greedy way he attacked was overpowering. Her body took on a life of its own, winding tighter and tighter until she thought she might lose her mind. She had no idea she was chanting his name until her lungs were burning for air and she had to stop to inhale.

Lightning seemed to strike through her body as that tension coiled and her body burned. Panic set in, but there was his voice talking to her in that whisper of dark, intimate velvet, commanding her to relax and let go for him. She'd do just about anything for him and her body always seemed to obey him, relaxing into the heat of his mouth and the stroke of his tongue. Fire raced, a million colors burst behind her eyes and she was thrown into the sky, soaring with constellations she didn't even know the names of.

Heart pounding like wild, eyes on his, she opened her mouth, but nothing came out. He grinned at her, shamelessly smug.

"Let's see if you can do that again," he said.

She shook her head, her gaze dropping to his body. So hard. So perfect. He'd come up on his knees, and she could see the heavy erection. Evidently, he'd enjoyed what he'd been doing to her almost as much, or more than she had. She couldn't imagine more, but that wasn't what she wanted.

"Not again?"

Did he look disappointed? "I want you inside me, Gino." She tried to sound assertive and firm.

"Baby." He let out another soft groan. "Don't tempt the devil. I'm trying to do right by you. The surface is hard. A mattress would feel a whole hell of a lot better. As it is, twice I nearly caught at your hips and I would have touched those lacerations that aren't quite healed. I don't want any pain for you when we come together."

"I know what I want, and I'm not feeling pain at all. Just the opposite." She kept her gaze fixed on his so he could see she meant it. She knew him well enough now to know if he decided against it, there would be no changing his mind, not even if she pulled out some of her seduction tricks she'd read about.

"Princess." His voice had gone husky. Sexy. Hypnotic. "You have to be certain. I planned this out in the bedroom where you'd be comfortable, not here where the ground is hard."

"I want here. I love being here with you, and this place is magic to me. I'm not hurting at all. I swear, I would tell you immediately."

He closed his eyes for a moment and she thought she'd lost. Her heart pounded. She counted her breaths, her heartbeats. She moved her body subtly, widening her legs, arching just a little so it drew attention to her breasts. He groaned, and she knew she won.

"All right, baby. I've got a couple of condoms in my wallet and we're going to protect you." He reached for his jeans, dragged them to him and pulled out his wallet and then a foil packet. "I've got two in here. That's the limit, Zara."

One of his hands rubbed her thigh, the other cupped the slickness between her legs. She gasped as he pushed a finger into her. It was slow, but she felt every inch.

"You're tight, princess, and I'm . . ." He broke off, shaking his head. "Your first time is going to hurt. There's no getting around that. I can be careful and make it as good as I can, but it can hurt."

He looked around at their surroundings and then back down to her body, laid out in front of him like a feast. She wasn't afraid and, although the pain part didn't sound great, she'd read about that too and knew what to expect. From that first moment of partial freedom, when she'd attended school outside the compound, she had realized that men and women gravitated toward one another. She'd wanted what others had. A man. A home. Children. She had been determined to be ready in case the opportunity was ever given to her. She had been unwavering in her desire to be the best partner for her man she could be.

She stretched her arms above her head, and lifted her hips, rocking a little. "I want you right now, Gino. I want to know I'm your woman. If it's going to hurt here, it's going to hurt in the bedroom."

His hand fisted his cock absently, doing several lazy pumps while he looked at her body lying there. A faint sheen covered her skin where tiny drops of water remained from the pool.

"Cup your breasts, baby. Remember what I did to your nipples? Do the same thing for me. I want to watch you."

She didn't know if that meant yes, but she followed his instructions exactly. Her body was already in a heightened state and just the brush of her fingers on her nipples sent streaks of fire straight to her clit. She gasped, and rocked her hips more, trying to assuage the terrible need building in her just from watching Gino's fist sliding on his cock and that one long finger pumping in and out of her. It wasn't nearly enough, and her breath came out in ragged little pants she couldn't control.

He pushed a second finger into her along with the first. It felt . . . too much. Too tight. Burning. Just the way he said. She gasped and pinched and rolled and tugged more. Harder. Needing the fire to overcome the burn.

"Relax, princess. The more you relax, the easier this is going to be."

Her body was already listening to him, the tension going out of her muscles, and almost immediately, the two fingers fit. She took another deep breath and let it out as he scissored them, stretching her even more. It felt unexpectedly sexy. Maybe it was the way he looked, kneeling over her like a conquering warrior.

"You're so fucking beautiful, Zara. I love that you do exactly what I ask of you, that you trust me that much."

Just the way he looked at her was a turn-on. Every sense she had was heightened, so acute, her skin was sensitive to the slightest brush of her fingers. His eyes were so black, so feral, the lines in his face carved deep with lust. There was that mixture of lust and some deep emotion she wanted to call love because that was the accepted word. Whatever it was, it was all for her and she gave herself completely to him.

Gino pulled his two fingers away from her and her body tried to follow them. He brought them to his mouth and licked them clean. "I love the way you taste. All mine. No one else is ever going to have that."

She liked that too. Watching him roll on the condom was hot. She didn't know why, but just seeing the glove come over his cock was exciting—although she was greedy enough to want to know how he felt inside her without it.

He caught her bottom in his hands and pressed the broad head of his cock to her entrance. He felt a lot bigger than his two fingers had.

"Just relax, Zara. You're giving yourself to me. Your body is a gift I'll always treasure. You'll never have to worry that I'll forget about taking care of it or you. Even now, this first time when we both know it's going to be a little uncomfortable, I'll make certain you feel pleasure."

His voice was so gravelly it was almost harsh, but it moved over her skin like the touch of fingers. Eyes on his, she nodded as he pushed steadily through her tight folds. She did her best not to tense up, but the burn wasn't a good one. She felt stretched beyond what she could handle. She shook her head. "I don't think this is going to work." She wanted it to, but it really did sting. Okay—hurt.

"I'll fit, princess. You were made for me. It's just difficult at first."

He retreated and then pushed in a second time. Slowly. Steadily. She couldn't decide if the sting was better or worse. The third time, he pulled out, replaced his cock with his mouth, and she nearly came apart again. Liquid heat nearly dripped like honey. Then his cock was back, and this time it was easier with her sheath slick.

He caught her buttocks in his hands, pausing. "Keep your eyes on mine. I want you to pinch your nipples hard. Right now."

She obeyed and he surged forward. Fire flashed straight to her sex, mixing with the blast of pain as he took her innocence. Then he was all the way in, buried deep, and she surrounded him. She felt every inch of him. His girth stretching her madly. The long thick vein. The way his cock pulsed with energy and hunger. Every one of his heartbeats. She didn't take her eyes from his, but she breathed deeply, trying to decide if she wanted to cry or beg him to move.

He remained very still, her muscles clutching him tightly, holding him in a vise. She didn't look away from his eyes, obeying his directive, feeling held by him, feeling soothed by the way his gaze held hers. The stinging and burning subsided slowly and her muscles began to ease their panicked grip on him.

"Feel better?"

There was pure gravel in his voice. The sound moved over her, stroking her skin, bringing her body to a fever pitch. His eyes were so intense for a moment she couldn't find her own voice to answer him. He looked like sin incarnate. If he was the devil, and she knew he wasn't from heaven, she wanted to burn in hell with him.

She nodded.

"Baby, I want to hold you, but if I lie on you, my hips are going to be cradled in yours and those lacerations might tear open even more. Just keep looking at me." Now his voice slid over her like velvet. She shivered. Trembled. Was desperate for something out of reach that only he could provide.

She nodded again, moving her hips experimentally. That got her a smile from him and it took what remained of her breath away. She noticed he didn't do it that often around anyone else, and that made it all the more sensual and intimate.

Gino stared down at the woman who had somehow wrapped herself around his heart. He didn't know how it had happened or even when, only that he couldn't do without her. She was beautiful to him, physically astoundingly gorgeous, but more than her looks, she was everything he wanted in a woman. He'd never considered that his dream woman really existed, or that if she did, he would find her.

Gino had no real respect for authority. He *was* the authority. Arrogant, yeah. Completely confident. Absolutely. Dominant. No question. He could be as cold as ice, not feeling a thing. He didn't mind what others thought of him and he didn't mind fucking someone up.

Zara was intelligent and had a sense of humor. She was soft inside. Empathetic. Sweet as candy. She followed his lead without hesitation. She never wanted to hurt a single soul. He was the complete opposite of her. She was quiet and soothed the demon in him, when he wanted to do violence to the world in general.

He wanted his woman to be *his*. He didn't want to share her with the rest of the world. Not in the sense that Zara couldn't go out and share her work, he'd be proud of her for that. It was about her focus. Her center. He needed to be that for her—and he was. He needed to be able to tell her what to do at times and have her do it just because she wanted to please him. He needed her trust in him. It was a lot to ask of a woman and he knew that. In return, he would give her anything and everything. He had the means and the desire. He needed to know he was her obsession, just as she was his. Maybe it was a fucked-up way to love, but it was his way.

He waited until he felt the viselike grip of her tight inner muscles relax their hold on his cock. Taking a breath, watching her closely, he withdrew slowly, feeling the friction around his shaft. The pleasure/pain was almost too much. It felt like a thousand fingers gripped him tightly and massaged. Her eyes widened, and he surged forward. Her mouth opened in shock. Her breasts gave a sexy jolt, jiggling for him, drawing his attention so he wanted to fill his mouth with her.

Moving in her body was paradise. Fire radiated from his groin, spreading out of control down his thighs and up to his belly. Flames rolled there, hotter than hell, hotter than anything he'd ever experienced. He knew she would be like this—surrounding him with that silken fist that was so tight he thought his head might explode.

Every time he withdrew to thrust forward, he wasn't certain if his cock could make its way through her sheath until he was buried deep. He was as gentle as possible, when he wanted to throw caution to the wind and drive home over and over, as hard and fast and as deep as possible. This was all for her. He tried to make it that way, but it was almost impossible when she was practically strangling his shaft. The head of his cock felt like it might explode. He could feel each surge of hot liquid as he pushed deep.

Her face and body flushed. Her eyes had gone wide with a kind of shock. Her hair had come loose, or maybe he'd pulled it free, and it was all around her, spread on the blanket like red flames glinting at him in the sun. Her body nearly glowed from the water, humidity and beads of sweat. Every hard thrust had her breasts jolting, the action drawing his attention to the curves of her body and the way his cock disappeared into her. Was swallowed whole. He fucking loved that. He felt every breath she took right through his cock. Every movement of her body, that was how tightly she gripped him.

Lightning streaked through his body, lashing his cock. He'd never been restrained. Not ever. When he took a woman, he took her hard. He satisfied the needs of his body, the violence that was always with him and always would be. He would take her the way he needed, he knew that, but not until she was ready. Right now, with his body a firestorm burning through him, he fought to make it right for her. To make it good for her. She mattered to him, and he was determined to stay in control to give her this.

Zara was the one woman who could bring him to his knees, figuratively and literally. His body trembled, trying to hold back. Looking at her spread out before him, the trust in her eyes, the rising pleasure, feeling those tight muscles begin to clamp down harder, more urgently, sent a firestorm sweeping over his cock and up through his body.

A shiver of awareness crept down his spine. He loved her. He was so in love with this woman. Zara Hightower. It hadn't been instant, even though they'd been together a few short weeks, but they'd spent just about every minute of every day together. Ordinarily, that would have driven him crazy. Now, he couldn't imagine being without her, and when he was away, he thought about her all the time. She would always be his obsession, his one and only love.

Her breath hitched. She was close. "Keep looking at me, baby. When I tell you, let go. Not before. Hold on until I say."

He wanted to watch her give that to him, see the beauty on her face. He wanted to know she'd hold on, even as inexperienced as she was, just because he asked. He wanted to feel her body take his, sweep him up in the sensual, overwhelming tsunami overtaking her.

Her fists clenched in the ground blankets, fingers dragging the material into her palm. Her head thrashed from side to side and little chanting sobs—his name and "please" escaped—but through it all, she never once took her gaze from his. Fuck. He loved her all the more for that. There was power and a feeling of humbleness. She was his, but it was her choice. Always her choice. This incredible woman had chosen him.

"Now, baby. Let go for me."

Her breath hissed out of her lungs in a rush along with a small scream that stilled the insects droning around them. Her sheath bit down hard on his cock, the hot, silken muscles milking him, forcing his seed to erupt like a volcano, bursting from him in powerful jets. Lights played behind his eyes and pure, fiery pleasure danced down his spine, up his legs and through his chest while her body drained him dry. It was an unexpectedly explosive reaction for him when he'd been so careful to be gentle, even tender with her.

He fought to get his breathing back as the fire subsided, the flames receding from his spine, dancing their way back to his roaring cock. He waited until the last possible aftershock of her body, wanting to experience all of it with her. Every second he could get. Every tiny feeling. All the while he watched her face for signs of discomfort.

Very slowly, he pulled out, seeing the evidence of her innocence staining the condom. He knotted it and set it aside to take away. He didn't believe in ever leaving indication of his passing out in the swamp. Stretching out next to her, he wrapped his arm around her waist and kissed her. God, he loved kissing her.

"You all right, princess?" He lifted his head to look at her.

She bit her lip and nodded, but her gaze slipped away from his. He didn't like that, but he didn't call her on it.

"I had no idea it would feel like that. That was more than amazing, it was beautiful. Once I got used to your size, it didn't hurt at all. I had no idea what I was missing."

She sat up slowly, and he let her. Let her scoot a little distance from him. She was still within arm's length so he wasn't concerned; he knew he could get to her if she tried to escape. He just waited until she let him know what was bothering her, and something clearly was.

"You're very good at this, aren't you?" she finally ventured.

He knew immediately he had to be careful. He promised himself he would always give her honesty, even if it meant they'd have to work through scary issues. He didn't make the mistake of giving her a smug grin or one hint of cockiness. To her, this wasn't humorous. "What are you getting at, baby?"

"That you've had a lot of experience."

"I'm not going to lie to you, Zara, I've certainly had my share of women. For one thing, I've got money. Women like money, and the thought of marrying it spread a lot of legs."

She winced and drew her knees up tight to her chest. "That doesn't sound very nice."

"I told you, I'm not a nice man. Yeah, I definitely went through a lot of women. It was easy. Eventually, it got old, so there weren't so many lately, just enough to give me relief when I needed it." He cupped the side of her face, his thumb sliding over her lower lip. "I don't cheat. I'm not a cheater, and I wouldn't do that to you. There's no divorce unless I'm physically or mentally abusive, in which case you take your ass straight to the men in my unit and let them know what's going on. Or if I cheat. I do that, baby, and you're welcome to take me to the cleaners."

"I don't know what that means."

"It means you'll be set for life. I may have had a lot of experience, Zara, but there aren't going to be other women for me. I swear that to you. I don't need variety, that was never the reason I screwed around a lot."

She moistened her lips. "I don't have any experience.

You're really good at this, Gino, but you have to tell me what to do half the time. You're the first man I ever kissed."

Gino leaned closer, this time brushing his mouth gently over hers. He told her the strict truth and hoped she could hear the honesty in his voice. "No other man ever gets your taste in his mouth. He never gets your kisses. He doesn't get any part of your body. I fucking love that, baby. Never thought in those terms before, but realize that you're only mine. No one else came before me and no one is coming after me. You're a gift, Zara, an unexpected treasure. A man like me likes to give instructions to his woman. I like to tell you what to do and watch you do it. It's hotter than hell."

"It is?"

If his woman needed reassurance then he was giving it to her. "Absolutely. I know that makes me kind of a prick, when I've had other women, but I love that you're mine alone. I love that I have something that is all mine. Just mine. I get off on telling you what to do in the bedroom, princess. It makes me hard as a rock. Just thinking about telling you what to do, teaching you things that will blow your mind makes me harder than I've ever been. You're perfect for me."

She gave him a tentative smile. "I think you're perfect for me." She looked up at him, suddenly shy. "When I'm with you, Gino, I feel so much more than I ever have been or thought I could be."

He caught her face in his hands. Looked into her eyes. Wanting her to see him. To know he spoke the absolute truth. "When I'm with you, Zara, I'm so much better. I've got things inside me, dark places, cold places, demons screaming to be let loose, but when I'm close to you, they're asleep. You have magic and you give it all to me. Thank you for that. Thank you for giving yourself to me. I know it has to be scary, so just know I appreciate it."

He took her mouth. That sweet curve that left him needing to kiss her every time he saw it. Or needing to feel her lips wrapped around his cock whenever he thought of them.

They spent the next few hours making out, talking, laughing, eating, cooling off in the pool and using the last condom in his wallet. He was even more careful, not wanting her to get sore. By the time the sun had set, he was ready to get her home and into a bathtub. He wasn't in the least bit sated. The more he took her, the more he knew he had to have her. Loving her and obsessing over her were intertwined until he wasn't certain where one started and the other left off. He only knew he was a lucky man and he didn't intend to blow it.

13

"You know, princess, we're building something here together, right?" Gino regarded Zara from over the top of his coffee mug. He found waking up to her was something he'd grown addicted to and he wanted confirmation from her that she knew this was going to be a long-lasting thing between them. He thought he'd made himself clear, but he wasn't taking chances. "I know this relationship is new and you don't have a lot of experience, but I'm talking permanent. I would definitely have a difficult time if you suddenly decided to play the field."

She put her teacup on the small table beside the bed and frowned at him. "Play the field?" she echoed. "As in another man? I don't want another man." That shocked her.

"That's just as well. I can be a complete bastard when I'm jealous. You might want to keep that in mind."

"I can't imagine you being a complete bastard about anything." She wiggled her toes and smiled up at him. "I can wiggle them without pain, which feels like a miracle. Nonny's poultices really are helping."

Gino put down his coffee and went to the floor to lift her feet up, so he could inspect them for healing. "I want Joe to take a look at your feet," he said, frowning. He slid his thumb over the top of her foot in a little caress. The bruises were gone and the lacerations had closed so there were only thin red lines to remind him that a monster had hurt his woman.

He dreamt about it sometimes, while he lay next to her. He dreamt he caught up with Bolan Zhu and had him alone in a place where no one could get to them before he had time to show him what it was like to hurt like that.

"Joe's a psychic healer. I'm not certain how he does it, but he heals from the inside out."

"Do you think he can help?"

"We can ask." He wanted her feet healed. Resting the tendons was helping, but she could mess up all their work by doing one wrong thing. She was becoming restless, having difficulty remembering not to put her weight on her feet. He couldn't blame her. It had been weeks and she was still having to be carried everywhere. She detested that.

Zara looked down at Gino where he crouched near her feet and met his eyes. The impact was like a punch to her heart. She had never really had the slightest interest in a man, and now she was completely enamored with Gino. Sleeping in the same bed with him had taken on an entirely new meaning now that he no longer considered her fragile. He'd taken her twice in the night and once in the morning.

She was becoming addicted to him and to the sex, because just looking at him turned her inside out. But she didn't like keeping anything from him. She didn't even know why. The smallest thing made her want to blurt out a confession. That didn't make sense when she was used to only sharing with Bellisia and Shylah.

"Baby, talk to me. I hate that look on your face."

She dared to push at the black, wavy hair spilling every which way. She liked that his hair was unruly. He was always so cool. Calm. Everything she wasn't. "It's just that I can hardly breathe without you, and it doesn't make sense. I don't want to be one of those clingy, needy women who can't make a decision without their man, but I'm terrified I'm really that woman."

His hands slid over her feet with exquisite gentleness. "You were made for me, Zara. We fit for a reason. You're hell on wheels when you're doing your research or talking about your ideas in your chosen field. I'm proud of you for that, but I don't want you making household decisions without me. Our home will be sacred. Ours. What we do there belongs to us and no one else. Our relationship is for us alone, no one else belongs in our choices. I like you clingy and needy. I like that you want to talk over decisions. That's a good thing, not a bad one."

She sent him a small relieved smile, but she knew it wasn't the real thing. Her nerves were coiled tightly in her belly. "I'm trying to get used to feeling that I'm okay just the way I am."

"Baby, you're still not telling me what's really bothering you, and that's not going to make me happy."

She should have known he would be able to see that she was holding something back. He could read her like a book. She took a deep breath and then made her confession, knowing he wasn't going to be happy when she told him. Either way . . . "I tried putting my full weight on my feet this morning when you were taking a shower."

His long fingers stopped stroking her feet. His black eyes met hers, and the impact sank her heart. He wasn't in the least bit happy with her, and she detested that she'd let him down.

"I thought we agreed you were going to wait."

She nodded. "I know. I know I should have. Please don't get upset with me."

He was silent for a long moment and then he lifted her into his arms and carried her through the house to the front porch. He put her very gently in one of the rocking chairs and then crouched down to lift her feet up, placing each on his knee, his hands moving very gently over them, while he examined them again, this time inspecting each carefully, bending her toes, moving her foot at the ankle. She did her best not to wince when pain shot up her leg and down into her toes.

"I need you to listen, Zara. To really hear what I'm saying to you. Not just for now, but for the future. Our future. I need you to hear me and remember what I say." He looked up, waiting until her eyes met his.

The powerful collision sent shock waves through her. Those black eyes gleamed at her, dark and compelling. A hint of anger swirled there. She found she couldn't look away, her stomach dropping and tension coiling deep. The obsidian could be as cold as ice, or on fire, like now. "I'm listening, Gino."

"I don't get angry over too many things. I'm not built that way. You hurt yourself, I'm going to get fucking crazy. You didn't have to test your feet. Nonny and I both told you to wait. We both said they were damaged and the healing was going to be slow."

She ducked her head. He was so right. Both had cautioned her repeatedly, but she hated being helpless. It was very, very boring to lie in bed or sit in a chair while people waited on her. She was used to doing for the others when she was in Whitney's compound. She loved cooking and she wanted her chance in the kitchen with Nonny like the other women. To do that, she had to stand on her own feet. When she'd wiggled her toes in the morning and they hadn't hurt, she'd decided to try to put her weight on them.

He caught her chin and raised it, forcing her to look at him. "Didn't we both say that to you, because I distinctly remember it?"

There was a bite to his voice that sent a little frisson of fear through her body. He was disappointed in her, and she didn't like it. It hurt that she'd disappointed Gino. Somewhere deep where she lived and breathed she wanted him happy, especially with her.

"I'm sorry." She touched his face because she needed the connection. His fingers were long and strong, stroking over her feet so gently it turned her heart over. She stroked the shadow along his jaw with equal gentleness. "I really am, Gino. Sometimes I feel desperate to walk."

"I know it's hard waiting, Zara. I hate this for you, but hurting yourself isn't the answer, and every time you put weight on your feet, it's going to hurt them. That only makes the healing process take longer."

She nodded, swallowing the lump in her throat. She needed the anger and disappointment gone from his eyes. There was no defense. Nonny had even sat with her one evening and explained that the damage to her tendons was severe and she might not ever be able to run or walk without some pain. The poultices were helping the healing process, but it was essential to give her feet the time to heal.

"Most of the time, caning the feet hurts like hell, but there's no permanent damage. Zhu knew what he was doing and he deliberately concentrated the strokes to do the most damage. He not only wanted to break you, he wanted to make certain that he slowed you down so you couldn't run from him."

The strikes to her feet had seemed to go on forever. She remembered screaming. She'd tried to stop, but there was no way when the pain was excruciating. He hit the arches of her feet repeatedly, so many times she lost count. Then he hit the heels and balls of her feet and then the sides. He'd done the same to the tops of her feet until they were mangled and bleeding. She'd begged him to stop, promised him anything to get him to stop. His expression had never changed, he just kept hitting her.

Gino brushed tears from her face. "Baby, don't cry. I'm not trying to be harsh with you, I just don't want you to hurt yourself or do any more permanent damage."

"Sometimes," she whispered, looking around her, trying to center herself back in Louisiana, in the States, "I feel it happening all over again. I can hear the whistle of the cane or the whip right before it strikes."

He cupped the back of her head in his palm and pulled her head against his shoulder, stroking his hand down the length of her hair. "You're safe now. He can't reach you."

She knew better, but she wasn't going to argue with him. "I'm all right, and I promise, I won't be silly and try standing again, not without you giving me the go-ahead."

He kissed the top of her foot and gently placed it on the pillow he'd brought outside with them. "What happened when you tried to put weight on your feet?"

"It was painful, but not like it was before. Not excruciating." She was silent, biting her lip when he continued to look at her. God, he was annoying at times. She couldn't help but confess, just blurt out the truth when he looked at her like that. He would never have to resort to torture. "It still is kind of bad."

"Were you going to tell me the level of pain?"

Her stomach did a slow roll. "Probably not." She wouldn't have told him she was in pain for any reason if he wasn't looking at her like that.

"Don't do that again. Don't keep important shit from me, you understand? You hurt, I want to know about it, even if it's stubbing your toe or jamming a finger."

He meant it. She could see it in his eyes and hear it in his voice. He wanted to know if she was hurt. She wasn't supposed to suck it up and keep quiet, she was supposed to tell him. "We weren't trained that way, Gino, especially me. I wasn't allowed to whine, not for any reason. Once, I broke my arm and Whitney was angry with me for going to the infirmary. I was supposed to keep quiet and try to endure the pain for at least a day or two, not be such a wimp that I left the others during training."

She pushed back her hair and looked at him, feeling shame all over again. "I didn't leave the others until the training was over. I helped them as best I could. When we were returned to the barracks, then I went. Honestly, Gino, I didn't desert my team."

"Zara, Whitney needs someone to put a bullet in his head and put him out of his misery. Seriously. A woman breaks her arm, she needs a doctor. Waiting can cause more damage. The man is an ass. You didn't do anything wrong and you're not a coward. He tried to make you feel like one, but any man or woman who took the kind of beating you did without breaking is no coward."

"I feel broken," she confessed. "I don't know why his opinion mattered so much to me."

He went up on his knees, cupped her face in his palms and kissed her. He brushed his mouth gently over hers, and then deepened the kiss. This one wasn't a wildfire like many of the others. This one was tender. Warm. Compassionate. This one said things that got to her. When he lifted his head, his gaze held hers.

"His opinion mattered to you because he was your only parent. Your father figure. You're not broken, Zara. You didn't break. You're a little damaged, but that's all. We're fixing the damage, and once we do, you're going to be so strong. The things he said will be a distant memory. You're smart, baby. You're so damn smart you were a threat to him. Whitney wants everyone to believe he's the most intelligent person in the room. He despises women and thinks they're inferior. You were a huge threat to him, so he had to make you feel like you were nothing. That was his goal and his way to make you do what he said."

She leaned down to brush her lips over his. "You make

me feel whole. I know I'm supposed to feel that way all on my own, but right now, when I'm with you, I feel safe and complete. Thank you for that."

"Believe it or not, Zara, you make me feel the same way. I looked for you, for the right woman to share my life with, and until I saw you, I didn't think there was anyone out there who could live with me. You think you're damaged? I know you're a little broken from the things Zhu did to you, but I know damaged. That's me, princess, not you. There was a gaping hole in me, maybe where my heart and soul are supposed to be, and that's gone too. You do that for me. We're meant to be. It's as simple as that."

She wanted it to be that simple. If she could just figure out what to do with the information stored in the SSD in her brain and get rid of it, she'd be very happy.

"I'm adding to the plans for the house. We have a lot of acreage, Zara. I want to know what you're going to need for your research center. Money isn't an object, so put down everything you can think of on your list as you make it. This evening we can go over floor plans, so I have an idea what to have drawn up."

"Research center?" she echoed.

He nodded. "Of course. You're going to want to continue where you left off with your work, right? You don't have to go anywhere if you don't want to. We can bring in whoever you need to assist you, and when you have to travel to the university, I'll go with you."

She got that he didn't ask her if she wanted him to go with her. She got that because she knew another woman might have pointed it out, but she was grateful he didn't force her to admit she didn't want to travel alone.

"I can't believe you'd have a research center built for me here."

"Your home is here. Someday we'll have children. I doubt that's going to stop you from wanting to continue your work."

It wouldn't. She loved what she did. She loved sharing it and talking with others interested as well. She wouldn't be alone. That was what she heard and what she clung to. "Do you really mean it, Gino? You'll go with me?"

He nodded slowly, his features very serious, and her heart sank again, afraid he would take it back. "I won't like you traveling without me, Zara, or at least without a couple of the others if I'm away. It's important to me that you discuss all your traveling dates with me ahead of time so we can work that out."

He wasn't asking again. She got that. She found herself smiling. "That sounds good, Gino, I can do that."

"And we have to get on figuring out how to get the information from the SSD into someone's hands so Whitney has no reason to try for you again."

"I'll talk to Bellisia today. I'm hoping to spend time with her and fix the problems we have. Mostly, I think, I really didn't understand relationships between a man and a woman. I would have a difficult time keeping something from you."

"I wouldn't like it, princess. Zeke might get upset and talk to Bellisia about keeping secrets, but you would have serious consequences for keeping anything from me. When someone wants to talk to you about something important, when they give you that kind of responsibility, you make damn sure they know they're talking to both of us before you take it. Understand?"

She was back on "serious consequences." "What kind of consequences?"

"Babe, really? Do you think I'm capable of hitting you? Hurting you in any way? You're what I've looked for my entire life. I'm not dumb enough to fuck that up by being an asshole."

She couldn't imagine him hitting her. She liked that he understood she did take responsibility for the things others told her and that he wanted to share that burden with her. She knew other women wouldn't want Gino taking that off her, but she was coming to understand that she wasn't "other" women, and her needs came first with him. He didn't want her to be embarrassed because she didn't like making those decisions. She could if she needed to, but when it was unnecessary, she didn't have to. There was freedom in knowing that.

"I like that you're building . . ."

"*We're* building," Gino corrected decisively. "The two of us, Zara. I want you to go over the plans for the house as well as the research center. It will be your house too, so you need to have it exactly the way you want," he reiterated.

"Our house, then. I like that Cayenne and Trap are going to be our closest neighbors. I like Cayenne." She identified with her in some ways. She wouldn't mind being neighbors with her. Cayenne wasn't the type to hang out at the back fence and talk and she wouldn't expect Zara to either.

Gino shot her a glance as he leaned one hip against the porch column. "Cayenne isn't to everyone's taste. Most people are intimidated by her. She's good for Trap and she's damn good to him."

"I've seen the way she is with him."

It was impossible to miss. Trap came in the day after Gino had removed the virus capsules, and he, Wyatt and Gino got lost in examining the virus under microscopes and a dozen other instruments they had in Wyatt's lab. Cayenne had come in with them, stayed to the back of the room to watch in silence, but every time Trap needed something, a pen, paper, a drink, whatever, she had it there before he asked. All he did was drop his gaze, look around him and she was handing it to him.

Zara couldn't help watching her, seeing the look on her face when she gave Trap whatever he needed. Once, she was certain, Trap needed Cayenne. He turned abruptly without a word to anyone in the room, walked out, his arm circling Cayenne's waist as he went by her, lifting her and taking her with him. When they returned, he was less restless and more centered, and she was glowing.

"She gives Trap whatever he needs and she does it without asking for anything in return. He gives her everything because she is everything to him," Gino said.

His black eyes burned into her, right through her skin to brand his name on her bones. She knew there would never be a time that the moment she saw him, her heart wouldn't beat faster and her sex wouldn't clench and go liquid with need for him. He would never have to worry about other men because she wasn't capable of seeing anyone else. Her world was completely centered around him and always would be, just as Trap was Cayenne's center. She didn't mind being like that woman at all.

"You going to give me everything like that, baby? Whenever I ask? Whatever I ask for? Is that the kind of relationship you want?"

His voice was low. Forceful, even though so quiet. Totally compelling, just like the man. If she could have walked, she would have flung herself into his arms. She detested not being able to go to him.

"Yes." She made the commitment because that was who she was. She would give everything to him because she wanted that for him—and for herself. There was something in her that drove her to please Gino, to make his life as wonderful as she could. It didn't matter that she'd get that same thing back, and she knew she would, it was just that she needed to be needed.

She'd never considered her need to please was the underlying reason she'd misled her sisters. She believed they needed to hear the stories of the outside world in order to have optimism that one day they'd get there. She felt it was her greatest contribution to the other women, bringing them hope each time she got back from her travels. Their smiles were always radiant, and instantly, no matter how she'd felt while she was gone, she would light up inside. Glow. Because they needed something she could give. Gino really needed someone to care for him. He needed a home and family of his own. She could give him the best one possible, the kind of home he needed, because she was that one woman for him.

"Gino, I'm giving you anything and everything you could possibly want. If I don't know how to do it, just teach me." She couldn't keep the shyness from her voice, but it didn't matter. He accepted her just the way she was and she loved that. He'd already taught her so many things in the bedroom. She'd enjoyed doing every single one and wanted more. The promise in his dark eyes excited her.

"Nonny tells me you like cooking."

She nodded. "That's part of why it's so frustrating sitting all the time. You've taken me into the kitchen when Nonny's giving a cooking class to the others, but I can't really participate like they do. I swear, sometimes my feet itch to jump up." At his look, she hastily held up her hand and laughed. "I didn't. And I won't. Nonny would smack me with her wooden spoon if I did that and you wouldn't be happy with me, so no jumping up, even though I can't always see how she's judging the exact amount of the spices to put in."

"You'll be able to stand soon enough, and I suspect at some point you're going to get tired of making all the dinners for us because I'm a lousy cook. When that happens, you tell me. Anytime, Zara, no matter how tired you think I am. I don't want you to suck it up."

She couldn't imagine ever getting tired of cooking for him and her family, but she supposed, day in and day out, it might happen. "Okay." She bit her lip, wanting to make her confession in a little rush, but not quite able to get it out. It was one thing for him to say to tell him everything she liked or didn't like, but another to do it. She wasn't used to it, as in, she'd never done it.

"Spit it out, princess."

"Do you like art? As in going to museums? Paintings? Sculptures?"

There was a small silence. He regarded her for so long she was afraid he wouldn't answer. He'd gone very still, as if holding himself frozen in case he might shatter. His features were expressionless, but something moved behind those black, black eyes.

"My mother loved art," he said eventually. "I can remember her dragging me to every fuckin' art museum in the country and abroad. She would look at paintings for hours. I wasn't always the best, although secretly I didn't mind as much as I made out. Now . . ." He shook his head and looked out over the river. "I wish I had those times back so I could be different."

Gino circled the porch column and kept his eyes on the moving water. She wanted to put her arms around him and hold him. "You were a boy, and she understood."

He looked back at her, that something in his eyes tearing at her. "She was gentle, like you, Zara. She would have loved you. My entire family would have. I didn't realize it until just this minute, but you're a lot like she was. Not in looks, but your nature. The way you care about me. The things you're willing to do for me. She was like that. She did them for my father. For me. We were the center of her universe."

"I hate not being able to hold you right now," she admitted.

He turned back to her, stalked the short distance between them and bent down to take her mouth. She expected gentle, but he was rough, his kiss a pure flame pouring down her throat. It was a claiming, and as inexperienced as she was, she still couldn't fail to understand. She took advantage, wrapping her arms around his neck, fingers finding his hair to tunnel in. She gave herself up to him, sensing he needed her surrender.

Gino lifted his head slowly. "We own a hell of a lot of art, Zara. You want it, I'll build us a room for it. She collected some beautiful and rare paintings. They need to be in a controlled environment. We can try to see how many art museums we can visit before we're so old we can't walk anymore, if that's what you want. I promise, I'll enjoy them all with you."

"I'd like that," she admitted.

He straightened and went back to the railing, leaning against it, regarding her with that serious expression he wore most of the time. "You like shopping?"

"I don't know." She flashed him a grin. "I've only ever really shopped in adult toy stores."

He burst out laughing. She loved what that did to his eyes. They crinkled at the corners and his dimple appeared, softening the hard angles and planes. "Yeah, you can forget going there without me. I'll take you myself."

A little shiver crept down her spine. "I'd like to try clothes shopping, although it probably would be intimidating the first time, but I'd get the hang of it. Bellisia might want to go with me into town sometimes." She liked talking about their future because it meant Whitney wasn't going to get her and neither was Zhu. Intellectually, she knew she was running out of time, but she needed this fantasy, this world Gino could give her if she survived.

He nodded. "Of course. She may want a girls' night out too. I want those things for you. Any of them ask and you want to go, say yes and let me know. I'll make sure you're safe. I imagine, depending on who goes, the others will make certain as well."

"I can't imagine Bellisia or Cayenne wanting anyone guarding them on a girls' night out."

"Doesn't matter, Zara. So, if you're talking about yourself, that's too bad. I can tell you straight up, Trap would never leave Cayenne hanging out there, and Zeke wouldn't leave Bellisia either. We have enemies and we're always going to have them. When you go out, you're going with guards. We can be invisible, but we'll make sure you all get home safely if you want to drink. No one's going to cut into your fun, baby, we want our women happy, and in particular, how you feel is important to me."

She thought it was a dumb thing to argue about because she really didn't mind if he watched over her when she was out with the girls having fun. She would definitely feel safer. "I get it. Everyone's lived here a lot longer than I have and I'm just trying to understand the rules, Gino, not really arguing against them."

"Tell me the things you dreamt of when you were going to the university. You had to have seen there was life outside Whitney's compound."

She nodded. "It was wonderful and terrifying at the same time. I was so young in comparison to the other students." She didn't always remember those days fondly.

"What was wonderful?"

"Being able to take back hope to my sisters. I realized what a family was. I watched some of the kids, and they were far older than me, get visitors—parents, siblings, grandparents—the people we never had in our lives. I wanted that for my sisters and I wanted it for me. I would watch television in my room, all the cooking shows and anything that portrayed families. The books I devoured were all about families. I read about them and saw them on television and then would tell the others."

"How many children do you want?"

She tipped her head up and looked to the sky. Clouds drifted across the wide expanse of blue, but there were very few of them, small wisps that made her think of lazy days. She'd never had that—a lazy day. They weren't allowed such a thing in Whitney's compound. Sitting on the porch or being with Gino at a swimming hole, with a picnic lunch, was a luxury.

"I don't know how many, Gino." She was honest. "I read books on parenting because, obviously, I wanted to know what I was doing, and I don't have a good example to follow . . ." She broke off and pressed her hand over her womb. Rubbed gently. "Can you imagine feeling a baby, a *life*, kicking inside of you?"

He gave her a small grin. It lit his eyes, giving them a glint of humor through all that unrelenting black. "Not really. But I'd like to feel my child kicking inside of you. I thought three or four, but I know that's considered a lot these days. Most people opt for one or two because it's easier to support them and they say the planet is exploding with population."

"Does that mean we're supposed to only have one to two?"

"We can do anything we damn well please, princess. You want a dozen, I'll fucking give you a dozen. We've got money enough. I can give you anything you want."

"What about what you want?" She kept her gaze steady on his.

"I never wanted much of anything until you came along. I guess I'm going to have to reevaluate what my wants are. You. But I consider you a need, not a want."

She laughed softly. "You're so crazy. You don't need me. You have all this. This wonderful place. And you have freedom." Her smile faded and she fought the sudden lump in her throat. "I don't have that yet, not all the way. Any minute I expect someone to come and take me away from here."

"I want you to stop worrying about that, Zara. Let me worry. We need to get the information out of your head. The sooner you tell Bellisia she can talk to Zeke, and get her to give you the okay to talk to Trap and Wyatt, then we can all put our heads together and solve this problem. Trap is hell on wheels with this kind of thing because he thinks outside the box. Wyatt as well. We'll get the information out and Whitney will lose interest."

She thought it was interesting that he stated she shouldn't worry and clearly expected that she wouldn't just because he said so. He was used to people doing what he ordered, or maybe it was because he always followed through and made certain there was nothing to worry about. Whatever the reason, she felt the now-familiar flutter in the region of her heart. He made her feel cared for. Loved even. But Whitney wasn't the only one they had to worry about.

"Zhu won't lose interest." She tilted her head, challenging him. "You know he won't."

"I've got eyes on him. When he makes his move, we'll get him. The boys and I have been talking over a game plan."

"You didn't tell me that." Her stomach tightened into hard knots. "That means you think for certain he'll come." It was one thing for her to be so certain, but an altogether different one for him to be. She thought she'd gotten over terror, but it had been waiting, it was right there, pouncing before she could control it. Zhu. The monster. He was in every nightmare. Gino holding her close to him helped, but sometimes she woke, her heart pounding and fear drying out her mouth.

"He'll come." Gino shrugged. "Let him." He crouched down in front of her again and took her hand, his thumb sliding over her knuckles. "Look at me, Zara."

He waited until her eyes met his, and she didn't like that she had no choice. She was compelled to look at him and if she didn't, he'd wait forever because he had the patience of a hunter. She swallowed hard at what she saw there.

"You've forgotten what I am, baby, and I'm okay with

you forgetting once we remove the threats to you, but not now. Zhu hasn't done anything I haven't done. I can guarantee you, my training started long before his, and he isn't enhanced. I am. Even if it was an even playing field, Zara, you're mine and that means I have an edge because I'm not willing to give you up. And that fucker is going to pay for what he did to you."

She took a breath and released it, knowing she should have conveyed everything to him when she first was telling him about Zhu, but she'd been so frightened in those earlier days that small details, no matter how important, tended to escape her. "When I first arrived, I was taken to Cheng's office. He had tea brought in for us. Zhu poured the tea and I watched very closely because I was afraid they were going to drug the tea. They had me sit in a certain chair and I had the feeling they could monitor my heart and respiratory rate."

"It would be easy enough."

She nodded. His thumb continued to slide over her knuckles and there was something in that simple gesture that gave her confidence. "He poured Cheng's tea first and then mine. He didn't put anything in the tea, but I saw his finger slide around the lip of the teacup and I knew immediately he'd put some kind of drug on it. I had a couple of choices, but decided to go ahead and drink the tea. I was careful to use the same spot every single time when I sipped it."

"So, you ingested the drug."

She nodded. "It was definitely a truth serum, but one that acted differently than the conventional truth serums. They've been researching obviously. But it was more than that. I got around the need to answer their questions by doing math problems and coding in my head."

"What was the more, Zara?"

He knew her so well now. They'd spent so much time together, and he could read her. He knew she was reluctant to tell him. "You know how Whitney was pairing couples? He wanted to get certain traits together so he paired us with one another? Well, I think Cheng's people were working on something similar, or it was a by-product of the truth serum. It wasn't exactly the same as Whitney's because I knew immediately that something was wrong. I was attracted physically to Zhu."

She tried to look away from Gino, ashamed that even for one moment, chemically induced or not, she'd been attracted to such a horrible human being, but Gino wouldn't let her.

"Princess, just tell me, don't let yourself go back there. They did that to you. They did all of this to you. Cheng. Zhu. Whitney. You aren't responsible for any of it. You're in a good place right now, don't let them take it away from you."

"I got over the attraction fairly quickly. I don't know if doing the math in my head helped, or my fear, or what, but he didn't get over it. He was attracted. It didn't stop him from hurting me, in fact he made it clear that he would continue to hurt me, so I don't think the physical attraction mattered that much to him. Maybe he's attracted to tons of women . . ."

Gino shook his head. "We've had a couple of our best people finding out what they could about him. Flame, Wyatt's sister-in-law, and Jaimie, the wife of another Ghost-Walker, are both very good at ferreting out things people don't want brought into the light. The clubs Zhu frequents when he goes to other countries are not for the nice or faint of heart. They aren't simple bondage clubs, they're clubs where men and women can inflict a lot of pain on others for their own sexual gratification. That's a lot different than tying up a partner for fun and sexual pleasure. Zhu gets off on causing pain. You're perfect for him in a lot of ways."

She shuddered. "I'm not, Gino. I hate pain. People like Zhu find women who get off on pain. That isn't me."

"No, baby, it isn't. But he's physically attracted. You're beautiful and intelligent. You can contribute to their coffers by leading their research programs. You're naturally passive or, for want of a better word, submissive. Best of all, for him, you don't like pain. He doesn't want a partner who gets off on it, *he* gets off on hurting people, seeing their pain. Where is he ever going to find a combination like that? My best guess is, he researched you thoroughly, watched you for a long time and then set a trap for you."

She was silent, hating that he might be right. "You think I'm submissive?"

"Yeah, baby, I know you are, and that suits my personality. Fortunately, you also have that temper of yours, so you'll keep me in line."

She frowned at him, thinking it over, and then she shook her head. "I like to please you, Gino, but I don't think I'm submissive. I assert myself. Even with Whitney, and he scared me. Not like Zhu, but I knew he didn't like me and he tossed me in solitary every chance he got. Knowing what would happen, I still defied him. Especially if he got upset with Bellisia or Shylah. It was easy enough to redirect his wrath to me."

"Being submissive doesn't make you a wimp, baby. You're strong and courageous. I have no idea how you could hear his voice telling you that you're a coward, when your brain has to tell you that you aren't. Submissive can mean many things, but it doesn't mean you lie down for everyone. It only means you prefer to comply with an authority figure."

She did, but only if he was just. She nodded. "Whitney was an asshole to everyone. I wouldn't call him in the least bit fair." Which was why she'd defied him over contraband and a zillion other things. He didn't deserve to be obeyed. She'd tried so hard to please him when she was young, but then, over time, realized nothing she did would ever be good enough. "Zhu was a thousand times worse."

"Neither man deserved your surrender."

She wasn't talking about that with him, not until she thought it over more. "Why did the pheromones work on Zhu but not me? Because I swear, even when he was beating the shit out of me, the physical attraction, for him, grew toward me while mine toward him was completely gone. Even before he actually hurt me it was gone. One of the things I was afraid of was that he might douse me with whatever that was and I'd feel something for him."

"Why would he ever use something like that on himself? If he wanted to get you to be attracted to him, he would use it on you, not him. It was to his advantage to make you want him, not the other way around. He had to have been naturally attracted. Probably the more he hurt you and you reacted the way he needed, the more it fed his attraction. Either you were right and the truth serum had a side effect, or they were trying out their own, obviously not as good as Whitney's creation."

"That information wouldn't have been included in the file Violet gave Cheng," Zara pointed out. "Whitney went through his computer very carefully. All details are compartmentalized. She gave Cheng the facts, that the United States had teams of soldiers enhanced both psychically and physically. There were some details, but mainly she counted on Cheng getting a soldier from your particular unit. She detested everyone here because they accepted the babies with their venom, and Pepper and Cayenne with theirs. Whitney was upset that he hadn't gotten rid of Violet a while back, when he first began to lose control. He paired her with him, thinking that would take care of the problem, but it didn't."

"Because he doesn't understand emotion."

"No, he doesn't," she agreed. "He doesn't seem to really feel much for anyone, unless it's his adopted daughter, Lily, but she's truly the only one, if he really does." She chewed on her bottom lip for a moment, thinking of all the talks she'd had with the doctor. "Although he even experimented on her. It bothered him that Ryland, her husband, was one of the first GhostWalkers because he considers all of that team flawed."

"They need anchors, someone to draw the overload of psychic energy away from them, or they get brain bleeds like Pepper."

She nodded. "Whitney never liked that she had a baby with Ryland. I know, if he got his hands on the child, he would experiment on him. He talked about it. Whitney often talked to me about experiments, mostly, I think, because he didn't have anyone he trusted that much and he was certain I'd never be able to get away from him."

"And you could understand what he was talking about." Gino stood up and moved back into the shadows of one of the porch columns. She liked him close. Touching her. She really was too far gone on him if he couldn't stand just a few feet away without her feeling the loss.

"Bellisia and Zeke are here, princess. Their car just pulled up."

"I don't see them." She leaned forward to look into the yard, but she didn't see Ezekiel's car. She hoped Gino was right. She really wanted to talk to her best friend. She needed to straighten things out between them. She'd chosen Gino as her partner and she'd fallen hard for him, but she owed it to Bellisia to give her permission to tell her husband what Zara was hiding and to clear things up between them. She had never been terribly good at asserting herself, but this time, she had to make Bellisia understand why she'd lied about wanting to go out into the world and give talks.

She wanted to get away from Whitney's compound, but traveling alone was terrifying. Surely, she could explain that to Bellisia's satisfaction. Of course, it wasn't that Bellisia wouldn't understand—it was the fact that Zara had lied to her.

"Zeke likes to park close to the road, just out of sight of the house, but also of anyone passing by. He parks where that big stand of trees covers his car. You okay? They're coming now. I'll disappear and give you time to talk to her."

She wanted to cling to him, but she wasn't going to be a coward. She loved Bellisia, and her sister deserved an explanation. "Thank you. And I'll have an answer for you about who to talk to when you come back."

"She'll tell you Trap and Wyatt are good men and they won't talk out of turn."

She hoped not. If they did, she knew there was a good chance the major general would send her right back to Whitney. If not him, someone above him.

14

"Zara? Gino?" Bellisia came running up the stairs leading to the porch. She was soaking wet, the water running off her in small rivulets. Behind her, looking protective, was Ezekiel. He was wet too, but he had a towel and was drying off as he watched them warily.

"I'm so sorry for the way I acted," Bellisia said immediately, making Zara feel worse. Zara shook her head to try to forestall her, but Bellisia continued. "I don't know why I'm so anxious for you, Zara. I just want to lock you away where no one can get to you. Just for a little while until I know you're whole again."

Bellisia looked down at her hands. Zara couldn't tell if tears were swimming in her eyes or if it was the water from the river. "I saw those bruises and lacerations all over you and it just about killed me. If I hadn't escaped, if I'd gone back, maybe Whitney wouldn't have sent you to Cheng."

"Of course he would have sent me, Bellisia," Zara said immediately. "We talked about escaping. All three of us.

We had an agreement. There's no reason for you to feel like any of this was your fault, because it wasn't."

"I shouldn't have told you I needed to tell Ezekiel, and I haven't." Bellisia sent Ezekiel a quick look of guilt. "That shouldn't have been my first response. It's just that I trust him so much and I guess I didn't think beyond that."

Gino shifted his body just enough to draw the attention of both women. "I'm going to get some of Nonny's strawberry lemonade. Bellisia? Zara? You good with lemonade? Maybe you could help me, Zeke?"

"Of course," Ezekiel offered immediately. He dropped a kiss on Bellisia's head as he moved past her.

Bellisia waited until the men had gone into the house before coming all the way onto the porch. She hadn't dried off because her body required moisture, so much of it that sometimes in the middle of the night she got up, filled a tub with water and immersed herself in liquid.

"I should have trusted your judgment," Zara conceded. "I know Ezekiel must have realized you were keeping a secret. Was he very upset with you?"

Bellisia shrugged and waved that away. "I feel like I drove you right to Gino because of the way I acted. Why were you able to trust him so fast? To trust his decisions?"

Zara could hear the hurt in her voice. Bellisia looked near tears, and she'd always been the strongest one of the three of them.

"I've been your sister since we were a year or so old," Bellisia continued. "It was always Shylah, you and me. All those years together, depending on one another, and yet you went to Gino instead of Ezekiel. I don't understand."

"I don't know what I expected when we talked," Zara said. "I wasn't being fair to you, I guess. You were saying things I didn't want to hear, things you had no way of knowing would hurt me. I realized your loyalty wasn't just to me anymore, it was to Ezekiel first, and that made me feel very alone. You had your husband, and I was alone. Not just alone, the one person I had come to depend on, Gino, you were trying to pull out from under me. I know you were trying to protect me, Bellisia, but at the time, I was feeling raw and hurt. Things haven't been good for me since you've been gone. Whitney retaliated against Shylah and me both. He thought we knew what you planned."

"I'm sorry." Bellisia leaned against the railing, staying out of the sun so the water wouldn't dry too fast on her skin.

"Don't be. None of this is your fault. You're supposed to trust your husband and put him first. I understand that now, and I should have taken the time to understand that then. I was being childish not wanting to trust him just because I was jealous that he had you and I no longer did. I just needed you so much right then and thought it was going to be the same. You. Me. Apart from everyone else."

"Why Gino?"

"Tell me why you don't like him."

Bellisia opened her mouth to deny that claim but then closed it and frowned instead, thinking it over. "It isn't that I don't like him, Zara. I don't know him. No one really knows him. I've seen men like him though. He's more at home in the woods or the swamp than in a house, although, I suspect he'd be at home hunting in a city. Anywhere he chooses could be a hunting ground."

Zara couldn't fault her for thinking that. She thought it herself. She *needed* the hunter, the predator in him. She was drawn to that part of him.

"He likes being alone and as far as I can see, the only ones he really spends time with are Trap, Wyatt, Draden and Joe. Even then, he looks out for them."

"And Nonny, Pepper, Cayenne, the children and you, Bellisia." Zara didn't think that was a fault at all. If anything, she admired Gino for it and she trusted and relied on him because of those traits. "I think all the Ghost-Walkers, including your husband, have that same trait."

Bellisia nodded reluctantly. "Yes," she conceded. "I think that's a fair assessment."

"That still doesn't say why you don't like him."

Bellisia sighed and went to Zara's side, lowering her voice so she was practically whispering in Zara's ear. "I don't know if I should tell you this. I've already screwed up big-time by trying to warn you off him."

"I want to know. I'm asking you."

"Joe Spagnola is the man leading this team. They all look up to him and respect him. He's kind and compassionate. A good man, Zara. His father is Ciro Spagnola, a rather infamous crime boss. Ciro and Gino's father, Jacopo, were close friends growing up. They served in the military together. When Gino's family was murdered, it was Joe who found them. They saved Gino's life when they took him in. Gino was raised by Ciro."

"Gino told me Joe was like a brother to him. I knew they'd been raised together," Zara acknowledged.

"Joe should have been Jacopo's son and Gino, Ciro's," Bellisia said. "Gino was raised as an enforcer for Ciro. Do you understand what I'm saying? Joe turned his back on that life, but Gino embraced it. He's done things that aren't good." She hesitated again. "An enforcer tortures and kills people, Zara." She kept her voice very low. "He did that for Ciro. For all I know he's done that for the military, and we both know if you can do that and sleep at night . . ."

"He couldn't have been very old when he joined the military," Zara pointed out.

She wanted to be more shocked and appalled than she was. Gino was quiet. Watchful. There was something ice-cold and dangerous in his eyes, and he could turn off emotion. She'd seen him do it. He was also the most protective man she'd ever met and she could imagine Ciro drilling it into him as a boy that he had to watch over Joe. Gino had lost his entire family. It stood to reason that he would do whatever Ciro deemed necessary to protect those remaining that he loved.

Gino had told her more than once that he wasn't a good man. He never lied to her, in fact everything Bellisia was telling her matched up with what Gino had implied. He had confessed that Zhu and he were the same in many ways, that he'd done similar things when needed. She was grateful he'd told her, so she wasn't shocked when she heard it from Bellisia.

"I know. He followed Joe. But the fact remains, he's capable of doing things most men aren't capable of. You were tortured, Zara. He's capable of that."

"He would never torture a woman, Bellisia," Zara said with complete confidence.

"Maybe not, but I'm telling you, honey, it isn't natural to be able to do some of the things he's done, both for Ciro and for the military."

"Are you saying none of the other men would extract information from a prisoner if it was needed to save others in their unit?"

Bellisia was silent for a moment, looking uncomfortable. "I don't know the answer to that. Okay, maybe. Yes. But the difference is, he wouldn't have a problem with it. He scares me for you."

"You think he would hurt me, but I'm telling you, he isn't capable of hurting a woman. If she was an enemy, he might shoot her, but he wouldn't torture her. He wouldn't hit me, or abuse me. I know that with everything in me."

"He's old-fashioned with women, and that isn't going to change. I want someone different for you. Someone who allows you the freedom you need."

Zara rubbed the hem of the shirt she was wearing. Gino's shirt. It gave her the necessary courage to confess.

It was a huge confession and she knew Bellisia would not only be hurt, but possibly angry, and she deserved it.

"About that, Bellisia, the truth is, Gino does give me freedom. He gives me exactly what I need to feel free and whole and safe. I have something I need to tell you and I'm going to warn you up front, you aren't going to like it. In fact, you're going to feel betrayed and I never meant it that way. I love you and Shylah. Both of you. I didn't have anything to contribute to us like the two of you. You both covered me on our missions, when Whitney would send us out. You know you did, no matter how much you want to protest. I wasn't made for being a soldier. I can fight, but I lack the killer instinct. It made me sick, and both of you covered for me."

"Honey. We love you. You held your own when it was needed."

"That's the point, you two made it so it was rarely needed. You gave me such a gift. I knew it was a gift. I never took it for granted. The two of you were so fierce. Shylah is sensitive, and kind, yet she kicked ass. You were like the sweetest, and you could do whatever was needed, but I let you both down every mission."

"You didn't, but keep going. So far, I don't see the betrayal," Bellisia prompted.

Zara rubbed the hem of her shirt again as if she could make a genie appear and whisk her away. Or Gino. She didn't want to admit any of this to Bellisia. She looked up to her. Loved her. She detested disappointing the few people she loved—the few who loved her.

"I needed something to contribute to the three of us. The only thing I had to give the two of you and the other girls was a taste of what was out there in the world."

"And you did. I can't tell you what that did for all of us. The stories you told. All the adventures you had. The parties at school. The walks through open parks and the various countries you were able to visit. The contraband you risked so much to get to us. You gave that to us, Zara. You made the world come to life for us and that instilled hope. You also kept us knowing there was something out there, either to fight for and keep safe, if our lives were always in the compound, or to escape and become part of the real world. You gave all of us that."

Zara nodded. "I know I did. I worked hard at it. I tried to become an observer, a recorder, a storyteller, so I could give the best of everything to you. You deserved it."

"We *needed* it," Bellisia corrected.

That was true. Zara had known that at a very young age. She'd known all the girls had to have hope. She became that hope for them, and she lived that lie for years. For them. She had nothing else to give them when they gave her so much. She hated telling Bellisia the truth, but she had to. It wasn't fair to be angry at Bellisia when Zara had deliberately deceived her.

"I don't like being out in the world alone. I felt exposed and vulnerable, just the way I did when we went into battle. I hated school when I was so young and everyone ignored me, made fun of me or tried to push me around. I was petrified. I was terrified when I traveled. Absolutely terrified. Of everything. Of taking a plane alone. Riding in a taxi alone. Checking into a hotel. The worst was standing up in front of all those people and talking about whatever project I'd headed, knowing I was stealing from them. It was a nightmare for me. The last thing I want to do is continue that life."

The words came out in a rush, and she didn't know if she'd said enough that Bellisia would understand that the person she'd grown up with and loved wasn't at all the real one. She was fake. Zara had manufactured her so that she could give them something—so she could fit in and feel as if she belonged. It wasn't at all the real Zara, but she'd done what she'd thought was right. Once she'd started down that path, there was no going back from it.

Bellisia stared at her for what seemed forever. She finally took a deep breath. "Baby, did you think we wouldn't love you for who you really are?"

"*I* didn't love me. I wanted to be like you and Shylah. I really did. Both of you are so beautiful, strong and funny and everything you do is right. I was the screwup and both of you always had to protect me. You loved the fact that I'm smart. You loved that I could go out of the compound and bring home those stories. I wanted to give them to you."

"Honey, don't you realize that Shylah and I loved you for you? Not your brain or your stories, but for you. That sweet, gentle girl who saw every hurt we had and attended to us. You matter to us. You're our sister. Whitney would have sent you out no matter what. In fact, he probably would have insisted you go out twice as often if he realized you didn't like it. I would have cherished those stories even more, knowing how difficult it was for you to go."

"I'm sorry for not telling you the truth, but I couldn't bear to be that person in your eyes. Whitney already despised my cowardice and I didn't want you to as well. I couldn't have stood to see that look in your eyes."

"Zara, how could you think that?"

"Because I thought it of myself. I still do, although I'm trying to get his voice out of my head and listen to the people I know care about me. I hate that I'm like this. I want to be like you. Like Cayenne. Even Pepper has a reason she can't fight. Gino told me she gets brain bleeds around too much violence. I don't have any excuse at all."

She looked down at her hands. Gino was slowly making her feel as if she wasn't the coward Whitney had called her, and now, Bellisia was backing up his claim. Better to believe the two people she loved than a man she had grown to despise. Now it just had to sink into her brain and override her lifetime of insecurities.

"You don't need an excuse. Not everyone has to be that person, Zara. You know you can fight if necessary. You're proficient enough to take on most people, and if push comes to shove, you always have your last line of defense. I don't fight on land. I'm too small, especially against Whitney's supersoldiers. You have to know your strengths and weaknesses."

"I know mine, I just don't want anyone else to know them."

Bellisia sank down into the rocker next to Zara's and drew her legs up. "Ezekiel is good for me. Maybe Gino's good for you, but he does scare me a little. I'm not going to lie about that." She hesitated. "Or the fact that I was a little jealous that you relied on him and not me."

Zara couldn't help but laugh. "Jealous? Bellisia, I was so jealous of Ezekiel I couldn't even look at him. The minute you said you wanted to tell him about the SSD I was so upset I couldn't stand myself. I don't know why I trusted Gino so fast, maybe it really is because he rescued me and I've relied so heavily on him, but it didn't feel that way even then. Now, he feels as if he's a part of me. Maybe the best part."

Bellisia shook her head. "I don't like that you sell yourself short, Zara. It isn't healthy. You can't get into a relationship if you don't know yourself and feel as if you're bringing something equally of value to that other person."

"I think I'm doing that for him," Zara said. "I hope I am. He says I am. I don't like being away from him, and he doesn't seem to mind sticking close."

"Honey, you can't even walk right now. Of course you're relying on him."

Zara glanced around the yard and then turned a speculative gaze on Bellisia. "Do you think it's Whitney? Could he have paired us somehow? Is that what you think?"

Bellisia frowned. "It's possible but not probable. In any case, what if he did? He can't do it emotionally, so that's all you and Gino."

Zara let out her breath. "We talked about pairing, but not in the context of us. I just want something real." She wanted Gino to fall in love with her, not have him want her because Whitney had decreed they should be together.

"Gino is about as real as it gets. I'm here for you, no matter what. If Gino's your choice, then I'll make every effort to get to know him and have an open mind while I do it, but promise me you'll take into consideration what I told you about Joe's father and Gino's background with him. Also, the fact that you still can't walk and can't do anything else but rely on him."

"Gino *is* my choice, Bellisia." She was decisive. Firm. Assertive. She recognized her path and she wanted to stay on it because, for her, Gino was the perfect man and she knew it. "Like Ezekiel's your choice. He's already making plans to build me a research center. He told me to give him the list of the things I need for it. He isn't expecting me to sit in a house waiting for him. He knows I need to work, that I want to and it's important to me. Because it's important to me, it's important to him."

Zara could see the struggle on Bellisia's face. She wanted to believe. She wanted Gino, if that was Zara's choice, to be right for her.

"Have you . . . "

"Yes. And it was awesome. He's awesome. I had no idea it could be like that."

Bellisia really smiled for the first time, her grin a little mischievous. "I have to know, all that practicing, did it pay off?"

"Most assuredly," Zara said. "You know how I believe in researching everything important. I was very happy I had because I shocked the heck out of him."

Bellisia laughed. "I'll bet you did." The smile faded

and she leaned into Zara. "Does he really make you happy? It was fast for you. I'm not saying it isn't real because I fell hard for Zeke right away, so I know it can happen. Neither of us has ever dated, or spent time with other men. I knew Zeke was right for me. Do you really *know*, Zara?"

"I know he's right for me. I'm hoping I'm right for him. There's a part of me that worries the moment I'm all healed, he won't feel the same way."

"That's Whitney talking. You're more than good enough for him."

"It's not that. He's so protective of everyone, you said it yourself. He might have the white knight syndrome. We read about it, remember? We used to look things like that up all the time. He rescued me and took care of me day and night. I looked far worse when he first got to me. He had to take me to the bathroom and stay in the room with me because I couldn't sit on a toilet alone, or take a shower by myself. I was completely dependent on him. Once I'm not, that part of him that maybe needs that . . ."

"Don't. Gino is many things, but he isn't a liar. If he says he wants you, you can bet that he does. He isn't a man to deceive himself. Not ever. He knows exactly what he's looking for. He's had the time to figure that out. If he wanted someone else, Zara, he'd have her already. And I can't believe I'm taking his side."

"That's because you love me and you want me to be happy. You know Gino makes me happy." Zara sent her a smile. "He does. Very happy. I feel safe when I'm with him and cared for. Loved even, although he hasn't said he loves me, but he gets this look on his face sometimes when he's looking at me."

"He can't help but love you, silly."

"So." Zara took a deep breath. She had to get this done. "I did tell him about the information I stole from Cheng's computers. He wants to tell Trap and Wyatt so they can help figure out how to extract it. I didn't want to let him do that until I talked to you. If you say Ezekiel will help without moving that information up the chain of command, then of course you have to tell him. I need to know if you think Trap and Wyatt are okay to tell."

"Zeke would tell Joe if he thought it was absolutely necessary and that we could protect you, otherwise, no, not if you didn't want him to. Trap and Wyatt are renegades. Like Gino, they go their own way. Joe has a tough time reining them in. Truthfully, all the men in this unit are a little bit renegade."

"You're sure about Ezekiel?"

Bellisia nodded. "Truthfully, he's as rogue as the others. I think GhostWalkers just are, Joe included, although because he has to lead, he has fewer choices. He has to bring things to the major general. Gino protects him, so it stands to reason he wouldn't give him this information about you. It would put Joe in a terrible position. Trap's impressive. He might be a difficult man, but he comes up with innovative ideas that are far ahead of our time. The strides he's made in the medical world are amazing. Believe me, Zara, no one will have to explain PEEK-carbon and nanotubes to him, or whatever you were talking about."

Zara found herself laughing with relief. She should have known Bellisia would forgive her and help her immediately. It was her own insecurities that kept making things between them difficult. She had to stop or she'd end up ruining every relationship she had. She'd be fulfilling Whitney's prophecy through her own stupidity.

"Do you really understand all that stuff?" Bellisia asked. "Because I looked it up and half the article sounded like a foreign language."

"You'd understand if you wanted to, you just have no interest in it. You're all about other things."

"You got that right." Bellisia glanced toward the screen door. "Do you think they're ever going to be bringing us that strawberry lemonade? No one makes it better than Nonny."

"I think they're waiting for a signal that we're finished with our talk," Zara pointed out, unable to keep the laughter away.

Bellisia laughed with her and then lifted her voice. "Zeke, Gino, where's the lemonade? We might die of old age before you get out here."

"At least of thirst," Zara corrected. "Although it was sweet of them to disappear so we could talk."

"Zeke might want to run, thinking about the two of us locking horns," Bellisia said. "But I'm surprised Gino didn't have an ear to the screen. He's all protective of you."

The screen opened and Gino came out carrying a beer and a frosty, tall glass of strawberry lemonade. Right behind was Ezekiel with the same.

"I was listening at the screen," Gino said, unrepentant. "Did you think I was going to let my woman get upset without me close?"

"I wasn't," Ezekiel said, his tone saintly. "I did my best to pull him away, told him if the two of you got into a catfight, then I'd come watch, just for the entertainment, but otherwise, no way. I didn't want my ass kicked by a girl."

"I would have kicked your ass," Bellisia said, taking the glass. "But because you were so good, I'll just kiss you instead."

"Did you really eavesdrop on our conversation?" Zara asked, trying to glare and not succeeding because he looked so Gino. Gorgeous in that rough way of his. So . . . hers. And she didn't really care in the least.

"Yep. Every word, princess. Good thing you're not in trouble for saying anything nasty about me."

Bellisia regarded him over her glass. "Eavesdroppers never hear good of themselves."

"'Awesome' is the word that I think best describes

me." He brushed a kiss on Zara's forehead and then slipped into his favorite place in the shadows where he could keep an eye on their surroundings even as he joined in their conversation.

Zara opened her mouth, but closed it, uncertain what she wanted to say. Gino sent her an unapologetic grin that kind of melted her. She glanced at Bellisia, who had one eyebrow up and a look that said, "*see.*"

Zara realized she did see. Bellisia would have been angry with Ezekiel and maybe rightly so. She wasn't in the least upset with Gino, although clearly Bellisia thought she should be. She considered that while Bellisia explained to her husband that Zara spied on businesses for Whitney and how it was done. Zara knew other women would be really angry with their spouse or boyfriend for blatantly eavesdropping on a private conversation, so how come she wasn't?

"It was private," Zara finally said, half whispering.

Gino shrugged. "Maybe, but someone has to look out for you. The last time you cried for a long time. That wasn't happening a second time."

She looked up at Gino, her heart sinking. Maybe something really was wrong with her because he made her feel loved and protected. He made her feel safe and like he would fight for her if she couldn't fight for herself. Was it so wrong to feel that way? She honestly didn't know. She pressed the frosty glass to her forehead, trying not to feel anything at all. Bellisia wasn't trying to make her feel like a fool for not caring that Gino had listened.

"Baby." Gino was suddenly crouched down in front of her, his hands cupping her face. His thumb slid over her lower lip. "Look at me, Zara. Only at me."

His voice turned her inside out. He could sound so completely gentle, so tender, at odds with his tough image. She forced her lashes up so she could look into those black, fathomless eyes of his. What she saw there shook her. Took her breath. For the first time, there was no doubt in her mind what he felt. It was there in his eyes. Not lust like she'd seen several times. Not a mixture of lust and love, which she thought she'd seen the night before. Just plain love. She might have never had it from a man before, but she recognized it.

Everything in her settled. All the doubts were swept away. He'd told her their relationship belonged to them, no one else. Bellisia obviously had a good relationship with her man. It was different from Zara's with Gino because they were different. Neither was wrong or right, just different and that was okay. She let her breath out, the last of the knots in her stomach unraveling.

He kissed her gently, his lips brushing over hers, sending a million butterflies winging their way to her deepest core. "Tell me you're okay. I can take you for a drive if you feel you need to get away for a little while."

She brushed at the strands of hair falling around his face. She loved the way his hair seemed impossible to tame. "I'm good, Gino."

"You really upset over me listening?"

She knew what he was saying. If she said yes, they would be talking about it more, but he wouldn't back down. She shook her head. "I'll tell you if I need total privacy."

He frowned at her. "Remember what we agreed, baby. You think about that. We don't have secrets."

"You'll have them," Bellisia said.

"Okay, baby, that's enough," Ezekiel said. "I'm done with this weird shit you're pulling because you're not one hundred percent behind your girl with Gino. He's a good man. He's in love with her. They can work out their own relationship."

Bellisia shook her head and looked down. Ezekiel instantly put his hand on her shoulder to comfort her. She lifted her head and looked at the couple. "I'm sorry, Zara. Gino. I don't know why I'm so afraid for you, Zara. I'm trying to feel it's right, but there's a part of me that knows you're very vulnerable and fragile. Not just now, all the time."

Before Zara could say anything, Gino sank back on his heels. That put him eye to eye with Bellisia. "I know she is," he conceded. "I saw it right away. She'll never have to worry when she's with me. She'll learn that eventually, but we're still new. She's getting there. I'm glad she had you to look out for her when she was at Whitney's compound. I'm glad you're here to be her family with me. When I'm away, I'll know you'll have her back, and when you're away, you'll know I have it."

Bellisia glanced up at her husband and then looked back to Gino. She nodded. "Thank you for being so understanding. It's difficult to let go of that role."

Zara cleared her throat. "I'm right here in case no one noticed."

Gino stood, leaned down to brush a kiss over the top of her head and then disappeared once more into the shadows. "Princess, I always know exactly where you are."

"I want to talk about the storage unit you have in your head. It's pretty damned innovative, Zara," Ezekiel said. "I'm with Gino, I think we should bring Trap and Wyatt in on this and if you don't mind, I can talk to them tonight. Trap will have all kinds of questions for you to answer. Who would ever conceive of anyone planting an SSD in the brain?"

Zara nodded. "If Whitney hadn't gone off the rails, he'd be so far ahead of the competition, the United States would never have to worry about losing the cyber war, or the one on the ground." She realized what she'd said after the words came out of her mouth. Whitney had really gone off the rails, he was insane. His genius had corrupted him. She was no longer willing to listen to his voice in her head telling her she was inferior, that she wasn't good enough for him, a failure and a coward.

"It's pretty cool that you can 'talk' to machines," Ezekiel said. "Trap may ban you from his beloved laboratory. Wyatt's is first-class, but you have to see Trap's. It's state-of-the-art. Once he and Wyatt disappear into that lab, we all know we might not see them for a week."

The others laughed, but she didn't. She understood. She knew what it was like to be so passionate about her work that she couldn't break for something as mundane as eating or sleeping. She'd holed up for more than a week a few times. When she'd been in her teens, Whitney had locked her in the lab and told her she couldn't come out until she'd solved the problems he'd put in front of her. She'd learned that behavior from those earlier days. First it had been Whitney keeping her there, but then she wanted to be there. She loved the various projects she worked on, and she could escape into her work.

Zara felt Gino's eyes on her and she slowly raised her gaze to his. He sent her a slight smile, but his eyes weren't smiling as he gave a slight shake of his head. A small shiver went through her. She knew what that headshake meant. He wouldn't have her staying for a week in a lab or anywhere else doing research. She would be coming in at night and sharing their table and their bed. He'd already made that clear to her.

Did she mind? She thought about that too. Not really. Again, she saw it as caring, the opposite of the way Whitney had treated her, or the way she knew Zhu would. Zhu would be like Whitney, force her to work no matter what if Cheng wanted something from her. If she wanted to work late, she was certain Gino would come to her, probably with food. His kisses would be enough to distract her into going to bed with him. She sent him a reassuring smile.

Gino never really looked tense, but she was beginning to read him after spending so many days and nights with him. He definitely relaxed when she smiled at him. She tried to keep her attention on what Ezekiel was saying. He was attempting to help, and it was important to remove the data from the storage unit so Whitney would lose interest in her.

"I love the idea of PEEK-carbon being used. It's completely translucent. The idea that you can walk into any lab and steal data right out of a computer without a single person having a clue you took it is extraordinary. Add building an SSD out of the nanotube of PEEK-carbon, and you're the ultimate spy."

Zara felt her body tensing up. Ezekiel had a lot of clout in the unit. He was an officer. She knew Gino was one as well, but Ezekiel had been running the rescue mission, and like Joe, his word was law. If he decreed she had to go retrieve data from somewhere, or suggested she do that for his major general, she would be in trouble. She'd be forced to continue a life she detested.

She loved her work on artificial intelligence. She saw it as the future—something that could really help mankind. She didn't mind talking about it with others equally as enthusiastic, or those wanting to learn. If she was stealing from those people, she felt tense and sick. There was no way to have light conversation when she knew she'd stolen their hard work just so Whitney or someone in the government could piggyback on the work others had done. She sat still, frozen in place, feeling threatened. Ezekiel's enthusiastic voice receded as she stared out to the river.

She needed a porch on her house. She began building it in her mind. It was the first time she didn't count or do math problems to go somewhere safe. She built her home. A two-story house with wide sweeping stairs. Little alcoves along the way where she could put pictures of the children. A closet under the stairs where she could put their backpacks and jackets—although she was in the swamp, so the humidity might stop them from having to wear jackets. She'd have to ask Nonny.

"Princess." Gino's voice was low. Gentle. It cut through

the large living room she was putting together in her mind. She looked up at him. "Zeke isn't going to throw you to the wolves. Neither is Trap or Wyatt. We've all had our share of shit, baby. Bellisia, and if we ever find your friend, Shylah, and you, have had too much as well. We're building something here together. Homes. Family. We look out for one another. You're mine, and, baby, make no mistake about it, nothing will ever touch you like that again. I'm a hunter. It's what I do best."

"Did something I say upset you, Zara?" Ezekiel said.

She heard the genuine concern in his voice. It was impossible not to see it on his face. "I think I'm still a little afraid of everything, Zeke." Deliberately she used the shortened, friendlier version of his name. "I never want to have to steal from people again. It felt wrong when I was doing it and even though I have the gift, I'd rather find better uses for it."

"Tell me you won't mind screwing with Trap," Ezekiel said. "Wouldn't that be great, Gino, to pull a prank on him just once and he wouldn't be able to figure it out?"

"When you confessed, and eventually you'd have to, he'd probably shoot you," Gino pointed out and took a long, slow pull of his beer.

"It would be worth it."

"After Trap shot you, he'd have Cayenne roll you up in silk and hang you from a tree upside down. All the others would laugh and point and take pictures to send to the other GhostWalker teams before he relented and got you down, fixed your wound and then dumped some kind of burning liquid into it just to remind you not to fuck with him."

"You're right, damn it. He'd do all that."

The two men grinned at each other. Bellisia and Zara exchanged a look.

"Are they joking?" Zara asked, needing confirmation, because it didn't sound like they were.

"Nope," Ezekiel said. "That's Trap."

"And Cayenne will do anything for that man, even take one of us down if she has to," Gino pointed out.

"I believe your woman threatened to end me," Ezekiel said.

Gino took another drink from the bottle. "True. She can get wild on me, but if I recall, it was only after your woman threatened to do me in permanently for a very small indiscretion."

"It wasn't small," Bellisia chimed in. She sipped at her lemonade. "You were trying to get into my sister's very pretty undies. She always wears really pretty underwear, which just pissed off Whitney, but he gave up throwing them out."

"I brought home underwear for you and the others every time I came back," Zara said, piously, loving that she was part of the camaraderie. "And really, should we be talking about my underwear? I came with zero pairs."

Bellisia feigned horror. "Are you telling me that you're going commando right this minute? Zeke, cover your ears."

"You were the one who brought up my panties and how Gino wanted in them," Zara said. "And I have plenty. Gino has very good taste in underwear and other . . . delicate garments."

"Gino, you are a despicable kind of man," Ezekiel said. "Looking to get into your woman's underwear."

"It wasn't her underwear I was looking to get into," Gino clarified.

Ezekiel raised his beer to his friend, and Gino raised his back before they drank. Bellisia and Zara laughed together over the ridiculous conversation. Zara was just happy that she and her beloved "sister" had come to an understanding.

15

$\sim$

Zara sat outside on the porch after dinner with the women while Trap, Ezekiel, Gino and Wyatt went into the laboratory. She didn't even care that the topic the men were discussing was her. They'd asked her hundreds of questions and she didn't want to be with them anymore. She'd spent yesterday answering queries most of the day until Gino finally called enough. She was grateful to him, because discussing anything relating to Zhu or Whitney was upsetting. Talking about how she could steal from the machines and seeing their faces light up made her uneasy, so she was doubly grateful Gino recognized she needed a break from the men.

She found herself sitting beside Nonny with the other women surrounding her. It felt good to be in female company and she was glad that she had gotten to the point that she could totally enjoy herself without the safety net of Gino right there. It was restful. Pepper had already put the triplets to bed, and the women were watching the sun set over the swamp. She found she loved the nights there even more than the days. Being surrounded by the women she was growing to care about made for a perfect evening.

"Gino mentioned to me that when things settle down, Zara, that all of us, Nonny included, should have a girls' night," Bellisia said. "I've never been on one and don't know exactly what girls are supposed to do."

They all looked at one another, apparently clueless. Zara broke the silence. "He talked about that, and I should have asked him. I was waiting to ask you. He mentioned drinking."

"I would have said I was too old." Nonny tapped tobacco into her pipe from a spicy-smelling cloth bag. "But if you girls don't know what that is, then it's my duty to show you. As soon as the boys say it's safe, we'll go. It's fun."

"Gino said they'd come along but stay in the distance," Zara admitted, half expecting the others to be upset.

"Did you think those boys would let you go unescorted when Whitney spends half his time trying to get you girls, sends his soldiers to try to scoop you up when no one is looking or just plain when he's feeling ornery?" Nonny asked.

"I didn't know what to expect," Zara said.

"Zeke would skin me alive if I went into town without him or one of the others," Bellisia said. "He's not half as protective as Gino, and no way would he let me go."

"Not Wyatt," Pepper said, rubbing her belly.

"Trap wouldn't either," Cayenne said. "But then I wouldn't let any of you go without an escort. It really is too dangerous. Whatever girls' night is, we'll have to do it with the men across the room from us."

"Being all macho," Bellisia added, rolling her eyes.

Zara really loved having the other women around her. She was used to female companionship, but spending the evening in such a picturesque place with them was surreal.

"This is the most beautiful thing I've ever seen," Zara said, gesturing toward the river, meaning it.

The trees were black silhouettes against a fiery red orange backdrop. The sun had poured fire into every space around the stationary objects. The pier appeared black; the trunks and knees of the cypress trees rising out of the water were black so that the red in the sky only accented them. The moss hanging like fringe from the branches seemed like a lacy black shawl against the red.

"Is it always like this?"

Nonny shook her head. "Sometimes, it's purple or gold. Other times it's a combination. It's never the same and yet, you can always count on the swamp to be the same." She took her pipe out of her mouth. "I've never wanted to be anywhere else."

"I can see why," Zara said.

"I love it here because I'm surrounded by water," Bellisia admitted. "Everywhere I go, I can just slide into the water and feel my body absorbing it. It's a perfect location for me."

"I love it because the girls are safe here," Pepper said. "Wyatt convinced me that if we raised them here, not only would they have family to watch over them and love them, but we wouldn't have to worry so much about them making a mistake and hurting someone. This place has been a miracle for us."

Zara glanced over at Cayenne. She was looking out into the swamp, her face impossible to read with the shadows playing across it.

"I love it because Trap is here," she said softly. "He feels like home to me."

Zara hadn't thought of it that way. She didn't know what home felt like. She smelled it in Nonny's house. That smell of fresh bread and spices. Nonny's pipe. She heard it sometimes in Pepper's soft laughter when she was talking to the triplets or Wyatt. It was only when she was with

Gino that Zara truly relaxed. Was that because he was already home to her the way Trap was to Cayenne? She knew it was certainly becoming that way, and that sometimes, she could barely breathe without him.

"Nonny, this place definitely makes me feel safe and happy," Zara said. "It's magic."

Cayenne turned her head, one arm around the porch column. "Happy is good, Zara, but we're never safe. You have to always remember that. If Gino tells you that you need an escort somewhere, you have to believe him."

A dog barked in the distance as if punctuating Cayenne's words. A frog croaked and several took up the chorus. The frog croaked again very loudly, trying to outsing the others. Zara found herself smiling. Of course she believed Gino, and she really didn't care if he wanted to watch over her when she went out with the others, but she needed to know that Bellisia and the others would be okay with it too, if they were there. Clearly, they were already used to the protection of the men.

Nonny stood up and walked down the steps of the porch to knock her pipe clean against the thick trunk of a tree before walking toward the pier.

"She takes a walk every single night," Pepper said. "She never seems to slow down. I hope she never does. It isn't just this place that's magic, so is Nonny."

Cayenne turned her head to smile at Pepper. "I have to agree. She's amazing. I still can't cook very well, but she hasn't given up on me, and she never would. I didn't know it was possible, but she taught me how to let others in. I really love her."

Zara kept her eyes on the older woman as she walked along the river and then out along the pier. A fish jumped and plopped back into the water. Nonny appeared to be a black silhouette along with the trees and the pier itself. Around her was that fiery backdrop, making her the center of a beautiful painting. Zara wished she had a camera.

It was all so beautiful. As many times as she'd been allowed out of the compound growing up, she'd never experienced anything like this. The quiet, sitting surrounded by others, just watching the sunset and the woman who was the glue that held a very large, extended family together.

She wanted to be like Nonny. Not the same person, of course, but a woman others would feel comfortable around. A woman dedicated to her family. She knew Nonny was fiercely protective of all of them. Her shotgun was leaning right against the house, beside her rocking chair, where it always was.

There was another splash in the water. Something larger moved. Zara narrowed her eyes and leaned forward, trying to get a better look. Alligator eyes appeared red at night. Around her, the women talked, but Zara no longer heard what they said, intent on the water surrounding the pier.

"Nonny." She raised her voice to carry across the yard to the long dock. Wyatt's grandmother had walked out onto the wooden landing as she did every night. "Come back."

Zara was on her feet, heedless of the pain. She caught up the shotgun as she began her dash, and actually leapt off the porch, running. She'd always been fast. That was one of the advantages of her long legs and she'd always had the ability to sprint, covering distance faster than anyone else in the compound. Her cat DNA probably helped.

Nonny spun around toward her just as something big and black, the fiery glow behind it, heaved itself out of the water onto the pier, reaching for the older woman.

"Drop!" Zara screamed it. "Drop, Nonny!"

Nonny did as she was told, and Zara pulled the trigger just as her feet hit the wood of the pier. The kick in the gun drove the butt into her shoulder hard, but she didn't feel that either. She threw herself over Nonny's body and fired again as a man dressed in a black wet suit came at them. The slug drove him back, but he didn't go down.

"Run," she hissed at Nonny.

Nonny got up slowly to face the big man who had stumbled nearly to the end of the pier. He straightened. Time slowed down as he looked over their shoulders, a smirk on his face. Bellisia slipped into the water as three more men in wet suits came up on either side of the pier. Calmly, Nonny took the shotgun from Zara.

"This was a present from my grandson," Nonny said softly. "Never knew why that boy wanted me to have a shotgun with the capability of shooting so many rounds. Never needed such a thing. Thought it was overkill." She lifted the barrel and shot the same soldier point-blank, this time in his throat.

The man's eyes widened and he toppled over backward. His body hit the end of the pier, rocked there for a macabre moment and then fell into the water. Wyatt, Gino, Trap and Ezekiel hit the dock running. Ezekiel went into the air, knees to chest. He shot his feet out and both hit the soldier just coming out of the water. The man flew backward into the river. Bellisia was on him instantly, her poisonous injection paralyzing him immediately and then killing him as he floated away.

Gino sliced the throat of the third man, one cut, the laceration so deep it nearly severed his head. He spun toward the fourth man, but Trap had him down into the water, holding him for Bellisia. The three GhostWalkers went into the water, going under as the last of the fiery sunset sank, leaving them in the inky light.

Wyatt reached down to help Zara up. She could feel her feet now. Every bruised and mangled inch, the torn, mangled tendons. It hurt like hell. She wasn't positive she could run as fast getting back to the porch as she had getting to Nonny. She glanced at the pier. There were bloody footprints she knew were hers. She forced herself not to

wince as she took that first step. Wyatt had his arm around
Nonny as he started her in the direction of the house.

Cayenne was there, one arm around her. "Can you get
on my back?"

Cayenne wasn't the tallest woman in the world. Zara
would feel ridiculous climbing on her back. She shook her
head.

"I'm really strong. Get on and let's get back to the
safety of the house. It's you they're after," Cayenne reminded.

Zara stepped close to her, closing her eyes, forcing her
feet to work as Cayenne turned around to allow her to climb
up like a child getting a piggyback ride. She put her hand on
Cayenne's shoulder and something wrapped around her
ankle like a vise and she was jerked backward off the pier.
She hit the water hard and was yanked under before she had
time to really take a breath.

Whoever had her by the ankle swam fast, propelling
both of them through the water at a rapid rate of speed. It
was so dark beneath the surface that Zara couldn't even
see the soldier taking her away from safety. Her lungs
were already burning, feeling raw, and panic began to set
in. She fought, trying to get the fingers from around her,
trying to indicate that she was going to drown if he didn't
take her to the surface. She would have used the venom,
but she couldn't get to his hand with her fingernails. The
soldier swimming with her ignored her. She realized his
orders were to bring her back dead or alive. Whitney
didn't need her alive, he only needed her dead body, or
more precisely, her head.

Something small shot past her, brushing her body,
streaking toward the soldier. An arm slid around her
waist. Gino swam with her, not at all dragging so the soldier setting such a frantic, fast pace would have no idea
Gino was swimming with her. He caught her face and
then his mouth was over hers and he was pushing air into

her lungs. His eyes looked directly into hers and she could feel his calm. Instantly, the panic in her subsided.

He signaled that he was going up for air, and she nodded. The little rocket that had brushed against her arm had been Bellisia and she knew the soldier hauling her through the water so fast was going to be dead very soon. No one was as good underwater as Bellisia. She stopped fighting, stopped thrashing and just let the soldier drag her dead weight, as if she had drowned.

Suddenly his fingers tightened on her ankle, a rigid shackle, and then the soldier was dropping to the floor of the river, taking her with him. Bellisia was there, trying to open his fingers. Knowing he was dying, the soldier gripped her ankle harder. It would take him some time to die, some time for the tetrodotoxin to paralyze him completely, and it looked as if he wanted to take her with him. She wasn't certain she could survive until his body relaxed completely. Gino signaled her to look away. She saw the knife in his hand and she closed her eyes tightly. The moment her ankle was loose, Gino and Bellisia rose to the surface with her.

Air had never tasted or felt so good. Around them, she heard gunfire out in the swamp. A sniper rifle, probably from up on one of the roofs. A bullet hit the water and zipped under. Something big sent waves crashing around them.

"They have a submersible," Gino whispered in her ear. His arm was around her waist, holding her close.

"They won't have it long," Bellisia said. "As soon as you two are clear, I'm blowing it up. I have a stash of weapons hidden in the bank, just behind that huge root system. Get her clear, Gino."

"Wait and I'll help you."

She shook her head. "Like you, I work better alone."

Zara couldn't help herself. There was no longer a red sunset to tell her the world was on fire, but she felt like it was. She hugged Bellisia hard. "Make it back to us," she whispered.

"I will. Now get out of here, they're trying to make a run for it." Bellisia pushed off them, swimming toward the root system.

Gino put his hands on Zara's waist and pushed her toward shore, toward the thickest part of the swamp, but where there was enough of a lip on the bank for them to climb up. The moment they made it to the steep bank, he waited, pushing her close to the wall of muddy dirt, his body covering hers, his head down as they heard three soldiers whispering into a radio.

He leaned into her. "Don't move."

She nodded her head to indicate she wouldn't. Gino moved around her to climb up onto the bank. There wasn't a sound. Not a single piece of dirt slid back into the water. He used hands and feet to climb, and then it was like the swamp opened up and devoured him. He disappeared. She was looking up so she could see two of the three soldiers looking out over the water, trying to spot anyone swimming without giving their own position away. The third looked behind them into the woods.

Zara tried to make herself smaller without moving. She was too afraid to move. She could only stare up at them, hoping they wouldn't spot her. As they turned away, one dropped a holdout gun from inside his coat. It fell into the mud just above her. He crouched down to pick it up as the others hissed at him to be quiet.

Her eyes met the soldier's gaze. Shock showed on his face. She tried to push away from the bank just as he reached down with both hands, caught her around her neck and yanked her out of the water.

He had her on the ground, one hand over her mouth, the other squeezing her throat closed in warning. She stared up at him, tears blurring her vision as her body fought for air. Above him, the tree came to life. Something heavy dropped onto his back and a huge gash opened up from one side of his neck to the other. Red blood poured onto the ground around her, dropping into her hair and even hitting her face.

The soldier slumped over top of her, his heavy weight pinning her to the ground. Turning her head, she saw the soldier's two partners aiming guns at Gino. Then Gino wasn't there and shots reverberated through the swamp.

"Get up!" the second soldier shouted to her while the first continued into position behind her. "If you don't want me to blow your head off, get up, Zara. Right now." There was just a little panic in the soldier's voice.

She knew he would shoot her. She knew it absolutely. Zara shoved the dead weight of the fallen soldier up while she rolled out from under him. She got to her feet slowly, and he caught her arm and yanked her to him. She reached up to his face and scratched deep claw marks down his vulnerable throat and neck. He gave a hoarse shout and slapped her hard enough to send her stumbling back a couple of steps. He screamed in pain and turned, pulling his weapon up. Two holes appeared in his throat simultaneously. She glanced toward the Fontenot home, knowing two snipers were somewhere in that direction watching out for her.

"Zara, get over here now." She recognized him as one of Whitney's go-to men, Glenn Ridges. He was always with Whitney, always ready to do whatever the man said. He liked his job just a little too well. He had moved back into the safety of the swamp, but aimed his semiautomatic at her head. "You know I'll kill you if you don't get your ass over here."

She knew he would. He also had taken the precaution to protect his body from her. His throat was covered with a thick wrap and his hands were gloved. She went to him because she had no choice.

"I ought to put a bullet in your fucking head just for

killing Harvey. He would have died from your venom even if they hadn't shot him."

She didn't respond; what was there to say?

Glenn caught her arm and dragged her to him before she was on her feet. He gripped his gun tightly. "Start walking."

For some reason, now, even with the adrenaline rushing through her veins, she felt the excruciating pain of setting her feet down on the uneven surface. Her breath hitched in her throat.

"Zara, stay very still."

At the sound of Gino's voice, the soldier froze, trying to keep her in front of him. "I'll kill her."

Gino stared at Whitney's soldier. The man had dared to put his hands on Gino's woman. She looked scared. He didn't tell her there was no need. He wasn't a man prone to bragging, and this dumb fuck was about to die. The soldier didn't have a finger on the trigger, but he was turning the weapon toward Zara's head. Gino fired, putting a bullet through the man's gun hand. Dead center. The soldier gasped and dropped the weapon.

"Down," Gino said.

She dropped. His woman. She was a soldier whether she wanted to think she was or not. He shot the bastard through the throat. A kill shot. He didn't want to kill him so easily, not with Zara looking so scared, not with the knowledge that this man and his friends had taken her feeling of safety from her. He would have liked to have spent a little time showing the fucker what happened to men who made war on his woman, but haste was a necessity.

He shoved the gun into his waistband and reached for her. It was easier to run with her over his shoulder, so he put her there. "We're going to go over the rules again, baby," he said, his voice a little grimmer than he intended, but hell, his heart had been in his throat when he saw her on that pier with that shotgun, facing the soldier coming out of the water. He'd nearly had a heart attack when he saw that soldier grip her ankle and drag her underwater.

She didn't answer, but she bunched the back of his shirt in her fists as he took her into the swamp and out of harm's way. The rest of the team had mopped up most of the men Whitney had sent to reacquire Zara. An explosion rocked the ground. Birds took to the air. An alligator bellowed. Bellisia had blown the submersible to kingdom come and anyone still in it was gone. Once the all clear was given, Gino took her back to the house.

Joe stood just to the right of the porch, his eyes like twin silver flames. His eyes only changed color like that when his energy went south. He was definitely in a shit mood and there was not going to be any putting off his questions. Gino took Zara right past him into the house, but Joe followed.

"Give me a minute," Gino said. "Got to get these wet clothes off her and get her clean." She had blood all over her. He could see that she tried not to see it in her hair or on her clothes as he reached into the shower and turned it on. Joe backed out of the room and closed the door.

Gino stripped the clothes from her shivering body and then from his. He took her into the stall and let the water pour over both of them. He was familiar with her body, the curves and valleys, the way she felt when he washed the muddy water from her. He kept his arm locked around her rib cage, taking most of her weight off the soles of her feet, all the while washing her clean and trying not to react.

He knew he wasn't a saint, and there was no controlling his body around her even when the circumstances weren't conducive for seduction. She had to feel the hard length of him, but she didn't say anything, nor did she object to him rinsing her hair and then his own, all one-handed. She didn't say a single word. He took her out of there, set her on the sink and wrapped a towel around her. He should have wrapped one around himself, but instead, he crouched down to examine the bottoms of her feet.

"Baby, what part of 'don't walk' do you not get?"

"They would have taken her, Nonny. They were coming for her."

"They were coming for you. They might have tried to use Nonny to get to you, Zara, but you were their goal, not Nonny." His fingers slid over her ankles. She would have more bruises on her ankles and around her neck, just as they were fading. "You nearly gave me a heart attack."

"I'm sorry. I couldn't let them take her, or worse, kill her, Gino."

Her voice was soft, appeasing, not remorseful, and he knew she would make the same decision again.

"Cayenne and Bellisia are fast, princess." Abruptly he yanked a medical kit out from under the sink and prepared an injectable painkiller. Her feet had to be hurting.

"Not as fast as I am. I got there. They didn't. I had the shotgun, they didn't."

He wanted to shake her. He was damned proud of her, but he never wanted her to do anything like that again. "You put yourself in danger. How is letting Whitney get you back going to help anyone?" He injected the medicine into her thigh and stood up. It was fast acting and would take effect soon.

"I'm so fuckin' pissed at you right now, Zara," he warned. He shoved both hands through his hair, trying to get his breathing under control. Trying to get himself under control. He could have lost her. Like his mother. His father. His grandparents. All of them. He could have lost her. He saw the exact moment when the drug hit and her breathing calmed. Her eyes went a little hazy. At least he could do that, take away pain, even if he couldn't keep her safe.

"If they pulled a woman in her eighties into that water and held her there, she would have drowned, Gino."

"Stop arguing with me. Let me just have this one, Zara. You took ten years off my life."

He looked up at her and her eyes met his. She seemed shocked at the level of anxiety he had, but he was a little shocked as well. He couldn't find his calm no matter how much he tried to breathe the fear for her away. He stood up abruptly and nabbed a towel, refusing to turn away from her. Let her look. Let her see what she did to him no matter the circumstances. Yeah. He wanted her. He wanted her no matter what kind of shit was happening around them. He wanted her every time he heard the sound of her voice, let alone looked at her when she was naked.

Her gaze dropped from his eyes to his chest and then lower. He heard the little hitch in her voice. Yeah. That was better. She wanted him too. He caught the front of her towel, so that his fingers curled between her breasts as he yanked her close to him. He pushed her thighs apart to allow his body to be even closer. When she tilted her head to look, he took her mouth.

She gave herself to him. There was no holding back. Her mouth moved under his, lips parting, and then he was taking every damn thing he wanted. Her mouth was pure flame. Sheer paradise. He devoured her, taking control the way he wanted, showing her who he was and what she could expect when she scared the crap out of him and he was pissed as hell.

Maybe it wasn't her fault and she'd done the only thing she could, but all that adrenaline and rage swirling in him had to go somewhere. Her arms slid around his neck and he yanked down the towel. She kept kissing him, not acknowledging that the towel was gone.

He was aware the moment there was nothing between him and her body. He was always aware of her skin. Her breasts. That tucked-in waist. The flare of her hips. That really nice ass and the way her curls were tight and silky over her mound. He kissed his way over her chin and down her throat to the curve of her left breast. His hand cupped her right one, thumb and fingers working her nipple while his mouth closed over the left.

She gasped, but she didn't pull away. If anything, she arched her body to give him better access. He took his time, making sure that she knew who she belonged to. He was gentle at first, judging her reactions. He suckled harder. His fingers got rougher. Her hips bucked a little, and he used the edge of his teeth. A sound escaped, a soft moan that she tried to suppress but failed.

He lifted his head, his eyes moving over her face. "Don't do it again."

"I can't promise you that," she said softly.

He retaliated, his mouth on her again, using his teeth and tongue on her breasts, the undersides, down her belly, his shoulder pushing into her until she had no choice but to lean back, hands gripping the edge of the sink behind her. He bit the inside of her thigh and then licked up her leg. "Don't do it again."

"Gino." Her breath came in ragged gasps. "I want to promise you, but you know I can't."

One hand to her belly, he pushed until she was lying on her back, only elbows supporting her. He put his mouth between her legs and lifted her to him. She tasted like she always smelled, that hint of citrus and vanilla. He had no idea where the scent came from, it wasn't in the soap he'd used on her, but the hot honey spilling from her had just a faint hint. Enough that he wanted more of that elusive taste. He loved the way she tasted, and twice that day, while he was supposed to be working with the others on solutions, he thought about that taste and craved her like a drug.

He gave her no mercy. She hadn't given him any. He'd watched her nearly be taken from him. He'd watched her leave the safety of the porch and run barefoot on her damaged feet straight into hell. In those few moments, he'd known, without a single doubt, he wasn't just making some decision that could be taken back, making her his choice because he was physically attracted to her. She was wrapped up inside him, tight. Wound around his heart. How the hell she'd gotten there when he'd protected himself for so long, he didn't know, but she was there and she wasn't going anywhere.

His heart had nearly stopped. His world had tunneled. He saw that run in slow motion. Wyatt, Ezekiel, Trap and he had sprinted for the pier, all four shoving guns in their jeans as they came out of the laboratory. Looking back, he had no idea what had warned them, but they opened the door to see Zara running toward the dock, Bellisia close behind her. Pepper had raced to get the triplets to the safe room, and Cayenne had stayed on the porch to protect the children.

Gunfire had erupted from the swamp, with return fire from other team members. The attack came from water, road and swamp. Nothing mattered to Gino but getting to Zara. They weren't going to take his woman.

Gino wouldn't have been surprised, when he looked in the mirror behind her, to see his hair gray. He used his tongue and teeth ruthlessly on her, driving her up. She gasped. Writhed. He didn't let her go over. He lifted his head.

"Baby, don't do it again."

"Gino."

Just his name. Breathless. Almost a sob. A little panic-stricken. He took her there again. And then a third time. Each time he punctuated his action with the same thing. "Don't do it again."

Her fists curled tightly in his hair. "I didn't know I was going to do it. It just happened. I didn't think first."

He closed his eyes. Of course she hadn't. She'd acted. And she'd do it again. It wouldn't matter if it was Nonny or one of their children. She'd go flying to the rescue because that was who Zara was. He rubbed the darker bristles along his jaw over her thighs.

"Coward my ass. You're going to make me old before my time, woman."

"I'm sorry."

"Not as sorry as I'm going to be over the years," he said, meaning it. She might not like pain. She might not like to go out into the world, traveling everywhere. She might think of herself as a coward, but she would never hesitate to protect the people she loved—including him. That was in her nature. The truth was, he'd known it all along. He knew it the moment he saw what Zhu had done to her, especially her feet, and he'd found out she hadn't given up any information. That knowledge had been reinforced when she'd revealed she had a lethal venom.

"What does that mean?"

Her breasts were heaving with every ragged breath she drew in. He had to cover her up because he wasn't such a dick that he'd take her in the bathroom with Joe right outside the door.

"We need clothes." He raised his voice, because Joe was still out there. He knew it because the man had always been as stubborn as hell and he wasn't going to go away without answers.

Gino pulled the towel around her again, just in case Joe decided to walk in. "It means, Zara, that you're no coward and I'd better not *ever* hear you say you are again."

She opened her mouth to protest, thought better of it and closed it. "Over the years," she echoed.

He sent her a look. "You're my fucking woman, Zara. What the hell do you think it means? And we're getting married as soon as I can arrange it."

She pressed her lips together and then swallowed. "You don't have to sound angry."

"I *am* angry. They nearly took you from me. I'm going

hunting the minute I have you safe. It isn't going to happen again."

"Do I have a choice in this?"

"In what? Marrying me immediately? Or me going
hunting?"

"Both."

"No to both." Abruptly he turned away from her when
Joe knocked on the door. Stalking across the room, he
glanced over his shoulder to make certain she was covered
up and to see how she took that particular bit of news.

"Okay, then. But are you really angry with me?"

A few of the knots in his gut relaxed a little. He took
the clothes from Joe, shut the door and turned back to
regard her. She looked beautiful sitting there on the sink,
holding the towel to her. It wasn't difficult to see his
marks on the upper curves of her breasts, and he liked
seeing them a hell of a lot more than he liked seeing the
faint whip marks still marring her skin. Most were closed,
leaving only long red marks. Nonny's concoctions and the
antibiotics had helped tremendously, along with the fact
that most GhostWalkers healed injuries fast.

"Are you, Gino?"

She sounded and looked upset at the idea that he would
be angry with her. He was across the room again, this
time to cup her face gently in his hands. "Baby, I'm angry
at anyone who puts their hands on you. Anyone who hurts
you. Anything that hurts you. Not you. You might get into
trouble, Zara, but I'm not going to be angry."

He bent down so he could brush his mouth across hers.
She'd been through enough and he didn't want her to be
upset. Certainly not because he wanted to go hunting. The
more he was with her, the more he saw who she really
was, the tighter those ties were around his heart. He didn't
even care that she'd wrapped him up like that. He hadn't
expected it. He'd been an idiot thinking he could claim

her and then she would fall like a ton of brick for him, not the other way around.

"What does getting in trouble entail?"

He dragged a T-shirt over her head. "Don't think that cute tone is going to get you off the hook, princess."

She licked her bottom lip, her eyes on him as he pulled up a pair of jeans. It wasn't the easiest adjusting his cock when she was looking at him, and that particular part of him refused to stand down even when he told it to.

He pulled on his tee and reached for her. "I need to see to your feet, and we can talk to Joe at the same time."

"Joe? As in the head of your team Joe?"

"The one you've avoided since you've been here," Gino said. He pulled open the door and jerked his chin toward his room where his medical supplies were so Joe would follow them there and not think Gino was avoiding him.

"Whitney is still after her, Gino. You want to tell me what's going on? You, Trap, Wyatt and Zeke are all up to something. I let it go, but once it affects the team and the women here, you don't get to keep your secrets."

"It's not my secret, Joe, or you would have been the first to know." Gino put Zara on the bed and reached for his medical bag, pulling it to him while he sat, dragging her feet into his lap.

Joe switched his gaze to Zara's face. She was looking at the sheets. "You're on my home turf, Zara. I want to know exactly why Whitney wants you back so much that he's made two tries for you. He lost a hell of a lot of men he can't afford to lose. My guess is he's got another wave of them coming at us soon. Spill it now."

Zara looked up at Gino, searching his face for a sign. He wanted to tell her that Joe was his brother, and trustworthy as hell, but it had to be her decision. She'd given him her secret and then allowed him to tell Trap and Wyatt. Bellisia had told Zeke. She was very scared that if they couldn't get the information out of her head, she would be taken forcibly from the team by someone Whitney was friends with. The worst of it was, her fear very well could turn into a reality. Gino would have no choice but to go AWOL and get her back if that happened.

"Don't look at him, Zara," Joe said. "Look at me. I'm the head of this GhostWalker team, not Gino."

"I'm not under your orders," Zara said.

That shocked the hell out of Gino. She was usually very passive. She would state her point, but then she refused to argue. She was shutting down Joe's authority over her. Gino stroked ointment on the soles of her feet and then over the bruised muscles.

"No, you're not, but Whitney just made a grab for you. I've got women and children to protect here. If you aren't willing to tell me why he keeps coming after you, then you aren't staying here."

Gino very slowly put Zara's feet back on the mattress. He stood up, feeling the familiar surge of adrenaline flooding his body. Heat coiled. "Joe. Just so you know, she leaves, I leave."

They stood toe-to-toe. It was rare for Gino to ever go against Joe. Ever. Gino protected him and had since he was very young. Gino followed him into the service and then the GhostWalker program for that very reason. There was no going back from this.

"Zara," Joe said very softly, not taking his eyes from Gino. "I never thought I'd see the day when my brother chose to put a woman before me. You must be very, very special. I'm asking, as his brother, that you tell me why Whitney won't let you go."

There was a small silence. Gino didn't drop his gaze from Joe's. He wasn't backing down. Behind him, Zara shifted her weight and then her hand was slipping into his. So small, her fingers delicate. She had such a grip on him, not with those small fingers, but with whatever it was that was between them. Gino broke the eye contact to look down at his woman. He nodded to her, and she took a deep breath before she gave Joe everything.

"Whitney knows I stole Cheng's information. All of it. Everything he collected over the last few years. Names of agents, weapons development by various countries, who is selling out their country, who is drug running, gun running, human trafficking, all of it. Whitney sends me in as an industrial spy. I give a lecture and collect data from whatever company he needs the information from. Cheng had the GhostWalker program. All of it had to be destroyed. I was capable of doing both, collecting the data and destroying everything he had so he couldn't recover it. Whitney sent me in. Unfortunately, if you tell your commanding officer, they will come for me, and eventually Whitney will get me and the information anyway."

"We didn't want to put you in the position of having to lie to Major General Tennessee Milton," Gino explained.

"Thank you for telling me, Zara. It can't be easy to trust any of us," Joe said gently.

"Gino trusts you," she said.

Her fingers curled into Gino's and he sank down onto the bed, knowing she needed reassurance. He was beginning to read her. She was nervous. She knew, just as well as Gino did, that Joe was in a bad position. The Ghost-Walkers might be handled differently than other military teams, but they had to answer to their commanding officer.

"So, Gino, what exactly have you geniuses decided to do about this?"

"Don't lump me in with them," Gino protested, tugging until Zara leaned into him. He brought her knuckles to his mouth and kissed them. "Trap, Wyatt and Zeke get that label, not me. I do the grunt work."

"Bullshit. In any case, what have you decided is the

best course of action, because we can't have them coming at us like this."

"No, but you could call Major General and let him know Whitney isn't keeping his side of the bargain. We were told if we rescued her, we got to keep her."

Zara tried to pull her hand away. Gino kept possession of it, holding it tighter, pressing her fist against his chest.

"That makes me sound like some kind of prisoner to be passed back and forth depending on who is in charge," she protested.

"You are a prisoner," Gino said. "Mine. And as far as you're concerned, I'm in charge."

She rolled her eyes and flashed a faint smile at him. "You're impossible."

"True." He was unrepentant. He'd been up front with her about his personality, his character. She knew him and she knew he wasn't joking.

"Let's get back to the problem, because it isn't going to go away, Gino," Joe said. "If they keep coming at us, someone is going to get killed. None of us want that."

"He's right," Zara said. "Maybe I should go, Gino. Whitney won't have a reason to attack any of you if I'm gone."

"That's not a possibility," Gino said. "You know that, so don't even consider it. You try to leave, baby, and I won't like it."

"Have they come up with any ideas?" Joe persisted. "Can you just pass the information to us and let us decide what to do with it?"

"The files are in my head. I don't know what's in them, and I can't get them out. Only Whitney could do that," Zara explained.

"In her head?" Joe looked to Gino for an explanation.

Gino told him everything, and they looked at one another for a long time. Zara sat very still as if she was half expecting Joe to change his mind and kick her out.

"Solutions?" Joe prompted.

"We're working on it," Gino said.

"Then work faster. In the meantime . . ."

"In the meantime, I'm going hunting. Whitney has attacked us twice. He's got another team somewhere close, probably the main one, waiting to attack. Most likely he thinks the first two softened us up, made us think he was finished. I'm pissed now, Joe. I need to take it to them."

Joe nodded. "I was afraid you were going to say that. When are you heading out?"

"As soon as I know Zara's covered. I'm talking to Bellisia and Cayenne. They'll make sure nothing happens here while I'm gone."

"Meaning you think they'll stop me if I try to leave," Zara said. "I don't want you to go off looking for supersoldiers. I know you think they're easy to kill, but they aren't."

"They are if you know how to kill them, Zara. I do. We all do. We work together to get it done. Whitney is going to run out of men."

"I don't want you to go," she whispered. "I hate that everyone is in danger because of me."

"Actually," Joe contradicted, "they're in danger because Whitney keeps coming at us. I'm going to talk to the three resident geniuses and tell them to step it up. You get your team together, Gino, and I'll call Major General and tell him his good friend Whitney needs to back off."

Gino watched him go and then he turned to Zara. "Baby, don't keep thinking in terms of leaving. I've got a house to build and you've got a home to make for us. We'll get rid of the threat to you. It might take a little time, but we'll do it. We're building something here. Something important."

He hadn't thought he'd have a wife. Children. Now he needed that fortress the GhostWalkers were building around their women and children. He had something to protect other than Joe.

"I don't like you putting yourself in danger."

"Worry about the ones I'm going after, Zara, not about me. When I'm out there, I belong. I'm part of that swamp. I'll come back to you. I'll always come back to you." He meant it. Now, he actually had a reason to survive.

16

~~

Gino moved through the swamp with ease. The night hid him, just as it did the other GhostWalkers, those moving in a loose line, spread out so they left no tracks and no evidence of their passing. There was no sound to give them away. They owned the night. When they moved in it, the darkness hid them, just as the swamp allowed them to become part of it.

He was known to his fellow GhostWalkers as the "Phantom Wind." He'd gotten the name after a few battles when he moved through the darkness destroying the enemy and no one ever heard or saw anything but the wind. He had an idea of where Whitney might have managed to hide his soldiers. There were only a few places he could have gotten them in without the locals gossiping about them.

Up ahead. The camp belongs to the Comeaux family, Wyatt said, his voice soft in Gino's head. *We've had a running feud with them ever since I can remember. If there is one family that would be willing to take Whitney's money and not get word to us or anyone else that his soldiers are around, it would be the Comeaux family.*

Gino was certain Wyatt was right. This would have been his choice, not because he was familiar with the family, but this was an entire section of the swamp where no one dared to go. Any other place, the locals would gossip, and Nonny would know about it. The Comeaux family was notorious for being unfriendly. They liked to shoot first and ask questions later. There were no trespassing signs up all along the waterway on both sides of the river and canal systems. He knew very little about the family, other than the men were big and mean, abused women and liked to fight.

The family bought up this land a hundred years ago, and the river has changed course since then, so that now, if you want to get near their property, you have to go off the main channel onto the much shallower stream. Boats can hang up there, making anyone caught in the shallows fair game. If you're caught, you're lucky to get off with a severe beating, robbed of course, and your boat confiscated, Wyatt added.

Do you really think they'd betray everyone in the swamp just to get at you, Wyatt? Mordichai asked. He was always cool under fire, with steady hands, scars and hair that was always that little bit too long and shaggy.

They'd betray their own father for money, Wyatt responded.

So yeah, without a doubt, Gino was certain they were on the right track. They were walking in. Even quieting the sound of their boats, something would have given them away. They could control frog and insect sound, dogs barking an alert, and they could muffle the sounds of a boat moving through the water, but that didn't mean they could foresee everything that might happen, and it was always that, the one thing not accounted for, that got soldiers killed.

Wyatt sank down in the grass and the rest of the team followed suit, crouching low, listening. They were going to have to move into the open soon. The small stream was wide enough to get a boat in, but shallow, the rocks, sand and debris making it difficult, but not impossible to maneuver over. The Comeaux brothers did so on a regular basis.

Gino studied the layout across the stream. It looked peaceful enough. The moss hanging in the branches of the cypress trees swayed with the wind. The grass was taller here, although he could see two distinct trails where humans had walked single file, forming paths leading back into the tree line. The tract of land between the stream and the swamp held only a few large boulders, grass and sand. The open space was approximately thirty feet wide. Maybe forty. Once into the swamp, the trees were thick and closer together than in a lot of other places. That gave the advantage to anyone guarding the property.

On their side of the stream, the bare tract of land between them and the stream was much narrower, perhaps closer to fifteen feet. Altogether, that gave them quite a lot of territory to cover without drawing attention from a guard.

Up in the trees, south end. The tall one with the wide branches, about two-thirds up, Rubin said.

Only Gino's eyes moved. If they had a spotter in the trees—and the soldiers would—any movement would draw his attention. It took a few seconds to find him. The soldier appeared part of the tree, his body partially hidden, the rest in plain sight but covered with a ghillie suit, making him appear part moss and part leaves and branch. The man was very still, but obviously hungry. Every now and then his arm would move, so that it looked as if the branch swayed upward toward his mouth and then came back down.

He can't be the only one. He doesn't have sight from

every direction, Gino told the others. He was already searching the trees in the area to the east. The second sentry would be in a similar tree—one tall and strong enough to support a heavy soldier. Now that he knew what he was looking for, and where the soldier would have to be, Gino spotted him. This one was sitting, not standing, and he was in a good position to shoot with his rifle. The cross-branch was perfect for him to set up shop.

I see him. These two know what they're doing. I'll take the one to the east. He's taking his job very seriously.

I'll take west, Draden said.

We'll be taking a little nap while the two of you go play, Wyatt said.

Gino dropped back into deeper cover to work his way to the east. He would have to cross the stream and grass areas in order to get to his goal. He knew he looked no more than a shadow, but any movement would draw the sentry's eye. That meant moving slowly. The one thing Gino had in abundance was patience. He could move like a sloth if that was what was required. He wouldn't be surprised if Wyatt and the others really did take a nap while they waited. It might take a couple of hours for Gino and Draden to work their way to their goals, and the others didn't have much to do.

He went to his belly and began to inch his way out of the trees into the grass and rock that would take him to the stream. The water was cold as he slid into it. It was so shallow that only his chest and legs were immersed, but he was inching over rocks, some sharp as he pressed down to make certain there was no sound to give him away. He didn't look toward the sentry, there was no use. Either the man would spot him or he wouldn't, and sometimes, scrutiny drew the eye.

The water was uncomfortable, but that barely registered. He was used to cramped, uncomfortable positions. Once, he'd stayed motionless, covered in mud, buried in the embankment of a river while the enemy camped just feet away. He killed seven of them before they discovered anything was wrong. They never saw him, but he watched them pack up and leave from that same mud bank.

He was on the other side, moving slowly now, using fingers and toes to slide forward over the rocky ground toward the grass. The grass was going to be tricky. He would have to follow exactly in one of the paths already trampled down, or the sentries would be able to see the grass being flattened as he moved.

Voices stopped all progress. Two men walked out of the trees. Both were big men with dark beards. They looked left and then right. Both spat at exactly the same moment. Gino recognized them immediately. One was Pascal Comeaux. He was the taller of the two brothers and had a reputation for beating his wife and children. Blaise wasn't married, but considered himself a lady's man, and he was every bit as mean as Pascal.

The brothers loved to fight, bully and drink. It was rumored they often shared women. Gino had, more than once, considered letting them pick a fight with him at the Huracan Club, a bar in the swamp they frequented. So far, he'd resisted, but it hadn't been easy.

"No one tells me what to do," Pascal said. "I want to shove my knife in that big bastard's gut and watch him die slow. He keeps telling me what to do, it's going to happen."

"There's only eight of them. We could take them. I was looking at their weapons, Pascal. If we kill them all, we could sell those weapons and make us even more money," Blaise said. "*After* they kill Wyatt."

"You see Wyatt's woman?" Pascal licked his lips. "I want that one for myself."

"If I help you kill these bastards, you're sharing that with me," Blaise protested.

They walked right past Gino, toward the part of the

stream where they had a boat beached. Clearly, they were experts at guiding their boat in the stream, going slow over the shallows until they made it out to the main branch of the river. Their voices faded a little as they pushed the boat into the stream.

"How we going to kill all eight of them?" Blaise wanted to know.

"Poison. They all gotta eat, don't they?" Pascal said. "The wife fixes something for them, and we dump poison in it. Even if it just makes them sick, it won't be hard to pick them off like rats in a sewer."

Gino took advantage of the fact that both sentries would be naturally looking at the Comeaux brothers. He slid toward the grass, covering a few extra feet much more quickly. He was right at the mouth of the path leading back into the trees. The Comeaux brothers were idiots thinking they could kill the supersoldiers. They had no idea what they had let into their homes. They'd be lucky if they managed to get out of the entire thing alive, and that was with keeping a low profile.

He dug his elbows and toes into the ground and propelled himself forward into the crushed grass. The soldiers and the Comeaux brothers had been using the two paths for some time. He could see that the grass was so compacted that it felt like a thick mat he was traveling over rather than actual grass. He continued dragging himself, careful not to touch the taller grass still standing upright on either side of him. Even with the Comeaux brothers leaving, he knew the sentries would be watching closely. They had been too still up in the branches of the trees to indicate they weren't taking their job seriously.

He made it to the trees and slipped behind the deeper foliage. His arms and legs needed a little break, so he stretched cautiously while he took stock of his surroundings. The Comeaux household was about a half mile from the stream. It had been close to the river until erosion had changed the course of the river, creating the little stream and veering the river away from their property. Like most of those living in the swamp, Gino knew, the Comeaux family had originally relied on the river for their livelihood. The family now had more money than most, but still, they hunted and fished and crabbed. Losing river frontage had to have upset them.

He caught movement to his left, and he rolled over slowly to get a better view. Soldiers moved, surrounding an outside fire pit. They were a good half a football field away, but he could see four of them. That accounted for six men if he counted the sentries. That left two more.

Comeaux brothers had conversation, stated eight soldiers here. I see four more back here. Don't have eyes on the other two. Draden?

No, can't see any of them. Nearing tree. Let me know when you're climbing.

Will do. Gino made his way toward the east and the tall tree where his target was. He circled around behind the tree, making certain that there was cover between him and the fire pit at all times. It wouldn't do for one of the soldiers to spot him as he was coming up on his goal.

He crouched at the bottom of the tree, looking up. He could see where there were gouges in the bark where the soldier had climbed up. *In position.*

Let's do it.

At Draden's go-ahead, Gino began to ease his way up the tree. He had the strength to use just his upper body, but he didn't want the trunk or branches to tremble as he moved upward. He couldn't displace bark or crack a limb. Any of those things would give him away to the soldier watching the entrance to the property.

He was into the heavier branches now, but he couldn't move fast and draw the eyes of the sentry. He kept his pace steady and made certain he was on the far side of the tree, away from the observant soldier and the one Draden was targeting. He finally came up behind his man. The soldier was stretched out along the branch, his rifle resting in the crook of two twisted limbs. He was using his night vision goggles, sweeping the area along the stream and the swamp behind it continuously in a grid pattern.

Gino waited a couple of heartbeats, looking along that swamp line as well. There wasn't one indication that his team was right there, waiting for the signal to attack. It was difficult to kill Whitney's soldiers. Sometimes they even wore mouth armor. The doctor had created an armor beneath the skin that kept bullets and knives from penetrating. The armor was made of a kind of spider's silk, but it rendered the soldiers a little stiff. Whitney had tried to experiment on a couple of the women, but this was relatively new, and he still made mistakes. It was a measure of his lunacy that he now used the supersoldiers he knew wouldn't last very long. They could move fast when necessary, but they didn't have the kind of agility and quickness they needed for fast hand-to-hand combat.

What Gino was going for was stealth. His GhostWalker team wanted to wipe out the soldiers without anyone knowing they were even there. It would be interesting to see what Pascal and Blaise Comeaux would do when they came home to a killing ground, especially after Whitney had to have paid them a fortune to house his soldiers in secret. The two men had gone to a bar to drink, something they were known for. Whitney had probably left orders that the two men stay away from the bar, afraid of loose lips. The two brothers had played right into the Ghost-Walkers' hands.

Gino crept up behind the sentry, his heart beating steadily. There was no adrenaline to deal with, no wild breathing. This was his world and he was damn good at it. The soldier moved, his arm going slowly down to pick up his water bottle. He raised it just as slowly to his mouth, tilting his head to drink. Gino's knife sank deep, straight into the throat to slice left and right. He left the knife in him while he caught the water bottle before it fell. Holding the soldier's body as the life drained out of it, he lowered the bottle back to the small box the sentry had set up next to his rifle.

It took minutes to station the body in the tree, laying him out, belly down along the branch, wedged in the crook, his hand on his rifle, so if anyone looked up at him with field glasses, they would see he appeared in position to shoot.

Clear to the east.

He moved to the far side of the tree, away from the sentry to the west. He leapt, landing in a crouch, and stayed at the bottom, close to the root system, waiting for Draden's report. It came a few minutes later.

Clear to the west.

Eyes on the last two soldiers? Wyatt asked.

Negative, Gino and Draden reported simultaneously.

There was a small silence while Wyatt debated. *We're moving toward you. Look around, see if you can spot them. They could be taking turns sleeping.*

That made sense, but Gino was uneasy. He didn't like the idea of two of the soldiers being absent. He knew Whitney's new army could go without sleep, just as the GhostWalkers could, for several days if necessary. If they weren't sleeping, where were they? Could they be watching the Fontenot home and if so, did they see the team leave? He doubted that or there would have been an ambush set up.

I don't like this, Wyatt. If they aren't here, and I don't think they are, they have to be watching our women and children.

Joe and Ezekiel have a five-man team there as well as Cayenne, Pepper and Bellisia. Nonny is no slacker, and neither is your Zara. She charged that soldier with a shotgun and bare feet. Keep your mind in the game, Gino.

Those two soldiers aren't going to try to take her them-selves.

Opportunity could just be as simple as chance. Zara could be alone on the front porch. He hadn't told her to stay indoors. The women liked to sit on the porch when they couldn't sleep. He doubted, with Wyatt and him gone, that either Pepper or Zara would be able to sleep. He should have been very precise in his orders. Instead, he'd fucked her. Okay, who was he kidding? It hadn't felt like fucking. He knew exactly what he'd done. He'd worshipped her. Paid attention to every square inch of her body. Memorized her. Etched her into his brain for eternity. He'd taken her twice and then, just before he left, he kissed her. Over and over. God. That mouth of hers. He was as addicted to it as he was her body.

He watched Wyatt and the others move out of the trees and denser foliage to belly crawl to the stream. Insects continued droning loudly. Frogs kept up their chorus. That reminded Gino that some of Whitney's soldiers did have some developed psychic abilities. They hadn't failed testing because of their psychic gifts—they'd failed psychological testing.

He swept the area behind Wyatt, Malichai and Rubin. There was no movement. Now all three were in the path created by the trampled grass. Draden joined him and the two went back-to-back, Draden facing the fire pit and the four soldiers there. Gino kept his gaze moving restlessly, quartering their back-trail, making certain that the missing soldiers—or the Comeaux brothers—didn't come up behind his team.

Wyatt took the field glasses and studied the four soldiers sitting around the fire pit. Clearly, they weren't expecting to be attacked; all four were looking into the fire.

One yawned. He glanced toward his sleeping bag and then toward the house. It was a good distance away. Several trees separated the house from the soldiers' camp.

"Wish that woman would cook for us," he said. "Rations suck."

"Gotta agree with you there, Tyler," another said. "The smells coming from that house are amazing. I'm pretty sure there's fresh baked bread."

"You ever get near the Fontenot house, Tom, you'll smell some great food cooking. That old lady has a rep around here. We ought to forget bringing Zara back and get that old woman. Get her to cook for us," Tyler said.

There was a great deal of laughter over that. Gino didn't like them even saying Zara's name aloud. It was said with familiarity. They knew her. They knew the way the women were treated by Whitney and still they went along with everything he did.

"Whitney would despise Comeaux," Tom said. "He's a greedy little bastard and doesn't have one ounce of patriotism. Not one."

"Neither do you," another soldier sneered good-naturedly.

Tom threw his hat at the soldier, hitting with deadly accuracy right across the flames. "I'm in it for the money. What are you in it for, Brax?"

"The women, of course," Brax admitted with a grin. "I've been trying to get Whitney to pair me with Zara. He says she's too smart for me. Who gives a fuck what they have in their head? Comeaux might not be a patriot, but he knows how to treat a woman when she doesn't give him what he wants. He beat the shit out of his old lady last night and then fucked her brains right out of her head."

That black rage in Gino's belly coiled into something deadly. Something lethal.

"How do you know?"

"Heard him swear at her in Cajun. Knew he was going to whale on her and I snuck up to his bedroom window and watched. He's like a bull. Funny thing is, his brother was there. Right in the bedroom, calm as you please. Watchin' right along with me. When Pascal quit beating her, he stripped her clothes off and the two of them went at it. Hot as hell watchin' that shit."

The fourth soldier rubbed the front of his jeans. "Just thinkin' about it makes me wish I could join them." He glanced up at the house. "We could kill the brothers and tap that. Afterward, just slit her throat and get out, no one would ever know."

The other three soldiers laughed. "You're a blood-thirsty bastard, Buck," Tyler said.

"Nope, just horny," Buck corrected.

Wyatt gave the signal, and Gino moved, making his way around the encampment to come up behind them. Wyatt and Malichai went straight toward them. Draden and Rubin came in from opposite sides. They couldn't make a sound and every kill had to be silent. If Comeaux's wife or children happened to look out the window, they couldn't see GhostWalkers moving stealthily in the grass.

I'll take the big guy closest to the fire. The one called Brax, Gino informed them. The sick fuck wasn't getting close to Zara or Comeaux's woman.

The others chose a target. Rubin wanted Buck. Draden took Tyler. Malichai had Tom.

Wyatt would back them up with his gun, if necessary. They would all slide forward in the grass together, get as close to their objective as possible before committing to the kill. This was a world Gino was very comfortable in and he began to move, easing his body onto the ground, using his toes and fingers to pull himself forward, eyes on target.

The soldier called Tyler let out a heavy sigh. "Whitney wants Zara bad. Wonder why? He usually doesn't care that much if they get away. They're always replaceable."

"He likes to get them when they're young and do his

work on them, then he gets pissed that they act like women when they grow up," Tom said. "I've been trying to get into his breeding program for months."

Tyler shook his head. "Not me. It's dangerous. None of the women want any part of it and unless they're tied down tight with a gag in their mouths and gloves over their hands, it's too dangerous to get it up. I prefer the whores in town to any of Whitney's creations."

Buck shrugged. "All women are whores. You just have to let them know you're not taking any of their crap. They'll do whatever you want given the right motivation." He leaned forward and spat into the flames.

In position. Gino was right behind Brax's chair. Buck actually turned his head and stared right at him without seeing him.

Wyatt waited until the three others had given the okay that they were in position. *It's a go. Three, two, one.*

All four rose up simultaneously, knives sliding neatly through throats, while hands muffled any sound. Each held their target through the death throe and only when the bodies had stopped twitching did they allow them to slide down into their chairs, feet dangerously close to the fire pit.

"I'd give anything to see that bastard Pascal and his filthy brother find the soldiers. They were talking about killing them and now, suddenly, they're all dead," Wyatt said.

"Is there a way to get his wife and kids out of here?" Gino asked.

Wyatt shook his head. "Nonny's reached out several times, but she won't leave. Too afraid, I think. She's never been away from home and the only life she knows is here. I'll have Nonny try again, but even doing that is dangerous. Pascal gets wind, he'll try to burn our home down."

"Maybe we should make certain he tries," Malichai

said. He sounded grim. Darker than they'd ever heard him. "Gives us an excuse to kill him."

"I could do it," Gino said. "No blowback. He uses the waterway as his own personal highway. He's always going to the Huracan Club. It would be easy enough to kill him."

Wyatt sighed. "We aren't the police here. I detest the bastard. Pretty much every decent family up and down the river despises him and his brother, but we've got enough going on without taking that responsibility too."

Gino shrugged and turned back toward the river. "There's still two of Whitney's soldiers out there. Let's go find them."

~

"It's hot tonight," Zara observed.

"Humid," Pepper agreed. She wound her thick braid on top of her head and pinned it into position to take the heavy fall of hair off her neck. "I can't tell you how often I've considered cutting my hair off. Wyatt would lose his mind though."

"Does it matter what Wyatt wants?" Bellisia asked.

"To me?" Pepper was already nodding. "Absolutely it does. If he prefers my hair long, then I'll keep it that way."

"What about you, Cayenne?" Bellisia asked. "Would you cut your hair if Trap said not to?"

Cayenne stretched and then pulled herself up onto the railing surrounding the porch. "Nope. Trap doesn't like something, I don't do it."

"Really?" Bellisia frowned at them. "I don't get that. I take into consideration what Zeke likes or doesn't like, but he isn't going to dictate to me."

"Why would you think Wyatt dictates to me?" Pepper asked. She unbuttoned the pearl buttons on her blouse and poured water on her chest, uncaring that it got on her blouse, rendering the material see-through. "I said he *pre-*

fers my hair long, so I keep it that way. I didn't say he told me I had to keep it this long. I don't mind doing things that make him happy."

"Trap dictates," Cayenne said. She shrugged. "I don't mind at all. I decide whether or not I'm going to do what he says. If it matters more to him, I do it, if it matters more to me, I don't. It all works out."

"Cayenne, marriage isn't a dictatorship," Bellisia said.

"Tell Trap that." A ghost of a smile appeared on her face. "The man doesn't know the meaning of the word 'ask.' I'm with Pepper, I don't sweat the small stuff. I like pleasing him, and he gives me the world, and I don't mean in material things, although he'd buy me a country if I wanted one. I know I'm his world, and that's good enough for me. The rest of it, Bellisia, is just diction. Trap has learned not to make the same mistake with me twice. I've learned to wait until I cool off—and he does—before I work out what's wrong and fix it."

Bellisia sighed. "I guess that's why we all are attracted to different men. What you can take in your marriage, I'd never be able to in mine." She went down the steps to the garden hose, turned it on and let the water pour over her head until she was soaked.

"I could use a little of that," Cayenne said. "Spray me."

"Me too," Zara said.

"You're both going to end up feeling sticky," Pepper pointed out. "It will cool you off for a few minutes and then you'll be steaming."

"With Zeke, I feel like I have a partner," Bellisia said, turning the hose on Cayenne.

Cayenne hopped off the railing and stood at the top of the stairs, turning around so Bellisia could really get her wet. She was wearing a white T-shirt and instantly the material was see-through just like Pepper's blouse. They didn't care; no one was around. Pepper joined Cayenne, putting her hands in the air and spinning around gracefully so Bellisia could soak her clothing and hair. When she was dripping she looked down at herself a little rue-fully.

"Since I've been pregnant, my breasts have grown. A lot. Sheesh. I can hardly keep them in my bra." Her white shirt was mostly open and the curves of her breasts were very much in evidence. "Wyatt and I are partners, Belli-sia, just different from you and Zeke, but I like the way Wyatt is with me."

"I *love* the way Trap is with me," Cayenne said. She reached toward the eaves, shot silk from her hands and wove a swing. She was fast at it. She sat in it where the slight breeze could fan her body. "I sometimes do things to get into trouble just for the fun of it."

Bellisia was really frowning now. "Get into trouble?" she repeated.

Zara fanned herself to keep the others from seeing the color creeping up her neck to her face. She wasn't about to say that she was certain she would prefer the relation-ship Trap and Cayenne had to any other that she knew of. She loved the way Trap looked at Cayenne. Since she'd been around them, there had been several times when he very abruptly would just turn to his wife, swing her over his shoulder and carry her out of a room. She wanted Gino to want her like that, and so far he'd seemed to be exactly that way. She didn't mind in the least pleasing him. In fact, she hated disappointing him. She wanted to know more about Cayenne's relationship.

Cayenne nodded, making little circles with her foot. "Yep. In trouble. He spanks me." She grinned at Bellisia. "It hurts so good."

"Are you kidding me?" Bellisia demanded.

"Nope, it's fun and it's hot. I especially love it when he tells me to do things."

"His voice," Zara said, startling herself that it came out of her mouth. "Well, Gino has this voice sometimes."

Cayenne grinned at her. "I know all about the voice. I should have realized Gino and Trap were friends for a reason."

"You two are hopeless," Bellisia said, shaking her head. "How are we going to cool Zara down? I think she needs to be sprayed with the hose too, because she's very red right now."

"She can't help thinking about Gino," Pepper teased. "It's a good thing Nonny went to bed or she'd be asking when you two are going to get married. She practically aimed a shotgun at Wyatt and told him he had to marry me."

"Well, you did have three children together," Cayenne pointed out. She hopped off the silk swing. "Come on, Bellisia, you're strong. We can make a seat and carry her to the edge of the porch. You can spray her with the hose there."

"You are not going to carry me," Zara said decisively. "I can walk a couple of steps. I ran to the pier."

"I saw Gino's face afterward," Cayenne said, holding out her hands to Bellisia so they could form a seat with their arms. "You do it again and he's going to put you right over his knee. 'Course, you'll probably like it. I always do."

"Oh. My. God," Bellisia said, rolling her eyes. "You are insane. All three of you. I wouldn't want Gino to smack you on the butt, Zara, so sit your ass down and let us carry you."

Zara couldn't help laughing. "I wish Shylah was here as well. She'd love this."

"I'd like to see some man try to smack her on the butt. She'd have them on the ground with a knife to their throat in ten seconds."

"She'd be too late," Cayenne pointed out, while Zara circled her neck with her arm. "Ten seconds with these men is far too long."

"You know what I mean."

"Don't knock it until you try it," Cayenne said.

The two women carefully deposited Zara on the middle step. Bellisia grabbed the hose and began spraying her. The water was cold and it felt refreshing in the sultry heat of the night. She sank back on her elbows. "This is heaven. Keep spraying, Bellisia."

Cayenne climbed back in her silken swing, and Pepper joined Zara on the middle stair so she could have the water running over her as well.

"Has Gino . . . you know," Bellisia asked. "And *not* with spankings."

Pepper burst out laughing. "*You know*? Is that how we say it? Has he touched you yet?"

"Yep," Zara admitted.

"It was a *lot* more than touching," Bellisia said.

"Details, woman," Pepper coaxed.

"He kissed me. A lot. And it was hot. That's a detail." She wasn't about to share anything else they'd done. It was hers. Gino was hers. "He did say I was his woman. That I belonged to him."

Bellisia groaned and made a show of gagging. "You don't *belong* to him. You aren't his sex kitten."

"I'm Trap's sex kitten," Cayenne said smugly.

Zara nearly fell off the stair laughing when Bellisia turned the hose on her. "I think your entire relationship is based on sex, Cayenne."

"Isn't everyone's?"

"You are so full of it," Bellisia said.

Pepper shook out her blouse and rebuttoned it to the pearl button just under her breasts. "She never says a word unless she's talking about that man of hers."

"What else is there to talk about?" Cayenne turned upside down and crawled down the long ribbon of silk. "You should see what I can do to him hanging like this."

"I am going to learn the moment I have this baby,"

Pepper decided. "I think your silks are the coolest thing in the world. And it's beautiful to watch you. I can imagine how much Trap loves that when you entertain him."

Cayenne flashed her a smile, did a slow somersault and planted her feet on the stair beside Zara. "Anyone want lemonade? Nonny made her fresh strawberry lemonade and it's fabulous. I tried it when she was making it. Best yet."

Immediately the other three nodded. Bellisia turned off the hose. "I'll help you carry the glasses out."

"I'm using the tall ones and filling them with ice," Cayenne said.

The two women hurried into the house. Two minutes later, Pepper glanced back at the house when sounds came from the interior. "Is that the girls? They better not have gotten out of bed. I swear, Zara, they're little escape artists. You know those dog crates? Why can't we put our children in them when they go to bed? It's the only way to ensure we get any time off at all." She was up and running into the house, laughing as she went.

Zara leaned back on the stairs on her elbows again and looked up at the night sky. Somewhere, Gino was out there. She sent up a little prayer that he was all right. Something rustled in the dry leaves at the corner of the house. She turned her head and saw a man standing there. He was in the shadows of the house, but she could just make him out. He held a finger to his lips and motioned her to come to him.

She shook her head, sitting up straight, glancing back toward the door.

"Zara, you know me. I'll kill every one of those women if you don't do what I say. Get over here."

She shook her head again. A darker shadow moved close to her, near the hose Bellisia hadn't wound back up. The long rubber tubing lay on the ground right next to the house. She looked at the man standing so close to her. He was grinning, staring at her shirt, the one that was practically transparent. She made no move to cover up. The loop slid over his head, the strands of silk so delicate he didn't feel them until they pulled tight.

Ezekiel came out of the shadows. "Seriously? What kind of soldiers watch a group of women spraying themselves with water in enemy territory and not figure out that they're keeping eyes on them? I bet my wife twenty bucks it wouldn't work and I lost."

The first soldier had eyes on the second one as he dangled off the ground, kicking and swinging macabrely in the night. He looked around at the five GhostWalkers surrounding them and then back to Zara.

"You bitch. Whitney's done with your disobedience. He wants you dead. Orders are to bring your head back to him. Sooner or later, someone's going to get you."

"Maybe," Ezekiel said. "But it won't be you. You were too busy looking at the show to figure out we spotted you the minute you entered our territory. It was only a matter of time before you got complacent enough to come look at the peep show."

"Just do it."

Ezekiel obliged, and killed him.

17

Gino stared down into Zara's upturned face. She was so beautiful it made his soul ache. That face. Skin so soft. Her bone structure. Her mouth so sinful every time he looked at it his cock got harder than a rock. Those eyes of hers. Pure slate blue. Unusual. Large. Framed with long lashes. All that hair. Red gold. Like silk, but so thick when it was spread around their pillows, it covered them. That was a fantasy in itself.

He could admit to having something seriously wrong with him. He came back higher than a kite, needing sex. Ciro had probably perpetuated that, telling him after every time they interrogated someone and then killed them that the best way to get over taking someone apart was to spend the night indulging one's body so you knew what life was all about. It made sense when he was a kid and now he was certain he'd been programmed, but it was different with Zara. With Zara, his need of her was real.

He pushed all that spun red gold from her forehead. He had her sprawled out on his bed, looking more beautiful than anything or anyone he'd ever seen in his lifetime. She looked the picture of innocence, and he was coming to her with blood on his hands. He swore his hands were shaking as he traced a finger from her throat to the curve of her breast.

"I swear, woman, I detest being away from you, even for a minute. I'm not sure what you've done to me, but whatever it is, there's no going back from it." His hand cupped her breast, thumb sliding over her nipple, all the while watching her eyes.

He loved the look she got when he moved in her. When his hands claimed her body. When she gave herself up to the beauty of what they were together.

"I don't like being away from you either, Gino," she admitted, arching into his hand.

The rain had started outside, falling on the roof and beating on the windows, the rhythm adding another dimension to his fantasy. The room was dark, but he could see easily and there was no way he was going to miss out on one detail of her face and body, not one small expression in her eyes.

"See how still you can stay for me." He whispered it, staring into her eyes, his hands filled with her soft breasts, fingers and thumb tugging and rolling her nipples.

She tried for him, because she liked pleasing him. He worked her body, using his mouth, tongue and teeth, his hands, gentle to rough and switching back. Watching her the entire time. Her breath came in ragged pants, providing a counterpoint to the rain's driving rhythm, but she stayed relatively still for him. Because he asked. Her hips bucked and her body writhed, but she held it under control, doing her best, those eyes never leaving his.

He lavished attention on her breasts, taking his time, leaving his mark, wanting to write his name there. He'd never felt like doing such a foolish, childish thing in his life, declaring ownership, wanting the world to know she was his, but there was something about her that, right from the first moment he'd read about her, had made him feel a bit primitive.

He lifted his head just a little as he slid lower. "Going to be a long night, baby. You ready for me?" He was asking if he could be who he was. Take her the way he needed to. Make sure she enjoyed every second of it. "Wet and hot? Just for me?"

"I'm always ready for you, Gino."

Her voice was a whisper but it slid over his skin like a sensual sin. He took his time, kissing his way over every square inch of the front of her. He used his tongue to taste her everywhere, his teeth to leave his mark, and his lips to suckle, bringing up faint strawberries here and there. Her breathing became frantic, her breasts swaying with every frantic inhale and rushed exhale.

He murmured to her, his mouth against her exquisite skin, telling her who she belonged to, letting her know he wasn't ever letting her go, that she was the woman he wanted to wake up to every morning and hold every night. He told her a million things, most that couldn't be deciphered between his mouth against her body and her breath hitching, exploding, rushing, moving through her so feverishly because she was desperately trying to keep still under his assault. For him. Always for him. He asked, and it mattered to her. God, he loved her.

"I can't stay still," Zara said. "I'm trying, Gino, but it's impossible."

He knew it would be, but he was pleased she tried. He spent a few minutes between her legs, devouring that addicting cream that belonged solely to him before kissing his way down her thighs to her ankles. He caught her ankles and twisted, flipping her over so he could claim every inch of her body.

"Your skin is the softest thing I've ever felt in my life," he admitted and then found the lobe of her ear with his teeth.

Zara said something, but it was muffled by the sheets. Her hips bucked again, almost as though she might dislodge him, but he clamped his leg over her thigh and held her down for his slow exploration. He moved the long, thick length of her hair, admiring the way the silky strands spread across the pillow in luxurious golden waves.

His mouth found the nape of her neck. She was particularly sensitive there and he spent a little time kissing and licking, nipping gently with his teeth, watching the slow burn spread through her body, her movements and little cries feeding his own fire. His cock was hard and thick as he dragged it down her spine, leaving a trail of wet. His mouth followed, kissing and nipping, finding every sensitive spot, until he made his way to her buttocks.

"I like the way you look a whole hell of a lot." He nipped her, right in the middle of a small dimple.

She yelped, laughed and pushed back against him, her breath hitching. "You do?"

"Mmm." He used his tongue, more exploring, widening her legs to give him access to what he wanted most. She tasted like heaven. He yanked her up onto her knees, at the same time pressing her head down so she went obediently to her elbows. "Like the way you look just like this, princess." He stroked her breasts, tugged on her nipples and then pressed his mouth to all that slick honey.

She cried out, pushed back against him, and he found his body on fire. No longer a slow burn consuming him, but a raging inferno. He licked at her one last time, pushed his finger deep while he stroked, flicked and circled her clit, wanting to ensure she was ready for him. Her cream coated his finger and he licked it clean, kneeling up behind her.

"Gino." She wailed his name. "Hurry up."

"Right here, princess. You giving me a royal order?" He loved her needy like this. Her body writhing. That little sob in her voice. His beautiful woman with that little hint of desperation drove him crazy.

"Yes," she hissed.

He pressed the head of his cock into her burning entrance. Scorching heat surrounded him, her body clamping around his like a vise, determined to pull him deep or keep him out. He was never certain with that first entry. His breath rushed out of his lungs in a long, slow exhale of pure pleasure or pain, he couldn't decide which, as he pressed deeper. Watching as her body was forced by his steady pressure to accept the invasion of his added to his pleasure. He could watch himself fuck her all night. Fast. Slow. Hard. Rough. Gently. Easy. It didn't matter as long as he was in her and watching her take his cock any damn way he wanted.

"Move."

The sob in her voice added to that mounting lust. "I am moving." He inched forward, forcing those tight muscles to accept him. Each increment was sheer bliss. Fire lashed his thighs, burned through his gut. The flames surrounding him threatened to burn right through his flesh, but it felt so damn good he didn't care.

He rubbed her left cheek, hoping her body would ease up just a little. She was so tight he wasn't sure he could fit, but it was always that way. Every time he entered her, there was this moment, the one he usually retreated and started again, letting her get used to his invasion. Not this time. This time, he was going to bury himself to the hilt, as deep as possible, all in one long assault.

"*Gino.*"

His name again. He loved the need in her voice. That little hungry plea that told him she wanted him just like this. He took his time, savoring every inch he got inside of her. It wasn't just a victory or a claiming; after the first three inches it was just plain paradise. He broke out in a sweat, holding back, feeling the boiling in his balls, the way his thighs hardened and every drop of blood rushed to his cock. All the while he watched as her body swallowed his, and it was better than any porn show he'd ever seen. Fantasies ran through his head, and he knew he would try every one with her. She was his woman and she liked to give him everything.

He used his thumb on her clit, stroking until her body coated her sheath in fresh liquid fire so he slid the last few inches all the way. His hands went to her hips. Finally, she was healed enough that he could hold her there, grip hard. He was going to need hard and she was as well. He withdrew. Her breath hitched. He heard his heartbeat. There was a roaring in his ears, like the sound of thunder.

He surged into her, dragging her hips back hard into his. Lightning streaked right through his cock and up his spine. "*Fuck*, woman." He didn't know what else to say. There was nothing else, she'd turned his brain to mush. All he could do was feel, not articulate.

He began to move in her, hard and fast, letting the sensation take him, giving himself up to it, riding that edge for as long as he could. Each time he was so close he thought he'd never pull back, he managed, even when he took her there repeatedly. Each time that she came, her body clamping down on his, that soft little sobbing of his name, drove his cock to a new level of hardness.

Gino lost himself in her body, in that incredible feeling, lost track of time and was unaware of his surroundings. He felt power gathering, heating, boiling until he was at the point of no return. His fingers dug deeply into her hips. He clenched his teeth and held on until she was there again, until he felt her coiling tight, so ready for release, so ready to soar with him.

In the end, it was more than soaring. He was flung into the universe, pinpoints of light glittering behind his eyes as his cock filled the condom with long, hard spurts while lightning rocketed through him. It seemed to go on forever, that euphoria he didn't want to come down from. His lungs were raw from lack of air and his body wanted to collapse. He circled her waist with his arms and hung on to her while they both fought for air.

When he could, Gino lifted his head. "You all right?"

"I think so," she admitted. "But I'm not sure."

He laughed softly. "Damn, woman. When I said you might kill me, I wasn't kidding. I'm going to ease you down." He slipped out of her, removed the condom, knotted it and tossed it aside so he could help her to the mattress.

She rolled over onto her side and looked up at him, her long lashes framing her slate blue eyes. "I'm not sure I can breathe."

"Then I'd better help you."

He took her mouth instantly, kissing her the way he wanted, the way he knew he was going to be kissing her as long as they both lived. Hot. Hard. Possessive. Demanding. She kissed him back, her mouth so soft, so perfect, he knew he'd never want any other woman's kiss. Her taste was so addictive, it was difficult to stop once he started. He spent time kissing her. Slowly. Burning for her all over again. Knowing it was always going to be like that.

If he'd thought about how he would be so obsessive over her before he met her, he would have been appalled at the idea of being so wrapped up in a woman. Having been with her, he could only count himself damn lucky that he'd found the right one.

A little giggle escaped her when he lifted his head. The sound pierced his heart just like an arrow. She made him happy when he'd all but forgotten what happiness was.

"I'm not sure that's helping me breathe, Gino," she said.

He surveyed her body. She was a fast healer and the marks of the whips were all but faded. His marks, ones of love and possession, had taken their places. He bent his head and kissed one that ran along the upper curve of her left breast. He liked to see them there. He liked that Zhu's marks were mostly gone.

"I'm so in love with you, woman." The declaration came out of nowhere. He knew it was true, but he hadn't meant to tell her. He smoothed back the silky hair tumbling around her face. "It's impossible not to fall for you, you know that, don't you?"

Her eyes searched his for the longest time, and then her smile came. It was slow and beautiful and it shook him to his core. Something about the way she smiled made his heart shaky, so much so that it actually hurt. He pressed his hand over his chest to try to ease that ache.

"I didn't know that, no, but I do know I feel that way about you. You're this incredible man, so amazing, treating me like the princess you call me, and I can't help but love you. So much, Gino. You're the first person I think about when I open my eyes in the morning and the last one I think about before I fall asleep. I know it sounds so silly, but just in the few weeks we've known each other, I think I've become obsessed with you. I think about you all the time." She gave him that little smile of hers, the one that always made him want to kiss her. "All those fantasies I have would make you blush."

"No, baby, they'd make *you* blush. I'd be happy to carry them out for you." He kissed her again because every time he kissed her, she got a look on her face. Dazed. Beautiful. Her lips a little swollen, her eyes dark with desire. When he lifted his head, he caught her hand and brought it to his cock. Already, he was stirring. That was the power of what her kisses could do. He watched her closely for signs she wanted to stop. There were none. Her gaze jumped to his face, a little awed. He liked that look a lot.

"Already?"

"Your fault, baby. You're lying there all laid out in front of me like an invitation to a feast. My body can't resist yours." He shrugged his shoulders. "Gotta admit, I did work damned hard. Tired myself out."

Her eyes lit up. "Did you? I guess you did, poor man. I

suppose you're deserving of a rest, although now that you've mentioned the possibilities, I'm kind of hungry."

She rolled over, giving him a good view of her very fine ass. He was partial to that part of her anatomy. Who was he kidding? He was partial to every part of her anatomy. He sat up, his back to the headboard and watched to see what she would do.

She crawled up the bed to him, looking so sexy it took control to keep from flipping her over and taking her again. As it was, his cock grew. His fist curled around the long, thick length. Her gaze dropped to the sight and just the way she looked had his lungs feeling raw, burning for air. She licked her lips, and his cock jerked in his hand.

Her fingers curled around his with one hand while the other slid under his heavy sac to roll and caress his balls. He let go, his eyes on her. Unblinking because he didn't want to miss one second. The sight of her as she lay down and stretched along the bed was almost too much. Her touch was an added bonus at that point.

She circled his shaft at the base with one fist and her tongue did a lazy slide up the heavy vein. The tip of her tongue delved into the spot just under his crown, licked and teased. Then her mouth engulfed him, and he lost the ability to breathe. Both hands went to her hair, his fingers curling in the silky strands, two tight fists.

He let her work him, her tongue dancing and teasing, her mouth hot and wild, a small sound vibrating right up through his shaft. It was beautiful to see, to feel, adding to the scorching pleasure. All the while that dark hunger in him spread. He transferred his hold in her hair, bunching the strands at the top of her head in a knot around his hand while the other curled around her throat.

He pushed her head down over his cock, thrusting gently at the same time, driving deeper into her mouth. She didn't fight him, but relaxed even more, relaxed her throat to give him that. God, he loved her. He loved the way she took him no matter what he asked of her. He held her there a moment and then let her take a breath. "Again, princess," he whispered. His voice came out husky. Dark. Compelling.

Her mouth clamped down over his cock, swallowed him down as he thrust upward. At the same time, he pushed her head down over him. She took him deeper. He stroked her throat gently with his fingers. His cock swelled even more.

She was tight and hot. Wet. The constriction felt like paradise, but more, it was what she did for him. The way she did it. One of her hands stroked caresses over his balls and then along his thighs. She didn't tense up. She trusted him to bring her up for air, which he did, although it was with reluctance.

"You have no idea how that feels, baby," he said, needing her to know.

"Good?" She licked the leaking drops from the crown.

"So good. Can you take me deeper?"

She sent him a look that told him of course she could, or at least she would try. She was willing to do whatever it took to please him. "I want this, Zara." It came out more of a command than he intended.

Her mouth was on him again, swallowing him whole, taking him deep. He began to move, thrusting gently, over and over, each thrust taking him a little deeper. That fast, he knew if he let himself he'd be out of control, but he didn't want it to end. He pulled her off of him, gave her air and repeated, each thrust a kind of paradise. It wasn't just her mouth and throat, it was the fact that she gave that to him. That she gave him her trust and that she wanted to please him. He wanted this, so she wanted it for him.

"I'm going to blow, baby. You don't want me feeding you, you've got to stop." He let go of her hair, making it her choice.

The suction never stopped, and then his body was an

impossible rocket again. So much more than he could have conceived. She took it all, and when he was done, her tongue was very gentle on him, just as he'd taught her. She rolled over and smiled up at him, looking angelic when she'd just given him something sinful and so much better than he'd ever had.

He slid down in the bed to lie beside her. "I'm going to give you an hour of sleep, baby, but we're nowhere near done tonight."

"I'm not certain I'll be able to keep up with you."

He laughed and stroked her breast. "You'll keep up." There was no question she'd keep up. She was made for him.

❦

"It's got to be Bluetooth," Trap said. He paced back and forth frowning, his eyes on Zara's head, as if he might cut it open just to see if he was right. "I've developed a proto-type, a device that is able to store vast amounts of infor-mation beyond anything the government or any private sector can imagine. It seems Whitney has done the same, otherwise the SSD couldn't hold that much data."

He pulled what looked like a regular cell phone out of his pocket, his fingers moving over it, giving commands. "I'm searching for all Bluetooth devices in close proxim-ity." He muttered the explanation, but his tone was one of annoyance, as if having to explain irritated him beyond belief.

"There's several, which I expected—the cars, the house, the lab—but we've got one here called Fiore Brillante." He looked up, his gaze meeting Zara's.

She swallowed hard. He was intense. She glanced at Gino. He was watching Trap carefully. They all were. Not carefully, expectantly. She found herself doing the same.

"It's Italian," Trap murmured unnecessarily.

"Brilliant Flower," Gino interpreted.

Zara knew languages and she knew what it meant. She didn't know how knowing the name of the SSD could help other than the fact that Whitney had an obsession with flowers.

Trap continued to stare at her until she was afraid he'd burn a hole through her skin with his laser-sharp gaze.

She leaned close to Cayenne. "He doesn't have an axe handy, does he?" she whispered.

"An axe?" Cayenne's frown matched Trap's. "Why an axe?"

"I'm pretty certain he'd like to see my brains spilled out on the table so he could go picking through them and find what he's looking for."

Cayenne choked back her laughter and sobered when Trap glared at the two of them.

"Do you have to be so distracting?" he demanded.

"Well, yes," Cayenne answered, clearly unafraid of her big, bad husband.

"You're losing control of that woman," Wyatt pointed out a little too gleefully.

Trap's expression darkened. "I never had control." He circled Zara and Cayenne like a shark, his gaze glued to Zara's head. Cayenne might not be intimidated, but Zara was. She knew exactly where Gino was, sitting back in the shadows right by the door. When he'd taken that position she'd thought a little hysterically that he was the guard, preventing her from leaving. She hated being under scrutiny, and all four men were staring at her as if she'd grown two heads. It threw her back to when she was a child in Whitney's compound and was under guard for one reason or another.

Now, she needed Gino. She felt very vulnerable and when that happened, she knew she could look to him and immediately the feeling would ease. He did that for her—

made her feel safe. It was silly to think she would be feeling apprehensive and insecure when she was surrounded by GhostWalkers, but she did. She accepted that part of her a little more now. She might always have moments when she was under scrutiny that she panicked a little, but that was just part of who she was.

Her eyes met Gino's across the room. A faint smile touched his mouth. He looked tough. Intimidating. Just as intimidating as Trap, only in a different way. It was significant that he had taken up a position there by the door. Gino was all about guarding others to keep them safe. He kept her safe.

Heat slipped into her veins. God, he was sexy. He just sat there with that faint smile on his face, and all she could think about was the things he'd done to her the night before. All night. In the morning. She'd hardly slept and she knew he hadn't.

"You've tried to connect with the storage unit yourself?" Wyatt asked.

Zara forced her mind back to the main problem and the men determined to help her. She looked around the room. There were Trap, Wyatt and Ezekiel surrounding her, looking at her like she might explode any moment. Joe sat across the room, very still, very quiet, making certain not to disturb the others. Gino guarded the door. Cayenne sat on one side of her and Bellisia had taken the other. They were in the middle of the room, sitting on slightly uncomfortable high stools, like ones that might be in a bar. The seats twisted from side to side and it was difficult for Zara not to swivel nervously when the men stared at her.

"Yes, all the time. Whitney has it password protected. I can't access the data in it. Whitney didn't want me to run and then give whatever information I had to someone else."

Wyatt nodded. "We've tried the various passwords he's been known to use and none of them have worked. I think he's made this simple for himself. You've got a permanent SSD that he never planned on removing. He injects you with something light, just enough to keep you from seeing him extract the files so you don't know where the SSD is located or how he gets the information. It's fast and you're not under more than a few minutes."

"The soldier pointed his gun right here," Gino said, pointing to the spot on his own brain.

"The where wouldn't matter if it's Bluetooth," Trap said. "And password protected. We know it is and the device is named Fiore Brillante." Again, the last was said speculatively, as if he was turning something over and over in his mind.

"Why make it difficult?" Ezekiel asked. "Whitney knows she can't get away. He has the virus. He has the other women. She's not going to give him any real trouble."

Gino added his assessment of Zara. "She's the gentle soul. The one that wants the best for the other women. She follows the rules."

"She didn't," Bellisia objected. "She brought us contraband and spent weeks in solitary."

"He would expect that. Those small rebellions were nothing to him. He wanted her to break the rules that didn't matter to him so he could punish her," Wyatt theorized. "Did she ever do anything that caused him to hurt her physically?"

Zara's stomach clenched hard. She pressed her hand there and once more looked to Gino. Of course she had. Once. One time. She looked down at her hands. It had only taken one time of Whitney inflicting real pain on her and she'd never gone so far again. In fact, she'd stopped bringing in contraband for the girls for nearly a year—until her anger at Whitney for his injustices and at herself for letting him make her a weakling overcame her fear.

"Zara?" Wyatt prompted. "I'm asking for a reason. He

put the device in your head. This all centers around you. The more we know about you and your life there, the better the chance we have of figuring out Whitney's password."

She kept looking at Gino, eyes unconsciously pleading with him. She'd told him. That one time she'd rebelled against Whitney's authority.

Gino cleared his throat, got up casually, in that fluid, catlike way he had that always made him look more dangerous and lethal than ever. "The girls wanted pictures of a real college party. They wanted photographs of the college boys." He stalked across the room, his body moving in very close to hers. He stopped right behind her, one hand sliding up her back, under her hair, to curl around the nape of her neck.

The hold felt claiming. Possessive. It also felt protective. The moment he was close to her, Zara felt safe and almost comfortable in spite of being under such scrutiny. She wanted to wrap herself around him, melt her body right into his. Be that close. Maybe others wouldn't like the way he took care of her, but she needed it and he gave it to her.

"She was young, only fourteen, but she snuck out of her apartment, right past three of Whitney's supersoldiers. At that time, she always had guards around her."

Gino leaned down and brushed the top of her head with a kiss. Zara knew he did it because he could feel the tension rising in her. "At fourteen, she was already outthinking her guards. She got past them just after midnight, snuck into the party and took lots of pictures, using her phone. She went through the rooms until she found a computer open, sent the pictures to her email and then stored them on a very small thumb drive. She wiped them off the computer and from her phone and snuck back into her room. She thought she was safe."

"I should have known better," Zara whispered.

Bellisia put a comforting hand on her knee. "You did it for us, honey."

"I know."

"Whitney, of course, monitored everything. He knew she had pictures. She refused to give them up, telling him she didn't have them, but it didn't matter. He had the three men who had failed in guarding her punish her."

"They used hoses," Bellisia said, her voice very low. "He made all of us watch."

"After," Gino took up the story, "he forced the girls to watch as he had each of the soldiers killed for failure to ensure Zara's compliance." He slipped both arms around her.

"So, you never defied him like that again," Ezekiel said.

Bellisia and Zara exchanged a long look. "I never got caught again," Zara clarified. She glanced over her shoulder at Gino, leveled her gaze on him and told the absolute truth. A warning. "I follow someone's lead until they prove to me they aren't worth it and then I don't."

"I got that," Gino said. "I'm crazy, baby, not stupid."

"Whitney's lulled into a false sense of security with her, thinking she'll obey his every directive in order not to get punished. So, he uses Bluetooth," Trap mused aloud. "Easiest way. He just knocks her out, puts his device near the SSD and types in his password and they connect. He keeps her under just long enough to extract the information and he's got what he wants. You didn't ask him questions, did you? By that time, he'd intimidated you enough that you wouldn't go against him."

She licked her lips, hating that her mouth was dry. "I didn't. Never. Not once." Mostly she hated that she hadn't even tried to figure it out herself. She was smart. She should have.

"So, we need the password," Wyatt said.

Trap continued to pace back and forth. He fascinated

Zara. Everything about him. The way he moved. The total concentration. He was absolutely silent. Zara became aware of how the room stilled. The clock seemed very loud as it ticked out the seconds. She held her breath, the beating of her heart overly loud in her ears. Gino's arms remained around her, but he also was barely breathing.

Trap moved with unbelievable precision, almost as if his brain was moving so fast, his body had to try to keep up and had become a machine. Trap passed the three barstools sitting in the middle of the room several times. He circled them and came to stand in front of Zara, using his long fingers like two rakes, shoving them through his hair until he looked wild.

"Simple. Simple," he repeated under his breath. "Fiore Brillante." He muttered the phrase over and over, looking directly at her. "Zara. Your name has several meanings. Gino calls you princess. He's Italian, but in Russian, Zara means 'princess.'" He looked to Gino for added confirmation.

Gino nodded.

"In Hebrew, it means 'seed,'" Trap said. "I'm not going there. Don't want to give Gino any more ideas than he already has. In Arabic, Zara means 'flower' or 'star.' In this case, I would say flower. It's spelled differently sometimes—Zahra."

"What does that have to do with anything?" Ezekiel asked. "Enlighten us and maybe we'll be able to help you with this line of thinking."

Trap shrugged. "I'm not certain myself yet. Just mulling things around in my head."

"In Italian, it would be spelled differently but it means 'orange flower,'" Gino said.

"That's a possibility, if he actually paired the two of you. He might go with that . . ." He broke off to look straight at Gino. "You think Whitney paired the two of you?"

"Yeah," Gino said, shocking Zara.

She whirled around on the barstool to stare at him in total astonishment. "You do?"

"Babe, we light up the world when we go at it. Been with a lot of women, no one does it for me like you. Might be the emotion, that's probably a good part of it, but"—he shrugged like it was no big deal—"chances are good he created a pairing."

"I thought the chances were slim," Trap contradicted. "Lately he hasn't been bothering unless he wants a specific genetic pairing for a child. Was the attraction between you instant and physical?"

Zara detested the idea that Whitney might have paired them. She wanted one thing without his taint on it. She loved Gino. She loved the way he made love to her, even when it was wild and crazy or he was introducing her to things she hadn't known could be done. She didn't want to think that Whitney was in any way responsible. Gino brought his hand to the back of her neck, his fingers massaging. She knew he could feel the tension in her. She wanted to leave the room, not be around anyone while she tried to decide if Whitney had really used pheromones against them. She actually made a move, as if she might leave.

Gino leaned into her, put his lips against her ear. "Do you really think Whitney could make me love someone? You've got my heart, Zara. He couldn't possibly make that happen. Settle. Let Trap puzzle this out. His mind is . . . something."

She took a breath, made herself relax under Gino's magic fingers. What did she know about Whitney? She was an observer. She'd trained herself to pay attention to the details around her. Whitney didn't understand emotion, but he did love his flowers. He always had a hothouse and he spent time there.

"Trap, he spends time in his greenhouse. A huge amount of time. If he loves anything at all, it's his flowers." The moment the thought escaped, she was certain whatever that password was, it had something to do with his obsession with his flowers.

Trap's gaze was fixed on her immediately. Speculative. "Simple," he murmured. "Zara means 'flower.' 'Orange flower' in Italian. Hothouse. His only real emotion." He repeated it, still rumpling his hair and staring at her. "Device named Fiore Brillante. Bright flower. Bright flower." Once again his gaze went to Zara, his laser-like stare focusing completely on her.

She realized he wasn't really seeing her at all. He was in his own mind, shuffling through a thousand possibilities and discarding them.

"You refer to the place he keeps his flowers as a hothouse, not a greenhouse, is that because he does?" Trap demanded.

"He never called it a greenhouse," Zara said. She glanced at Bellisia for confirmation.

Bellisia shook her head. "It was always hothouse."

"He thought the entire green conversation for the planet was taking too much attention off the military when we needed it most."

"Try ZagarAINHothousE," he said suddenly to Ezekiel. "Capitalize the first and last letter of each word. He likes to do that. With Bluetooth we don't need the exact location of the SSD in her brain, just close to it, so get close."

"Why that combination?" Ezekiel objected. "What's your reasoning, Trap?"

"It's Arabic, and a fusion of two words. Zara for 'flower' and 'Zahara' for beautifully bright," Wyatt provided. "Zara is beautifully bright and she's one of Whitney's flowers."

"Still doesn't make sense. Why that specific spelling? Trap, how could you possibly come up with that phrase?" Ezekiel demanded.

"He named Zara after the word for flower in Arabic, so

it means something to him. He has a hothouse and grows flowers. Citrus flowers vary, but zagara specifically indicates sweet orange and bitter orange trees. If you travel and want to keep citrus, you're going to have to grow it in a hothouse. Citrus can't be grown everywhere. Then there's the Italian input. Zara means 'orange flower.' Zagara has been in literature, specifically Italian literature. In the work, they mention a hothouse variety of zagara." He shrugged. "I could be far off, but his mind works like that. He believes he's very clever. We know he likes to capitalize the first and last letter of every word. It all comes back to Zara. She's his shining star. His bright flower."

"He didn't think that of me," Zara objected. "That I was beautifully bright."

"He didn't let you know he thought that," Gino corrected. "Baby, no one could see you, know your skills, and not feel you shine bright. It just isn't possible."

Zara stiffened when Ezekiel moved very close to her and began typing into his small device. Her heart beat so hard she pressed her hand to her chest. What if they couldn't get the information? Would she have to leave Gino? What if they got it and it fell into the wrong hands? She became aware of Gino rubbing his hand down her back soothingly and knew her breathing had changed enough to give away her fears to him.

"It's entered, and the SSD seemed to accept it. Can you do your thing, Zara?" Ezekiel asked. "Tell the SSD to download to our device?" Clearly, he wanted to see if she could do it.

She held her breath, but nodded. Reaching for the machine, she gave it orders to connect with the device Ezekiel held. She felt the response, the way the machine accepted her energy and immediately, as if she were part of the hard drive, did her bidding. There was a moment of silence and then Ezekiel's breath hissed out as he stared at Trap's storage prototype in his hand.

"Holy fuck, Joe, she's really got these files. They're downloading right now. I can't believe this. She didn't do anything, say a word. Zara, has anyone ever told you that you're a miracle? Because you are."

"She is," Gino agreed, "in more ways than one."

Zara shivered, glancing warily toward Joe and then Trap. These were men who thought in terms of weapons and how they could use them. She had a gift that was unparalleled. As far as she knew, no one else could talk to machines, let alone give a speech and talk to them. Why had she let Whitney make her think she was worthless?

She glanced at Bellisia. Immediately Bellisia reached out and took her hand, smiling at her, pride in her eyes. "I knew you'd be able to do this."

"I think Trap and the others helped."

Trap shook his head. "The hothouse thing was the deciding piece in my mind."

She had no idea how he could get *Zagara in hothouse* as a password, even after he explained it. Joe stood up and took out his cell phone, indicated to the others that he wanted silence. It was only a matter of seconds before it became apparent why.

"Whitney? Joe Spagnola here. Just thought I'd connect with you. Really hoped this phone number still worked. We just extracted the information from the SSD you installed in Zara's brain. Very clever. She has a one in a million gift, doesn't she?"

Joe was silent a moment, nodding his head. "Yeah, Trap figured it out. That was your main worry, wasn't it? You knew once Trap was brought in it was going to be over. Stay out of Zara's life. Keep your word this time. You want to send your supersoldiers against us once in a while to test them, we accept that, but you know Gino's a wild card. You don't want him set loose on you, and you take his woman, he'll be coming after you. They'll be no stopping him."

Again, there was a small silence while Joe listened to Whitney. "No chance that I'll send you any of that information. None, Whitney. I won't bargain with you. You knew Violet was flawed, but you sent her out anyway and in the end, you may as well have pulled the trigger that killed her. You sent Zara after Cheng knowing what would happen to her. You're never going to be my favorite person. I'm not the man who will help you. I'm telling you to back off Zara and giving you the warning that if you don't, you'll be contending with Gino."

There was another silence. Joe shook his head. "Not happening. You can figure out who will end up with the information, if anyone does. For all I know, it will be destroyed." They all knew better. Joe shrugged. "Don't know. Don't care. Just leave her alone, or you're going to find out what happens when four teams of GhostWalkers decide to make you their number one priority. You need to start thinking about that."

Again silence. Then Joe sighed. "I get it, Whitney. You're a great patriot, blah, blah, blah. I'm getting damned tired of seeing the havoc you wreak with your fucked-up experiments on these women. You have no right to hold them prisoner. I'm hanging up now. Things happen if my temper gets loose, but you already know that, don't you?" He ended the call and looked at Zara. "I believe he's smart enough to take me seriously, honey."

"Thank you." She indicated the device where the information was stored. "What are you going to do with that?"

"I'm hand delivering it to Major General. It's his problem, not ours. I wouldn't want to be in his shoes when he gets this little bomb. It could blow up in his face. Again, not our problem. I'm leaving tonight."

18

⚘

"So, this is a girls' night," Bellisia said, lifting her feet up onto the chair like she did at home. She looked around her at the crowded bar with a small smile on her face. "I always wondered. Is the objective to get drunk?"

The music blared so loud it was difficult for Zara to hear her. She leaned forward, across the small table where the other women, Cayenne, Nonny and Pepper, were crowded together. "I think it's to have fun, Bellisia."

Nonny laughed at both of them. "When I was your age, I had two best friends, Lona and Melissa. They were both married as well, and we'd get one night off a month. Our husbands would watch the young ones, and we'd go into the swamp to the bar. At that time, the Huracan Club wasn't named that, but it was this same bar. It's had a makeover, been remodeled a couple of times since then. Still, there were peanuts on the floor, no piano, but music blastin'. The three of us loved to dance and we did, all night long. We didn't have to worry about men 'hittin' on us,' as you young folks say. They all knew our husbands.

In those days, a man comin' after your woman was a killin' offense."

"This was the bar?" Bellisia asked, looking around her.

Nonny nodded. "It's been in the Thibodeaux family for a long time. We tend to hand things down, father to son, mother to daughter. 'Course, I never had me a daughter." She looked around the table at the four women. "Not until now. We're only missing Flame, Gator's wife."

Zara loved that Nonny included her. She'd never had a mother, and as role models went, Nonny was perfect.

"So, the goal *is* to have fun," Cayenne said. "Like going over and giving my husband a lap dance and then walking away. That would be fun."

The women burst out laughing. Nonny tried to scowl, but only ended up laughing harder than the others. "Of course you would think of that, Cayenne. Trap would carry you off. You know he would."

"Isn't that the idea?" Cayenne sent a smoldering look Trap's way.

"I want to know how Nonny knows what a lap dance is," Bellisia said. "I had to look it up on the Internet when Cayenne told me she sometimes gave Trap lap dances. And worked a pole and did silks. She's got the moves."

"Wait. I want to know how to do a lap dance," Zara said.

"There's video," Bellisia said. "And instructions on some. Seriously, Zara, we have a lot of catching up to do."

Zara tried to look pious. "I actually saw a lap dance once, at a frat party. I snuck in because I heard they were going to be giving them to the guys. It looked very interesting."

"And you didn't share?" Bellisia feigned outrage.

"I didn't want you practicing on me." She managed to say it with a straight face.

Another round of shared laughter went up.

"Now do you see why girls' night is so important?" Nonny asked. "We didn't have the Internet and cell phones. Mostly, we came together to share knowledge and answer one another's questions and learn." She lifted her hand and immediately beer was brought to the table and set in front of each of the women.

Delmar Thibodeaux bowed slightly as if he had royalty in his club. "Grace Fontenot, what a privilege. I'm not takin' your money," he added, pushing back the bill on the table. He eyed Cayenne. "You're sittin' with Grace, so you're welcome, but I expect you and your man won't be causin' trouble." He lifted his gaze toward the back table as if he could pierce that darkness and see Trap.

Cayenne smiled at him but didn't reply. Nonny patted his hand. "I'll be responsible for all of them, Delmar. Thank you for the round of beer. Please allow us to pay for any other rounds we drink tonight."

Delmar looked as if he objected, but there was no getting away from Nonny's determination. He nodded his head, gave Cayenne one more serious glare and then went back to the bar.

Bellisia whistled softly. "Cayenne, you've been holding out on us. What exactly did you do to get that kind of welcome?" She picked up the beer and took a healthy drink. "There's nothing better on a hot, sultry night than an ice-cold beer," she added.

Cayenne shrugged. "Which time? I started out with a bad reputation, and it seems to grow through no fault of my own. You know Trap and his jealousy. It was just a little fight this last time. We were making out on the dance floor and maybe some other stuff, but it was dark and he was hot and anyway some man wanted in on the fun and Trap got kind of upset. Wyatt pulled him off the man and his three friends and we left. We paid for the damage though."

Bellisia rolled her eyes, but couldn't help but laugh. "There's no saving you, girl."

Zara let her gaze slide from the group of women over to the darkest corner of the bar, where she knew the men were kicked back, hopefully relaxing. She could barely make them out. Trap was there, but she couldn't see him at all. There had been no question that Trap would be there if Cayenne was. And Wyatt. Pepper was a very sensual woman, and one touch of her skin could set up an addiction to her. Supposedly her pregnancy helped suppress the hormone hidden so cleverly in her skin, or whatever it was that Wyatt called it, but no one was taking chances.

Ezekiel had accompanied them as well, saying there was no way his woman was going to a bar where danger might be lurking, without him. Gino had made it clear that where Zara went, he did. The last man at the table was Malichai. He said he was watching out for Nonny. He said he knew the woman could drink them all under the table and then she might take it into her head to cause some kind of ruckus. Nonny had rolled her eyes, but she hadn't objected.

"Did you come here very often with your husband?" Pepper asked.

Nonny nodded. "My friends and I came up with a plan where we watched one another's children so the other could have a night off with our man. Berengere, my husband, liked to dance and he would take me here on our night. He was a good man. A very good man." Her voice drifted off and she looked away, lifting the bottle of beer to her lips.

"I really do want to learn to lap dance," Zara said, changing the subject because she detested seeing Nonny sad. "Gino would love it."

"I could show you," Cayenne said, half rising.

Nonny put a hand on her arm just as Bellisia did too. "I'm not near drunk," Bellisia objected. "Let me get a few beers in me. I have to be feeling just a little tipsy."

"I can't drink," Pepper said. "You can have my drink, Bella."

"Pepper has been with me the longest," Nonny said. "She graciously has stayed in my home rather than asking Wyatt to build her another one. Her generosity allows me to see my great-granddaughters every day, and they are the light of my life." She raised the beer bottle. "Thank you, my girl. You surely have become my daughter."

The others raised their bottles toward Pepper, who smiled at the older woman. "I think you're the generous one, Nonny, to all of us. None of us knew anything about homes and families. You took us all in and put up with our strange behaviors . . ." She raised her glass of water while the others again raised their beer bottles and took another drink.

"I just can't figure out cooking," Cayenne said. "Zara had to sit out the first month and now, after just a month with your lessons, she's top of the class. I don't get that. I really do try, Nonny. When I'm at your house, I totally get it done, but then I'm home and I suck at it." She lifted her beer bottle. "To Zara and her expertise at cooking."

"Hear, hear," Bellisia said, and they all took another swig of beer.

"You don't pay attention when you're cookin' at home," Nonny said to Cayenne.

"I do," Cayenne objected.

"You do when you're in my kitchen with all the girls and me, but when you're home alone with Trap and he's in the kitchen with you, I doubt you give your cookin' the same focus."

There was silence while comprehension slipped into Cayenne's expression. The women around the table erupted into laughter.

"She's *so* right." Pepper nudged Cayenne with her glass of water. "You and Trap can't go long enough to boil water without having your hands on each other. Here's to finding out the *real* reason Cayenne can't cook."

Everyone drank down the last of their beers, and Nonny raised her empty bottle into the air. Delmar must have been waiting for her signal because he returned with another round. This time, instead of bringing Pepper a beer, he brought her an ice-cold water.

"You want something else?" Delmar plopped a tall frosted glass on the table in front of Pepper. "Your man says you're gonna have a baby and you can't drink beer. This is my own favorite drink, lemonade and lime with sugar and soda water. Just try it. I put some mint in there. Grow it myself out back."

Pepper glanced at Nonny as if waiting for a cue. Nonny inclined her head slightly, and Pepper smiled carefully at the man, trying hard to keep the wattage down. "Thank you, it looks lovely," she said.

The moment she spoke and smiled at him, it wasn't difficult to see he was a bit ensnared by her. His face turned a dull red and he sputtered his acknowledgment. A chair scraped near the back wall, the sound coming from the darkest corner, breaking the spell so Delmar stepped back away from the table.

Nonny lifted the money up, but he shook his head. "Your men have a tab, said they'd pay it. Want you all to have a good time." He kept backing away until he was nearly halfway across the room. No way was Nonny going to be able to spend her cash.

"Even pregnant you've got sex appeal," Bellisia said. "Most everyone thinks I look like a kid just because I'm short."

"I'm tall. A giant," Zara said.

Nonny rolled her eyes. "You girls are all beautiful and should know it by now. Your men certainly tell you enough. In my day, men didn't speak much about looks. I worked alongside Berengere on fishin' boats, we crabbed together and hunted alligators. We hunted for meat and pulled the moss from trees to dry it out for our mattresses every year. It was hot work, and mostly I felt I looked a mess."

Zara caught those words, the way she said it. "Mostly you *felt* a mess. Does that mean your husband didn't feel the same way about you?"

Grace Fontenot lifted a hand to her hair to tidy it. Not a hair was out of place and Zara couldn't imagine her, even hunting and fishing, having her hair dare come loose when she put it up. "No, he never thought I was a mess," she conceded. "He always looked at me with that look, the one that told me I was a very lucky woman."

Zara found herself falling for Nonny too. How could she not? How could anyone not fall under her spell? It might not be sexual, the way Pepper's enchantment was, but the attraction to Nonny was like a magnet. Strong. Lasting.

The door opened, and Zara watched as two men came in. They scanned the entire bar before they shut out the night, as if they might be expecting trouble. They appeared Cajun and looked similar, as if they were related. Both men seemed hard, but then quite a few men living on the river were tough. They had to be. Living in or around the swamp could make for a difficult life.

Simultaneously, their gazes hit the Fontenot table and took in the women. At once both men swiveled left and right searching for what Zara could only assume were the men in that darkest corner. The eyes came back to the table and then to each of them. Their gazes lingered on Pepper and then Cayenne and then jumped to her and then Bellisia. Finally, they settled on Nonny. Both men made their way to the table.

"Delmar! Beer!" the taller of the two men yelled. His

voice was booming and filled with command. Clearly, he was used to getting whatever he wanted.

"Your house beer!" the second one called out.

"Comin' right up, Pascal, Blaise!" Delmar shouted.

"Ms. Fontenot," Pascal, the taller of the two men greeted her. There was the slightest deference in his voice. "I've never seen you here before. I'd like to buy a round for your table."

"That's sweet of you, Pascal," Nonny said. "I was over the other day visitin' your *mère*. We played a long game of cards and she managed to take all my money again."

A smile broke out on his face. "She does look forward to your visits, ma'am."

Nonny smiled up at his brother. "Blaise, so good to see you out and about. I rarely have the chance. The two of you have made something of yourselves. Your *mère* is very proud of you."

"It's nice you visit so regular. Since she took sick and can't get around, she doesn't get many visitors," Pascal said, sounding a little bitter.

"Most of us have gone away or died, boys," Nonny reminded gently. "We're all gettin' up there in age. Your *mère* had you late. Lost so many with all the hard work. Back in those days we had to do the work of the men. Your *mère* was no exception."

The atmosphere in the room had changed since the two men had entered. Zara could feel the tension in the air. It seemed to stretch tighter and tighter, like a wire being pulled taut. It took control not to glance toward that corner where Gino was. She didn't know why, but she felt vaguely threatened.

"You goin' to introduce us?" Pascal asked. "I've met Cayenne." He leered at her, sounding as if they had a history. "But the others . . ." He looked at Pepper and his mouth seemed to drop open.

"Girls, this is Pascal and Blaise Comeaux. This is my

daughter-in-law, Pepper, Wyatt's wife," Nonny said. "Bellisia, married to Ezekiel, and Zara. She's engaged to Gino. We're just out havin' a bit of fun. I should have asked your Alida to join us. She needs to get out once in a while according to your *mère*. We all do, come to that. I know your *mère* watched the children occasionally for you so you could take Alida out. If you'd like, call me, Pascal. I'll do it for you." Nonny deftly turned the attention back to her.

"Nice of you to offer, Ms. Fontenot," Pascal said. "I might take you up on that some time. Blaise and I try to keep her entertained, don't we, brother?"

Blaise nodded and snickered at the same time. He looked at Zara. "You want to dance? See how a real man does it? Not some Italian foreigner?"

Zara kept her smile with difficulty. "I'm not certain how Gino is a foreigner, as he was born in the United States, but perhaps you mean a foreigner here in Louisiana. Thank you for the offer, but we're just hanging out together tonight." She gestured around the table at the other women.

"Too bad. Your loss." Blaise turned away from the table and sauntered across the crowded room, moving others with his shoulder when they didn't see him coming.

Zara noticed some turned fast as if they might decide to fight, but stopped whatever they were going to say or do when they saw who had shoved them. Pascal remained, staring down at her. "I've never met your man. Has he been in the area long?"

Zara glanced helplessly toward the dark corner again, needing Gino. She detested being the center of attention. Nonny leaned over and patted her hand. "Gino's been with me for well over a year now, maybe longer or a little less." Deliberately she was vague. She shrugged. "Time runs together for me, Pascal, same as it does, I suspect, for your *mère*. Gino doesn't like to be indoors, so he avoids town and most places you might run into him."

The Cajun nodded, but his gaze didn't leave Zara's face. "Don't understand how these men get such beautiful women."

Zara forced a smile. "Thank you, that's sweet of you to say." She dropped her hands into her lap and twisted her fingers together. Something about both Comeaux men repelled her. She didn't know what it was, they both had been very polite. Even Blaise, although he hadn't taken her refusal very well.

Pascal stepped away from the table and made his way to the bar. The four women looked expectantly to Nonny. Nonny shook her head. "Those boys are bad, all the way through. Reckon they have reason to be. Their *père* was the meanest man in the swamp. Why Shanty married him, I don't know, but I suspect her *père* sold her to Jean-Baptiste. In any case, Jean-Baptiste was a mean, vile man. Any crime in these parts, you could bet he had his hand in. He drank and beat Shanty and the boys. He brought home women. He even brought home women to his sons."

The four women exchanged a long look. "Pascal appeared to be genuinely concerned for his mother," Zara pointed out. "I could almost like him for that." Almost. He made the hair on her body stand up in alarm when he pushed close.

"I think the boys, and there were five of them, their oldest brother is dead now, love and hate Shanty. She was weak. She didn't protect them or leave their father. Jean-Baptiste taught them to think of women as playthings, inferior to them, only servants. Their older brother was involved in kidnapping and selling women. He got away with it for quite a few years until my grandsons did something about it. It wouldn't surprise me if the rest of the boys had a hand in it but weren't caught."

"How sad that they really had no chance," Zara whispered.

"They had plenty of chances," Nonny corrected. "People all over the world have terrible childhoods. Look at you girls. Pepper lived her life in a cell. Cayenne's life was even worse than hers. Bellisia and you were in Whitney's compound. He experimented on all you girls. He gave Flame cancer time and time again. Gino's family was murdered. So many lives are difficult and start off bad, but people overcome these things. Pascal and Blaise and their brothers, they like livin' a life of crime. They like scarin' people and hurtin' others. It makes them feel like big men."

"Well, that's sad too," Zara said. She snuck another glance toward the dark corner where Gino sat with the other men. Gino had been affected by the murder of his family, he'd turned his back on the life his father had built and he'd embraced the life Ciro Spagnola had given him.

She took another drink of the ice-cold beer, thankful for the cool liquid. The room was hot. Outside, the humidity and temperature hadn't gone down much from the daytime. Occasionally, rain would pepper the roof and just as abruptly stop.

"It is sad," Nonny agreed. "But nothin' any of us can do about it. Many tried. We all thought we'd be able to get Shanty free of Jean-Baptiste, but she stubbornly refused to leave him. Just like Alida. History repeatin' itself. I suppose the woman Blaise eventually settles with will be beat and abused and she'll stay too. Let that be a lesson to you girls. You respect yourself and demand respect from your man."

She looked at Cayenne. "That man of yours thinks the sun rises with you, but he can be demandin'. Don't you ever let him cross lines. You understand me? You set boundaries, ones you can live with. They're yours, no one else's, but you make certain he respects them."

"I will, Nonny," Cayenne agreed. "I'm not shy about telling him if I don't like something, and he never does it again."

"Good." Nonny looked around the table, her gaze settling on Zara. "That goes for all you girls. Zara, you have a sweet, giving nature. I can see that in you. Pascal and Blaise could see it as well."

She sat up straight. Alarmed. What was wrong with her that men like Pascal, Blaise and Zhu all saw something in her that wasn't in Bellisia, Cayenne or Pepper? What about Gino? Was she deluding herself into thinking he was a good man?

"What's wrong with me?" She supposed she needed to face it. If she didn't know, she couldn't do anything about it.

"Nothing is wrong with you," Nonny assured. "Nothing at all. Because they can see you're sweet and accommodating doesn't mean you wouldn't walk away from abuse. I think you would in a heartbeat. From what Bellisia has said, you defied Whitney many times. I just want you to remember, you're as important as your partner."

Zara pressed the frosty bottle of beer to her forehead. "This relationship thing can be confusing. When I'm with Gino, everything feels clear. Safe. Perfect. Then he's away from me and I find everyone around me questions our relationship and I think maybe I don't know what I'm doing. Why does it feel so right with him and everyone thinks it's wrong?"

Cayenne leaned forward and, for the first time, touched her hand to Zara's in a gesture of solidarity and sisterhood. "No one understands my relationship with Trap. On the surface, it appears to others that it's all about sex. Our relationship is very sexual. It's intense. But we fit. I love everything he does, and when we're at odds, we fix it fast. I know he's the only man who will suit me. He knows I'm the only woman for him. We work. If you work with

Gino, it's no one's business how you work, as long as he doesn't in any way hurt you."

"Cayenne is right, Zara," Nonny said. "I know Gino's a good man. He looks at you the way Trap looks at Cayenne. There is no one else in his world, and there won't be. I don't worry he'll abuse you. My husband was a strong man. He wanted a partner, but he wanted me to always follow his lead. Juggling the two wasn't always the easiest, but I loved him and he loved me. We made it work. I do know that men have to be reminded every now and then that you have needs outside of them. You remind Gino, Zara. Every now and then think of something he can do for you and let him do it."

"That is not what you told me," Bellisia said, waving her hand in the air for Delmar to refresh their drinks. "I believe you said I should give Ezekiel my entire adoration." She sounded indignant.

Nonny's eyebrow went up. "*I* said that?"

"Ezekiel said you said that."

All of them burst out laughing. Relief swept through Zara. She didn't like not knowing the right thing to say or do. She felt as if she spent most of her life trying to fit in, to figure out the right moves, what to say in any given circumstance and how to act. The only time she could remember relaxing was around Bellisia and Shylah. When it was just the three of them at night when no one was around and they were far from the cameras. Gino had given her that again.

"Ezekiel does walk on water," Nonny said. "Ask his brothers or Rubin and Diego. They'll tell you."

"So will I," Bellisia admitted, "but I'm not telling him I think so."

"That's best," Nonny agreed.

"I have to admit, I think Wyatt can walk on water," Pepper said. "He's amazing with the girls, and he always seems to know what to do when I'm overloading. I had no idea how to take care of children and make a home for them, and he's so good at it." She smiled at Nonny. "He says you gave that to him. And you definitely give it to me and the girls, Nonny. I don't know what we'd do without you."

She took another drink of the lime lemonade that Delmar had brought her. "By the way, this is really good. It isn't alcohol, but it doesn't need to be. That's how good it is."

"Delmar's *mère* used to make that drink when we'd have a big celebration, music, food, good friends and neighbors comin' together. It was refreshin' and every one of us loved it." She sounded nostalgic.

They drank another round of beer, laughed a lot and spent some time on the dance floor in a group. Nonny had moves she taught them and they tried teaching her some of theirs. Zara and Bellisia had learned and practiced dancing by watching videos. Pepper and Cayenne had done the same, although Cayenne's taste ran to the more exotic and provocative.

Zara was certain it was Nonny's presence that kept the men in the bar from continually hitting on them, because, as promised, the GhostWalkers stayed away from them. She liked knowing Gino was close. She liked having him close because ever since Pascal and Blaise had singled her out from the other women, she'd been uneasy.

Pepper was the sensual one. Cayenne was sexy as hell. Bellisia was exotic. Zara knew she was pretty, but with the other three women there, especially given Pepper's allure, it didn't make sense to her that the two Cajuns had *both* made a point of talking to her. She was very happy when the brothers left about an hour before closing.

The women danced and laughed and drank until Delmar was ready to throw everyone out because they hadn't noticed it was well past closing. Lights and laughter spilled out of the bar as they exited together. Nonny was all no-nonsense, stepping into the boat and reaching back to help Zara. Zara was a little tipsy, but the buzz felt good. She took Nonny's hand and stepped aboard, feeling very proud of herself for not falling into the water.

Bellisia started to board the boat, but ran back to fling herself into Ezekiel's arms. He and the others were saying good night to Delmar, up on the bank by the bar. Cayenne had jumped into Trap's arms the moment he exited the bar and he had her pinned against the outside wall, hands and mouths all over each other, oblivious to anyone else. Wyatt curled his arm around Pepper's shoulders while he talked to the bar owner.

Zara blinked rapidly, trying to find Gino. "Is he still inside?" She murmured the question aloud, not really expecting Nonny to answer it. Part of her wanted to get off the boat and go find him. Was he upset because, like the other women, she hadn't jumped him when he came out of the bar? That odd flutter in her stomach worsened. She widened her search pattern, although she didn't see how he could have gotten in front of them without her knowledge. Her radar was usually very good at telling her where he was.

She took a long, slow perusal of the surroundings while they waited for the other women. The Huracan Club was located fairly deep in the swamp, where most authorities would never bother looking. The building was located up above the river on the highest part of the bank, with the swamp reaching for it every moment. Trees and brush crept around it and spread out on three sides as far as the eye could see. In front of it stretched the canal. Boats tied up to the pier and then the occupants had to climb the stairs carved into the bank to get to the bar.

Something moved just for one moment in the heavier brush on the right bank. A face appeared, peering at her. It was so fast she thought she might have made a mistake, but it looked like Blaise. She stared at the moving leaves, her stomach dropping. There was no breeze.

"Nonny, I think the Comeaux brothers are spying on us," she whispered, turning her back to the swamp just in case they might see her lips move and know what she was saying.

"I believe you're right, Zara," Nonny said. "Why don't you step back onto shore real casual-like. Take my hand, I'll help you."

Zara glanced toward the bar and stiffened. Men in dark clothing emerged from the interior and spread out. Each of them carried an automatic weapon. More came out of the swamp on either side of the canal, all training their weapons on the women in the tight circle the Ghost-Walkers had formed around them.

"We're not lookin' for trouble," the leader said. "It's a job. We're to bring that one"—he jerked his chin toward Zara—"to a plane waiting at one of the private airstrips. Man's payin' us bank. Too much to pass up. One woman for all the others. You can afford to give up one."

"Who would that be?" Ezekiel asked. "Who's paying for her?"

The man shrugged. "He said he wanted her to know I was delivering her to him. Zhu. Bolan Zhu."

Zara's heart sank, but she'd known the moment she saw them pouring out of the bar. She would never be able to prove it, but she was certain the Comeaux brothers had led them straight to her. It wasn't like outsiders knew where the Huracan Club was. Only locals knew. And the way wasn't easy, with lots of twists and turns. One had to access it by the waterways. Outside mercenaries—and these men certainly were mercenaries—would never have been able to find it on their own.

"My wife is pregnant," Wyatt said. "I'd appreciate it if you'd allow the bar owner to take her inside while we work this out. I don't want her to have a miscarriage. She's very sensitive."

Pepper shook her head and tightened her hold on his arm.

"Can't do that for you, man," the leader said. "All the more reason for you to cooperate."

"Pepper," Wyatt said. "I want you to get behind me. Close your eyes, baby, and keep them closed until this is done. You're pregnant, and I don't want you getting a brain bleed with all the violence surrounding you. Delmar, would you mind making certain my wife stays put? Just stay close to her." Wyatt pointed to a spot right behind him and waited until Pepper reluctantly did as he said, Delmar moving with her.

Zara caught movement as Cayenne stealthily made her way up onto the roof and disappeared into the darkness. Bellisia had inched her way closer to the embankment. She was above the canal and with one turn and a dive, she would be in the water and gone. The mercenaries would never be able to find her, or if they did, they wouldn't live through it.

She counted five at the bar and three on either side of the canal. It occurred to her Malichai was unaccounted for as well. She reached for Nonny's hand and the older woman took hers immediately and pulled her close, wrapping her arm around her.

"Stay very still, Nonny," she whispered. "They're up to something."

The words had barely left her mouth when something screamed. It was a male voice, the sound haunting, in agony, filling the swamp, quieting the drone of insects and croaking of frogs. Stillness settled over the swamp as, shocked, everyone turned toward the sound. It had come from the right side, where three of the mercenaries had been, covering them all from the distance with their weapons. Now, no one stood there.

She glanced to her left, icy fingers creeping down her spine in spite of the oppressive heat. The three men who had been on that bank were gone as well. Her breath hitched in her throat. Vaguely, as if a long way away, she heard a splash and a grunt. She turned back to look at the five men surrounding the GhostWalkers. Four of them lay on the ground, one hung from the roof, his body swaying macabrely. She realized that agonized scream had been a diversion, allowing Wyatt, Ezekiel, Trap and Cayenne that moment to kill the five mercenaries who had come to take her back to Bolan Zhu.

She didn't realize she was shivering until Nonny wrapped her arms around her. "You're all right, Zara. The boys took care of it."

"What do they do with all the bodies?"

"Someone comes. Zeke calls and they send someone out. Mostly we don't ask those questions. Delmar will keep his mouth closed. He's a good man and hard as nails when he has to be. These men are outsiders . . ."

"I thought I saw Blaise Comeaux in the swamp just before the mercenaries came out of the bar."

Nonny sighed softly. "I wouldn't be surprised, but if he was there, I hope he scoots on home fast because your man is loose in the swamp. I would guess anyone out there is in danger."

She shivered again and rubbed her hands up and down her arms. "I want to see him. I need to know he's all right."

Nonny gave her a smile. "Child, your man is safe. Never fear that. He's doing what he does best. I need to get you home now." She lifted her head and signaled to her grandson. "Wyatt, I need to get these women home."

Wyatt kept his arm around Pepper, keeping her head against his chest as he walked her toward the boat, shielding her from the sight of the men dead on the ground. Cayenne trailed after him, Trap by her side. Ezekiel hurried down to the water, peering all around it as if he could spot his wife.

"What the hell, Wyatt?" Delmar demanded.

"Sorry," Wyatt called back without turning. "Gotta get the women home. You make yourself scarce for a few hours, Delmar. I'll have someone clean up the mess." Even as he spoke, Malichai came striding out of the swamp and dumped a body by the side of the canal.

Delmar swore under his breath. "Anyone messin' with you Fontenot boys had better know you play for keeps." He closed the door of his bar and followed Wyatt down to the pier. By the time he reached it, Malichai had dumped a second body on top of the first one. Delmar shook his head and watched him disappear back into the swamp.

Zara was busy inspecting the other side of the swamp, straining her eyes to catch a glimpse of Gino. Two bodies had rolled out of the swamp onto the embankment, but there wasn't a third one, and no Gino.

Wyatt glanced at his watch. "Let's move, ladies. We don't have a lot of time."

Zara couldn't imagine why they didn't have time. "Gino isn't here yet."

"Don't worry about him," Trap drawled. "Worry about the other guy."

"That doesn't help." Cayenne glared at him, then let her gaze travel around to the others. "You all obviously suspect or know something we don't. I don't like being in the dark. Did you know these mercenaries were going to attack us tonight?"

"Not a clue," Trap answered. He stepped onto the boat and tugged until she fell into him. At once his arm swept around her. "Just luck."

"Where's Gino?" Zara summoned up the courage to demand. "I'm not leaving here until I know where he is." She took a step toward the front of the boat where it was tied up to the pier.

Wyatt stepped casually in front of her. He'd already seated Pepper. "Gino's tracking the last merc back to the airstrip. If he can't take out Zhu right there, we'll be following."

Zara's breath caught in her throat. "Following? As in following the plane?"

"He'll get a tracker on it."

"But you know he'll head for Shanghai."

Wyatt shook his head. "We don't know that for certain. We hope. He has a favorite little place he likes to go to unwind. We think, if he managed to reacquire you, that he planned to take you there. Now that he didn't, he could go there to let out his frustration."

"How could you know that?"

"He waited for a couple of months in order to make certain we forgot all about the threat. He thought we'd just buy that he let you go. The time gave us the opportunity to find out more about him. That was his first big mistake. The second was underestimating Gino. We were ready for him." Wyatt indicated the seat.

Zara tried to stare him down, and then glanced anxiously into the swamp where she knew he was. That sound. The agony in the man's voice. She knew Gino had caused that. It had given the others the necessary distraction to prevail. Intellectually, she told herself that, but emotionally, she feared Gino had been the one to make that terrible sound.

She sank onto the bench seat and gripped the edge, all the while staring into the swamp. Nonny sat beside her and reached over to take her hand. "He's going to be fine. That man of yours comes alive out there. He's a hunter. It's what he does. He's going to eliminate the threat to you as any man would want to do."

Zara shook her head, tears blurring her vision as Wyatt started the engine and took the boat into the middle of the canal, heading home. "I don't want him to," she whispered. "I really don't, Nonny. I don't want him to put himself in danger in order to protect me. He does that enough for everyone else. I just want him to come home. How many times is Zhu really going to hire mercenaries? After a while, he'll give up." But she knew he wouldn't.

"You had to know Gino would hunt him down," Nonny said.

She nodded because she had known. Before, she'd felt safe with him because he was the kind of man who would hunt down Bolan Zhu, but now that wasn't at all what she wanted. She wanted him just as safe as he made her feel. She held herself very still, almost rigid, in spite of Nonny's close proximity and her reassurances.

"So much for our girls' night out!" Bellisia yelled. She was soaking wet, but as usual, refused to dry off, even though she'd been handed a towel by her husband.

"We always seem to have adventures," Cayenne agreed.

Pepper nodded and sent them all a shaky smile. Energy created by violence could affect her. Just like the first team: Ryland Miller's team could get brain bleeds when using violence. Ryland's team was the first group of psychics Whitney had experimented on. With each group, Whitney got better, freeing the GhostWalkers he enhanced of most of the problems that came with his improvements. Because of Pepper's brain bleeds around violence, Wyatt was very protective of her whether she was pregnant or not. Zara noticed Cayenne was as well.

The water was dark and choppy as the boat sped toward the Fontenot home. Zara couldn't help but think, as laughter spilled around her, that everyone had someone, but she was once again alone. This time, she wasn't thinking of herself, but of Gino, somewhere out there where he could be killed. Alone.

19

Zara stood at the window, one hand to her throat, staring out into the night. With the light off in the room, the only illumination was from the moon trying so valiantly to shine through the gathering clouds. Thunder rumbled ominously, and she rubbed her arms in an effort to soothe herself. She didn't bother to check the tears running down her face. No one was around to see her weakness and she could cry all she wanted.

As soon as they'd returned to the house, a flurry of activity had ensued. The men seemed to be getting ready to take off, presumably to join Gino, wherever he was. Wherever he was going. Chasing Zhu was madness, but no one would listen to her. Zhu was like a wounded animal, lethal and angry, raging at the world around him, but disguised under his handsome features and his civilized clothing.

Rain hit the roof in a long wail. Not soft and light, but a furious pelting, as if the heavens had opened up and the water was pouring over the highest falls. She watched the drops hitting the window, obscuring her view of the thick swamp and the river. What would she do if Gino didn't return? She touched the glass with her fingertips, a small brush that didn't remove the heavy wash of raindrops from the other side. It didn't give her mind any clarity either.

With a sigh, she turned back to the room, looking a little helplessly around her. The women had gone to bed finally and she was alone. In spite of the rain, it was still hot. The fan was going at high speed and not even that seemed to alleviate the relentless heat. It was strange that when Gino was around, the heat felt different. Sultry, yes, but sexy, as if the nights were made for sin and pleasure. Now it was just plain hot.

She paced until she could barely stand the pain in her feet and then she took a long, cool soak in the bathtub, hoping she'd just drift off there. But it didn't happen. She was certain she cried enough to raise the water in the tub an inch, but all she did was give herself a headache to go along with the persistent ache in her feet.

Wrapping herself in a silken robe that felt like heaven against her skin, she gave up and made her way back to the bedroom, where she put her hair up on top of her head to get it off her neck. Tossing the short robe aside, she lay under the fan without a stitch on. She clasped her hands behind her head and stared up at the rotating blades.

Gino. She'd been with him nearly three months and in that time he'd become her everything. Of course Zhu would try to lull them into a false sense of security. He thought they'd dropped their guard down. She was shocked at how the GhostWalkers worked so fast and so perfectly in sync to eliminate the threat to her. She shouldn't have been. She had been trained as a soldier, and so had Bellisia. Maybe differently, because mostly, once they were adults, they had worked alone, but when they were younger, they ran missions together.

Bellisia had known exactly what to do. The moment Gino had provided the distraction, she was in the water, exactly where she could have done the most good had they needed it. Cayenne had participated, both women blending in seamlessly with the GhostWalkers. She had stayed on the boat, uncertain what to do. She didn't want to leave Nonny, nor did she want to mess up whatever plan the GhostWalkers had.

She sighed and lifted the pillow next to her, inhaled Gino's scent and then switched it with her own. She stared at her pillow a few moments and then punched it hard. The pillow went flying across the room. She wanted to get up and kick it.

"Is that a substitute for me?"

Gino's soft voice set her heart pounding. She closed her eyes tightly, hoping she wasn't hallucinating. None of the other men had come back. There was a skeleton crew there and they'd called a friend, Donny, to help watch over the house. Two men she recognized from the compound where she'd been trained were there as well. They'd worked for Whitney and had defected with Bellisia to the GhostWalkers. She was still a little afraid of trusting them.

"Yes." She whispered her answer, but it wasn't true. "No." She looked around the room into the darkest corners. She couldn't find him, not even when she knew the direction of his voice. "I was afraid for you."

"Princess, you need to be afraid for the other guy, not for me."

Her eyes strained to see him, bouncing from one wall to the next, shifting to the floor, trying to cover every square inch of the room. She sat up and turned toward the door. "I don't care about the other guy, whoever he may be, I care about you. You went into that swamp and you didn't come out." There was accusation in her voice.

"I had to tail the remaining merc back to Zhu and his

plane so I could put a tracker on it and make the necessary arrangements to follow it. I've got a plane standing by and we're leaving in under an hour."

"No." She said it sharply. Asserting herself. "Absolutely not. That's like following a wounded animal into his own territory. He'll know if some strange plane enters Shanghai. He'll know it's you."

"I have businesses all over the world, Zara." His tone was gentle. He emerged out of the shadows, almost right in front of her. "Including China. What's the point if I can't commandeer my own airplane? He won't know it's my team following him. He's arrogant, baby. He's arrogant and thinks he's above retribution. He believes he owns Shanghai. He's gotten away with murder too many times and walks around thinking himself invincible. He's not. Retribution is coming his way."

He walked toward her, one hand pulling his T-shirt over his head and tossing it into a corner. He wore no shoes and she had no idea how that had happened. She could see them now, his boots, set neatly in a corner close to the shadow he'd just come out of. Both hands dropped to his belt as he got to the side of the bed.

"He'll know," she argued. Breathless. All that muscle. He looked invincible himself.

He kicked his trousers away and put one knee on the bed, right between her legs. "No, he won't." He took her mouth with exquisite gentleness.

Her heart fluttered and her sex clenched hard. Her arms crept around his neck and she gave herself to him. To that kiss. His mouth was fire. But so much more. Tears burned behind her eyes. The way he touched her was as gentle as his mouth, one arm curling around her back and locking there, sliding her beneath him, so she lay looking up at his beloved face, those eyes that burned over her body and then rested on her mouth.

"Did I remember to tell you that I'm crazy in love with

you, woman? I should have told you that before I let you out for your girls' night out." He punctuated each word with soft kisses over her eyes and down her face. "Because I am. So in love. I didn't know it was possible to love this much."

He wasn't a man to say such things, and it meant all the more to her that he did. He kissed her again, stealing her breath. He'd taken her heart some time earlier when she wasn't paying attention. Now he owned her soul. She lifted a palm to his face. Those lines cut deep with desire. With hunger. For her. Those eyes, so dark and compelling, alive with love for her.

"I love you so much, Gino. I don't care about Zhu. I'd rather live with a few bad moments of worry than to ever have you put yourself in danger."

He caught her hand and pressed it to his mouth, making her heart skip a beat. He kissed the center of her palm and then nipped at the end of her finger, sucking the sting away. He stroked a caress down her body, his mouth following. Her breath caught in her throat. He could make her come alive with a look, let alone the way he touched her. Everywhere his hands and mouth went, he left flames licking at and over her skin. In her belly. Deep in her core. Between her legs. Everywhere until she couldn't think, only feel.

Then he was moving in her. His fingers threaded through hers, stretching her arms above her head, eyes staring down into hers, intense, loving, possessive, connecting them on such an intimate level she could barely breathe. He never once looked away from her, his body moving slow, a burn that spread through her, growing hotter and hotter with each stroke.

She slid her foot up his leg to his thigh and then wrapped her leg around him. She did the same with the other foot. Still, he moved with the same slow intensity that was earth-shattering. She couldn't look away from his gaze. She was mesmerized, caught by him. Held spell-bound. Love was overwhelming. She shifted under him, writhing as the need crawled up her spine and heat coiled tighter and tighter in her.

He kept moving at the same pace, and it was beginning to drive her crazy. It was too much and not enough. And then suddenly, just that fast, her breath was hitching. Her lungs felt raw. He never looked away. Never let her look away. Her body came apart and she saw herself in his eyes, saw the wide, shocked look, the dazed pleasure that only he could bring her and then her body clamped down like a vise on his, taking him with her. It was heat and fire, a blaze she didn't anticipate, consuming her. Consuming him.

He lay over top of her, still staring into her eyes. A slow smile lit the dark intensity of his eyes. "I forgot the condom."

She didn't look away. "You don't forget things like that. I do. You don't."

His smile widened into a grin. "That's true."

"Gino, you haven't even lived with me yet."

"What do you think we've been doing, princess?" He brushed kisses over each eye. "We've been living to-gether. I'm sure. Aren't you?"

"Yes, but I want to be with you for a little while before we bring someone else in. I need time to do research on parenting and homemaking. I need time with Nonny."

"No, baby, you don't need any of that. Nonny's won-derful, but she isn't you. I want you exactly as you are. If you like to research those things, just for fun, go ahead, but you don't need to do it for me. Our home is about us. You. Me. Eventually our children. What you learn online isn't how it has to be. It's how you feel."

She loved him even more for that. "I don't want to do something wrong, Gino. Not for you." But really, she was beginning to have much more confidence in *them*. They fit. They could do anything together. She wasn't as weak a link as she had first thought. That knowledge was growing stronger in her every day with him and the others. "You can't go." Just thinking it, let alone saying it, sent panic skittering through her.

He kissed her again. Long. Hot. Wet. Taking away the anxiety. He kissed her until she forgot to be afraid of anything and there was only the two of them, locked together in the privacy of his room. When he lifted his head, she chased him, one arm hooking around his neck to pull him back down to her. She kissed him, teasing with her tongue, stroking along his until he was growing in her again, stretching her until she felt tight and he felt hot and hard. He rocked in her, sending little tremors spreading through her body like a building wave of pure heat.

"You make us a home, Zara," he said, "however you want that home to be. I want to come home to you. If you're there, it's going to be perfect."

"I don't know things," she reminded.

"Then we'll have fun doing them together. Furniture hunting, decorating. I want our home to be yours, baby, and whatever that is, it will be perfection."

He suddenly pulled out of her, flipped her over and brought her hips back to him so he could surge deep. The contrast between his gentle and his rough sent her careening right over the edge. That didn't stop him. He pistoned into her, pulling her hips back into him with every stroke. She couldn't think. Couldn't breathe. Only feel. Over and over, until she was lost in him and everything was gone from her mind. Every worry. Every silly detail that had been looping there, making her fear she would disappoint him.

There was only Gino and the way he made her feel. Beautiful. Perfect. His. Made for him. Then there was only their bodies, soaring together, his hoarse cry mixed with hers. He collapsed over her, pinning her to the sheets, both of them trying desperately to catch their breath.

The love she had for him was stronger than anything she'd ever known. She was better for being with him. She knew that. And she knew he would be better for being with her. There was that cold, dark place in him he could disappear into. It was dangerous there. The more he went, the easier it was to get lost. He would be in that place when he hunted Zhu. She knew it just as she knew he slipped in and out of it more easily than any human being should.

She closed her eyes and took long, deep breaths, trying to find a way to make him understand it wasn't worth risking his going after Zhu. Gino had gotten too comfortable with that side of himself. It had probably saved his sanity. Trauma had pushed him there when he was a child, and Ciro Spagnola had deliberately grown that coldness so Gino could better protect his son, his business and himself.

Very slowly he rolled over and then slid up to the headboard. She rolled over as well and lay looking at the fan.

"I don't want you to go, Gino."

"He's a loose cannon, princess, and he hurt you, neither of which I am willing to tolerate."

"He's sick. Demented. He likes hurting people, and he wants you to follow him. He's probably waiting for it."

Gino shrugged and reached down to stroke a caress over her breast, his fingers lingering, and then his palm covered her in a claiming hold. "Doesn't matter."

"It does though." She sat up slowly and crawled up the bed to him. "Gino, you don't have to mete out vengeance because he hurt me. I'll admit that in the beginning, I wanted to be with you because I knew you were probably the only man capable of going up against him and coming out alive . . ."

"That's not true. I might be the only one who won't kill him fast, but any member of this team, or one of the others, is capable of killing Bolan Zhu. Don't for one moment think they aren't."

"That's exactly what I'm talking about," she said. "They would kill him fast implies you wouldn't. Sit up on a roof with a rifle. Shoot him from a distance. Does it matter how he dies?"

"It matters to me. He took something from you."

She knew what he meant. Her feeling of safety, but she'd never really had that, not even with Whitney. She knew Whitney terminated some women. He put others into a breeding program. He sent them out on dangerous missions. "You gave it back to me." He had. Gino had made her feel safe almost from the first moment he had come to rescue her.

"I'll be home soon."

She shook her head. "Just tell me you'll kill him from a distance."

"I can't give you a promise like that, baby. I don't even *want* to kill him from a distance. That bastard hurt you. He tried to permanently damage your feet. He'll never stop."

"So shoot him if you have to, but don't get close. He's dangerous. I know you're good at what you do, but you're underestimating him, and that could get you killed." Worse, if he went to that cold, dark, dangerous place, he might not come back from it. She couldn't say that, because she didn't know how to put it to him.

"It's going to be all right, Zara," he murmured, gathering her to him.

She crawled onto his lap, feeling as small as Bellisia, wanting to melt into him, to share his skin, to keep him with her. "I'm so scared, Gino." She lifted her gaze to his face. "Really, really scared. I don't want to have to live without you. In my entire life, I never thought I'd have a man for myself, let alone a man like you. I really didn't. You seem like such a rare gift. You've somehow made me feel it's okay to be me, that there's nothing wrong with me. You make me feel beautiful and extraordinary and loved. You're all those things to me and more."

"Zara, you're not living without me, but you are living without the threat of Zhu hanging over your head. If I don't go after him now, when we have children, you're going to be worried sick."

That was true. But . . . "I'm not trading having children for you. I'd rather spend all my days with you alone, Gino, than have you go after him because we're worried about what he might do when we have children. I want them, but I want you more."

He kissed her. She loved when he kissed her. He had stolen her soul with kisses. She snuggled her head under his chin, breathing him in. She loved his scent. There was something wild and undefined she could never put her finger on. Gino might have companies that belonged to the modern world. He might have all the money in the world, but there was something very feral and predatory about him.

"Zara, you need to hear me. Really hear me. Nothing is going to happen to me. We're the last soldiers Whitney experimented on. We don't get brain bleeds. We don't need anchors. We don't have any of the problems some of the other GhostWalkers have experienced. He gave us all the enhancements as well as enhancing our psychic abilities. Zhu has no idea what's coming for him. It's like taking a lamb and dropping it alone in the middle of a wolf's territory."

She liked that image—the team a pack of wolves hunting Zhu. She chewed on the end of her finger. "How can you catch him alone? He's probably locked up in Cheng's fortress right now."

He took her hand and turned her finger up to his mouth

for kisses. "Leave that to me, baby. I have a plan. I'll take care of Zhu and come straight home to you."

"Cheng . . ."

"Is a vengeful asshole. I know that. But he'll check to see where I was, where you were. The plane we're flying in on is a regularly scheduled flight to Shanghai. I have never once been on it, nor will I be on it this time. He won't know who killed his brother. Most likely it will cross his mind and he'll check, but we'll look as if we never left Louisiana. He'll think it has something to do with the club Zhu likes to visit."

"Club?"

"It's a vile place, baby, not a real BDSM club, but a place where sick fucks can get off hurting or even killing others. It appeals to very wealthy men and women who fly in from all over to visit. They pay big money to participate and the club provides men, women and children of all ages for their clients to hurt."

"That's truly horrible."

"Very demented." He tipped her chin up and kissed her again. "I'm going to have to go. I'm on a timetable here, baby. I have to make that plane before it leaves."

There was no winning this battle. She drew a long, deep breath and pressed closer to him. "How long will you be gone?"

"I don't know." He kept her face tipped up to his, forcing her gaze to meet his. "Know I am coming back. Nothing will keep me away. I'll get back to you, Zara, even if I have to break out of hell to do it."

She wanted more than that reassurance. She wanted to know he'd come home still Gino, not some dark, twisted version of him. "All right, honey," she whispered. "Just know I'm right here waiting for you."

"Lie down for me. I've got seven minutes and I'm out of here."

"How are you getting to the airstrip?"

"Helicopter. Trap has a couple of them. I can see we're going to have to have our own plane and at least one chopper."

He lifted her off his lap and back on the bed, his hands on her shoulders urging her to lie down. She did, but only because she knew nothing she said or did was going to stop him from getting on that chopper and she wasn't going to send him off with her being a sobbing baby. She could wait until he was gone to do that.

~

The club Razor's Edge was located in the red-light district of Shanghai. The GhostWalkers stayed away from the streets and alleys, moving instead on the rooftops. They used signs and fluttering wires to stay above the garish lights. The deeper they went into the streets lined with strip bars and clubs, the seedier the establishments.

They could have easily followed the dark-tinted-windowed vehicles bringing elite clientele to the club. Too many, as far as Gino was concerned. They'd discussed going in as rich patrons, an easy enough thing to change faces and fingerprints, but they didn't bother. They were there as hunters, and they didn't need to blend in with their prey.

Flame, Wyatt's sister-in-law, had sent them quite a file on Bolan Zhu. Between Jaimie, Lily, and Flame, they had gathered a tremendous amount of intelligence on him. All three were very good at hacking and they seemed to know where to get information. Bolan Zhu was born Bolan Allen Cheng. He was Cheng's younger brother by nearly twelve years. He had been a sickly child and his father had hidden him away, embarrassed at having a son he didn't deem good enough to share his blood.

To toughen his son up, he turned him over to sadistic teachers, men who taught him to fight. To condition his

body. To use weapons. To become a weapon. He trained
night and day, frequently yanked from his bed to go work.
He was caned when he didn't take down his opponents or
if he made a sound when being punished. He grew strong
enough for his father to claim him, but by that time, having a son he could use as an executioner that no one knew
of was too good to pass up.

Zhu excelled in his service to his country, interrogating
prisoners and keeping his men in top shape. They were the
elite sent on impossible missions. He had his own army
now, a private army of men loyal only to him, pulled from
the ranks of the soldiers who had followed him. They traveled with him as a rule, and many of them were frequent
visitors of the same club Zhu preferred. Like him, none
were married. It was whispered even Cheng feared him
and his army.

The GhostWalkers spread out, Ezekiel and Malichai
taking the roof of the building to the left of the club.
Mordichai and Trap took the roof to the right of their target. Gino, Rubin, Diego and Draden waited in the shadows, just outside the back entrance where bodies were
brought out. Three bored guards smoked and paced, occasionally exchanging words. Clearly, they'd seen it all
and weren't in the least caring about what went on inside
the building or how many were killed in a night.

Twice the largest of the three men nearly stepped on
Gino's hand where he lay in the ditch at the side of the
building. Diego stood upright, pressed into the corner,
blending in with the tawdry colors splashed on the siding.
Rubin was above the door, lying prone on the roof, his
eyes the only thing in sight. Draden, even Gino couldn't
spot. That was Draden, the male model who had graced
so many elite magazines, a dangerous predator there in
the darkness.

Two men on the roof. Both armed. They mean busi-

ness. They aren't like the guards you're facing. These have to be two of Zhu's men. Ezekiel reported in.

I'm looking at two roaming to the front of the building, Mordichai said.

Two roaming to the back, Trap said.

Zhu's guards number twenty-five when he comes to this club. He likes his show of force and he gives some the privilege of participating in club activities, Ezekiel said. *Count it down so we don't miss any of them.*

Cover us, Gino said.

Like a lizard, Rubin moved over the roof until he was looking down at the two guards in the front. The men paced back and forth, meeting briefly in the middle of the street, but not acknowledging each other. They continued walking partway down the road, turned and walked back, their pace unhurried, their semiautomatics very much in evidence and their eyes moving restlessly, scanning the entire block, roof to ground.

The problem was, it was too big of an area to cover for two men. They were good, but they had established a pattern and that allowed for movement. Rubin signaled to Diego, the soft moan of the wind, and Diego waited until the three guards had their backs to him and then he was gone, sliding into the night to get into position.

Gino had to take out the two men on the roof of the club without being seen or heard. Rubin and Diego would take care of the roving guards in the front of the club, and Draden and he would take out those to the rear. No one could move without the snipers on the roof gone first.

He rolled back to the darker shadows that took him to the side of the building between the club and the bar beside it. A man had a woman pinned against the building not more than five steps away from Gino when he entered that three-foot space. The two were going at it so hard, neither saw him as he climbed to the roof without a sound.

He was strong, unusually so, and he used only his

hands, pulling himself up fast, not taking a chance his foot might scrape too loudly or push debris loose to fall on the couple doing their thing. He pulled his body up high enough to allow him to see the roof above the club. It was long and flat. The two guards went from one side to the other, and they were very systematic. He stayed still as the guard walked away from him. Had Gino wanted, he could have shot him, but this had to be silent work. He pulled himself all the way onto the roof.

He froze right over the thick railing, remaining very still. The other guard walked toward him in the same cross pattern the guards on the street maintained. Gino had to time it perfectly. He needed the first guard to keep his eyes forward, scanning the rooftops of the other building, while the one he stalked, coming at him, examined the left side. As the guard passed him, missing his prone figure by no more than two inches, Gino rose up, slammed his knife through the base of his skull, his hand over his mouth to muffle any sound. He caught the heavy weapon and lowered both man and gun to the roof.

He moved to his right, already having picked the darkest parts of the roof. He didn't crawl, but walked fast, coming up behind the second guard. Something must have alerted the man because he began to turn his head to look over his shoulder. It was already far too late for him. Gino repeated the same kill, slamming his knife home, lowering man and weapon to the rooftop.

Eyes on roof taken out. That's one and two, Gino reported.

It's a go, Ezekiel gave the order.

Gino moved fast to get off the roof and down where he could do the most good. They had to take out all the guards in seconds and then get inside to find Zhu and the rest of his men before someone inside tried to contact one of the dead guards.

The moment Gino gave the all clear, Rubin and Diego

went to work. Gino slipped back into the alley, noting the man and the woman were walking back. He was just a little ahead of her, walking quickly, making it plain he didn't consider her anything but a whore he paid for her services. She didn't seem to mind or notice, she chattered away, trailing after him. The moment they rounded the corner to the front street, he ran down the alley in the opposite direction.

I'm in position, Gino, Draden said. *I'll take the one facing north. He's within a few steps of me.*

I'm in position, Gino echoed. *I've got the one facing south.*

Rubin and Diego had chosen their respective kills and said so.

All four men waited.

It's a go, Ezekiel gave the order.

Gino moved out of the shadows to walk silently into the street, where Zhu's soldier paced away from him. He fell into step behind him, just as Draden, Rubin and Diego did the same with the prey they stalked. Two more steps and Gino had him, taking him in their classic kill method, driving the knife deep into the base of the neck, severing the spinal column. He kept his hand over the mouth while he caught the gun. Quickly, he dragged the dead weight to the side of the building, pushing him into the darkest corner and wiping his knife on the man's shirt.

One down, that's three.

One down here, that's four, Draden said.

One down, that's five, Rubin reported.

Down here, so six altogether, Diego added.

Gino was already on the move, heading to the back of Razor's Edge, where the three bored club guards were still lounging. One flipped his cigarette onto the ground, looked furtively around without seeing the four Ghost-Walkers surrounding them and pulled out a flask to drink. He was a civilian guard, one the club had hired, and he was probably more interested in whatever perks the club gave him than doing his job. Another guard sniffed cocaine up his nose.

Gino took the one closest to him, walking right up to him in plain sight, as if to ask a question. He just kept walking, and as he passed the guard, he slit his throat. He never even paused or slowed down. Rubin and Draden did the same with the two other club guards and Diego pulled each body to one side and dropped them in the darkness.

Club guards dead, going in, Gino reported.

He yanked open the door and entered the club. The music was pounding and loud, spilling out from various rooms. Screams, moans and laughter could be heard over the music. He glanced back at Rubin and Diego and then at Draden. Draden knew what to expect, but he didn't know about the two brothers from the Appalachian Mountains. He hoped they'd keep it together.

He walked down a narrow hallway that opened almost immediately to a large common room where a bar curved along one side and tables stretched across the floor, giving ample seating to the patrons. Naked waitresses and waiters, all wearing collars, served the men and women at the tables. Two waitresses dropped to their knees at one of the larger tables after handing out the drinks, to crawl under and open trousers. A waiter was doing something very similar at another table.

Gino signaled and Diego and Rubin split up, each going up the side of the wall, clinging like two lizards, nearly impossible to see with their blurred images. They would be the eyes in the room. Each of Zhu's men wore a red armband sewn into the sleeve of his shirt, making them easy to identify. Zhu wanted those armbands to strike fear into anyone who crossed them—and they usually did. The men liked to wear them because no one ever opposed them.

Small table to your left, Gino. Three sitting together.

One just got up to go into another room. Rubin gave the report.

I'll go after the one leaving, Gino said.

No worries, I've got the two at the table, Draden said.

Gino fell into step behind the tall man with the red armband. The club was like a giant beehive. All around were rooms, the walls glass so anyone could see in. Many visitors stood and watched as a woman was being whipped, the skin flayed from her back. Two men had their cocks out, stroking excitedly to the sight. Zhu's man stopped to watch, grinning as the woman begged and pleaded for her tormentor to stop.

Gino took him right there, while the others stood staring, fascinated at the window. He killed Zhu's soldier and dragged him over to a chair, where he positioned him with his legs sprawled out before walking in a circle, looking into each of the windows.

Another down, that's seven. Keeping track of their enemy was a common thing when spread out and they were certain of the numbers. That way, no one would accidentally be left to come back at them.

The common area was dimly lit so the hexagonal cells could be blazing with bright lights. He simply walked around, looking into each cell, noting the ones that held men with red armbands. There were three. On the fourth cell in, he located Bolan Zhu.

Eight and nine are down, Draden reported in. *I left them sitting at their table, drinks at hand.*

Gino should have known Zhu would draw a large crowd, and he had, the onlookers two feet deep around the window. They smelled of alcohol, drugs, sex and excitement as they regarded the man they'd come to expect a huge show from. He knew it too, and he played to his audience.

Zhu was angry that Zara had escaped him once more and he was taking it out on the two women and one man he had chained and hanging from the ceiling. The two women were bound in extremely painful positions, their bodies contorted, the ropes so tight the bonds cut into the skin. The ropes had tiny hooks woven into the strands, so they ripped at skin each time the women moved, or even took a breath. Weighted balls hung from their nipples, adding to their agony, but it was the man Zhu heaped humiliation and punishment on.

Zhu was naked, his body rippling powerfully with muscles. He beat the man unmercifully, every part of his body, then tied him in a pose that left him contorted but exposed his cock and ass to his tormenter. Zhu left him hanging and went to work on the women, clearly getting aroused at seeing them suffer.

Gino was shocked to feel sick to his stomach. He had seen torture, but not like this, not for pure pleasure. One shouldn't get aroused by hurting others. There was no doubt that Zhu was getting off on what he was doing, and a good portion of those watching were as well.

Find the others. They have to be in this club. I want someone to start finding dead bodies and start a panic. I can't get to Zhu in the blinding light. Nor did Gino want to. He wanted to kill his men one by one and then have a little time alone with Zhu. Gino had always thought of himself as a demon—a man belonging in hell—but the things Zhu was doing to his three prisoners were evil. Vile. The man was sick and twisted.

Red armband in crowd at fifth window, just past Zhu. That was Diego.

Gino hated that Diego was inside the area where the well-lit cells were. Each scene was something out of a horror movie. He hadn't realized he felt so protective toward Rubin and Diego. It wasn't that they were that young, or that naïve, but they were both good men.

Gino walked in plain sight to the next cell and stood next to the man with the red armband, just back two steps.

The man actually glanced at him and then looked away. Gino waited for recognition to happen, but none did, not face recognition. It was more the fact that he was a man to look out for. A predator, just like Zhu. Zhu's soldier swung toward him, but Gino wrapped an arm around his neck, and wrenched hard. The crack might have been audible if the music wasn't so loud. Keeping his arm around the man's neck he dragged him to the middle of the room to the rows of chairs placed back-to-back to view the scenes in the cells.

That's ten. Fifteen to go. Anyone spot those outside? Gino walked back to see Zhu raping one of the women, his hands around her throat, squeezing the life out of her while he took his pleasure. He wanted to kill the man more than he wanted to breathe. He might have used a gun at that moment, but there was no guarantee he could shoot through the glass.

At your six, Gino. And again, another coming out of a room and heading toward the one at your six. He's covered in blood. The girl he left barely alive looks to be about fifteen if that. That was Diego. His voice was steady, but there was something there that had Gino wanting to order the brothers from the room.

Two just came out of the cell at the end of the hall, right side. They're laughing and looking back into the cell. Both men have blood on them. Looks like arterial spray, Rubin reported. *Moving closer.*

Don't. Gino couldn't help himself. He was beginning to feel a little desperate. This club was one of the sickest places he'd ever been in. He needed to kill Zhu, but he didn't like exposing Diego and Rubin to the kinds of things happening. He had a feeling he knew what went on in that cell. *There's no need to see what they did.*

I've got them, Draden said. *Hang back, kid. You're our eyes. We have to know the minute someone spots one of our kills.*

Gino walked casually with a man and a woman, the woman dressed in a luxurious fur, her ears dripping with diamonds. Her eyes were bright, and she was clearly as high as her man as they wandered over to the cell where the two men with red armbands talked just outside the lit room. The woman giggled when she saw the young girl, naked and barely moving, her body covered in blood.

"We're too late," she whispered, excitement in her voice. "I wanted to see this one. So many ideas to bring home with us to our own little darling."

Fur coat, black suit. They come out, kill them, he ordered Ezekiel and his brother. He wanted to burn the club down with everyone in it.

You can't kill them all, Ezekiel's voice steadied him. *We're here to take out Zhu. Keep your heads in the game, all of you.*

Maybe not, but these people don't deserve to live.

20

~

The woman in the fur coat turned to the man who had just emerged. "I saw you were here and they'd brought in a young girl for you on the program. I was hoping to see your performance."

The guard looked her up and down and then back at the girl trying to push up to her hands and knees. "She was delicious."

Gino took his friend, right there while the other man was basking in the glow of being some kind of star for hurting young girls. He slammed his knife into the base of the skull of the ex-soldier and dragged him back a few feet. Others crowded in to see the teen fall back on the floor. Applause broke out. Gino hauled the dead man to the row of chairs. *Eleven down.*

He felt grim, drained of all humanity, but he had to have something left because the club and its inhabitants twisted his stomach. More, the thought of Zara in Zhu's hands made that sick feeling inside him worse. He crept up behind the man responsible for the young girl lying in a pool of her own blood and waited until the man got his fill of laughing at his handiwork. Abruptly Zhu's soldier spun on his heel and pushed his way through the crowd, spotting his friend sprawled out in a chair.

Gino let him walk almost right up to him, shadowing his every step. When the soldier halted right in front of his friend, he halted as well.

"What are you doing? We have to relieve the others," the man demanded. He stepped closer when there was no movement.

Gino heard his swift intake of breath, the recognition that his friend was dead, and then Gino killed the man. There were no guns to catch. These men were relaxing in their favorite way. The ex-soldier liked hurting others. Zhu had gathered an army, personal bodyguards, whatever he wanted of them, but the men were sadistic just like their boss.

That's twelve. There was satisfaction in killing this one.

Thirteen and fourteen down, Draden reported. *Sick fucks. I would like to be able to kill them again. Maybe three times.*

Gino watched the woman in fur come across the room to the chairs. There was purpose and determination in her step. "We'd like a private demonstration. We can get you another virgin, one even younger if you prefer," she started and then narrowed her eyes, stepping closer.

Gino slipped up behind her. He didn't like killing women, but she was every bit as sick as Zhu. She screamed. Loudly. Loud enough to be heard above the pounding music. The club members were used to the sounds of screams, but hers were persistent and without the notes of agony included. She was also screaming from the common area, not the cells. Heads began to turn.

Security came out of the shadows as Gino melted into them. He went up the side of the wall, just as Draden did.

They all clung there, high, nearly to the ceiling, blending in like lizards. Gino kept his gaze fixed on the hexagonal cell where Zhu indulged his sadistic nature. The scene in the common areas was chaos as people began discovering the dead bodies positioned throughout the club.

Zhu glanced up, looking impassive as a man wearing a red armband rushed into the brightly lit cell. His gaze never left the window as his man informed him of what was happening. He never once changed expression. He said something, turned back to the man hanging in such agony and shoved a knife into his belly, twisted as the man shrieked, cut up to spill the intestines onto the floor, his expression never changing.

His men, what was left of his army, gathered around the cell waiting for him to come out. He didn't seem to mind keeping them waiting.

Zhu walked to the first woman, who shook her head and pleaded. He stabbed her repeatedly, making certain that none of the knife wounds were fatal. She would suffer, bleed and be disfigured if she didn't bleed out. The second woman had stared in horror, and when he turned to her, she begged. Cried. He pulled the ropes to him, licked the tears from her face, and took her mouth in a savage kiss. At the same time, he shoved his knife deep into her body.

The ex-soldier who had come to warn him laughed and shook his head as Zhu calmly went to a basin and washed the blood off. He didn't look back at the wrecks of human beings he left hanging in ropes. He simply dressed and walked out to join his men. He waited while one helped him into a long coat, listening as they tried to raise the outside guards. Again, it didn't seem to faze him that not one of the men outside answered their radios. He had to know those men were dead and that left him with eleven out of his twenty-five guards.

Gino didn't look at the remains of those hanging or

lying in the cells. He couldn't do that and still stay in position. For the first time since Ciro Spagnola had taught him, he couldn't find that cold place inside that allowed him to disassociate. There was no way to see such suffering, the aftermath of sadistic torture on innocents, and not want to embrace a berserker's rage, so he kept his gaze fixed on Bolan Zhu.

They're coming out.

All vehicles surrounding the club have been rendered useless. There was satisfaction in Malichai's voice. He might not have been in the club, but the things Draden and Gino revealed with just their snippets of conversation were enough to tip him that it was ugly inside.

Zhu and his men started wading through the chaos of the crowd. They had no problem using the butts of their weapons to slam into the other patrons' heads to get them moving away. The very wealthy weren't used to such treatment. They tried to run for the exits, and that just added to the pandemonium, allowing Gino, Draden, Diego and Rubin to follow unseen, hiding in plain sight in the middle of the panicked crowd.

The hallway leading to the bar was short, but narrow. Zhu's guards had to go into it two abreast. Draden and Gino came up behind the last two men who were trying to keep the wealthy patrons from knocking them down in order to get out. One swung his semiautomatic toward the ceiling and let loose a burst. The screams amplified and the crowd flung itself forward, a living, breathing wall.

Gino took advantage, pulling the ex-soldier back into him from behind and cutting his throat in one smooth move, dropping him with a shove back into the crowd. He fell, blood spraying toward those coming at him. More panicked screams. More pushing. *That's fifteen.*

Zhu's guards picked up the pace, pushing toward the front, and, knowing they were followed, urging the others to hurry. They kept turning their heads, trying to see an enemy, but the GhostWalkers were too good at blending in.

"Kill them all," Zhu snapped.

That was distinctive, and Gino and the others went up the wall fast to cling to the ceiling just as several guards stopped, turned and, fingers on the triggers, swept a hail of bullets across the crowd trying to follow them to get to the exits. They mowed the patrons of the club down so they fell like dominos. Gino didn't mind in the least. They'd all come to torture others, men, women and children bought from traffickers. They frequented the club to hurt others. He had no problem with seeing their bodies drop and hearing their moans. In the end, the guards left no one standing.

When the sound of the guns died away, the silence in the club was eerie. The two guards at the rear of the line stepped into the pile of the dead and dying, uncaring that they stepped on fingers or chests. They scanned the building carefully. Inside the lit cells was the only movement. A few of the lucky wealthy were pressed tightly against the walls, hoping they would remain unharmed. The guards stalked them and systematically shot each one in the head. As far as Gino was concerned, the men were doing his work for him. He had fully intended to return and take out as many of the foul, vile people as he could and then rescue the victims.

Zhu called out another order and they returned. Inside the bar, they stopped for a brief consultation. "Burn it down. Kill anyone you come across," Zhu ordered.

The GhostWalkers had followed their prey, staying above them, moving slowly so as not to draw attention. There were enough moaning and dying patrons to keep the attention of the ex-soldiers. Still, they were careful, not tempting fate by moving too fast.

We have to get the victims out. They couldn't leave them to die.

Already, Zhu's men had gone into a closet beside an office door and pulled out some kind of flammable cleaner. They began to throw it on the walls. One went behind the bar and broke bottles of top shelf bourbon and poured it over furniture.

We'll get them out, Diego offered. *You and Draden kill these bastards.*

Ezekiel swore. He wanted the team to stay together, but they couldn't leave victims to be burned alive. *Hurry and get them out. We can't leave Gino and Draden without backup.*

I'm good alone, Zeke, Draden assured.

I'm better that way, Gino added. He was grateful he had Draden though. The man was a machine when it came to killing or saving lives. Either one.

There was more swearing. Gino ignored and began his move. The bulk of the guards had surrounded Zhu as best they could as they went out of the club onto the street. Three were left behind to burn the club to the ground.

Fuckers are doing our job for us, Draden observed.

One less job for us, tonight, Gino said. *Let's get this finished. You boys watch your six,* he added to Rubin and Diego.

He waited until the guard finished pouring the alcohol along the bar and had lit a match. As he tossed it, the man turned, and Gino was standing in front of him. Close. The knife bit deep into his throat. His eyes went wide with shock. He tried to speak, but only a gurgle could be heard. Gino withdrew the knife, staring into the man's eyes as he helped him down to the floor. He watched the life ebb right out of him and then turned and walked slowly after the other two, who had both tossed matches into the hive where the victims trapped in the cells were unable to get out.

Sixteen is down.

The guard tossing the match laughed and waved at a

naked woman banging on the cell door before he turned to leave. Draden dropped down on him and snapped his neck. The naked woman stopped screaming and stared at him. Tiny flames licked along the bar and ran up the sides of the walls, the light illuminating Draden as he dropped the body to the floor.

The third guard turned back just as the GhostWalker let go of the dead guard. Gino's knife took him through the throat as he lifted his weapon.

Seventeen and eighteen, Gino said.

Thanks, man, Draden said, glancing over his shoulder. The blaze was fast moving toward all the bottles lined up on shelves behind the bar.

Diego and Rubin were opening cells, pulling people out and sending them toward the back door. Those that couldn't walk, they carried on their shoulders, running to beat the flames. The fire was picking up speed, accelerating with so much fuel in the silks hanging on the walls and draped over tables. Elegant sheets were on some of the beds, because no matter how much agony their victim was in, the patron had to have all the comforts imaginable.

The sound of the fire was loud now, crackling and popping. Neither man even glanced toward it, rushing the women and children out first and then the injured men.

Gino lost sight of them as he paused just inside the door to the club, scanning the street. Zhu had to have left a guard behind, just in case. By now, he had to know the cars up and down the streets were useless. He would go into the narrow alley and make for the warehouse district located right behind the red-light district.

Gino threw a vase that was sitting on a small table in the foyer through the plate glass window. Outside, near the street, a guard leapt into view, his finger on the trigger of his semiautomatic. Gino threw his second-favorite throwing knife. A knife could fall over that distance, but what he loved about this particular blade was that it just kept going. It buried itself deep. *Nineteen.*

All clear. To your left, heading into the alley, Trap said. *Wish we'd brought my woman along. She'd have nooses all along their way out.*

It wasn't a way out. The GhostWalkers were herding Zhu and his men exactly where they wanted them to go. Zhu hadn't caught on yet, nor would he. Gino was certain he was too arrogant to ever conceive that a force would be able to outthink him in his own territory. He hadn't counted on the women's ability with computers to ferret out his every secret. He hadn't counted on the fact that Gino was a meticulous planner and had no problem biding his time in order to exact revenge. He had patience, and he'd learned that from Ciro Spagnola.

Mordichai and Trap, get down there and help Rubin and Diego get those victims out. The fire is spreading fast. People are coming out of the other clubs and very soon we're going to have company. I want us gone before anyone else gets here, Ezekiel ordered.

On it, Mordichai answered for both of them.

Gino ignored the byplay. He ran with Draden, feeling for his surroundings. In the seventeen-plus hours on the plane, he'd run it a hundred times in his mind, finding his way with his footfalls, making certain he could do it fast and yet remain silent. Ezekiel had taken them through every detail of their mission, over and over until every move was automatic. With the detailed information the women had gotten for them, they had put together a good plan of attack.

Draden kept pace, running practically in his footsteps, yet he couldn't even hear his breathing. Rodents scurried out of the way, but other than that, as they ran down the alley and across the next street toward the warehouses, there was no one to see or hear.

Zhu was left with six men. He'd lost them one by one

and no one had seen what chased them. GhostWalkers came out of the night and took their prey. That had to spook Zhu's elite force just a little. If he was Zhu, he would send one up high to be the eyes for him. Gino had even chosen the spot. There was a long bank of warehouses, rows of them, but the first bank had the ability, on the connecting roof, to hide a man with a weapon. He could wait up there and see if anyone followed them. The entire bank of warehouses was protected by a very high chain-link fence.

The first and second row of warehouses belonged to Cheng. The third row was exclusively Bolan Zhu's. Intel was, he housed his own armory there as well as armored vehicles kept in the best of shape. He was definitely headed there. At the street facing the first long bank of warehouses, where Gino was certain a guard lay up on the roof, Draden and he split. One went to the left, the other to the right, until they were each at a corner. There were no lights back there; Cheng and Zhu didn't want anyone seeing what they were doing.

Under cover of darkness, both sprinted across the street, again in absolute silence. They had to chance that the guard was watching the alleyway. It would stand to reason that if anyone was following, they would come from there. Draden went up one side of the building, Gino the other. It was Draden's job to take out the guard on the roof.

Ezekiel and Malichai lay up on the roof across the street, eyes to scopes, waiting just in case. They wanted this operation done in complete silence if possible. Any evidence left behind was evidence damning Zhu and his men. Nothing remained of the GhostWalkers. Every knife had been retrieved, and no fingerprints were left behind. They couldn't risk an international incident. Major General would never have sanctioned this operation and he wouldn't be able to get them out of it if they fucked up.

Gino was up and over the chain-link fence in seconds.

He heard the running beat of several shoes. His enhanced speed enabled him to fall in line behind the last guard.

Twenty, Draden said. *Coming after you, Gino.*

Gino took the guard as he ran, matching steps, getting close and driving a knife deep into the base of the skull. He had to swerve around the body, but before it actually toppled to the ground, he was on the next one. The others had rounded a corner, leaving the guard alone for a few steps. It was enough time for Gino to kill him.

Twenty-one and twenty-two.

He paused at the corner. It would be suicide to blindly run around it, but he needed to get inside Zhu's warehouse with him and the rest of his elite guard. Without the one on the roof, Ezekiel and Malichai made their way to the same rooftop, setting up to take their backs and give them eyes from above.

Gino went up, scaling the side of the wall to the second bank of warehouses. Running across the rooftop in a low crouch, he saw Zhu with the remaining three men surrounding him as he unlocked the door to his warehouse. All looked back, waiting for the other guards.

One swore when no one came. "Who is doing this, Bolan? I haven't even seen the enemy and he's taken out just about all of us."

Zhu shrugged and swung open the double doors. "I suspect I saw him once at the American embassy." He said no more. He didn't run. He walked inside.

"It's only one man? It can't be one man," the same guard protested.

Gino was already in the shadows just to the side of the door. Draden had joined him. The two slipped inside just before the doors were pulled closed. Instantly the warehouse went dark. Gino and Draden both could see easily in the dark. Their DNA enhanced by Whitney gave them that advantage.

Zhu leveled a cold gaze on his bodyguard. "Does it

matter if it is one man or several? We have to leave this place. We'll get them another time, Dai." He snapped on a single dim lightbulb that hung from the center of the very large room. That left a lot of darkness for a Ghost-Walker to hide in.

Dai shook his head. "We didn't even hear him. Or them. Did anyone see or hear anything? Feng?" He looked at one of the remaining men, who shook his head.

"I never even saw a single one of our men go down, Dai."

Dai looked expectantly at the remaining ex-soldier. "Longwei?"

Longwei shook his head. "Nothing."

"Bolan, seriously, we've never come up against anything like this. I don't like you exposed this way. Call your brother. Have him send reinforcements," Dai said. "I can't protect you against something I can't see."

"You would have me whine to my brother that we cannot protect ourselves against a single man? Or those with him?"

"There are three of us left to protect you. Every one of us was trained in all special forces under you. You know what we're capable of. This man or men following us isn't human."

"I suspect they aren't. Not fully," Zhu said. "It would be a great thing to kill one and bring his body back to my brother so we could have these same kinds of advantages. I will not go crying to my brother. He would forever look down on us. Right now, he fears us. He would think he could make a move against us."

That was news. Zhu and Cheng weren't completely in sync with each other. Zhu's bodyguards were in a tight cluster, but they would have to fan out at some point.

Clear, Diego reported in. *We got everyone alive out. Some of them were in very bad condition. Found the*

*owner of the club hiding in one of the cells. Chained him
to a pole with enough evidence for the cops to prove that
he was dealing in human trafficking and using them for
sadists to torture and kill. Found a small group of women
being held below the club. Name's Moffat of all things.
He's good friends with Cheng and Zhu. I know this because he told me multiple times.*

He see your faces? Ezekiel asked sharply.

We weren't born yesterday, Zeke.

Just making sure you're in the clear. Gino, report in.

*Just standing around here sucking my thumb, boss-
man,* Gino said.

He never took his eyes off his prey. Zhu stood there,
his features as impassive as ever. Looking at him, no one
would ever think he could have done the sadistic things
he had to the three victims. Gino couldn't help but notice
that the woman he kissed and then cut so badly had red
hair. She hadn't looked exactly like Zara, but she was
probably a substitute for her. The other woman—the one
he'd stabbed repeatedly and disfigured—had blue eyes
and skin like Zara's.

If Zhu didn't die tonight, he would make another try
for Zara. Gino knew that with absolute certainty.

"Bolan." Dai was obviously the head of Zhu's security
team. "It doesn't matter what your brother thinks. I can
hire another crew. I can find the right ones, men who like
the same things as us. We allow them to make life or
death decisions for their sexual partners and the power
will be addicting. It won't take that long to build another
force and then we can go after this man."

Zhu shook his head.

Dai persisted. "Cheng would learn to fear you very
quickly again. We visited his bedroom more than once
when he got out of hand and we can easily do it again.
Remember his face when he woke up to find the dead

women sprawled all over him? Sheets coated in blood? He will fear us again. Better he has one moment of false triumph than something happening to you."

"The car is armored." Zhu had made up his mind.

Dai shook his head and shrugged. "Let's go then, before all hell breaks loose. Our men are strewn all over that club and probably down the street as well. They're known by everyone. We have to move before we are found and questioned."

"Don't be ridiculous. No one would dare to question me."

"That was before the Razor's Edge burned down and everyone inside it was shot. That was before the club was exposed for the things going on inside. This might not be so easy to sweep under the carpet." Dai was reluctant to leave what he thought was the safety of the warehouse.

"Get more weapons," Zhu ordered and then ignored his head of security.

He stalked over to the side of a large black SUV with tinted windows and special armor plating. The windows were bulletproof. He leaned against the door while Dai, Feng and Longwei hurried over to the large crates sitting to the back of the warehouse.

"Need a crowbar," Dai muttered and pointed toward the far corner of the room.

Longwei immediately rushed to get it. None of them wanted to stay, but they didn't want to leave either. They didn't know where safety was. Gino dropped in behind Longwei, a silent shadow, following him right into the corner where a long table held a variety of tools. Longwei took out his cell phone and shone a light along the table. Gino handed him the crowbar with one hand. Longwei took it, murmuring a polite "thank you." He stiffened, his head swiveling around, eyes going wide with shock.

Gino was on him, one hand over his mouth, muffling any sound as he shoved the knife into the guard's throat.

He stared down at the man. Eyes to eyes. Nose to nose. Gino breathing, Longwei unable to breathe. Gino took him to the floor, removing the crowbar from his spasming fingers and pulling the blade from him. Very carefully he wiped it on the guard's shirt.

Twenty-three.

"Hurry up, Longwei," Dai snapped. "We have to get these open."

Silence met his demand. The crowbar hit the floor with a loud metallic sound. The tip was in the light. Dai, Zhu and Feng turned toward the sound. Zhu tried the door, frowned when it was locked and then walked around the armored car to the other side, putting it between the clattering sound and his body.

The crowbar was lifted from the floor, but Longwei didn't step out of the shadows to hurry back to Dai. He just stood there. Unseen. In the dark. The three remaining men couldn't see his body, they could barely make out that it was a man standing there.

"Stop playing around," Dai demanded. "You always make jokes and play pranks at inappropriate times."

Gino had gone up the wall, moving sideways until he was so close to Feng he was afraid the man would lean back into him. Feng had taken refuge between the row of large crates and the wall, hoping by keeping his back to the wall, no one could sneak up on him. He was sweating, and Gino could smell fear.

Draden stood where Longwei had been, the crowbar held loosely in his hand, keeping the attention of Zhu and Dai. Gino moved down the wall like a spider, until he was directly behind Feng. He reached out with both hands, one clamping tightly over the man's mouth while the other slit his throat. He held him upright, waited until the guard began to slump and then slowly lowered him to the floor behind the crate.

Twenty-four.

Dai glanced over his shoulder toward Feng but the area was empty. When he looked back at Longwei, no one was there. Instantly he moved toward the armored car, his eyes bouncing around the warehouse. "Bolan, we have to get the hell out of here. Get into the car."

"The locks are jammed. I tried all of them," Zhu said. "We can't use the car."

"We have three others," Dai pointed out, making his way warily toward his boss.

"It stands to reason the locks are all jammed on them as well."

"Send for more men. Make it clear to your brother that we need them now."

"I've done so and told him I uncovered a conspiracy to kill him. In doing so, I set myself up as a target and am now in danger. If he believes the threat is to him, he will want us to live to help protect him," Zhu said.

"At the word 'conspiracy,' he'll kill an entire floor's worth of employees," Dai pointed out.

Zhu nodded with a slow, cold smile. "I believe he will. He's descending into madness, just as our father did."

"Is Cheng sending help?"

"He answered immediately that they're on the way. Relax, Dai. We are fine right here if we stay together and under this light. Even if this man is in this warehouse with us, he will make a mistake."

"He hasn't so far."

Zhu looked around the cavernous room with a cold smile. "But he is close to his goal and eager to get to me. He stole something of mine and he doesn't want me taking it back."

"The woman."

Zhu nodded. "I searched years for her. The perfect one. She would grace every public event I went to, especially after my brother meets an untimely death. She dislikes pain to the point that it terrifies her. She's intelligent, and her brain will be very useful. More than anything, she's American, like my mother, and I will have her complete obedience."

He looked around the warehouse and tried taunting the man who had come for him. "I have so many plans for her. She'll crawl under tables and blow my guests if I demand it right in front of everyone." He smiled as he looked around the warehouse again. "Think about that, GhostWalker. Think what I'll do to her. Those women suffering at my hands were mere substitutes for her. That was mild torture, mild compared to what I plan to do to that woman. She'll suffer for going with you. She'll be in agony for days, weeks, months. She'll beg my forgiveness."

Gino shut out that snide voice. Zhu wanted to shake him up, have him make a mistake. The mistake was Zhu's. He paced while he mocked and jeered at Gino. In pacing, hands behind his back, looking nonchalant, he had separated himself from his private bodyguard, the head of his security.

Dai made the mistake of watching Zhu, of keeping his eyes glued to his boss while occasionally looking around the warehouse, but not behind him. The armored car was behind him and he thought himself safe. Gino went right over the top of it, lay for a moment on the roof and then slithered down the other side. Dai didn't want to take his eyes off Zhu, afraid of someone coming out of the night and killing him.

Gino hooked him around the throat, cut off his airway by clamping a hand over his mouth and nose while he rolled with him under the car and out the other side. It took all of one and a half seconds to get into the dark and break Dai's neck. *Twenty-five. Draden. You need to leave.*

I'm on you.

Not for this. It isn't going to be clean or pretty. Get the hell out of here.

Gino wasn't going to shoot the bastard. He wasn't even going to cut his throat, at least not right away. He'd been good to the others, killing them fast, almost before they were aware. They didn't have time to suffer as they deserved.

Not going to happen.

Zhu became aware of the silence. He turned and realized Dai was no longer behind him. He crouched low and took a long look around the warehouse. "You're good. I'll give you that. Every one of these men were specially trained. The senator assured us the GhostWalker program was worth whatever she asked for, and clearly she was right."

He stood slowly and walked to where Dai had last been, inspecting the area, looking for Dai's weapon. All the guns were gone. Zhu had been too arrogant to carry one himself. He had surrounded himself with men with weapons and didn't believe he needed one, not in the club he frequented. He could go in looking every inch the gentleman. He liked dressing in his suits, the ones custommade, the shoes the same. He liked buying men and women and knowing he had the power of life and death over them. That didn't mean he was without weapons, and clearly the GhostWalker preferred silence to guns.

You aren't going to have the stomach for this, Gino tried again. *It doesn't bother me to have you see what I do to him, but you're never going to look at me the same.*

Just get on with it.

Gino walked out of the shadows into the open to face Bolan Zhu.

Zhu smiled at him. "You didn't like me sending a few stupid mercenaries after Zara and you came all this way just to tell me. They weren't nearly as good as I was led to believe."

"I was always going to come for you," Gino said. "Did you think I'd let you do that to her and get away with it?" He glided closer, watching Zhu, getting a feel for his energy, how he moved, the slightest hint that the man would attack.

"Ah yes, little Zara and the whip. It was beautiful to see those stripes across her breasts. It was all I could do not to take her right then, with her blood dripping everywhere and her little body shuddering in pain. Her tears were beautiful. You have to admit, you get off just looking at those tears. Didn't you fall just a little bit for her, looking at her bruised face and those gorgeous stripes? A woman is so beautiful with her face contorted in pain."

For one moment, another woman's face rose up, his mother, lying in her own blood, pain making her almost unrecognizable. Gino slammed the door hard on the memory. He couldn't allow Zhu to shake him in any way.

"It's delicious to have a woman at your mercy. Don't tell me, with all your strengths, you never even tried it? Not once? I am not certain I believe you."

Gino remained silent, watching him. Zhu kept his expressions blank, but he couldn't stop the movements of his body. Tiny. Subtle. His fingers twitched.

"Society tells you not to give in to your nature, but you're like me. A woman belongs to you and she should follow your every command. Your every desire. That's your right as a man."

Gino smiled at him. "Everything about Zara is beautiful. She does belong to me, and yes, I want her to follow my every command, my every desire. I don't think it's my right as a man, but it is my right to protect her, to see to her care, her pleasure and happiness. That's what I'll be doing while you're long dead."

He knew Zhu thought of himself as a fighter, but he didn't have a prayer. Gino was in that distant, cold place. It didn't matter what Zhu said. He couldn't make him lose his temper or make a mistake. He could taunt him all he wanted, but Gino wouldn't break. He'd learned in a hard school.

He remembered that moment when Joe pulled him out from under his dead grandparents and his father. His dead mother stared at him, her face contorted with pain, the flames of the fire the murderers had started to cover up their crime drawing closer.

Gino had tried, over the years, to forget how much he loved her, the way she'd looked at him, that soft glow on her face whenever he came into a room. Whenever his father had. She'd loved them both, and in spite of how he tried to stomp it out of himself, the moment he'd laid eyes on Zara, he knew he was capable of that deep, abiding love.

Ciro had known what Gino was trying to do and had taught him how to compartmentalize. There was no room for rage, he'd always said. There was no room for personal emotions. You did a job and you did it thoroughly so no one ever fucked with you or your family. Not. Ever. Family was sacred and any threat to them had to be eliminated.

Bolan Zhu was a threat to Zara and he always would be. More, he was a threat to every decent man, woman and child he came across.

"Every one of my men experienced what it was like to have a woman or a man at their mercy. What it was like to have sex any way they demanded. To be treated like a king. You have so much and yet you refuse to give in to your true nature. I see it in you. I see what you would like to be."

Gino knew better now. He had thought himself like this monster, because he could take apart a human being. But he wasn't like this man. Not even halfway. He could never do the sadistic things Zhu enjoyed. He had never looked at the marks on Zara and thought her pain was sexually stimulating. He wanted to take care of her. He wanted to provide for her and see to her every need. He wanted to give her the things in life that would make her happy, and if that meant her freedom to work outside their home, although it would be difficult, he would do it for her. He was many ugly things, but he was not a Bolan Zhu.

"You think you have what it takes to best me?" Zhu asked softly. "I cut my own father to pieces. Cheng was the golden boy, his favorite, the one he was so proud of. He wouldn't even claim me. My mother allowed him to treat me that way. She didn't deserve to live either. I whispered that to her all the time. That someday, I would end her life." He laughed. "Do you have those kinds of balls? Maybe I'll find out. I like to fuck with men who think they're macho. It's all the sweeter when I cut off their cock and balls. You were in there today. You didn't get to see the grand finale because Dai insisted I leave before I was finished."

As he talked, he edged closer, within striking distance. There was no way for Zhu to know how fast a Ghost-Walker could be. He exploded into action, flying at Gino with his front foot. Gino knocked it sideways and slammed his fist into Zhu's throat. Hard. He had always been strong, and the enhancements added even more strength. Zhu fell to the floor choking.

Gino methodically beat him. He used the hardened edge of his hand, his fists, he stomped him, kicked him, making certain there wasn't a place on his body that hadn't been touched, that wasn't hurt and painful. Zhu tried to roll over, and Gino knelt down and stripped him, cutting off his clothes to leave his body naked and vulnerable like so many of his victims'.

Zhu began to laugh insanely, spitting blood, trying to look defiant, but there was no way to hide terror. There was a smell to it. There was a look in the eyes. Zhu did his best to act unafraid, but he winced when Gino came at him again. Gino walked away and Zhu tried to stand, crawling to the car and trying to pull himself up by the door handle.

Gino returned with several of the tools that had been laid out on the table, tools Zhu hadn't put there but recognized as his own. *Last chance, Draden. Get out of here.*

Get on with it. That fucker deserves whatever you're going to give him. I saw what he did to those women and that man. I saw what he did to Zara. Just do it and let's get the hell out of this place.

An hour later, the screams died down, the babbling started and there was nothing left of arrogant Bolan Zhu. There was only a shell of a man. Gino was tempted to let him live, to have to be cared for by nurses, but he didn't want to take the chance that a man that evil might have even a small part of his brain left to harm anyone. He cut his throat and left him on the floor.

Let's get the hell out of here, Gino, and go home, Draden said.

They left the warehouse, locked it and moved into the shadows where their team waited. There were police and ambulances as well as the fire department the street over, so they went up to the rooftops, making good time out of the area.

"Cheng's men never came," Gino said, as he pulled open the door to their vehicle.

"I noticed that," Draden answered.

"We watched for them," Ezekiel said. "We were prepared for a shoot-out, but he never so much as sent a man to see what was going on."

"I guess there wasn't much love lost between them," Gino said. He closed his eyes. All he wanted was a thousand hot showers to wash the stink of Zhu's blood off of him and remove the images from the Razor's Edge from his mind for the rest of his life. And then he'd go home to his woman.

21

~

Gino woke abruptly, his heart racing, sweat dotting his forehead and trickling down his face. He pushed himself into a sitting position, one hand pressing on his chest to try to gain control of his wild breathing. He didn't have nightmares anymore. All those years ago, he had woken nightly seeing his mother's face, watching his father's body drop to the floor. His grandmother and grandfather lying in a pool of blood.

Ciro had awakened him one night and urged him to get up and come with him. He remembered he was still in his pajamas. Ciro had told him to put his shoes on, and they left the house without Joe, just the two of them and the bodyguards. Gino had been taken to a restaurant they frequented a lot. They'd gone to the back and down a flight of stairs to an underground labyrinth he hadn't even known existed.

The men who had killed his entire family were there, tied to chairs, their eyes bouncing around. Gino had never felt so satisfied in his life when he saw them looking afraid. Ciro had stood with him, one hand on his shoulder as he directed his men to make them pay for the death of his best friend and Gino's father. All Gino could think of was his mother's face as she lay dying with her beloved husband already dead beside her and flames licking all around her.

He didn't think about what was being done to the men. In his mind, they deserved everything they got and more. He couldn't see them as human. He had already disassociated.

"Gino?" Zara's voice was soft, her hand whispering over his forehead as she pushed at the damp hair spilling around his face. "What is it, honey?"

Her voice. Her touch. He never thought he'd have that. He caught her in his arms and dragged her onto his lap, holding her too tightly because he needed to know she was with him. She wouldn't leave him. That she could love him as fucked-up as he was, because the things he'd done in his life for Ciro, indulging himself with Zhu, that was fucked-up.

"Tell me, Gino."

If he had insisted she tell him something, it would have been a demand, an order, and he would expect her to obey him. He would insist on it. Zara wasn't like him. Her voice was an invitation to share with her. If he didn't, she wouldn't be upset with him. She would simply cuddle into him and hold him, taking her cue from his body language.

"I don't deserve you." That was the strict truth, but he was keeping her. He needed her. He had been so close to losing his way. Somehow, she pulled him back from the edge.

"Probably not." There was a touch of humor. "But you're not getting rid of me, so tell me what's wrong."

He considered her reaction if he told her the truth. He found he needed to. He didn't know why. He wanted to hide the things he'd done from her. From himself. "I did something I know you wouldn't like or agree with." It was the first time he'd ever had a nightmare that had to do with the justice he exacted—and it had. He'd played the scene out with Zhu a hundred times, and none of them had been pretty.

"Was it really bad?" Zara brushed at the strands of dark hair falling onto his forehead. Her fingers felt cool on his skin. Light, the way she was light.

"I did to Bolan Zhu what he did to you and then some."

There was silence. He could hear her breathing softly in the darkness. He held his breath—waiting for condemnation. For judgment.

"You didn't just kill him outright?" It was a soft inquiry, strictly neutral.

"I thought I would. At first. Before we got there and I saw him with two other women and a man in this disgusting club. People paid to buy human beings so they could get off torturing them. Others watched and got off." He pressed his fingers to his eyes. "I can't get the images out of my head. The things Zhu did to those people. The way others gathered around to watch those suffering. Cheering Zhu on like he was some star performing for them."

He looked down at her, waiting for her eyes to meet his. When that slate blue gaze finally lifted, he felt the impact and it rocked him. There wasn't apprehension, or judgment, only concern for him. *For him.* Zara only thought of him.

"It didn't seem right to me to just kill him without his knowing how what he did to others felt."

She leaned into him, giving him her body. Her breasts pressed tight against his chest. So soft. Her face nuzzled his, her lips sliding along his cheek to his jaw. "Like an eye for an eye," she guessed, her tone gentle. Accepting.

He had woken in a rocky place. Heart pounding. The

flames of hell burning through his mind. Why did Bolan Zhu's death bother him so much? Not his death, but the things Gino had done to him before he killed him.

"Like that. There should be justice in the world, Zara. Shouldn't there? A man does that kind of thing, sadistic torture, shouldn't he at least experience the same before he dies?"

She pulled her head back to look him in the eye. "If you have to ask that question, honey, you already know the answer to it."

"They should," he argued.

"I'm not you. I don't have to do the things you have to do. I don't have to see the things that haunt you, that keep you up at night, that put that look on your face when you woke up, so I will never judge you. Never, Gino. I love you absolutely. Terribly. With everything that I am. I can only tell you that maybe we aren't the ones that have to tip those scales equally. Maybe someone else does that. Or not. Maybe he just had to die to keep him from hurting others, because in the end, who did you hurt more? Bolan Zhu is dead. He can't feel anything. He isn't suffering. You are."

He was silent, turning her counsel over and over in his head. He brought her fingertips to his mouth and bit them gently and then sucked the sting away. Her other hand slid over his chest, and traced the muscles of his abdomen. He couldn't be this close to her without wanting her. Without needing her body.

"I wanted to hurt him."

"I know, Gino." Her fingers danced down his belly, stroked back up to the heavy muscles of his chest. "I would think that would be a natural reaction. It isn't wrong to feel the need or want to hurt someone who hurt us. That's human." She tipped her face up and kissed his jaw. Her lips traveled to his throat.

"I don't have bad dreams. I don't know why this haunts

me. If anyone deserved to suffer, it was Bolan Zhu." But he did know why his actions haunted him and she was sitting in his lap, sliding to one side, so she was on the bed again, her hands moving over his body with gentle persistence. With possessive insistence. His woman was the reason his actions bothered him enough to wake him from sleep.

"Ciro made me feel safe," he admitted. "I admired him. He was a man no one ever fucked with. No one would ever try to kill his entire family because they knew what would happen to them."

She kissed his chest. Her tongue flicked his nipple and the heat rushed through his body, taking him over. He felt the lick of flames in his belly and growing in his groin. He put his head back, savoring the way she made him feel.

"You admired and respected Ciro, Gino. That's natural too. Of course anything he said or did would be gospel to you."

"He's a good man." Gino heard the defensive note in his voice. Was he? Was Ciro a good man? There were many sides to Ciro. To his wife and family, he was good. To the many charities he gave to generously, he was good. He sighed, letting his breath out.

"I don't know, princess. I really don't. I don't know if I'm a good man, so how the hell can I judge Ciro?"

"You don't, Gino." She was practical. "You can only decide who you want to be. What kind of man you want to be. What example you set for our children. We all have choices. If you don't like something about yourself, you work on changing it. It might take a lifetime, but that's a gift you can share with your children. With me. That kind of lifetime commitment to change something in yourself you don't particularly like."

She kissed his nipple, curled her tongue around it and began a journey down his belly. His breath caught in his throat when her arm wrapped around his hips and her mouth found his cock. She blew air over him and then he was inside that warm, moist haven. There was nothing to sort out when he had his woman and she was giving him the ride of his life. When she hollowed her cheeks and sucked hard, she took away every bad memory, every bad image until there was only that mouth and the fire she surrounded his cock with. He knew he would always strive to be a better man because of her—to deserve her.

~

"Stop squirming," Bellisia said. "Good grief, Zara, calm down."

"I can't calm down. I'm really doing this. Were you scared when you got married to Zeke? I'm petrified."

Bellisia stepped back and glared at her. "Don't you dare chicken out after all the talks I gave you advising to take your time and you wouldn't listen. Now Nonny's got her preacher man friend back, and I'm taking you out there even if I have to get the proverbial shotgun and hold it on you through the entire ceremony."

"I *want* to marry Gino," Zara admitted. "I'm crazy in love with him. I can't stand it when he isn't close to me, but I don't know the first thing about relationships, being a wife, making him a home and making him happy." The last came out in a wail.

"Sex," Cayenne said. "Lots of sex. All the time. Anywhere. Be inventive, it's so much fun. Wear all kinds of very provocative clothing and that leads to even more sex. Keeps me happy too, so it's a win-win situation."

Pepper nodded. "I have to admit, she's right. Lots of sex. Wyatt definitely keeps me happy in that department and he's all for it anywhere, anytime, so win-win for me too."

Bellisia sighed and pushed at her blond hair, which was up in a swirling chignon so she looked very sophisticated. "Yeah, go for the sex, Zara. It can get you out of a lot of trouble."

"Or in it," Cayenne said complacently.

The women laughed and Zara had to join them. Cayenne and Trap had no problem with public displays of affection. Sometimes he barely managed to get her into the tree line before she was peeling off her shirt and trying to get his off at the same time.

"You might cook for him," Nonny advised with a smile. "You want to keep your man's strength up. Feed him so you can have plenty of sex." Her smile faded and she looked very serious.

Zara leaned toward her, eyes on Wyatt's grandmother. The other girls sobered as well and stopped everything to listen.

"Make a home for him. *You* be that home for him so the moment he sees you, he not only feels he's home, he knows it."

"How?" Zara asked.

"You don't worry about what you're getting from him. Worry about what he's getting from you. If you married the right man, he's doing the same for you. Don't think he's going to anticipate or know what you need, communicate it to him. Talk to him. Let things go that are trivial. Laugh every chance you get with him. It's the little things that make or break a relationship. Put him first and hope he puts you first. That's the best advice I can give you. I was married for a lot of years to my man, and I loved every minute I had with him."

For a moment Nonny fell silent and then she smiled at them. "You girls make me feel young again and you make me wish I had that time back with him. Cherish your man. Show him that, Zara, and you'll never go wrong."

Zara was absolutely certain she wouldn't have a problem with that. She had grown over the last few months in confidence. She didn't listen to that voice that had always told her she wasn't good enough or that she was a coward. She knew she was different from Bellisia and Shylah, but it didn't matter. She had things to offer as well. And she had Gino.

Ezekiel poked his head in the door. "You ready? You look beautiful, Zara."

"Thanks, Zeke."

Cayenne and Pepper hurried out the door to get to their seats. Bellisia was standing up for her. Zara was suddenly anxious to see Gino. The music started, and Nonny leaned in and brushed a kiss on her cheek.

"You'll do fine. Gino's a good man." It was said with authority.

Zara knew that. She knew Gino was a good man. On cue, she started down the aisle, just an opening between the two rows of chairs, but she didn't notice because she had eyes only for the man waiting for her. Gino. Standing there in a suit. Waiting for her. He was perfect, her man. Perfect for her.

Her eyes met his and her stomach did a slow roll while her heart melted and a million butterflies took wing. She hadn't thought she'd ever have this. A family. A man of her own. A home. She felt like she had everything she could ever want just looking at him. She walked up the aisle to him, completely confident. Completely happy. Feeling beautiful. Certain of her future. Gino took her hand and pressed it over his heart as both turned to face the preacher.

KEEP READING FOR AN EXCERPT FROM
THE NEXT LEOPARD NOVEL BY CHRISTINE FEEHAN

LEOPARD'S RUN

AVAILABLE NOVEMBER 2018 FROM JOVE

Timur Amurov cursed under his breath using his native language, something his brother—and boss—strictly forbade. Striding from the town car with its tinted windows and black paint, he moved easily through those walking on the sidewalk. His trench coat swirled around his ankles, the inner lining filled with many loops to hide the weapons he carried.

People moved out of his way. It was the set of his wide shoulders, the scars on his face, his expressionless mask, the threat in his cold, dead eyes. He saw their reactions and he knew exactly what they would do—step aside for him—so he never broke or deviated from his pace. He looked dangerous because he *was* dangerous. He looked like a man who would kill—and he was.

He didn't pretend to be anything other than who he was. A shifter. A bodyguard. A weapon sent out when it was deemed necessary. If he showed up at someone's door, they weren't going to see another sunrise. He looked the part because that was exactly who he was. A stone-cold killer, a legacy given to him by his father. And grandfather. And uncles. There was no hiding the truth, not even from himself, and he didn't care to. Life had handed him a shit deck of cards, but he was playing his hand until he couldn't take it anymore and then he would go out his way.

He didn't let down his guard for many people. First and foremost was Fyodor, his older brother. Fyodor had risked everything to save Timur and his cousin Gorya, a man brought up with them in their sick, twisted environment. Timur and Gorya had taken the position of bodyguard to Fyodor, but Fyodor just refused to stay out of harm's way. He was the head of a large territory and might as well have gone around with a target painted on his back. No matter what security measures Timur and his security team took, Fyodor seemed to just ignore them.

In his defense, Fyodor had been a bodyguard, a soldier, long before he ascended to the throne, but Timur considered that he should know how difficult it was to guard and keep safe a man who ignored every security protocol.

He loved his brother. Not that they talked of such things. That had been forbidden growing up. They'd been taught never to feel affection for anyone—especially a woman. Fyodor's wife, Evangeline, owned and operated a bakery in San Antonio, and that meant Fyodor worked out of it sometimes. Most times. He had an office in the back. And despite their upbringing, Fyodor made no bones about loving his wife. No bones about showing it, either. The thing was, Timur loved her too. He loved her as a sister but couldn't express it. A childhood of savage beatings had seen to that.

Timur yanked open the glass door to the bakery. He'd had the door replaced and bulletproof glass put in it, along with the banks of windows that made up the shop's storefront. Evangeline looked up quickly and sent him a smile. His heart contracted. She was sweet. Beautiful. Perfect for his brother. More, she kept his brother's leopard from trying to break loose to hunt and kill. His own leopard raked and clawed, angry, violent, moody as hell.

"Everythin' all right, Timur?" Evangeline's little Louisiana accent always made him feel warm, like he'd come home. Her smile began to fade when he didn't return it.

Hell no, nothing was all right. His fucked-up brother was so smitten with this woman that he risked his life—and hers—every damn day. He kept that to himself. Fyodor wouldn't want him upsetting Evangeline, nor did he want to.

He gave her a curt nod as he moved across the floor, checking every table as he made his way to the restrooms. He scanned them quickly, around the legs, under the table-tops, to ensure no incendiary device or explosives had been placed there.

"Timur?"

Evangeline was being insistent. What was he going to say? Fyodor had received more death threats? That was a common enough occurrence. However, this particular threat he was taking seriously, but his brother wasn't—as usual. Timur knew they'd taken too many chances and sooner or later their luck was going to run out. His gut—never to be ignored—told him their luck was long gone and this time the threat was very real.

"Make me a double latte."

"A double latte?" She was clearly shocked.

He needed the caffeine. He needed her busy. He gave her another curt nod and shoved open the men's restroom door. He checked it carefully, every stall, making certain his brother was safe from any assassin, and then he checked the women's room. The moment he put his hand on the door to push it open, he knew, by the way his leopard went crazy, that it was occupied. He didn't care. He wasn't there to cater to anyone's sensibilities. He was there to make certain Fyodor wasn't murdered.

She stood in front of the mirror, lipstick in her hand, and her eyes went wide when he strode in. Her eyes caught him first thing. They were almost too big for her face. A very light brown, amber really, like a fine whiskey you sipped at night when you just wanted to lay it all down. The amber was ringed with very thick, dark lashes that made her eyes stand out. Those lashes feathered down in long sweeps, curling at the ends.

She turned toward him, lipstick held slightly in front of her, as if that could stop him if he came at her. He knew he was intimidating. He was tall, had wide shoulders and a thick chest. Ropes of muscle rippled along his arms, back and chest and down his abdomen. His heart thudded unexpectedly. Hard. An ache he'd never experienced.

She was beautiful. He could see her front, those breasts pushing at her thin tank. The small, tucked-in waist that wasn't in the least hidden by her shirt. She had hips and a very nice ass, which he'd noticed the moment he walked in. She filled those soft blue jeans to perfection. He kept walking right past her and yanked open each of the stall doors. It wouldn't have mattered to him had they been locked. He still would have made the inspection. Fortunately they were all empty; she was the only occupant in the room.

When he'd stepped past her to get to the stalls, he'd inhaled instinctively. She smelled faintly of grapefruit and fresh-cut cypress. Who smelled like that? Evidently he liked it, or, more importantly, his leopard did. Usually if he got too close to a human being, male or female, his leopard raged, wanting to kill. Needing to draw blood. For the first time the cat had gone entirely quiet. That never happened. As in *never*. Even when he was close to Evangeline and his leopard settled, the cat was never like this. Quiet. Almost purring.

"You are?" he demanded. *Shit.* There was no denying his Russian accent or his growl. Both came out overly strong.

He doubted if the top of her head came up to the middle of his chest, but she narrowed her eyes at him in what he suspected was supposed to be a scary look.

"I'm in the *women's* bathroom, which is supposed to be private to *women.*"

Sass. The woman had sass in abundance. Stupidity as well. He stepped closer to her, close enough that the tips of her breasts brushed his abs. She had to tilt her head all the way back to look up at him.

"You don't fuck with a man like me," he advised.

She nodded. "No, I won't. Not ever. Thanks for the advice."

Her voice was even enough, but she was totally fucking with him now, using his own words against him. He had to hand it to her—she kept a straight face and even managed wide-eyed innocence.

God help him, his body chose that moment to betray him. His physical reaction to her was intense. His cock lengthened and grew into a monster, roaring at him just the way his leopard always did, painful now. He didn't dare step forward or back. She had to feel it. There was no hiding it and he kept his expression blank, but he did a hell of a lot of inward cursing—and he used his own language too. Never once in his life had he had such a problem. Now, of all times, his body had decided to react on its own.

He took a breath and resisted the idea of patting her down. By now Fyodor was going to be restless. He wanted to see his woman and he would just . . .

"Is there a problem, Timur?" His brother's voice came smoothly over the tiny radio.

Looking straight into her eyes, Timur answered. "No problem. Give me a minute." His men were up on rooftops, watching over the car and keeping Fyodor safe while Timur checked out the interior of the bakery.

He was met with silence. That could mean anything. Fyodor might decide to not give Timur any shit for once and stay in the car, or he could just come striding in. In any case, Timur had to get away from close proximity to the woman. She was wreaking havoc with him and his leopard. For once, instead of demanding blood, his cat was acting weird, rolling around and practically purring. It was not only annoying, it was throwing him off his game.

"Tell me your name."

"Ashe Bronte."

"You made that up."

"You're just the nicest man I've ever met." Sarcasm dripped from her voice. "If you don't like it, you'll have to take it up with my parents. Unfortunately they're both deceased, so you might have a little trouble finding them."

She pushed past him, and he let her go. She had hair. Lots of it. It was thick and wild, a light blond that also emphasized her unusual eyes. It was only after the door closed behind her, and he was left to stand alone in the cool of the ladies' room, that he realized his leopard had been calm the *entire* time. *Silent.* There was no vicious raking. No demand for blood. Not even when his body had touched her body. For the first time in years he knew respite from his cat's constant fury. But the minute the woman was out of his sight, his leopard reacted, going insane, fighting for control.

This was what Fyodor had found with Evangeline. She tamed the beast in him just by being in close proximity. Timur refused to allow his heart to accelerate or for the adrenaline to be released into his bloodstream. Just because, for a few short minutes, his leopard hadn't clawed for freedom and blood, it didn't mean this woman would do for him what Evangeline did for Fyodor.

He turned abruptly and followed her out. She was walking across the shop floor, straight to the counter. The way she moved in her jeans was a work of art. His heart did a funny stutter as he watched her talk to Evangeline for a moment and then step behind the counter.

"Evangeline?" It was a demand. Nothing less. She couldn't hire someone, as she'd clearly done, without following protocol.

Evangeline tried to win in a stare down, and it wasn't happening. She sighed and came out from behind the counter to catch his arm and guide him across the room, presumably out of earshot, although the bakery wasn't that large and he figured whatever she said was going to be overheard.

"I know. I'm sorry, Timur, but she needed a job and she has experience. I can't keep having your men, who break my things, try to pretend they're baristas. They aren't. I know why you want them in the shop, but they're losing me customers. She's fast, knows her drinks, remembers customers' names and doesn't glare at them or intimidate them in any way."

"Damn it, Evangeline. She could be anyone. What did she do? Just wander in off the street?"

"That's how most people come in. And she is someone." Evangeline sounded more defiant than sorry. "I need the help."

"You could have told us and we'd have found you someone. Fuck. Her name is a joke. Ashe Bronte? That's ridiculous. No one is named that. Maybe a fucking porn star."

"Keep making fun of my name and every time you order a drink, I'm going to put something in it you aren't going to like," Ashe muttered under her breath.

She said it softly enough that he knew she didn't think he could hear. He hadn't bothered to speak that low, but still, she had good hearing. Her jeans were tight enough that he could see she wasn't hiding a weapon, but her breasts were generous enough that she might conceal a knife there. A garrote could be sewn into clothing, and she wore boots that had room for a gun.

"That isn't very nice, Timur," Evangeline pointed out. She lowered her voice even more. "Is she a porn star? Have you seen her in movies? She's gorgeous enough."

"How the fuck would I know? You think I spend my time looking at porn movies and jacking off? Why is it that

I always get into very inappropriate conversations with you? Sweet God in heaven, woman, you're the bane of my life."

Abruptly he spun around and hurried out of the shop, swearing again under his breath when Evangeline's soft laughter followed him. He looked right and left, and then studied the rooftops before he opened the door to allow his brother out onto the sidewalk. The moment he did, Gorya slid out and flanked Fyodor, covering his back. They walked in step and Timur noted that Fyodor was getting used to having bodyguards. He was much more in sync with them than he had been.

They'd already gone through an attack on their family. Evangeline had been targeted. Mitya, a cousin, had been badly wounded when those targeting her tried to kill Fyodor. Timur knew Fyodor felt responsible for that. He had been a little more cooperative ever since. All of them knew it was only a matter of time before the real enemy discovered where they were—hiding out in the open.

Fyodor had been living as Alonzo Massi, but after the attack that had nearly killed Mitya, he took his real name back. Timur was grateful for that. He was Russian and proud of who he was, but he was also a bodyguard; chances were, by taking his real identity back, Fyodor was going to have some serious enemies coming after him. They would be coming for all of them.

Timur opened the door for his brother, but stepped inside while doing so. He wanted to keep an eye on the newcomer. If she went for a weapon, she was dead. The idea of killing her didn't sit well with him, and he kept his body between the new barista and Fyodor at all times. It was easy enough when Fyodor had eyes only for Evangeline.

She came to him immediately, no hesitation. Timur knew better than to look at them. He kept his gaze sweeping the sidewalks through the glass and then back to the new woman. She was looking at Evangeline and Fyodor, and color had swept into her face.

Gorya wandered over to the counter, pretending he wanted a coffee, but clearly what he really wanted to do was flirt. Timur stepped closer to her. At once his leopard settled, curling up contentedly and leaving him the hell alone. Even so, he could feel the leopard snarling, head up alertly. He might be content to be close to the woman he'd dubbed the leopard whisperer, but his cat didn't like her near his cousin.

"Baby, who is this woman you've hired? You know this is dangerous, not only to us but to what we do," Fyodor whispered to Evangeline. "You said nothing about this woman to me, or to Timur. He's responsible for our lives. Can you imagine how he would feel if he failed in his job and you were killed? Or I was? Evangeline, you know better than this."

Timur nearly fell down he was so shocked. It was all he could do to keep his mouth from dropping open. Fyodor had never once indicated to him that he knew his personal security was a nightmare for Timur, especially since the attempt on his life as well as Evangeline's. His brother never reprimanded Evangeline, let alone in public.

He glanced up and met Ashe's eyes. The impact was just like a bullet through his heart. That intense. That visceral. She'd heard, and Fyodor and Evangeline were clear across the room, huddled together in a little corner while Ashe was behind the counter. Her hearing was more than excellent. She looked away first, ducking her head and concentrating on making Gorya's drink.

"I'm sorry, Fyodor," Evangeline whispered. "I really, really need the help, and none of the men you had working for me worked out. They drop things. They ruin the machines. Do you have any idea how much those cost?"

"Baby." There was a sigh in Fyodor's voice. "We can afford a new coffee machine. We can't afford a new you."

"She isn't a threat to me. Or to you. Please, honey, just let this one go."

Something in Evangeline's voice alerted him. Timur moved closer to the counter. Evangeline knew Ashe. There was some connection between them. He watched as Ashe handed Gorya his coffee and took his money. Her hands appeared steady enough, but they were trembling. Just slightly, but they were trembling all the same.

Timur didn't like puzzles, especially when it came to Fyodor's safety. Gorya signaled to him. His cousin had been raised as a sibling with him, and they had continued to be close as adults, although if he kept flirting with Ashe, that closeness might end. Timur was a little shocked that the thought went through his head.

He joined Gorya at the table his cousin chose. It was always the same one. It was small, a table for two, and it was positioned so that Gorya had his back protected and yet could see the front door and the sidewalks through the window, and still keep the counter in sight. Rather than take the chair opposite him that would put his back to the wall, Timur toed one around and sat straddling it, facing the door as well.

"She's scared," Gorya mouthed around his coffee cup. "My leopard went quiet, just the way it does when Evangeline is close."

"Maybe it's Evangeline," Timur pointed out, but he knew it wasn't. He knew it was Ashe. His leopard was practically purring.

"She has to be leopard."

Timur had to agree with that, and if they were both suspicious, that meant she was close to the emerging—a time when the female leopard's cycle and the woman's cycle synchronized. "Where's she from?"

Gorya shrugged. "I asked, but she didn't answer. She didn't answer any of my questions."

The bakery was beginning to fill up. Fyodor slipped behind the counter to the back room he used as his office. Gorya went with him. They took turns, one up front, one in the back. Two more patrolled the alley behind the bakery, and two were on the front walkway. One was on the roof above the shop and another was across the street on the roof.

Timur watched Evangeline and Ashe work together. They were fast and efficient. They moved in sync, as if they'd been doing so for years. They laughed occasionally, and when they did, Ashe's laughter seemed to move through his body, teasing every one of his senses. Again, that was so unusual that he didn't trust it.

His cat hated everyone. The leopard had been raised in violence, just as he'd been. His father had lived to control the world around him. He'd done so through fear. He'd liked everyone to be afraid of him. He'd *needed* that. Timur and Gorya, a few years younger than Fyodor, *had* been afraid. They hadn't dared befriend anyone because their father would have been very likely to force them to kill that person. It wouldn't have mattered if it had been a child, a woman or a man responsible for providing for his family, Timur's father would have laughed when he forced them to kill.

It had been impossible to be with a woman. Well, not impossible, but the risk had made it very difficult. When his need had become too great, Timur had found a willing woman in a bar, had sex with her and then left before his raging leopard could get loose and kill her. He'd talked to Fyodor, and his brother had the same problem with his leopard. Gorya had as well. Timur had suspected his other cousins Mitya and Sevastyan had the same difficulties when it came to women.

The leopards had been subjected to too much violence, too many killings at a young age. Timur's leopard had been forced to come out, to shift against Timur's will in order to stop the brutal beatings Timur had suffered at the hands of his father. The moment the leopard had come out, he'd been forced to participate in his father's cruel, sick games, training the cat to kill for pleasure. For blood. Human blood.

He tapped the table, watching the sidewalk. He wanted a home, just like any other man might want, but he knew that was impossible for him. Fyodor had found Evangeline, but they were still in a kind of prison and always would be. There was really no place anyone could hide anymore without being found. They'd all known it was a matter of time before their crimes caught up with them. Timur wasn't going to have a wife and children. He would never have a home or feel a woman's touch on his skin. Not again. Not when they were hunted like animals.

"Can I get you anything?" Evangeline offered during the next lull.

He'd been aware of her approach and knew she would attempt to fix things between them. He was upset with her for hiring Ashe without consulting with him. He needed a background check. He needed to know everything there was to know about the woman before he allowed her close to Evangeline or Fyodor. By hiring the woman herself, and then going to Fyodor, Evangeline had made certain that wasn't going to happen.

She slipped into the seat opposite him the moment he straightened with a small shake of his head. Ashe was watching them. She held herself a little too stiff, the smile fading.

"You don't want to do this with me right now," Timur said, his voice gruff. He couldn't control the rasp in his voice, the near growl. He wanted to shake some sense into her. "I'm angry with you, Evangeline."

"I know. I'm sorry. You have every right to be."

"Sorry doesn't cut it. You could get my brother killed. Or you could be killed, and then what would he do? I don't want to hear your excuses right now. We're not in a place of privacy."

That should tell her he had a lot to say, things she

wasn't going to like. As it was, she'd winced at the lash in his voice, especially when he'd rightly pointed out that it was Fyodor who could pay the price for her willfulness.

"I really am sorry. It won't happen again."

"I'm sure it won't. You can't know that many women who worked with you in a coffee shop." He kept his eyes on her face, although he really wanted to see Ashe's reaction.

Color swept into Evangeline's face. She glanced over her shoulder to look at Ashe.

"Don't bother to deny it, *mladshaya sestra*, that would just piss me off more. I don't like lies, and you're not very good at them."

"I don't want to lie to you," Evangeline admitted. "I just can't say anything. I'm really, really sorry, Timur, but she isn't a threat to us at all."

"You don't get to make that call and you know it. When you married my brother, that went right out the window. I make the call, not you. You want your friend to stay, you come clean with me. Make this right, because if you don't, she could disappear."

Evangeline's face went pale. "Timur . . ."

"Don't." He snapped the order at her, leaning across the table, staring her in the eye so she knew he meant what he said. "I'm responsible for you both. For your lives. I've spent a lifetime shaping myself into a weapon to ensure Fyodor's safety. And now yours and those of any children you have. That's my sole purpose in life. You don't get exceptions. You can talk to Fyodor, insist he fire me, it won't do you any good. I'll still watch over you both. Come clean about your friend or send her on her way."

The thought of Ashe leaving hurt. His cat protested with a mean snarl and a vicious swipe to his gut. That didn't matter. He'd meant every word he'd said, and Evangeline had better take him seriously.

"I'll talk to her. If she gives me permission, I'll tell you everything. If she doesn't, I'll tell her she has to leave. I promise, Timur, you'll either have that information by the end of the day or she'll leave."

Timur sat back in his chair and gave her a slight nod. She knew him well enough to know he meant what he said. His gaze was on the sidewalk outside. He noticed the two men approaching and a small sigh escaped. Cops. He knew them; they knew him. One, Jeff Myers, had been undercover as Brice Addler, and had tried to steal Evangeline out from under Fyodor's nose. His partner had gone by Reeve Hawkins. His real name was Ray Harding.

"I never noticed before, but you're actually further gone than Fyodor was, aren't you, Timur?" Evangeline said softly, compassion in her voice.

He didn't want her sympathy. He didn't want anything from her that might somehow change who he was, because then he might not be as sharp, and his brother—or Evangeline—would pay the price for his weakness. He waved her back to work, jerking his chin toward the door. He didn't want Ashe serving either of the cops. They'd hit on her. Both were like that and he didn't want the woman telling them a single thing about his family.

Jeff strolled in like he owned the shop, Ray beside him, both in plain clothes. Timur kept his mask in place as they stared at him. It was impossible for either cop to win in a stare down and they knew it from experience, so they didn't try. They barely acknowledged his existence before they were at the counter, flirting outrageously with Evangeline.

Evangeline had wisely told Ashe to take a break in the back room. That allowed Timur to breathe easier. The last thing he wanted was for his leopard to make him any edgier or moodier than he'd felt the moment he'd seen the cops. They didn't like him, and he sure as hell didn't like them.

He kept his gaze on the street, but always had the cops

in his vision. Hopefully, Gorya was standing in front of the door to Fyodor's office just in case Ashe took it in her head to be friendly and go talk to his brother, or worse, decide this was a great time to kill him, if she was an assassin. He nearly groaned aloud. Now he was worried.

"Keep your eyes on the new girl, Gorya," he ordered, talking softly into his radio.

"Eyes are on her," Gorya confirmed with a little too much enthusiasm for Timur's liking.

"I said eyes, not hands or mouth or any other part of your anatomy that I might have to cut off if you disobey that very direct order."

Gorya's laughter was offensive. Not because Timur didn't understand it, but because his attraction to Evangeline's friend burned through his body, making him so uncomfortable he felt surly and edgy even without the help of his leopard. He didn't trust himself to address Jeff and Ray and the way they flirted with Evangeline. Any other time he might have gotten up and broken up the flirt-fest, but right then it was far more important to sit in his chair, legs sprawled in front of him, and contemplate ways to kill them. He had already thought of at least fifteen and that was without really trying.

He breathed a sigh of relief when they left and told his leopard to calm down and stop making an ass out of himself. The cat answered with a snarl, a show of teeth and a pithy attitude, stating that was all Timur and not him. For once, Timur knew the leopard was right. Still, that didn't stop him from stalking to the counter and glaring at Evangeline.

"Have they seen or talked to her?" he demanded.

Evangeline didn't pretend not to know who he was talking about. She shook her head. "Not yet. If they caught a glimpse of her when they were walking through the door before I sent her into the back, they didn't say, and I think they would have."

"Try to keep it that way."

She nodded abruptly, and then the door between the kitchen and the main shop opened and Ashe stepped through. It was easy enough to see why her parents had given her that name. Her hair was a thick mass, colored ash and platinum with a little gold thrown in. He turned his back on her, but watched her in the mirrors he'd installed in strategic places throughout the large room. She didn't take her eyes off him until he was once again settled in his seat. There was some satisfaction in that.

The next hour saw a steady stream of customers. He took the opportunity to walk around, stretching his legs, keeping his muscles loose. He knew they needed a larger security force around Fyodor, but he wanted leopards and there were only so many. Shifters were faster, and if push came to shove, they could call on their animal counterparts to aid them. Every sense was far more acute, and a leopard sensed danger and knew when other leopards were close—with one exception: female leopards.

He sank back into his chair, his gaze fixed on Ashe. She was making drinks and handing out pastries. There was always a smile on her face, but he didn't quite believe it. Each time the little bell tinkled over the entrance, signaling another customer, her eyes jumped to the door. She was worried. Scared. That presented an entirely new set of dangers.

If she was leopard—and he was certain she was—and her leopard hadn't emerged, it would be like his uncles to send her in to assassinate Fyodor. His uncles were reputed to be even crueler and much more vicious than Timur's father had been, and they had sworn to see Fyodor dead for killing their brother. It didn't matter to them that the kill had been justified.

Fyodor had walked in on a bloodbath. Their father had already brutally murdered their mother and had been beating Timur and Gorya to death because the two boys had tried to stop him. Fyodor had killed him and then gone after the senior members of his father's lair in order to stop them from killing the women. Now their uncles were out for their blood. They'd put bounties on their nephews' heads, and now that Fyodor and his brother were no longer hiding behind false identities, the assassins would come to collect. It would make sense to send a female.

Timur studied Ashe as she worked. She was fast. Really fast. Sometimes he thought she would make a mistake, but she never did. Her handoff was smooth, and she moved with a fluid grace that seemed too honed to be entirely natural. As if she were in complete control of every muscle, every movement.

He really wanted to yell at Evangeline. Ashe made no sense at all, but she was strikingly beautiful. The more he looked at her, the more he thought so. She was model material, but then she didn't have the height. Her skin looked so soft he found himself wanting an excuse to touch her, just to see if it was as soft as it appeared.

She had tied her hair in some messy knot that kept falling out and she'd have to redo it. That told him she hadn't worked in the food service industry in a while, otherwise she wouldn't have forgotten to wear her hair back or covered. Instead, she kept pulling her hair up into that silly mess that had him thinking about bedrooms. Or sex. Or both. The bedroom didn't matter nearly as much as the sex.

The fact that her hair was so thick even though it was blond told him the odds that she was leopard were even higher. Leopards tended to have a lot of hair no matter what the color. The way she moved was an indicator as well. She suddenly looked up and stared right into his eyes. She caught up the coffeepot and came out from behind the safety of the counter, stomping right toward him. Not a good move.

"Stop staring at me," she hissed as she poured coffee

into his cup. "I mean it. You're making me uncomfortable. I get that you're royally pissed that I'm working here. I get why now that I've seen Evangeline's husband, but I need the work, so please just back off."

He caught her wrist as she turned away. Very gently he removed the coffeepot from her hand and set it on the table, just out of her reach. The last thing he wanted was for her to dump scalding-hot coffee in his lap, and he had the feeling that not only was she capable of it, she'd been considering it. He kept possession of her wrist. "You're better suited to be a bodyguard than a barista."

"Why do you say that?"

Her voice was strained. She sounded smooth, but he had a good ear and caught the stressed notes she tried to hide.

"The way you move. You're trained to protect yourself, and, I suspect, others."

"Maybe so, but I'm not in that line of work. I'm good at this, and I need the job."

"How do you know Evangeline?"

"Ask her."

"I'm asking you."

She sighed and glanced toward the counter. "I have to work. We're getting busy again. I know you need answers. Maybe after work I could meet you somewhere."

"I work until late. Where do you live?"

She hesitated.

Timur sighed. "I'm going to find out anyway. Just fucking tell me."

"I'm living in Evangeline's house. The one she used to live in."

He was glad she didn't argue about telling him where she lived. Tonight he'd be with her. Alone. He even liked the idea, which was dangerous for both of them. He let go of her. She immediately rubbed her wrist as if he'd hurt her—or she was trying to get the feel of him off her skin.

The entire time she'd been close, his leopard had been acting like a complete fool, rolling around and making absurd rumbling noises, which, fortunately, no one could hear but him. He ran his finger down her arm to her hand and then indicated the coffeepot. "You forgot something."

Soft color raced up her neck to her face. She caught up the glass pot without another word and hurried back to the safety of the counter.

His heart settled to normal again and he pressed his hand over his chest while he breathed away the hard-on he hadn't been able to control and, thankfully, she hadn't seen. Or at least he thought she hadn't. She'd kept her gaze studiously away from that portion of his anatomy. It had been far too many years since he'd had problems controlling his body. He had to put it down to his leopard and the fact that a potential mate was in close proximity.

Did she know? Most women didn't have a clue about their leopards, not until the emergence. Evangeline had known. She'd had a relationship with her leopard almost since infancy. If Ashe didn't know, then her leopard would as it rose, making her inclined to flirt with every man coming near her, including Gorya and the two clowns that passed for cops. That didn't sit well with him.

A man came down the sidewalk and passed the shop, barely glancing in. There was nothing about him to catch Timur's interest, but everything in him went still. His leopard snarled and came to attention. He lifted his coffee cup to his lips and kept his eyes on the man dressed in a dark suit. The man paused just at the edge of the window, glanced at his watch and turned around to go back the way he'd come. As he did so, he took a long look through the glass.

Timur cursed inwardly. He should have had that glass tinted more. The shop was busy, and there were a lot of customers, two deep by the counter. He watched as the man hesitated by the door and then went on past it.

"Man in dark suit. You on him? Tall, dark glasses, mirrored."

"Got him, boss," Trey Sinclair said. He was on the roof across the street. Timur had two more of his security patrolling the streets and another on the roof of the bakery. *"Right in the crosshairs."*

"What about you, Jeremiah? Can you follow him without getting tagged? This is important. You're not out in the jungle." He added the last because the kid needed to be a little humbler and a lot more vigilant. He was young and eager, and he wanted Timur to take notice of him. Timur didn't like sending the kid into dangerous situations, and he had a gut feeling this man was very dangerous.

"No problem, boss."

"Cocky little son of a bitch, you listen to me. That man will kill you if he spots you. Don't fuck up. You do, there aren't any second chances."

There was a small silence. Jeremiah might be cocky and full of attitude, but he'd learned that when one of them said something, it was worth listening. They'd grown up surrounded by danger, by vicious monsters; he hadn't. They had a built-in radar for danger; Jeremiah was just beginning to hone his skills.

"I hear you, Timur. I'll be doubly careful."

"I'd rather you lose him than get too close."

"I understand."

Timur could only hope the kid did, because even with the target out of sight, every warning bell he had was shrieking at him.